WITHERPOOLS

WITHERPOOLS

A STORY COLLECTION

JASON DURANT

"Tiger Walk" is original to this collection. The other stories in this collection, in different form, first appeared in *Johnny Apple: Dark Tales*.

ISBN: 978-1-7334407-3-8

Book design by Maureen Cutajar
www.gopublished.com

Contents

Captive

Oh, how he hated judges! Those meddlesome ... Those ...
"Tisk, tisk, Alfred." The judge, presiding over the Divine Court of Retributive Justice, peered down his nose at the newly convicted and soon-to-be-sentenced Alfred Haas.

"Tisk, tisk," the judge said. "Alfred, if I were to bend all the rules in your favor"—the judge leaned forward and Alfred shrank back—"your world would be just peachy. The cat's meow. Wouldn't it? Confess, Alfred!"

He can read my mind? Alfred thought.

"Tisk, tisk, Alfred. Of course I can read your mind. How did you think I got to be a judge?" He slammed his gavel down, and Alfred Haas jumped—a neat, clean little jump that just about took him clean out of his clothes.

"Tisk, tisk, Alfred." The judge glanced away and studied a vague spot high on a distant wall of the spacious courtroom. "I'll take a slight recess as you ... ah ... kindly get yourself dressed."

Alfred, his embarrassment turning into a rosy redness that quickly began to feel like a third-degree sunburn, hopped around and squirmed until he was fully inside his clothes once again.

"Tisk, tisk." Judge Thaddeus Favor, Supreme Potentate of the Divine Court of Retributive Justice, shifted his eyes back to the forlorn, shrunken, and shriveled Alfred Haas. Then, with a great show of disgust, he gaveled the courtroom snickers—which had broken out due to Alfred's impromptu act of partial disrobement—down to a silence.

Bang! Bang! Bang!

At last, a dropped pin could have been heard in the courtroom.

"Now, Alfred. Tisk, tisk. You are hereby sentenced to ..."

Oh, how he hated judges! Those meddlesome ... Those ...

Alfred Haas found himself nodding. *Poosh, poosh,* he said to himself, quickly and forcefully, coming to in a panic. He had been gone only a moment, but the judge, courtroom, and all had seized his mind once again, like always, whenever he dozed off.

Oh, how he hated judges!

Poosh, poosh.

He had to concentrate, stay alive to the situation, the place, etcetera.

Poosh, poosh.

Better, now.

It was the only way to escape from a life sentence. *Stay alive, Alfred!*

He clipped the fading remnants of the judge and courtroom from his mind, willing himself to stay afloat on ... this cursed sea of consciousness ... that he was obliged to flounder on until ... until ...

Tisk, tisk, Alfred. Until death, Alfred, the judge said.

Poosh, poosh. No! Not until death. I'll get out of here. *Poosh, poosh.*

Tisk, tisk, Alfred. Keep trying.

Poosh, poosh.

Push your potentials, Alfred, the judge said. Keep pushing your potentials. That's your only hope.

Poosh, poosh, Alfred said to himself, dashing the judge from his mind again. *Poosh, poosh.* I'll get out of here.

He came to full awareness, waking to a beautiful sun-splashed summer day. It was his birthday, his seventy-fifth birthday. It was the middle of July, in the year 2047, Alfred's ninth year of confinement.

Ah, but what a confinement it was! It was the Age of New Potentials, and all humans in this age were confined. All had been tried, convicted, and sentenced to *poosh, poosh* those new potentials into existence.

Alfred had spent nine years learning how to spin cocoons around himself.

Tisk, tisk, Alfred, the judge had said at his sentencing. You can only do what your awareness allows. So, *poosh, poosh,* and expand your awareness.

Alfred had *poosh, poosh, and pooshed ...* spinning cocoons around himself. It seemed the most natural thing in the world to do. But his cocoons were generally miserable specimens.

Damn ... damn ... he thought, mulling over his sentence again, for the millionth time. They had consigned him to a hateful place, to be with hateful people.

Tisk, tisk, Alfred, the judge had said. This is the Age of

Retributive Justice. *Poosh, poosh,* or suffer the consequences. Sentence passed!

Bang! went the gavel.

But ... but ...

You engaged in witch hunts, Alfred. Shame, shame. Your self-weaved hang noose is now swinging full circle, coming to get you, Alfred, the judge had said.

Bang!

To his dismay, Alfred found that the judge had the power of nature, of matter itself, of the very forces of the universe, behind him. He had walked from the courthouse a free man, surprised—considering his conviction and sentencing. For a wild moment, he thought he had escaped. Looking around, he saw no one dogging his footsteps, no official-looking menaces on the horizon.

He had skipped home, thrilled. Witch hunts? *Phooey!*

But things *had* changed. It *was* a new age. And Alfred, somehow or other, ended up obeying his sentence to the letter. Tunnels of magic seemed to dog him, funnel him, twist him and turn him, until he was exactly where he was supposed to be, doing exactly what he was supposed to be doing.

But with that one important difference—allowed for everyone—that one saving grace.

Poosh, poosh.

Everyone had *poosh, poosh.*

New potentials.

Tisk, tisk, Alfred, the judge had said at a latter parole hearing. Cocoons? Ha! Ha! You're spinning cocoons around yourself? That's how you're using the power of *poosh, poosh?* Tisk, tisk, Alfred, you are a disgrace.

But ... but ...

Bang! went the gavel.

But ... *Arrrrh!*

This is the Age of Nemesis, Alfred had thought.

Now, on this sun-splashed summer day, his seventy-fifth birthday, Alfred Haas sat at a picnic table in the Graham Graham National Park, buried in immense beauty, with rocky woodlands and grassy meadows all around.

Danger was lurking all around, also, and Alfred was busy spinning cocoons once again, now that he was free from the Judge Thaddeus Favor dreams.

Tisk, tisk, Alfred. You're never free from me.

Poosh, poosh.

Alfred Haas juggled his cocoons, matching them to the lurking dangers that ebbed and flowed, trying to protect himself well enough so that he could go back to his favorite pastime—reading the newspaper. Yes, even now, for diehard fans, newspapers existed.

It was harrowing work. Alfred was now entering his third hour at the picnic table. Sweat trickled down his brow. Seeking asylum was not for the faint hearted.

Poosh, poosh. Alfred's mind, like an invisible thousand-headed ant colony, began to repair the weblike cocoon that ran helter-skelter to various points on the picnic table and across his face.

Poosh, poosh. Cocoon matter marched, filling out the network. Alfred turned his head one way and then the other to test it. The web felt stronger, not much give to it, and he could see to the front and to both sides through slots he purposefully left open.

Poosh, poosh. Getting stronger.

Damn ... damn ...

Alfred felt something nibbling on his right elbow. His

mind involuntarily went *ush, ush,* and the cocoon to his front, losing the support of Alfred's mind, began to diminish.

He looked to the right. An animal—a fluffy, white goat thing, complete with horns and floppy ears—was eating his shirtsleeve.

Damn ... damn ...

Poosh, poosh. Alfred began to repair the cocoon that stretched in various odd shapes across his right side, focusing on the elbow.

Poosh, poosh. The cumulus—that was the name of the creature, a species *poosh, pooshed* into existence by the new potentials—skipped around to Alfred's left side.

Alfred swung his head that way. The cumulus now had his left shirtsleeve in its mouth and was playfully tugging and nibbling it.

Poosh, poosh. The cumulus jumped back, fearful of the advancing cocoon that began to pop up on that side of Alfred.

Poosh, poosh, poosh, poosh, poosh, poosh ...

Alfred nearly blew the cumulus away, back into the forest from where it had come. It retreated to the deep grass near the trees, a good sixty feet away, and then began to circle back, crossing into Alfred's blind side.

Damn ... damn ...

Ush, ush ... With his mind faltering, nearly giving up, Alfred's cocoons fell into a sad state and were soon waving in the breeze like tattered laundry.

Judge Favor cropped up in his mind again. Tisk, tisk, Alfred. Is that the best you can do? Ha! Ha! You can't even spin decent cocoons, Alfred. Doesn't that tell you something?

Poosh, poosh ... Alfred huffed and puffed and blew the judge away, and then began to repair his tattered cocoons, trying to spin the whole works into one big monster of a cocoon. He knew he must hurry; he sensed the cumulus still wandered somewhere behind him.

Suddenly, laughter and voices sprang out from a grassy field beyond a grove of blue spruce trees to Alfred's front, growing louder. It was Alfred's kin, the Sedlocks—Ruth, Marty, and their two children—and the Swansons, neighbors of the Sedlocks', returning to the picnic area. The troupe had hauled Alfred, against his will, to this place for the birthday-party picnic.

Damn ... damn ... I hope they're not coming back yet, the birthday boy thought.

Poosh, poosh ... Alfred pushed his potentials even harder, hoping to build a solid cocoon all around him, one so solid that he could spend the rest of the day reading his newspaper in peace. Anticipating the upcoming pleasure, Alfred gripped the curled-up newspaper tighter, vowing to swat the cumulus with it if the worthless thing should return before the monster cocoon was up and running.

Now ... *Poosh, poosh, poosh* ... With the *poosh* portion of his mind racing almost on automatic pilot, Alfred allowed his thoughts to drift, recalling odd fragments of the day, and then odd fragments from his entire life, since some odd fragments tended to bring other odd fragments to mind.

The Graham Graham National Park (named after Archibald D. Graham, former President of the United States) was a huge park in the state of Colorado, adjacent to an equally huge military reservation that harbored, among other things, the Academy of Light Sciences.

The Academy of Light Sciences, founded in the early twenty-first century, had been the harbinger of the Age of New Potentials. Time travel was its crowning achievement.

Phooey! Alfred thought. Time travel destroys the natural rhythms of life and endangers everyone. Intrusions into the past result in alterations of the present, annihilating millions of us.

Alfred Haas, growing to adulthood in this trembling era of flux, had sided with the naysayers, with all those who said *no ... no ... no ...* to the idea of digging into realms that were ... *better left alone, damn you!*

Alfred became a journalist and hounded the Academy of Light Sciences with all of his formidable naysaying vituperation.

Tisk, tisk, Alfred, Judge Favor said. Witch hunts.

Phooey! Alfred said. Time travel will annihilate us all!

Tisk, tisk, Alfred. You're grasping at straws, Alfred. The Academy of Light Sciences employs time travel without paradoxes not only to the past, but also to an unlimited, unbounded future.

Arrrrh! Alfred would not hear of it. He had screeched loudly at his trial whenever the judge had tried to speak of such things.

Arrrrh!

Alfred had left the courtroom, newly sentenced, and had begun to live a life of new potentials, just like everyone else on the planet, nine years ago.

And then things began to happen mysteriously.

Tisk, tisk, Alfred. There's a guiding hand behind it all.

Arrrrh!

His employer, a Washington, D.C., newspaper, retired him, which was almost unheard of in the Age of No Retirement if You Can Still *Poosh, Poosh.* Alfred squawked, but to no avail. Then his pension dematerialized. Squawking again proved futile.

Suddenly, Alfred could no longer afford to live by himself free and unencumbered, so he was auctioned off by the state, as was the custom for those in Alfred's sorry condition. His granddaughter, Ruth Sedlock, submitted a bid for Alfred, the only bid, and got him.

Alfred, having no choice to speak of, moved into a bungalow located in one of the dozens of picturesque villages that ringed the Graham Graham National Park. Ruth's husband, Marty, was one of the time travelers. Ruth and Marty lived in a mansion in another, nearby village.

Alfred hated the new arrangement. Hated it with a passion.

Tisk, tisk, Alfred.

Shut up!

The judge's pronouncements had come true. Every single one of them. Alfred's sentence had sprung fully to life.

A guiding hand, Alfred.

Shut up!

It's my birthday, Alfred thought gloomily, and with immediate regret, for the thought took on a life of its own—*poosh, poosh*—and became a swarm of flies buzzing around his head, and then attacking his head, as if it were a pile of dung.

Ruth Sedlock, his lunatic granddaughter, had traipsed into his bungalow that morning.

"Alfred, it's your birthday," she had said, presenting him with a present, a new coat. "Were going on a picnic."

Alfred had screamed. He hated going out. For thirty years his bespectacled visage, with its long beak and bald dome, had been before the public eye, plastered at the head of his syndicated column. He was known far and wide, and people hated him, especially the time travelers.

Arrrrh! But it was useless to argue.

Tisk, tisk, Alfred, the judge had said nine years ago at his sentencing. Ruth Sedlock will wither you with her fire-brand attack.

This morning, Alfred had withered under Ruth's firebrand attack.

Alfred thought of the coat Ruth had given him. It was a Nonconforming Materials brand, suitable for the cool days of autumn and spring, but on a cold winter's day, Alfred knew he would freeze to death in it. And never mind Ruth's nonsense about the coat acquiring a winter's growth—a fur lining—automatically when the season changed. *Phooey!* and *Arrrrh!* had been Alfred's responses when she trotted that out.

Nonconforming Materials. Now there was a corruption.

Tisk, tisk, Alfred. Witch hunts. Rejoice! Nonconforming Materials bestows godlike powers upon us, the ability to mold matter to our will.

Consumer fraud, your honor.

Nonconforming Materials, Alfred.

Fraud!

Tisk, tisk, Alfred.

It's fraud!

New potentials, Alfred. Whatever you want. Whatever your awareness can *poosh, poosh* through.

Phooey!

Alfred stole a moment from his mental wanderings and turned his attention to the newspaper article he had been reading. With one clumsy hand, he reached up to adjust his trifocals, which kept sliding down the long, narrow slope of his pointed beak. He tucked them back into place with a grimace, willing them to stay put, and then rotated the newspaper, which was still rolled up like a tube—ready to swat the cumulus—and read about an arson fire in Denver that had killed fourteen people.

Tisk, tisk, Alfred thought, mimicking Judge Thaddeus Favor. New potentials, tisk, tisk. We still have deaths, arson, murder, mayhem, you name it, judgey fudgey. Ha! Ha! A gleam shot from Alfred's eye, triumphant and sparkling.

For a moment, Alfred was taken away from the sunsplashed meadow in which he sat, webbed in cocoon armor to the picnic table, and was transported to heights unknown. He felt exhilarated, expansive. Then he abruptly snapped back to himself, losing the transcendent flavor of the moment, losing the spell.

Damn!

He heard crashing sounds in the deep, dark woods that lay behind him. The noise intensified, and then tugged at his cocoon and began to unravel it. Actually, the noise tugged at Alfred's consciousness, pulling out a thread of Alfred's mind, and the cocoon had no choice but to follow suit, unraveling as Alfred's mind unraveled.

His mind and cocoon unraveled faster and faster, and Alfred fought frantically to reel everything back into place.

Damn!

The crashing stopped, and the woods—creatures, birds, and all—settled into hushed silence, as if obeying some mysterious command. Alfred heard only the whispering chatter of the breeze as it rippled through the pines. His

11

mind whirred back into place, and as he began to repair his tattered cocoon, his thoughts turned dark. The crashing and subsequent silence was symptomatic of a time traveler's search for a good landing spot.

He heard soft, enchanting words.

Is he clear in the present, or lost in the trees?
Like lightning his thoughts, but his mind is the breeze.

Another symptom.

Damn!

Such words heralded the arrival of a time traveler. One of Marty Sedlock's friends from the Academy was coming to the picnic, journeying from some other century.

Damn! Who did he kill there? My antecedents? Am I dead now?

Tisk, tisk, Alfred, the judge said, setting up court in Alfred's mind again. You're grasping at straws.

Phooey!

He heard footsteps in the woods behind him, moving closer.

Damn!

And then another threat: the cumulus was back, nibbling at Alfred's right shirtsleeve.

Damn!

It had eaten through Alfred's cocoon.

Suddenly, to his front, laughter and voices sprang out from the grove of blue spruce trees that bordered the grassy field where Ruth and Marty and their two children, David and Kimberly, had gone to play, along with the neighboring couple, the Swansons and their two children. He smelled the fresh, sweet aromas of picnic food, which were just being released to the air from the picnic cart that sat somewhere in the area, out of his sight.

Phooey! They're coming back. The food is ready.

Suddenly, another catastrophe reared its head. The cumulus took hold of Alfred's cocoon and shook it. This time it seemed to mean business. It was a tug of war: Alfred's mind verses the fragile, fluffy creature. With one impressive tug, the cumulus won, and stripped Alfred bare of his cocoon. The cumulus shook it furiously, and then wandered with it a few feet, only to discard it and wander back to Alfred.

Alfred was in a panic.

Voices rolled in from the spruce trees.

Footsteps swept through the forest behind him.

The cumulus was back at his right elbow, nibbling away. *Arrrrh!*

Tisk, tisk, Alfred, the judge said. You have been sentenced.

Why can't I have peace, peace, peace?

Poosh, poosh, Alfred, the judge said. You can have whatever your awareness allows. Expand your awareness.

Phooey! Alfred mentally spat at Judge Favor. With the effort, his trifocals slipped down the long, narrow slope of his pointed beak, and he imperially shoved them back into place.

Marty Sedlock shouted something. Alfred bent his ears to the voice while frantically trying to spin a hasty cocoon and heard, "David, David, dinner's ready! Come out, come out wherever you are!"

David was their five-year-old.

David's not with them? Alfred thought. *Oh, no!* David was renowned for sneaking up on people and pouncing on them. Alfred spun harder and harder, his panic shooting to the heavens.

He saw the merrymakers break from the grove of blue spruce trees in a broad front: Ruth, Marty, Kimberly—their three-year-old—and the Swansons and their two children.

"David, David!" Marty called again.

Then came the stern, strident tones of Ruth. "Kimberly, quit playing with that rope and go keep Great-Grandfather Alfred company."

Alfred's fledgling cocoon fell away and shriveled up to nothing.

Tisk, tisk, Alfred, Judge Thaddeus Favor said, holding court in Alfred's sinking mind. You were sentenced, Alfred.

To her I'm just a job. Does she get paid for keeping me on in retirement?

Tisk, tisk, Alfred. What else? You were raffled off by the hand that guides the universe. Would you deny her a pittance? You got what you deserve.

Footfalls swished through the grass, converging on him, closing in from all around.

Alfred's jangling nerves coiled themselves into tight springs. He wanted to bound away, but his seventy-five-year-old posterior seemed glued to the picnic-table bench.

No, don't! Stop that, brat! The words flew through Alfred's mind but could not find expression through his vocal cords, which were frozen in a stricture of fear.

Kimberly was playing with a springy red rope that resembled a dog's leash, but wasn't. It wasn't even a rope, though that's what her mother had called it. It was another Nonconforming Materials product, and its introduction a few months ago had sparked a growing craze among children of all ages. They swished it on the grass for a few

14

seconds, released it, and watched it slither on its own like a snake for several yards. It drove the kids wild.

Run, Alfred!

A willful segment of Alfred's mind ordered him to get up and run. In his mind's eye, he saw himself loping across the meadow in long, graceful strides, heading toward his peaceful bungalow.

"Kimberly!" Ruth cried.

Alfred had seen her do it, had seen her playfully release the red thing toward him. It was slashing its way through the grass with astonishing energy, and Alfred thought the little girl must have whipped it just right to send it into such a frenzy.

"Cu ... mu ... nuss!"

He heard the child's piping voice, her last syllable whistling into an excited shriek.

"Look, Mommy!"

"Oh, Marty, look at the cumulus over by Grandpa. I hope it doesn't get into the food."

The red thing rushed on.

Panic stricken, Alfred braced himself, and then turned to peer at the cumulus, which was still calm, still rooted to the same spot, nibbling on Alfred's shirtsleeve.

Noticing Alfred's attentions, the cumulus lifted its head and peered back. Its liquid-blue eyes, set in a narrow face, regarded Alfred with an odd wistfulness that bordered on imbecility.

For one revolting moment, Alfred imagined he was seeing his own reflection in a mirror. He began to feel a strange kinship with the cumulus, as if they were shipmates on the deck of a ship that had just come under attack by enemy torpedo. A supreme wistfulness settled into Alfred, and he imagined the gurgling torpedo passing harmlessly beneath the ship.

That was not to be. The red thing—that's what most people called them—did not pass gently under the picnic table. It hit the wooden table legs with a smack that would have pleased the most jaded masochist. Since its drive intensified when it collided with solid objects—that's why its manufacturer recommended it be used only on grass, well away from solidly anchored objects—when it hit Alfred's slender shanks, it was like a bullwhip.

His lower left leg took the brunt of it, resulting in clean breaks of both tibia and fibula. His posterior became unglued, and Alfred rose from his perch on the picnic-table bench with such rapidity that he looked like he was being catapulted into the air.

In fact, something like that did happen. Razor-edged ribbons of pain, rocketing through Alfred's leg and exploding into his mind, propelled his consciousness into flight. In the twinkling of an eye, Alfred was clipped from his physical form and found himself roosting on an invisible perch high above the meadow.

He watched the events below with only mild interest as his body jackknifed backward over the picnic-table bench and completed a somersault before striking the ground. His body danced crazily across the grass, and then came to an abrupt halt, flat on its back. His left leg appeared to be skewered to the earth as the rest of him did an eerie fandango.

Then, just as abruptly, his body uncorked itself into a wobbling stance, and Alfred saw the dome of his bald head under the sharp shadow of a pine tree. He idly wondered if the shadow felt cool upon his scalp.

It was pleasant, viewing from above. Alfred thought he had finally found peace, perfect peace.

Tisk, tisk, Alfred, Judge Favor said.

Phooey, Alfred thought.

Bang! went the gavel. Sentence is passed, Judge Favor said.

An instant latter, Alfred was sucked back into his tottering body. His body lost its balance and fell. Through terrified eyes, Alfred watched the ground rush up to hit him.

He felt the impact with the earth. The blades of grass that touched his face felt like poison spikes. The white-hot flares of agony that came screaming from his leg quickly supplanted this strange torment. Alfred writhed about, as if doing an eerie fandango.

The red thing had continued into the trees. Alfred listened in terror. It smacked about as if it were intent on hacking out a new clearing. Kimberly squealed with glee. Alfred heard a loud swat and hoped her mother had clobbered her.

The cumulus had retreated a few steps, but appeared to be untouched. Alfred gave it a sidelong glare with one bulging eye. His other eye was closed, as if it sought to protect itself, since Alfred, in his pain-driven insanity, was digging a hole in the earth, using one-half of his face as a shovel. Though he didn't know it, he held his glasses by one lens, gripped tightly between his teeth.

Great flapping wings of darkness swooped through Alfred's mind. The wings became giant hawks with opium-drenched talons. He begged them to descend upon him and caress his misery away. None chose to alight. He cursed them and the shadowy flock scattered. A few remained along the periphery of his vision, skittering about as if looking for worms to eat.

Alfred felt strong hands roll him onto his back. He grappled with them, but they pinned him to the ground.

"Easy ... easy ..."

Looking up at the stranger, Alfred heard himself scream, but it was something pitiful. He felt something pressing against his tongue, something large. He stopped screaming and tried to spit it out, but the object seemed welded to his face.

The man holding him down removed the object and Alfred saw that it was his glasses. He opened his mouth to scream again, but managed only a loud gurgle. His chest heaved as he sucked for air. He started to scream again, but stopped, his energy depleted. Alfred sobbed uncontrollably, feeling his whole body quake in irregular spasms.

He glimpsed the stranger's jersey and saw a silvery phantom wolf with sharp fangs, poised to attack. He shuddered, looked away, and then looked back, realizing what it was. The wolf emblem embossed on the man's jersey was worn by only a select group of Academy specialists. The man holding him down was a time traveler.

Alfred felt doomed and began to struggle again, feebly attempting to scream. The man pushed down harder on Alfred's arms, and then placed a hand heavily upon his chest, stilling him.

"Sir, do not move." His voice was low but reached Alfred's ears with command authority. He obeyed.

"Your leg is broken. You must lie still. I have signaled for an air ambulance."

Alfred stared at the man's square jaw, his thick neck, his piercing eyes. The man stared back, and a flicker of recognition lit up in his eyes.

The man glowered at Alfred, and then abruptly stood and left his view. Despite his fear of the man, Alfred felt abandoned. Then the pain in his leg drew his full attention again, and he began to squirm and moan and sob.

Voices swirled about, intruding into his bleak coffin of pain. In Alfred's decaying mind, the voices took on physical form, becoming strong hands trussing him up for his funeral.

He heard someone crying in the distance. It sounded like Kimberly. He hoped her mother had clobbered her good.

They were doing something to his leg. He screamed in agony.

"Hold still." The voice, barely above a whisper, came from near his leg.

"Hold still." Another voice, carrying strains of urgency.

"Ruth, will you come here now? He's quieted down."

Ruth stepped into Alfred's cloudy view and knelt by his head. She reached her hands out as if to place them on his shoulders, but quickly drew them back.

"I hate these situations," she said.

Alfred wanted to reach up and strangle her. *What? I'm suffering but you're not?*

Tisk, tisk, Alfred, Judge Thaddeus Favor said. You've built your nest, now lie in it.

Phooey, Alfred thought. *Oh, how he hated judges!*

19

Tiger Walk

Tara Brewer keeps telling herself she doesn't have much to fear, but somehow fear is the only thing that fills her mind. And her self-appointed champion and escort, Doug Chamberlain, has not been helping matters. Heavy-browed and intense, he has been more interested in scrutinizing her than in anything else. Of the eight people in the back of the battle-scarred Toyota truck, Doug is the only one who hasn't been scanning the scrub jungle for tigers.

And now he's leaning into her, whispering that loathsome refrain, "Tara, Empress of the World," so that everyone can hear, his tone implying: What's wrong Tara? You look anything but cool. You look terrified.

She pushes Doug away for the umpteenth time. This time it will be permanent. She is fed up with his infantile behavior. He skulks to a far corner of the wheezing truck, where he keeps up his vigilance of her.

Under normal circumstances, Tara does try to make everyone believe she is cool under pressure, but these are not normal circumstances. She is standing in the back of an open truck, and there are tigers out there. She almost never swears, but right now she comes awful close to calling Doug something obscene.

She regains her equilibrium.

She thinks she handled it very well—with one aggressive, anger-inspired shove, she eclipsed Doug from her life. She must have been crazy to take up with that childish jerk in the first place.

Good riddance. Now, focus on tigers.

Whew, it's nice to be rid of Doug. What good would Doug do in the face of a man-eating tiger anyway? Not that they are likely to encounter any man-eating tigers in Ranthambhore National Park. But you'd think an enterprising young tiger would have to start somewhere, maybe with a tasty young American chick.

Doug, what an arrogant and hopelessly shallow guy he is. What if a tiger ate him? What would I do? Stand by and watch? Yell at the tiger?

Shoo, go away!

She stifles a giggle.

"What?" Doug asks, bellowing from across the truck.

Why does he think everything revolves around him? She whips around and says, "Nothing." And then she laughs and looks at the blue-gray whiskery brush that's creeping up on the truck from both sides. Shivers go up her spine.

"I was just thinking, Doug, what if a tiger ate you? I wondered what I would do, and I decided I would do nothing."

"Nothing?" He grips the handrail and stands his tallest, about six-two. He steps closer to her. "You'd do nothing, Tara? How could you?"

"Well, I don't have a gun, and you don't expect me to go after it with my bare hands, do you?"

"I'd go after the tiger for you, Tara. I'd tear him off you with my bare hands, or die trying."

Tara's eyes mist up, hearing this. You fool, she thinks. That was sweet. But still, Doug, keep your distance; we are through.

The truck rumbles along. Low hills, green trees, and golden grass trickle by.

Tara shifts a little and looks at Doug. She realizes he is frightened. She can see it in the tightness of his body, the strain in his face.

"Hey, Doug, don't let those tigers see your fear, or they'll be in the truck before you can say boo," she says.

"Huh?" he says, apparently absorbed in thoughts all his own.

Tara swings around, looks at the others. "Hey, is anybody else frightened?" Jill, Benny, and Lucas, standing near the back of the truck, glance at her.

Jill smiles. "Oh, a little." She does look frightened, Tara thinks. Benny looks a little apprehensive. Lucas looks vacant, like he doesn't have any thoughts.

She looks at Dave Gallagher. She has a lot of empathy for Dave. A drunk driver killed his wife and daughter two years ago, and she senses he is still hanging on to them, probably in an unhealthy manner. She wishes there was something she could do, a way to penetrate his protective shield. But maybe Dave is dealing with it the only way he knows.

And then there are Rose and Jerry Quinn, a middle-aged couple from California, sitting in the cab of the truck. And Omar Khan and Rajiv Das, their official

Ranthambhore National Park guides; Rajiv up front, driving; Omar standing in the back near the oddball surfer dude from California, Zachary Knight."

Lots of dudes from California, Tara thinks.

She looks at Omar. He is tall and extremely dark and brooding most of the time, and he always seems to be looking off to the side in some furtive manner. At times he appears deeply troubled. Not right for a tour guide, she thinks. He should be happy, or at least pretend he's happy.

She eyes Zachary Knight, the blond surfer dude, the mysterious one who keeps a professional distance from everyone. She has no idea if he is a surfer, if he is even from California, or if he is real at all. He just stands there and does whatever, and is not at all concerned with any of them in any way, and sometimes he seems to go all inside himself and drop off from humanity. Paradoxically, he looks responsible, as if he is watching out for all of them. He is tall and muscular, about thirty years old. If anyone here can beat a tiger with his bare hands, it is the blond surfer dude, she thinks, and she wishes Zachary would pay some attention to her.

"So, have you seen any tigers yet, Omar?" Benny asks, in his surprisingly deep voice.

Everyone looks at Omar, and Omar looks as if he's been caught doing something bad, like a dog that pooped somewhere it shouldn't and now must look around with an innocent face and isn't quite good enough an actor to do it.

"No," Omar says. He looks away and scans the brush as the truck shifts into low to traverse some deep ruts. He looks back at the group. "No, no tigers."

"But we will see them, won't we?" Benny asks, in a hopeful voice.

"With our luck they'll be out sunning themselves on a big rock somewhere where the truck can't go," Jill says.

"Right, Jill," Tara says. "We've got to stop this truck and go for a walk. Good idea. Omar, you are a man of authority. Go tell Rajiv we're walking from here. Scoot, go on now." She advances on Omar with mock haughtiness.

Omar looks at her, his eyes suddenly going wild.

Good God, she thinks, what's he got going on that he's so deceitful about? He's hiding something.

"I will, Tara," he says. "I will accommodate you." He runs to the back of the passenger compartment and pounds on the window. "Stop, Rajiv. Tara wants to walk."

"I want all of us to walk."

"She wants all of us to walk," Omar says.

The truck dutifully comes to a halt and the engine turns off.

Tara sees Doug staring at her, his eyes sinking as if into a desert sandstorm. She looks at Zachary, surfer dude from California. He's studying her. Nothing shows on his face.

Tara mindlessly steps to the back of the truck. Jill and Benny are already on the ground. Tara sits, dangles her legs, and slides off. The ground feels like mush, but as she walks around, she realizes it's her feet that feel like mush.

She watches Doug ease himself off the truck, and then Zachary, surfer dude. A real pro, that Zachary. A nifty move off the back of the truck. Is he a gymnast or what? The others follow with varying degrees of deftness.

She hears a door open, sees Rajiv step out; then sees Rose and Jerry Quinn emerge. Everyone but Zachary is walking around with an incredulous look, each pausing to stare at Tara.

Tara wants to get close to Zachary, surfer dude from California, and find out why he's so mysterious.

She sidles up to him, and suddenly, Tara and Zachary are walking down the road the truck had been following, the others falling in behind them.

"I thought it might lead to this, Jerry," Rose tells her husband, with no small measure of irony. "You've got to watch that Tara."

They've known me less than a day, Tara thinks, and they already know me very well.

Mindlessly, she walks along. She doesn't want to think about what she has done. And why they obeyed her. Are they crazy? What if I wake up one day and discover that everyone in the world has to obey me?

"Say, Zachary." She takes him by the arm, glances up at him. He seems to be listening to something inside himself. Always adrift within, she thinks. She whispers, lunging at him with each breathy utterance. "Why did they do that? Why did they stop the truck? Why are we walking? Isn't this crazy? I'm so scared I think my pants might fall off."

He doesn't break stride; he simply allows her to hold on to him, and they walk along.

Suddenly, Zachary speaks. "I'd be concerned if a person was alone out here, but with all of us in a group ..."

"With all of us in a group, a tiger isn't likely to attack, right?"

Zachary nods, his face a granite rock. Tara lays her eyes on this granite rock and asks, "So what have you learned about India since you've been here, Zachary? We hardly know anything about you. I'll tell you what I've learned." She looks back at the others. They're all marching along, looking to the sides, especially Omar; he always seems to be looking off to the side, as if there's an escape route he must find.

"We've been all over India, Zachary, did you know that? Six or seven places so far, not counting here, in six weeks. Six or seven more places before we go home. How about you? You never say where you're from."

"I'm from San Francisco."

"Oh? I thought so. California surfer dude. The Quinns are from Orange County. Did you know that?"

"Yes, I knew. No, I'm not a surfer dude."

"What do you do, if I might ask?"

"I'm a business consultant for high-tech firms that want to open markets around the world."

"Oh, that's interesting. So, you're here to study India, like we students."

"Yes, you could say that."

"Have you learned anything unusual yet?"

"Well actually—"

"You can call me Tara."

"Tara, I knew quite a bit about India before I came over here. I do my homework."

"But there's nothing like getting your feet wet, right, Zachary? Getting your feet dirty with the natives?"

"Uh, yes."

"You can read about the poverty, but once you're here it's ubiquitous. And everywhere we go, groups of activists speak to us about how the government oppresses them and how they refuse to hear them out."

"It's a democracy, Tara."

"Yes, but hardly anyone bothers to vote. The people tell us it wouldn't do any good anyway."

"Probably not. Sounds like America."

She laughs. "We have to wash our clothes here by hand, Zachary. That's not like America. And what do you think of Hindus and Muslims getting along so well? That surprised me."

"Well, Tara, actually Hindus and Muslims don't always get along so well. There's fighting up north—"

"Yeah, we've read about rebels executing prisoners. True?"

"True."

"How do you know it's true, Zachary? Do you just accept what the media reports? How do you know for sure the rebels execute prisoners?"

"It's been documented by all kinds of people unassociated with the media."

"We've been told by some of the people that the government controls the press and that they lie to make opposition groups look bad. We've been told that Indian Army troops engage in torture and summary executions of separatists. Zachary, I've seen ordinary citizens walking around armed to the teeth. This country is an armed camp sometimes."

He nods at her, and she thinks he is even more mysterious now.

"Tara," Zachary says, looking around at the brush, and for the first time she thinks he isn't buried inside himself. "I don't know if you recall, but a few years ago, Indira Gandhi was assassinated by her Sikh bodyguards and all hell broke loose. In Deli in one night, something like five thousand Sikhs were murdered. The authorities could do nothing, of course; what could they do in a situation like that? To quell such religious hatred is impossible. It's like a tsunami roaring in from the deep ocean; when the sea-floor rises, the wave becomes colossal. In India, there is an ever-present undercurrent of hatred that can be tapped by politicians or terrorists."

"Yes, it does sound like things got out of hand, Zachary. Couldn't the Army do anything?"

"The rioters were Hindus. The Indian Army is comprised primarily of Hindus. It's not likely that Hindus would step in and save Sikhs at the time. Emotions were too high. Innocent Sikhs were endangered by Indian intolerance. In rural areas maybe people of different religions can live together peacefully, but in cities all dangers are magnified, and like a tsunami approaching shallows, hatreds pile up and engulf everyone."

"Thanks for telling me, Zachary. But we've got to watch for tigers now. I think there's one up ahead somewhere. Don't you?"

Rajiv rushes up beside Tara. He's a good-natured fellow most of the time, but unduly influenced by the moods of Omar.

"The lady say—" Rajiv begins, but Tara interrupts.

"You mean Rose, Rajiv? It's okay for you to use our names, my good man."

"Rose?"

"Yes."

"She say the tigers come to where the sambar drink water. They lie in grass and charge the sambar. I checked with Omar, he says, 'Yes,' he says he knows where the sambar come to drink and where tigers might lie waiting."

"Oh, great, Rajiv. Can you ask ..." She looks back at Omar, who is bringing up the rear and is looking very nervous, swinging his head back and forth like it was a pendulum, looking for all the world as if he were insane. She also takes a look at Doug. Poor guy. But she won't go back to him. Jill is beside him. Benny is looking forlorn just ahead of Omar. Rose and Jerry Quinn are off to the side having a grand time. Dave Gallagher is walking alone, gazing at the brush, not sweating a thing. And poor Lucas, also walking alone, looking half-frightened now. We're heavy on California types, she thinks. Zachary and the Quinns. California surfer dudes.

"Hey, Omar," she yells. "Come up here and lead us, you're the man of the hour. Get up here pronto. Something's going to die today and we must get in our blood sport, you hear? We want blood," she chants, flying her hands around as if she were a cheerleader. "We want blood. We want blood."

Omar comes running up. "God, why is everyone obeying me today?" Tara says, under her breath. "I don't always want them to; sometimes I'm just fooling."

"Tara," Omar says, "the lake is this way." He points. "Also, I think ..." He bends close to her, his dark face inches from her.

God, no offense, Omar, she thinks, but your breath could kill birds in flight. "Yes, Omar?"

"I think your friend, Doug, is going to leave us soon."

She steps away from him, looks at Zachary. It's clear Zachary heard what Omar said. She looks at Omar. "Leave us?"

"He is feeling bad," Omar says. "He is looking for a way to revenge you. Maybe good for you to walk with Doug, Tara." He looks at her with pleading eyes.

"But I'm not going to babysit him," she says. She doesn't want to mention that Doug has been intruding over her boundaries, staring at her too much and trying to get his hands all over her. That's not Omar's business.

"You mean"—she tries to read Omar's face—"Doug might trek off into the scrub and then have us worry over him, given there are tigers out there who might take exception to his trespassing on their territory?"

Omar looks at Zachary, and Zachary nods. Omar makes a face like a perplexed bear and nods at Tara. "Yes, little one, I think so. Doug will wander away. I've seen it happen before with tour groups such as yours. With a young lady and a young man who have recently broken up, one or the other will revenge the loss and place themselves in harm's way to teach a lesson."

"Very well put, Omar," she says. She looks at Zachary, and he smiles at her, for the first time. "I think I understand you perfectly well, but I need time to think about this. You see, Doug and I are on the outs, and he will not have his way just by scaring me. I don't scare that easily. But could you have Jill come up here?" She yells at Jill. "Hey, Jill, come here, will you?"

Omar nods and takes his leave.

Jill rushes up to Tara.

"Why is everyone obeying me today, Jill? Never mind." She takes Jill aside and whispers, making sure Zachary hears, but not letting her voice carry beyond the three of them. "Keep an eye on Doug, will you? Omar says he's going to wander off into the clutches of a tiger to get back at me. Savvy?"

"Tara, if Doug wanders off, he's on his own. If a tiger eats him ..." She smiles. "I trust their intestines are tough enough."

"Okay, it'll be our war story, then," Tara says.

They walk along, Jill sticking with Tara and Zachary. After a moment, Tara says to Jill, "Maybe you'd better go back and keep Benny company."

"Forget it, Tara, Benny is tiger bait. War stories, you know. I'm staying here with you two."

"Thank God, Jill, someone finally disobeyed me. I was beginning to wonder if I was becoming God or something. That reminds me, Zachary, you haven't asked us where we're from. Aren't you curious?"

He smiles again, but is lost in himself, as if he were playing a chess master. "You're American college students on tour. I've gathered that much."

"Well, actually," Jill says, "we are on more than just a tour. We're spending half our year in India, to learn as much as we can about the culture. Our program is called Spiritual Paths of India. It counts toward our graduation, and of course it prepares us for the real world back home: no toilets, no toilet paper, no personal hygiene products, no—"

"Tigers lurking," Tara says. She doesn't want Jill to keep rambling on. Jill sometimes embarrasses the hell out of her. But they are the best of friends. She doesn't understand why Doug doesn't go for Jill. She's prettier. Her figure is snappier. So, Doug, why don't you paw her for a change?

"Tigers, tigers," Tara says, looking around. "Now I'm getting frightened again."

She looks ahead at Omar. He's leading the way to the lake where the sambars drink and is continually looking over his shoulder at them and to the sides. He's a crazy man, she thinks, and is suddenly glad Zachary is along.

Zachary looks tough. Someone put steel inside Zachary. If Omar gets any ideas about me, I'll call for Zachary. Omar looks like he wouldn't take no for an answer. Maybe I'm just being paranoid. The same could be said for any man. They're all animals, aren't they? Not Zachary. Or is he? She looks at him out of the corner of her eye and doesn't really know for sure.

"Zachary, each day when I get up, I try to figure out what's going to happen, if I'll be glad by the end of the day, or if I'll be sad, if I'll have learned anything of lasting value, or if it's been just another wasted day. What do you think will happen today?"

After a pause, he says, "If we get lucky, we'll see a tiger up close."

Tara wonders what Zachary does that makes him so blasé. Something tugs at her mind. She looks back at Dave Gallagher. Dave does not seem particularly bold, yet she thinks he would face danger with more alacrity than any of them. And then something profound penetrates her mind: Dave Gallagher has a death wish. She is certain of this and averts her eyes from him. This is awful. She locks eyes on Zachary; he is her savior, for the moment, with his calm demeanor.

"I mean, Zachary, what do you think we'll learn today?"

"Like he's going to open up a textbook for us, Tara?" Jill says. "Expectations can set up barriers to learning. Do you want us to just hang loose, Zachary?"

"Hang loose, Jill," he says. "You too, Tara."

"Excellent, Zachary," Jill says. "And what is your game, by the way? What are you listening to, if I might be so bold as to ask?"

"Listening?"

She's stealing my thunder, Tara thinks. She elbows Jill, wills her to fall back in the pack. Go see Benny.

Jill elbows Tara back and continues. "Inside your mind, you're always listening. It's obvious. So, what are you listening to? Anything you'd care to share?"

Zachary walks along in silence, his lips pursed.

Tara mouths to Jill: *Don't push it.*

"Well, Zachary," Jill says, "if you won't share your thoughts, at least share your plan if a big tiger jumps out at us."

But Zachary remains silent, and Jill answers for him.

"Oh, that's easy. We stay together in a group. We make like we're one big organism. Tigers and other predators have a survival instinct that warns them away from anything too big, such as an elephant. They prefer to pick on smaller beasts. So, if I pig out to the tune of a thousand chocolate bars a day for a year and tip the scales at nine thousand pounds, I'd be safe walking in tiger country."

"That's a partial truth, Jill," Zachary says. "I can't say for sure, but if you're nine thousand pounds and walking beside Tara, I think the tiger would go for Tara. I know I would."

They laugh. But Tara is jealous; Jill is working her way into her mystery man.

Almost imperceptibly, Zachary stiffens in his walk, and Tara looks ahead. Omar has stepped from the road and is standing near a wall of brush. He motions for them to follow and disappears into shadowy places.

Tara feels her heart jump. Running along with Zachary, she looks into the sky, as if getting her bearings for the last time. The sky is soaked with a milky haze that burns off visibly before her eyes, promising an afternoon hotter than the cool morning.

Pulled along by Zachary's hand, she ducks into a tight corridor where the bushes morph into fire-tipped cat whiskers that brush the bare skin of her arms. As they penetrate deeper, the air announces itself forcefully, and savory brush peppers her nostrils.

They wind through the brush, cross a grassy area, and enter a scrub forest, where the shadows lie bunched and thick. They walk through the silent beauty, crouching low as the scrub presses in. They break into a savanna, walk up a hill, follow a ridgeline, and then pass down into a marshy-looking area that turns out to be dry. They enter flats with tall grass that flares out in golden arrays. They see rocky outcroppings in the distance and blue sky overhead.

They form up in the golden grass. Tara feels energized. She looks at the others as they pull up. She sees a bobbing sea of rosy cheeks and hears the heavy machinery of breathing—but of people excited, people on an adventure, not people worn out.

They walk a bit farther.

"There." Omar stops and points. A green field of grass, stirred gently by the wind, greets their eyes, with blue water beyond.

"Do you hear how quiet it is?" Rose Quinn says. "I sense we're being watched."

At the sound of Rose's voice, something starts crawling inside Tara's skin. She shivers. "I agree," she says. "It is quiet. Preternaturally quiet. I think we are being watched."

"If it's a tiger," Omar says, "monkeys and deer will tell us. They will call when Raja near."

"You mean you know the tiger's name?" Tara asks.

"No," Omar says. "But it is good practice to name a tiger. Then it is less likely to eat you."

"Oh," Tara says, smiling at the others, then scanning the grass where Omar pointed. "Raja," she calls. She looks around. "Hey, where's Doug?"

Everyone looks around. Doug is not with them.

Dave Gallagher calls out, "Doug, get over here right now." A sheepish Doug walks toward them across the grass.

"He will try again," Omar whispers to Tara. "He will take revenge. It is written in his face and in every step he takes. I beg you to walk with him and to not walk with Zachary anymore."

"Look, Omar," she says, keeping her voice low, "I don't live in a society where I obey men as if it were my duty, like maybe it is here in India or in your Islamic world. Doug has violated some of my rules and now he is cast adrift. He'll have to deal with that however he can; I will not be swayed by his passive-aggressive attempts to get me to take him back. If a tiger eats Doug, I'll feel bad, but I'll get over it quickly. Are we clear?"

Omar leans away from her, a worried look on his face. But he appears resigned. "I won't say it again, Tara. You are powerful, like the tiger. I think Raja won't eat you."

"Right, Omar, he'd get indigestion. Let's go." She sets off toward the tall grass.

With Tara leading the way, they wind through grass so thick it twines around them as they try to walk. Eventually they become stuck. Tara realizes she doesn't know where to lead them, so she tells Omar to lead the way.

Omar leads them back out, and avoiding the impenetrable grass, finds a path for them. As they walk, the air becomes thick with the buzz of insects and the calls of birds.

They come across a game trail. Omar points at fresh deer tracks. Something bounds up in front of them and races away. Tara's heart leaps into the air. She's about ready to turn tail and run the other way when she recognizes the bounding thing as a deer. It tears away, its hooves pounding.

They hear calls and barks—sambar deer warning each other of their approach. They creep along the game trail, crouched and wary, listening with nervous attention. Tara can barely take the suspense, thinking a tiger might leap out at them any moment.

They reach soggy ground, the grass so thick they can't see more than five feet in any direction.

"We go back," Omar says.

They retrace their path and enter a drier area, where the hooves of animals have pounded the grass down.

"I should warn everyone," Jerry Quinn says. "There are freshwater crocodiles in these lakes and sometimes they creep out and get a deer."

Omar and Rajiv nod. Everyone looks at Tara. And it makes her feel guilty. She knows she has led them into danger.

"Let's get away from the water and find a herd of deer grazing," she says. "Maybe we'll get lucky. Omar, lead the way."

Omar begins walking, tentatively at first, then with purpose, as if he has sniffed out some deer. They walk to higher ground, and then they see, on a large, flat rock thirty yards away, the sun turning it into a fiery apparition, a tiger.

They stop. Rose, not watching, bumps into Rajiv; both grunt. The tiger stirs, lifts its head, and stares at Tara's group.

"Excuse me, Rajiv," Rose begins, but her husband taps her on the shoulder, points at the tiger, and she falls silent.

The tiger languorously rolls to its feet, crouches, and stares at them, its shoulders impossibly huge, muscular. They remain frozen as the tiger flows down from the rock, its eyes fixed on them. It flows into the green grass at the foot of the rock, flows along as if a ship on the sea. The tiger sinks low, and they can barely see it in the grass as it creeps closer.

Tara is petrified, frozen tight in a stricture of fear. She's sorry she got them into this spot. She thinks she was motivated to get off the truck and walk because of Doug; she thought she would fare better on the ground, keeping him at a distance. And now this tiger, a big male, she thinks, is stalking them. She's seen tigers in zoos and in pictures and knows the males are much larger than the females, and this big male is winding through the grass right at them. She knows they passed this outcrop on the way down to the lake; the tiger might have been there camouflaged and no one saw it. Or maybe Doug saw it but said nothing, the creep. She wishes the tiger had eaten him.

She watches the tiger inch its way toward them and hears Rose exhale and whisper in that marvelous California surfer-dude accent. "Look at that magnificent tiger."

And Rose inhales and exhales again and now Tara hears and feels a ripple move through the group and sees a ripple move through the grass—the tiger's ripple—and she feels the group squeeze closer together and she hears Zachary say, "Let's close up, and let's ..."

The tiger is still sailing along in that near-frozen posture, oozing through the grass, its eyes peeled on ...

Tara zeros in on the tiger's eyes and relief sweeps over her. Relief so sweet she is almost tempted to kiss Doug—no, maybe not that sweet after all.

She wants to say something to the group.

"I was in a zoo once," she says, "a few years ago before I knew much about tigers. And I stood in front of the tiger's cage and stared at the tiger a good long time. It was lying on a bench and suddenly it noticed me. It noticed I was staring at it. We made eye contact. It got up and crept to the bars of its cage, its eyes on me, staring right back, its teeth bared and its face in a ferocious squall. It was crouched and moving just like that tiger there, Raja. And its eyes were locked on mine. It would have gotten me if there hadn't been any bars there. I found myself moving down the way, away from that tiger, and it followed me as far as it could until it had reached the end of its enclosure. Eye contact with a tiger is not something I recommend, especially not here where there are no bars, so please everyone, no eye contact with Raja. Okay?"

"Sure," Jerry Quinn says matter of fact. "A predator sees eye contact as a challenge. But this tiger clearly is not interested in us."

"Slowly ..." Zachary says.

Tara has tuned Zachary back in.

"Slowly," Zachary says as the tiger inches closer. "Turn. No abrupt movements and keep turning ..."

Zachary turns his body; they all do the same, matching his movement.

"And when you can, turn your heads and look behind us."

"Ah," Rose Quinn says with a resonance of understanding in her voice. "Ah, yes ..."

Tara looks at Rose, sees the enchantment in her eyes. She looks at Jerry, sees Jerry enthralled at the tiger's advance.

Too many heads are in Tara's way for her to see what's behind them, but as the group rotates and as the tiger stalks close to them and comes up and passes so close they could reach out and touch it, Tara hears Jill say, "It's stalking deer."

Jill takes her camera out, points at the tiger, and clicks. Tara takes her camera out, points at the tiger, and clicks, also, as does the entire group, still turning and now violating Zachary's rule to stick close together, now that the tiger is past them and oozing through the grass beyond them, its big shoulders like a bulldozer through the sea of grass.

They spread out and snap away at the tiger and look into the distance where a herd of sambar is grazing.

"The tiger was using us as a shield to stalk the deer," Jerry Quinn says.

"A very opportunistic animal, our Raja," Tara says.

"I have seen this before, using shields to stalk," Omar says.

"We are having an experience here," Tara says. "Record it for posterity. Cameras at the ready. Anyone want to make any bets on which deer Raja will kill?"

"The largest," Omar says. "The tiger will sneak close and rush it."

Jerry nods. "The largest." He points. "Big cats go after big prey."

"I see," Tara says. "What do you think, Zachary?"

"I think I understand the evolutionary underpinnings of what we are witnessing. Tigers that go after the largest deer fare better. Those genes are the tiger genes of today. Raja knows this. He's a tiger driven to succeed."

"Well, put, Zachary."

They watch in fascination as Raja creeps ever closer to the deer, freezing and flowing, then stopping within striking distance. But the wait becomes interminable for Tara as the minutes drag on and the tiger does not make its move. She hears the whine in her voice.

"When's he gonna rush one of them?"

"Tara," Jill says, "can't you just accept the pace of nature?"

"Yeah"—she yawns—"I guess I'll have to."

The tiger springs up and bounds after the deer; they scatter and the tiger veers toward the largest sambar. The tiger is on the sambar in a flash and takes it down. All that is visible now is rippling tiger muscle rising above the sea of grass.

"It's shifted its grip to the throat," Jerry says. "It's strangling it. It'll feed from the hindquarters forward and it won't let anything else come near the kill."

"Right," Tara says. "Well, what do you say? Shall we mosey on down and take a closer look, tempt fate maybe? Maybe get ourselves killed? Or should we head back to the truck? I'm famished. I could also use a restroom. Omar, will you lead us back to the truck? Maybe we can rumble on to the next rest area."

They quickly agree that the truck is the better alternative to getting killed by Raja, so Omar leads them though the wilderness. They hear grunts and snarls from the tiger as they go. Gradually the sounds diminish and the normal sounds of the scrub jungle serenade them on their way.

Tara tells everyone to close up ranks. They had straggled out into a long, undisciplined line, studying the flora and fauna and snapping pictures. She counts the troops. Omar and Doug are missing.

"Hey, everyone, where are Omar and Doug?"

They spread out and call for Omar and Doug.

Tara says they'll keep walking. "When Omar and Doug show up, I'm going to bring them up on charges."

They reach the road. Military vehicles loaded with Indian Army troops cruise past them. They continue walking toward the truck.

When they get back to the truck, some military vehicles stop and soldiers surround them. Rajiv explains he is the park guide for the group. The soldiers take down the names and hometowns of the Americans and warn them that it is dangerous for anyone to be about, especially in the cities, and to stay here in the park.

Tara tells the soldiers that Omar and Doug are missing. She explains that Doug is probably taking revenge against her for spurning him.

They tell her not to worry. They tell her that Omar is probably trying to console Doug and talk him into pursuing her more forcefully.

"What an awful thing to say," Tara says. She waves her arms at them. "Scoot, go!"

The soldiers get in their vehicles and drive away.

"Let's all try to stay together now," Tara says. "We are faced with a serious situation. We need to go to the next rest area and spend the night there. If they have a landline, we'll call out."

She glares at Dave. He has a satellite phone, but she doesn't like him using it. She's concerned he'll call the

American Embassy and tell them the group wants to leave India prematurely. No one uses Dave's phone anymore, not even Dave. Tara won't allow it.

Omar and Doug ride up in a vehicle with some soldiers. They get out and explain that they had kept walking when the group stopped and had gotten lost when they tried to backtrack.

"You're both under arrest for desertion," Tara says.

They drive to the next rest area and find a telephone. Tara calls the American Embassy. A voice reaches her dimly through the mist of wires that lie between Ranthambhore and Delhi. She asks for news and is told that terrorist attacks have provoked rioting in Deli and elsewhere and that death squads are roaming about. She is told that war between India and Pakistan seems imminent. She asks what the United States is doing about it, but the connection flares out. When it flickers back, she is told not to come back to Delhi until things settle down. She has shivers when she hangs up.

Tara informs her group of the trouble in Delhi.

"We're staying put in Ranthambhore. Rajiv, lead us to the mess hall and break out some food. Afterward, Omar and Doug will stand court-martial."

After nightfall, Tara's group gathers in a large room layered with ghostly lamplight. Everything dates back to an earlier era: screened windows, a hardwood floor, scuffed and polished tables and benches. Tara sits at the front of the room. Lucas approaches her.

"I file a motion to dismiss," Lucas says.

"Motion denied."

"I file a motion against pre-trial confinement."

"There has been no pre-trial confinement."

"I file for a delay. I need time to consult with my clients and interview prospective witnesses."

"Motion granted. Make it snappy."

Lucas goes to the defense table, where he confers with Omar and Doug; to the prosecution table, where he questions Jill; and then to the spectator section, where he questions the others.

He approaches Tara. "Can I question you, too?"

"No. You shouldn't have questioned Jill, either. She's the prosecutor. But it's too late. Does the defense want to enter pleas?"

"Yes. Not guilty for both of them."

"Okay. This is the arraignment. Now we begin the court-martial. Take your seat, Lucas."

Lucas returns to his seat, and Tara tells Jill to read the charges.

Jill stands. "The United States versus Omar Khan and Doug Chamberlain. The accused are charged with desertion under conditions of war. The government is seeking the death penalty."

"Are you going to make an opening statement, Jill?"

"I am. Today, the defendants left their unit under conditions of war. Everyone here is a witness. They weren't seen for quite a while, until enemy troops returned them in a vehicle. We suspect collaboration with the enemy."

Lucas jumps up. "I object."

"Not now, Lucas," Tara says. "Not during the opening statement."

"The prosecutor is erroneously calling Indian soldiers the enemy, and she is suggesting an additional offense, which my clients have not been charged with. There was no collaboration with the enemy."

"Sit down, Lucas. You will have your chance. The prosecution can proceed."

"I will prove my case abundantly," Jill says. "Furthermore, I think Omar is a spy. I also think Lucas should be charged with dereliction of duty. He's supposed to be wearing a black hood and carrying an AK-47."

"Noted. Lucas, I am going to include you in this court-martial as another defendant, charged with dereliction of duty, unless you can produce a black hood and an AK-47. Can you get them?"

"I don't have them with me. May I proceed?"

"Sure, Lucas, but you'll stand charges, son."

"I'm not your son."

"Sit down, Lucas. Jill, are you going to start calling witnesses?"

"Yes, Tara. I call Zachary Knight to the stand."

"Good," Tara says. "It'll be our chance to question our mystery man."

But Lucas objects. "Hey, judge, I haven't made my opening statement yet."

"Sorry, Lucas. We're getting ahead of ourselves. You can make your opening statement now."

"My clients are innocent of all charges. There is more than just a reasonable doubt. The doubt is so enormous it would blot out the sun. I will prove that the government has no case, and that there is something strange going on here. I believe the judge and prosecutor are in cahoots, and both of them should be charged with subverting the legal process."

"Lucas, I must warn you," Tara says. "Leveling unsupported charges against superior officers is illegal. It can result in court-martial, termination from military service, and prison time. Do you wish to withdraw your comments concerning Jill and me?"

"No. My comments stand."

"We will proceed. And Lucas, you are faced with additional charges now."

"Fuck you, judge!"

"That's another charge, Lucas. I've never heard you swear before."

"You're an asshole, Tara."

"That's another charge. Lucas, I will have you removed from this courtroom unless you behave."

"Thought control, that's what this is. You broads are always into thought control and intimidation. That's the only way you can win. You're cold-blooded weasels."

"You are looking for trouble, Lucas. Sit down."

"You're a broad, Tara."

"I never call you names."

"Someday you're going to suffer, Tara, and then you'll know what this world is all about, you fucking broad."

"Lucas, your comments will cost you dearly."

"Tara, you're a fucking broad."

"Ah, I think we'll proceed with Lucas gone."

"More thought control. Tara, I'm the best defense attorney available. If you kick me out, my clients will not have adequate legal representation and the case will likely be overturned on appeal. You will look like a dumb broad."

"You are a criminal, Lucas. I will have you prosecuted."

"You're a dumb broad, Tara."

"Lucas, if you behave, I'll let you stay, and we won't charge you with anything. I'll also reduce your clients' charges to dereliction of duty. How's that?"

"Tara, after this trial, I'm going to tell my clients to kick your ass." Lucas sits.

Zachary Knight has taken the witness stand and Jill has sworn him in.

"Zachary," Jill says, "where I live, in Montana, an owl establishes its territory by killing and eating the insides of competing predators. Do you do this, also?"

Lucas is on his feet. "I object. The question is irrelevant and repugnant."

"Jill, are you trying to establish something here?" Tara asks.

"I'm trying to establish the expert credentials of this witness."

"Proceed, counselor."

"Zachary, let me rephrase the question. Are you attempting to establish your territory here in Ranthambhore? Remember, you are under oath."

"Jill, all I can say is that someone is attempting to establish their territory here."

"You?"

"I can't say."

"Zachary, I insist that you answer. How are you doing this?"

Zachary doesn't answer. Something seems to shift in Jill. She leans forward, her eyes capturing Zachary with a wild intensity.

"Zachary, where is the enemy?"

Zachary leans back. "I don't know."

"You must know."

"I don't know, Jill. You've asked me this before."

A spell seems woven between them.

"I thought men were good at fighting wars, Zachary."

"This time the enemy is too well hidden."

Lucas stands and the spell snaps. "Tara, I'd like to approach the bench."

Tara nods.

Lucas walks to her and Jill joins them.

"What do you want, Lucas?"

Lucas keeps his voice low. "Did you and Jill have something in mind concerning this witness?"

"He's mysterious. We wanted to unravel him."

"Tara, we are the mysterious ones. He's going to unravel us. Can't you see that?"

"Oh. Do you want me to stop it?"

"I do."

"Okay, I will. But we'll let Jill proceed a while longer."

Lucas returns to the defense table.

Jill glances at Tara, frowning. She's about to say something, but shrugs instead. "I have no further questions, Your Honor." She takes her seat.

"Lucas, do you have any questions for this witness?"

Lucas walks toward the witness. "Zachary, do you know why the defendants were separated from the unit today?"

"Yes."

"Are there any military personnel present in this room?"

"Yes."

"You?"

Zachary does not respond.

"Zachary, do we need to do something tonight to survive?"

"As I understand it, yes."

"Can you tell us what we need to do?"

"No."

"Did Omar Khan have criminal intent when he became separated from the unit today?"

"No."

"Did Doug Chamberlain have criminal intent?"

"No."

"Zachary, is our group being used for something here in Ranthambhore?"

"As I understand it, yes."

"Zachary, why? What's going to happen?"

"We can't know that."

"Zachary, we saw Indian soldiers today. We know there are death squads operating in India. Is there a death squad in Ranthambhore?"

"As I understand it, yes."

"Were the Indian soldiers looking for the death squad?"

"As I understand it, yes."

"That's enough," Tara says. "Lucas, do you want to make a motion?"

"I move to have all charges against my clients dismissed."

"Motion granted. I dismiss all charges. The prisoners are released."

Tara stands. "All rise. The court-martial is adjourned. Let's go outside."

They file outside. It is pitch dark. They stay close to the building. Rajiv wanders off with a flashlight and soon yard lights from the various buildings flick on and they are bathed in misty, yellow glows.

They wander, but not far. A while later they go back inside. Rajiv is carrying a stack of blankets. They settle in for the night, lying about on the floor. Tara turns off the lamps, but keeps one burning.

Lucas, lying on a blanket, holds up a bottle of water. He drinks from it, and then holds the bottle still. He stares into the liquid, illuminated in the glow of the lamp, and watches the water settle.

For a while, he sees nothing but undisturbed water, and then he sees motion, a tiny disturbance, barely perceptible, and then waves building and running at each other.

He saw this on the beach at Somnath, in Gujarat State, on the Arabian Sea, when Tara was in the water, bigger waves then. He was certain an undersea goliath was after her. It churned up the water. He nearly jumped off his towel and ran in to save her. Fear kept him back.

Tara hears a noise. Moments later, she is standing at the door, watching someone walk into the darkness.

A knock sounds on the door, sharp and insistent, startling Tara awake. Who would be knocking at this hour? Or at any hour? She looks up from her blanket, and then rises, as Benny, the closest, picks up the lamp and goes to the door.

"Get up, everyone," Tara hisses. She regrets not having posted a guard and gives herself a mental kick as she scurries to a table.

She sits and watches the others shake loose from their sleep. She doesn't know what to expect, but if there's trouble, she wants everyone awake.

Benny opens the door and a tall man enters, his boots

clumping across the hardwood floor. A thick musk accompanies him and the room quickly fills with his scent. Lamps flicker on as several more men follow him in, the mass clumping becoming a menace to Tara's equanimity. They are dressed in khaki uniforms and carry submachine guns, unslung and in their hands. All have beards; none wear headgear. They hustle about the room, staring at each face.

Tara makes eye contact with the leader. She remembers the tiger in the zoo and the dangers of doing this, but feels he is an intruder and must face her challenge. They stare at one another.

He walks toward her.

He stops and slips into a perplexity of nerve-twitches, as if he were no longer certain of his purpose, and then closes himself off to her. His attention drifts about the room but quickly comes back to Tara. His eyes do a rapid-fire dissection of her and seem to find something amusing. He laughs silently, and then shifts his gaze elsewhere, not concerned with her anymore.

Are they Indian soldiers? She doesn't think so. She thinks they're unofficial, and that's scary. Or maybe they're official, but deniable, which is even scarier. She wants to ask Omar. He's incredibly adept at reading people. She sees him across the room and asks him with her gaze. Who are these men? What do they want? But Omar's eyes are muted with a meekness she hasn't seen in him before.

The leader is turning about, his eyes sweeping everyone up. "Line up. Show ID. Passport. Answer questions." His voice has claws that dig in. His English is as uncomplicated as a road accident.

"Saeed," a gruff-voiced soldier calls. The leader glares at him. "I will wait outside." The soldier stalks out the door.

That name. Saeed. She has heard it before. She takes a closer look at him. He has a beard, like all the others; a large head; dark skin; and eyes that stab as much as look. She sees toughness in the cast of his shoulders and in the massive architecture of his hands. She sees that he is not a young man. The terrain of his face is deeply etched; his flesh sags.

Saeed is too old for this, she thinks. He should be in a grotto somewhere, issuing orders to subordinates. The one who called him by name is probably his second in command. She thinks he will hear about it later from Saeed, and that he and Saeed will joke about it as both try to dip the other's nerves in ice water.

A line forms and Tara pushes away from the table and joins it. Saeed begins checking IDs.

"Name. You first."

"Dave Gallagher."

"American?"

"Yes."

"Where from?"

"California."

Saeed walks down the line.

"Name?"

"Jill Ripley."

He stares at her, eyeball to eyeball. "Where from?"

"Montana."

"You?"

"Tara Brewer. I attend college in California, but I'm from Virginia."

He checks the other Americans and then comes to Omar and Rajiv.

"Name?"

"Omar Khan." Omar looks resigned to whatever fate these men represent.

"Name?"

"Rajiv Das." Rajiv looks defiant, puffing himself up.

Saeed looks around at the group, and then steps up to Dave Gallagher again. "How long have you been in Ranthambhore?"

"Since yesterday morning."

"How long do you plan to stay?"

"We don't know. A spokesperson at the American Embassy told us not to return to Delhi until things settle down." Dave looks around nervously.

Saeed seems indecisive.

Tara observes her group. Jill looks worried, terrified even. Benny looks like a ghost, all wispy and blown away. Doug looks as if he is on death row and contemplating his last hours. Rose and Jerry Quinn are trying hard to mask their panic. But Zachary looks nothing more than concerned, keeping Saeed in sight and being attentive. The difference between Zachary and us, she thinks, is one of degree. We feel our lives are about to end and he is focused on the moment. Now more than anything, Tara wants for these men to leave.

She catches Saeed's eye. He walks toward her.

"Can you go now?" she asks.

Saeed laughs, a deep and hearty laugh, and wanders away. He whispers to one of his men. The man rushes outside and soon another man enters with a large radio.

"One by one," Saeed says, "we will send word of your survival to the American Embassy in Delhi."

Tara hears exhalations from everyone in the room and sees Jill almost collapse in relief. Everyone comes alive and lines up by the radio and then Saeed says, "No, only one at a time, all wait outside, and one at a time will be brought in, in case sensitive information will be departed." He says only he and the radio operator will be present during the broadcasts.

They rush outside.

Tara waits her turn, lined up with the others. "Why all this bother just to have us talk on the radio with the embassy?" she asks one of the guards. The guard stares at her for a moment and then walks away.

She catches Rose's eye. "What do you think, Rose?"

"Tara, I think this is India, not America."

"Oh, yeah?" But Tara doesn't think that's all there is to it.

Dave emerges from the building; he's had his turn at the radio. And now the guards take Benny in.

She sees the guards take Dave away through the dimly lit yard. They disappear behind a building. She wonders if Dave still has a death wish. She holds her breath waiting for shots to ring out.

She hears no shots.

Benny emerges after an interminable wait and Jill enters. Tara can't contain herself any longer. "Benny, did you speak with the embassy?"

"Yes." He smiles at her. "Hey, it's cool, Tara." Benny, under escort, disappears behind the same building as Dave.

She wonders what Zachary would think of that, Benny so happy at speaking to the embassy. Hey, no big deal.

She turns and looks at Zachary. She roams around in his mind and tries to get a handle on his thoughts. What are you thinking, Zachary? Why would they want us to call the embassy? There must be thousands of Americans across the length and breadth of India. Imagine all that radio traffic in and out of the embassy and all the phone calls. Why not just a list of names and hometowns? We wouldn't be speaking to anyone who knew us personally.

She watches Jill emerge from the building. She can't get a reading off Jill. Nothing.

The guards motion for Tara to enter. She rushes up the steps and sweeps through the door. Inside, Saeed motions her toward a chair by the radio.

She feels something is not right in here; something oppressive is weighing the atmosphere down. She wants to be anywhere but here, even out there with Raja, alone at night with Raja hungry and willing to settle for an American college student.

"Here, you can have Doug," she says, whispering to the imaginary Raja as she takes a seat.

Saeed and the radio operator look at her with interest.

"Okay, what do I do?"

The radio operator hands her a microphone. "Just speak into it," he says. "Answer the questions."

Tara hears a click. A voice speaks from the set. In the most sterile English she has ever heard, a man says, "Please state your name."

"Tara Brewer."

"What is your hometown?"

"Ah ... Virginia."

"Your school?"

"UCLA." She half expects the voice to ask her to spell everything, but it does not. She thinks it's not an

American, but an English-speaking Indian employed at the American Embassy, with a voice from the grave.

The chilling graveyard voice asks her if she is being treated well.

"Of course, we're having a blast. A tiger almost ate us today. It was stalking some deer and used us humans as a shield to work its way closer." She looks at Saeed; he is studying her. Impossible to read his thoughts.

"Say, are you really at the American Embassy?" she says into the microphone.

Silence.

Saeed shifts in his chair and looks about. He studies Tara again.

"We haven't seen any ID from these soldiers or whatever they are."

Saeed puts his hand over the mic. Someone clicks the radio off. He stares at her. "Answer the questions only."

The radio comes back to life and a new voice is on the air. "Tara, have you seen anything unusual today?"

"Only soldiers in the park, and now these people, and it's hard to tell who they are."

"Oh, I can assure you they are legit, Tara." This sounds like an American voice. "They're a contingent of India's Special Forces. If they aren't answering questions, it's because they can't."

"What are they doing here? How do we rate this special treatment?"

"I'm afraid some very bad things have been directed against Americans during this disturbance."

"Very bad, huh? If you mean no toilet paper and no toilets or running water, yes, it is very bad."

"No, Tara, I mean executions."

Her heart sinks.

"Not the executions of Americans, mind you, that would be intolerable and would be met with the gravest possible response. No, this is something else. Mobs are inviting Americans to watch the executions of Muslims or Hindus, whichever the case may be. It's largely a Hindu show and it's mainly Muslims being executed. We have reports from all over."

"Are they getting many takers?"

"Do you mean are many Americans deciding to watch?"

"Yes."

"Disturbingly, yes, Tara, in the streets of Delhi. We don't know what to make of it. People are, of course, much safer if they don't venture outdoors and—"

Saeed cuts the radio voice off with a smile, snapping a switch on the set.

"Tara, I have news for you. We are going to execute Omar. Do you want to watch?"

Saeed's smile broadens. He chuckles soundlessly, his chest convulsing. The sharp glint of his teeth startles her. His breath creeps over her depositing a sickly layer of oppression.

He's kidding. She knows he's kidding. He's putting her on.

"I want to speak to the—"

"It is dead."

She reaches for the switch, and a finger-crushing grip stops her.

She pulls her hand away from Saeed's coarse palm, shakes it, her eyes watering.

"I know you're kidding." She can barely keep herself from crying. "Why would you want to execute Omar? He's done no wrong."

Saeed laughs. "He is a crazy person. Do we need another reason?"

"He guided us through the scrub today. He showed great courage. He saved everyone's life from the tiger."

Saeed stands and roams the room, laughing. "What is the matter, Tara? Don't you want to see someone die today? The others, without exception, said yes. We are not kidding. Omar is to be shot and we feel duty bound to ask witnesses to be present."

"What did he do?"

"You did not notice perhaps that Omar was a bit erratic today?"

"Yes, I did."

"That Omar continually looked like he wanted to escape?"

"Yes, I did."

"He was always looking around."

"Yes. Is that a reason to shoot him?"

"There was a body found in the brush a week ago. We do DNA matching in India; the results came in today. Omar's body fluids were on the victim. This has nothing to do with the current crisis. He knew there would be trouble for him today."

"I don't believe you; DNA matching takes longer than that. Omar's extra sensitive. I don't think he would harm a flea."

Saeed shrugs. "The others have said yes."

"I don't believe you"

"They said yes."

"You must have used coercion."

"What is your answer, Tara?"

"You obviously want me to watch Omar get shot, don't

you? Why? Because I'm an American and you don't think I can take it?"

"Americans have no concept of death like we do. We are always with death, and each of us can walk to his death with an undisturbed mind. You are merely a student here on holiday."

"We are here to learn. India is our classroom. We are here for our spiritual immersion."

"Then learn, Tara, about death, about a man who walks to his death with joy, a man who does not fear death but has absolute faith in what lies beyond. Any of us could walk to his death like Omar. We are all the same. We are all believers in what lies beyond."

"Would you let me shoot you, Saeed?"

His eyes turn fiery. "Yes, Tara. I would let you shoot me. I know what lies beyond."

She doesn't know what has come over her, asking this psycho if she can shoot him. "If I shoot you, will you let Omar live?"

"Yes."

Before she can stop herself, the words are out of her mouth. "It's a deal." She stands and shakes Saeed's hand.

She is being led out the door into the night, passing by the rest of them still in line. The soldiers lead her to the back of a building, where everyone is sitting at picnic tables. Omar and Rajiv are laughing, Jill is laughing, Benny is laughing, but Dave is not laughing; he looks disturbed.

"So, what did they do with you, Tara?" Dave asks. "Who did they tell you was going to be shot?"

"Omar."

"They told me Rajiv."

"Oh?" Tara looks at the others.

"They told me Benny," Jill says. "I had a hard time believing that."

"They told me it would be Dave and Doug," Benny says.

"You're confusing me," Tara says. "I got Saeed to agree to let me shoot him in return for letting Omar live."

Omar and Rajiv roar.

"They tell me Jill was to be shot," Rajiv says. "I hoped it wouldn't be true. Now I know they won't shoot her."

"You know, I'm beginning to think this whole thing was a setup," Tara says. "We're here to learn the ways of India, and summary executions have been penciled into the curriculum. Don't tell me it's not a setup."

Zachary joins them.

"What do you think, Zachary?" Tara asks. "Is this whole thing on the up and up?"

"The radio call, I don't know. The rioting in Delhi, that's real."

"My feelings exactly. Who did they tell you was going to be shot?"

"They told me you, Tara, but that Omar volunteered in your place."

"What?" She is stunned. Many things hit Tara all at once and she feels her body sink into the earth under the force.

"Why were we told different things?" Dave asks. "It doesn't make any sense. Tara, do you know?"

She has to compose herself before answering. "Dave, this is horrible. Nothing has come into agreement yet."

He gives her a strange look.

She goes to Jill and whispers in her ear.

"Jill, I'm about to go nuts. Everything is crazy right now. The clock is still ticking. When things come into agreement, all of us might be facing a death squad. I have a responsibility here and so do you. At the right moment, you have to help."

Jill gives her a scared look, and backs away.

In about half an hour, everyone has had their turn at the radio, and all are gathered at the picnic tables. Saeed's men walk up, their submachine guns at the ready.

"Omar, it is time," Saeed says.

Omar stands and bows to the Americans. A soldier ties his hands behind his back and blindfolds him. He is walked to a tree and secured.

"No!" Tara is aghast. She stands. She looks around at the others. "No! Why isn't anyone doing anything? Doesn't everyone have to obey me? Saeed, get over here. What was our agreement? I can shoot you and spare Omar. Give me your gun."

"Tara." Zachary has a hand on her shoulder. He whispers, "Sit down. Our lives depend on it. Don't warp the process. We can only be swept along right now. They are practicing an ancient tradition, a public execution to entertain visitors. It is their way."

Tara sits. The soldiers line up, raise their submachine guns. Saeed gives the command to fire. She hears the shots, sees the barrels spitting fire, sees a spray of bullets strike Omar's chest, sees Omar slump.

Tara is dazed. They are cutting Omar away from the tree and dragging his corpse away.

"Just for you, Tara, to prove that this is no trick." Saeed takes a machete, hacks off Omar's head, and holds it up. Then he and the soldiers take Omar and his head away.

After several minutes of silence, Jerry Quinn says, "We had to watch. There really wasn't an option. I guess Omar

just accepted his fate. His faith must be very strong. This
is quite unlike America."

Tara is sick. Omar walked happily to his death. Why?

The radio operator walks out and stands before the
group. "All names and hometowns have been registered
with the American Embassy. Thank you for your cooper-
ation. You are encouraged to stay here at Ranthambhore
until the trouble in Delhi has subsided. Very bad to go
there now. You will be quite safe here. Army units will be
patrolling the park."

Tara stands, tears in her eyes. She addresses the radio
operator. "Why did they kill Omar?"

"Omar looked forward to going to heaven, my dear.
Don't be upset. He is pleased. Don't you have a religion,
my dear?"

"Yes. But we don't line people up and shoot them."

"But, Tara," the radio operator says, "Christians worldwide have put millions of people to death in the name of
Jesus. Personally, I think it was sick. But what I meant was,
won't you embrace death someday, knowing it awaits you?"

Her eyes drying, Tara looks at the radio operator. His
words had hammered her. It awaits everyone.

The soldiers are gone and Tara wants to look for Raja in
the scrub jungle to test her new-found idea that it is she
who is responsible for everything that happened, not
other forces such as the trouble in Delhi or anything else
at all.

But Jill sees her wander off into the darkness and grabs
her.

"It's me, Jill," she says. "I did all of this."

"No, Tara, it wasn't you."

"But I'm a central spirit."

"I know, but it wasn't you."

"If not me, who?"

"Who knows?"

Jill coaxes Tara back to camp.

The next day, Tara heads off into the scrub jungle again, but finds she is picking up a following as everyone tags along, even the radio operator—it turns out he is a park employee, also. She wants to confront Raja, sit down with him and no one else.

"Go back, you, go back, I tell you. I'm going to find Raja on my own and have a conversation with him."

They pull her back to camp.

Various ideas float through Tara's mind as she sits at a picnic table sharpening a big sword Rajiv found in one of the buildings. She realizes several pleasant days are about to pass as she and her group wait out the unpleasantness in Delhi, unless she can do something about it. Unpleasantness in Delhi should mean unpleasantness in Ranthambhore, too. That's what she believes. But how can she bring about this unpleasantness?

Tara decides she is through mourning Omar. She wants to go exploring. She wants to take her group and Rajiv on another tiger walk. Omar is dead and nothing will bring him back. Maybe it was okay. Maybe Omar had to die. Or maybe not, but fretting over it isn't going to make a difference.

They head out, Rajiv driving the truck, the Quinns inside with him, everyone else in back in the open air, watching for tigers. They wind along a road that Rajiv says will take them to a drier area of Ranthambhore, away from the lakes and crocodiles. Tara has decided they will leave Raja's territory alone for a while and maybe go look for him later.

It isn't long before she is telling them to get off the truck and walk. "Come on, everyone, let's get on the ground with the tigers."

They walk through a wooded area where sunlight falls in dappled patches, turning the earth a fiery orange. Tara sees how natural selection has favored tiger stripes.

"Rajiv, you devil. You have taken us to the den itself, haven't you? Can't you see it?"

"I see it, Tara. Yes, this is tiger habitat. They hide here and catch deer. They will catch us, too, if we don't watch out."

"I hope we get caught. I need an encounter with a man-eating beast."

"Tara, don't tempt the tigers."

"I'm with you on that, Rajiv. Let's keep going. Nothing bad will happen."

They walk a long way through the shadowy woods, silent and watchful, and then pass into a meadow swept with tall grass and a few gnarly trees. Sunshine erupts around them. Rajiv navigates as if he's been here before, taking them on a mazelike path. Tara glances behind her repeatedly, keeping tabs on the others. She doesn't want anyone to lag. She tries to sense if there are any problems with her group, but she can't read anything.

They break into a meadow choked with tall, golden grass, the sunlight so bright it forms a white necklace around them. Tara feels the pleasant warmth work its way into her, and then she stiffens.

Lucas is gone. She watched him leave the night Saeed and his soldiers came. Why did he go? She can't know that, not now. She shoves him from her mind.

They walk a long way and enter into another type of ecosystem, a meadow, but different from the one before. The grass is not as golden; it is streaked with green, creating a mosaic of color. Some of it is trampled down, some of it sparse, some of it luxuriant. In the sparser places, tiny green plants hug the ground like mist. Tara gets down on hands and knees to study the fuzzy little plants. While eyeballing them, from the corner of her eye, she sees something move.

She gets up. A wall of grass stands five feet away, a place where a tiger might hide. She realizes the trampled areas are places where deer might have lain, and that a tiger could be lying in wait nearby.

"Rajiv, let's look for tracks, shall we? Here, where it's been trampled. What do you say, good buddy?"

"I say we should, Tara. But we should also post two guards to watch for tigers. A tiger behaves differently when it sees a face. It is more comfortable if it sees the back of your head. Then it might want to kill you. We should have two guards that show their faces in opposite directions. What do you say, Tara?"

"Good idea, Rajiv. We don't want the tigers to get too comfortable. Rose, Jill, you watch first. Break it into two sectors. Don't wander, stay close. We'll relieve you before long so you can join in the search."

She watches Rose and Jill take up positions, and then she squats and studies the closely packed grass.

"Beyond the park," Rajiv says, "this habitat does not exist. Cattle eat the grass. Villagers chop the wood. It is barren, like a desert. Ranthambhore is oasis."

"I hear you, Rajiv."

"They take the tigers' home away from it. Soon there will be no home left."

"We won't let that happen, Rajiv. We won't let our animal friends be wiped out. They remind us of who we are. We are animals, too, just like them."

"Does your God permit a thought like that, Tara?"

"I no longer think of my God as outside myself, Rajiv. If I am capable of that thought, so is my God."

"Tara, I think your holy men do not like that. I think they would execute you for such a statement."

"In olden days they would burn me at the stake. But these aren't olden days. We're beyond that, Rajiv. Holy men can't touch me. They can't know God like I know God. They don't know God at all."

"Tara, you are powerful. You are like tiger. So, I think your home might be gone someday, too."

"My home is everywhere."

Tara and Zachary relieve Rose and Jill. The group searches a while longer and finds lots of tracks, but none of them were made by a tiger. They are deer tracks.

Jill asks everyone to be silent. She says she hears a foot stomping far away. She says deer will stomp a foot in alarm. They decide to go investigate.

Jill leads. Moments later, she asks everyone to stop and be silent again as she listens.

"I'm hearing bird alarms."

She leads them through brushy terrain, picking up the pace. Tara tells her they are making a lot of noise and Jill says it's good that they are making a lot of noise.

A cawing of epic proportions sounds in the distance. They stop again.

"Crows," Jill says. "I hear snarling, too. I think there's a kill, and I think there's a dispute over it. I want everyone to make lots of noise. Pick up sticks and rocks and bang them together as we go."

She continues to lead them through the brush and soon Rajiv is beside her, informing her of a road that passes nearby.

"The road can take us close to where the crows are gathering," he says. He lowers his voice. "There's a tiger there, Jill."

She scans Rajiv's face and is surprised at what she sees, for there is no fear, only excitement. She glances at the others; excitement is everywhere. She leads them toward the road, telling them to keep making noise.

Minutes later, Jill holds up a hand and their footsteps cease. The road is right in front of them.

A wild scream erupts in the distance and is strangled off. The air vibrates into lyrics of terror as more screams are heard and then a deafening silence.

They draw close together. Jill looks at them. They're edgy. The fun has drained out of them.

"What was that?" Tara asks. "That sounded human."

"No," Jill says. "We heard animals. Listen up. Fan out in the bushes, stay near the road, and remain silent. I'm going to do some scouting. Tara, you come with me. Keep an eye out. We're likely to draw the attention of whatever is on that kill."

"Jill, maybe we better not go."

"Do not go, Jill," Rajiv says. "It is very bad."

"Rajiv, stay here with the others. Watch over them. Before we bring the unit up, we have to do some scouting. There's no tiger."

"Jill, people who say that get eaten."

"Scavengers are feeding off the kill. There is no tiger. It would chase them off."

"Jill, there is always a tiger."

Jill steps onto the road and walks with a purposeful stride. The crows are squabbling in the distance; a black cloud of them hangs in the air. The kill is probably large, she thinks, given the interest it has drawn, and that means it's probably a tiger kill. This gives her pause. A sambar stag can weight seven hundred pounds. She doesn't understand why the tiger isn't around to protect it. The crows are making ghoulish sounds.

She looks behind her. Tara is following, but she is taking nibbling steps, her eyes unfocused.

Jill looks ahead. The scrub jungle is creeping up on them, the shadows closing in. She has to think this through. All predators and scavengers in the area are likely converging on the kill right now, including the resident tiger.

Her legs are turning rubbery. She thinks they should go back. She runs to Tara. Tara is like a zombie, her eyes nowhere, her breathing almost paralyzed.

"Tara, I'm having second thoughts."

They run back to the others. Jill pulls them from the brush, tells them to form up. She posts a guard and then speaks to them.

"It's too dangerous. Even if I had a rifle, I wouldn't go down there. I'm sorry I led you into this."

"It's okay, Jill," Tara says. "But I'm glad you had second thoughts."

"Jill, you stopped the tiger walk," Zachary says.

Jill looks at Zachary. She notices that Tara is also looking at their mystery man.

"I did?"

"You had us make noise, but when we reached the road, you had us be silent. You hid most of us, and then you and Tara went on a scouting patrol. It was no longer a tiger walk."

"Uh, Zachary?" Jill's voice falters. She tries to smile. She takes a deep breath. Her heart is pounding, her mind tumbling with what Zachary said. "Zachary, why did I stop the tiger walk?"

Tara's group is on the road, walking toward the crows. They are in two files, one on either side of the road. Each holds a stick in one hand, a rock in the other. They are silent, except for their footfalls and Zachary's voice.

"This is dangerous work," Zachary says. "Your emotions can overwhelm you. There is never a precise plan."

Zachary speaks for several more minutes, describing their battlefield and the wounds they will encounter, and then he gives it over to Jill.

Jill steps ahead of the group. The scrub jungle is overwhelming them at this point; she can't see the crows in flight, but she thinks more are coming in all the time; they are still making that awful racket. They're feasting on something, and will continue to do so until something big and aggressive drives them off.

She turns around and monitors the troops. She sees fear on everyone's face, except Zachary's. She's going to talk to them.

She knows that what she wants to convey is best expressed by the ideas that came to her on the beach at

Gujarat, on the Arabian Sea, when Lucas nearly jumped off his towel and ran into the water to save Tara. She talks about life, about death. The ideas resonate at a deeper level for her now. Suddenly, everything is clear: the battlefield, the enemy, the long misty river of souls entering life, departing life.

"Zachary, did I say everything right?"

"You did, Jill."

The road curves, slopes down, levels off. The scrub jungle is replaced by grass ten feet tall. The claustrophobia gives way as a clearing opens and treetops swing into view, altars for the crows.

Jill leads them into the clearing. The crows are warring in the trees about fifty yards away. Their discordant voices mix with her senses, and she is jarred into a strange connection with the physical world. It causes her to jump back.

She clacks her stick against her rock, clack, clack, clack, and resumes her march.

Zachary steps up beside Jill. They are all clacking their sticks against their rocks as they walk.

Jackals are standing over the kill, watching their approach, their faces black patches in the shadows. They loft their ears and back away.

Jill watches the jackals slink toward a thicket and then returns her attention to the kill. A crow alights on it, pecks at the flesh, tears something off, and flies away. She decides she'll post a guard while they investigate.

"Doug and Benny, take up positions left and right. Watch through the trees. Tara, run forward past the kill and take up a position. Watch the thicket. Rajiv, watch our backs."

She watches Doug and Benny fan out and Tara run ahead. Tara passes the kill and stops a few yards beyond it.

Jill is standing over the kill now, her stick and rock silent. It's a large deer. The head and hindquarters are nearly obliterated. She takes a close look at its neck. It's a tiger kill.

Yips saturate the air. Jill snaps her head up. Jackals are scattering. A huge tiger has stepped from the thicket.

Jill loses her sense of self. She does not know if her body is standing, floating, or doing anything at all. She is hovering on the edge of darkness and feels a portion of herself dip low into shadowy places. Her consciousness is opening to an underworld of souls, ticking clocks, negotiable dramas, and things that come into agreement.

This underworld notices her presence and gathers something before her. What she sees scares her. A huge tiger is creeping toward Tara.

Jill is coming back to herself. She thinks her mind tricked her. None of what she witnessed could be true. She feels her fingers and toes ignite, her hands and feet, her arms and legs.

She walks around, anchored to her familiar world. The stick and rock are still in her hands. She clacks them together. Clack, clack, clack.

She walks over to Tara.

"How's it going, Tara?"

"Jill, I think I killed Raja."

"Tara, the tiger must have wandered off. I'm sure he's okay."

The others wander up, and Jill looks them over. Most of them look a bit shocked.

71

"Jill, I could have sworn. The tiger came out of the thicket. I was dancing ..."

"Tara—"

"Jill, don't you remember? After they executed Omar, I wanted to go out and have a conversation with Raja. I think I just had that conversation."

Jill looks around. Zachary is inspecting the ground where the tiger walked. She catches his eye. He walks to her.

"Jill, we have to leave."

As they walk toward the road, he asks if anyone has any injuries to report. No one has any injuries.

"What happened, Zachary?" Jill asks.

"I don't know, Jill. Give it some time."

Jill senses a shadow pass over them. An odd thought captures her. Lucas? She looks around. Where is Tara?

Tara thinks of a sweltering night in New Delhi, and of a cat creeping along, silhouetted against the glowing sky. Its tail is up, and the cat, driven by a constant inferno of desires, is alert to the wiliest of movements. A darting, and the cat's tail switches, and the cat creeps along with a prize in its mouth.

Having heard a sound, the cat is crouched, turning its head in the halo of light, searching with something rich and glistening in its jaws.

The cat has the look of an animal that is still hungry despite a recent kill, but hungry for what?

Tara wonders if cats can be as metaphysical as humans. She wonders if she can be as metaphysical as cats.

She wonders what she is doing now, drawing her shadow across the thicket, dancing toward the tiger.

Dancing toward her soul.

Human

At first, in the minds of the beholders, the cumbersome vehicle cruising the main drag of Pacific Terrace, California, registered as an old-fashioned circus wagon, and a carnival-like atmosphere soon prevailed. Ambling through wide turns and hugging the curbs, it mirrored the pace of the amused citizens on the sidewalks. But when a prehensile periscope of sorts sprang from the vehicle's side to poke at the crowds, and when a self-possessed voice shook forth from this contrivance, the circus wagon, by slow turns, like the haze-twisted California night itself, began to look outer spacey.

The police were called.

Two Pacific Terrace police cars, with red and blue flashing lights, pulled alongside the circus wagon. Officer Noel Jenkins, in the lead car, peered at the vehicle. The thing had no windows, no doors, no headlights, no taillights, and no turn signals. It looked like a flying saucer on end.

He glanced at the mob on the sidewalk. Arrayed in a semicircle, they crept along with the vehicle, keeping well away from a whiplike appendage that flogged at them from its side. A determined voice jetted from the vehicle. Though he could not make out the words, Jenkins got a sense of it. It seemed to be castigating someone in the crowd.

Jenkins pulled his cruiser in front of the circus wagon and stopped. The other police car drove alongside it and hemmed it in. The circus wagon came to a halt, its voice silent, its whip languishing over the crowd.

Jenkins got out. Montero, the other cop, got out. They stood beside their cruisers, watching the circus wagon. The red and blue flashing lights on their cruisers slashed the night like bloody daggers. Montero called over to Jenkins.

"What is it, an oyster on wheels?"

Jenkins did not share Montero's humor. He eyed the circus wagon and then glanced around. Traffic, what little of it there was, posed no problem. Drivers slowed to a crawl and trickled past. The people on the sidewalk were a concern. They would have to be dispersed. All because of some college punks who thought nothing of disturbing the peace, Jenkins thought. The state of California was saturated with high-tech slackers who thought nothing of flouting the law, while showing off their cracker-barrel brains. And, of course, they never went to jail. To top it off, the cocksure bastards always looked like they were laughing at you.

Jenkins seethed with barely suppressed anger. He rested the palm of his hand on the butt of his sidearm. What he wouldn't give to blow them all away.

"Officer!"

A man from the crowd ran at Jenkins, bellowing at the top of his lungs.

"Officer!"

He was in his late fifties, with bushy white hair and sideburns, his face tanned and creased. He wore casual seafaring garb—a blue-and-white striped shirt, white shorts, and beige sandals. To Jenkins, he looked like a freshly scrubbed sea captain out on the town. A tall, blond woman tagged along behind him. Too young to be his wife, Jenkins thought. Though one could never know. She had an aristocratic face and wore a dress that hit her figure like a dance of rainwater held in suspension.

"Officer!"

Jenkins held up his hands.

The man screeched to a halt.

"What can I do for you, sir?" Jenkins eyed the blonde, who stood in a pool of light a few feet behind the man.

"That thing!" He shot a hand toward the circus wagon. "That abominable thing!" The man uttered a curse beneath his breath. "They are so wrong, Officer. Thank God someone finally called the police."

Jenkins took a closer look at the man. His face, bobbing around in half shadow, looked less like a sea captain's now and more like that of an incensed professor's. So the high-techies rubbed you wrong, huh, bub? And you want them arrested for that? Jenkins stared at the woman. He had half a mind to squeeze her ass right in front of the old geezer.

"Let's step this way, sir." Jenkins ushered the man and the woman around the circus wagon and back onto the sidewalk. He laid eyes on the woman's ass as they walked. It bounced just right, shivered just right. Jenkins began melting into puddles.

Montero was already shooing the crowd away, but without much success.

"They won't go," he said to Jenkins.

That's not surprising, Jenkins thought. He looked at the assembly. They were milling around, pretending to leave, and then coming right back, clogging the pedestrian byway. No one had respect for the law these days. One shot, fired overhead ...

He noticed a well-dressed man with an icy stare, and gave him an extra going over. You've got hard eyes, pal. Do I know you? I've got to think. No, I don't believe so, Mr. Business Suit.

Jenkins took out his notebook and pen.

"Your names, sir?" he said to the professor. "You are witnesses." He scribbled as they talked. The man's name was Ronald Dillingham. The woman's, Sadie Woods. He recorded their addresses and phone numbers, exalting the day he decided to become a cop. Who else on the street could have gotten personal information from the woman so easily? And she wasn't the geezer's wife after all.

"Watch out for that thing, Officer," Dillingham said, pointing at the mechanical whip that stretched from the side of the circus wagon. "They'll smack you with it, sure enough, if you have the temerity to disagree with them."

"We can't arrest someone for having a disagreement with you, sir. That's not the province of the law."

"But surely there must be ..." Dillingham stammered, threw his hands up, and then looked helplessly at Sadie Woods.

While Montero rode herd on the spectators, Jenkins approached the vehicle, feeling Dillingham and Sadie at his back. First, he inspected the whip.

"That thing swings around like an elephant's trunk," Dillingham said. "It's remarkably fluid; it can even telescope. Look here, Officer." He pointed at the fist-sized end of the whip. "Don't get too close. They'll rap you on the skull with it, sure enough."

Jenkins looked at the vehicle itself. It was made of panels that glowed in varying hues: violets and blues at the bottom, greens and yellows in the middle, oranges and reds at the top. The saucer's wheels, partially hidden beneath flaring sections of the vehicle, were about a foot and a half in diameter.

"It isn't street legal, is it, Officer?" Sadie Woods asked.

Jenkins gave her an appraising eye, her voice still sailing through his mind. "No, it isn't street legal, Ms. Woods. That's the most intelligent thing I've heard yet." Feeling Dillingham bristle, Jenkins looked at him and said, "That's the province of the law, Mr. Dillingham. That's what we focus on. Is it legal? Not, do we disagree?"

Jenkins ran his eyes over the saucer, estimating it to be about eight feet high, ten feet long, and five and a half feet deep through the center. The high-techies went to a lot of trouble, he thought. He pictured them inside the saucer, looking out somehow, laughing their fool heads off, thinking they would parlay this stunt into lucrative jobs someday. I'm wise to you, pals, Jenkins thought. Stunts like this don't cut it anymore. High-tech companies are wise to you, also. Your skills are a dime a dozen these days, pals. You lose, bums. They prefer to hire true geniuses, like Sadie here, not troublemakers.

Jenkins cast another appraising eye on Sadie Woods and then walked to the saucer and rapped on it.

"Police, open up."

Nothing happened.

Jenkins rapped on it again.

"Police, open up."

"Maybe it's empty," a voice from the crowd said. "Maybe it's remote controlled."

Jenkins turned toward the voice. "Sir, remote-controlled vehicles are a dime a dozen these days." He threw his hands up. "Please, let us handle this."

"No, someone's in there," Sadie said. "I saw them."

Jenkins spun and looked at her. He saw Dillingham give her a peculiar look.

"But how, honey?" Dillingham asked.

So it's *honey*, is it, Dillingham? Jenkins thought. Getting overly familiar with the female, are we, Dillingham?

Sadie pointed at the middle panels of the vehicle. "They became transparent for just an instant. I saw three children in there. They're real small." She searched the crowd, as if looking for support.

"I doubt they're children, Ms. Woods," Jenkins said. "They're likely adults, in full possession of their faculties, and know full well what they're doing. But what they don't know is that it won't do them any good."

He rapped on the saucer again.

"Police! Open up! You're just making it worse on yourselves." He boomed his voice at the vehicle, feeling the thick muscles in his neck stand out.

"Sadie, honey," Dillingham said, "they can't be children. What they were saying—it's not what children would say."

Jenkins glared at Dillingham. *Stop calling her honey!* Then he glared at Sadie. *Children? My ass!*

Montero ran up.

"Jenks, they're children, all right." He glanced at the crowd. "Several people say they saw them. And like the lady said, they're real small." Montero drew his hands about twelve inches apart. "They say they look to be about seven or eight years old, but real small."

Jenkins searched Montero's eyes, looking for anything off-key. He glanced at the crowd and saw Mr. Business Suit's hard stare.

"Okay," he said to Montero, "children of tiny stature were observed. Offhand, Monty, I can think of two possible explanations for this oddity. One, the children were video projections, not people. Two, the children were distortions, the people inside presenting themselves as smaller than they really are, through the use of mirrors, lenses, or whatnot."

"Jenks."

"Yeah?"

"The children are Caucasian, two boys, one girl. Beyond that the descriptions vary too much to be reliable."

"Thanks, Monty."

Montero walked back to the crowd.

Jenkins faced the saucer, an idea hitting him. High-techies don't like anyone monkeying with their equipment. It riles them up like nothing else. Jenkins walked to the whip, grabbed it, and shook it.

The whip sprang from Jenkins' grasp. He stepped back and watched as some of the panels on the craft lit up with bright glows. The saucer rolled forward, crashed into the back of Jenkins' cruiser, and stopped. The whip shot at Jenkins; he ducked. It made another stab at him, but he spun out of its reach. The whip pulled back and hovered like a searching cobra as voices erupted from the vehicle.

"Watch it!"

"Don't do that again!"

"Leave it alone!"

"It's them!" Dillingham shrieked, running to Jenkins. "Now listen, Officer, and you'll see what I mean. If you have the temerity to disagree with them ..."

Jenkins gripped Dillingham by the arm and walked him to Montero, handing him to the other cop.

"Stay back, sir, for your own safety."

Jenkins walked back to the saucer. He'd heard children's voices coming from it. Sadie, the intellectual, was right.

Keeping a wary distance from the whip, he directed his voice at the saucer. "I won't touch it again if you cooperate."

Silence from the saucer. He reached for the whip, knowing they were afraid he would maltreat it. Children or not, high-techies were paranoid about their equipment.

"Stop!" The voice halted Jenkins' hands.

"Come here," the voice said.

Several panels on the craft became transparent. Jenkins walked to the saucer and looked inside. A small boy with dark hair sat at a control panel, staring at him. A girl and another boy were bouncing around on colorful cushions, which were strewn about the interior of the craft. The girl had long, honey-blond hair. The boy bouncing with her had brown hair.

God, they were so tiny.

Jenkins scanned the interior of the craft. Other than a mad scramble of cushions, which seemed to serve as playthings for the kids, the interior was like an aircraft cockpit, jammed with instrument panels.

These kids are test-tube nightmares, he thought. Someone's been conducting experiments. Or maybe they caught a contagious disease and needed to be quarantined. We'd better get them back to wherever they escaped from.

"Sadie!" Jenkins yelled. He needed help from the intellectual.

She ran to his side and looked into the craft.

"What do you make of it, Sadie? Is there some place in the area that might have harbored these kids? Some medical-research facility? Some genetic-engineering lab? I think they escaped from somewhere."

"Hmmm, I'm trying to think."

The dark-haired kid moved a control stick and the whip sprang close to Jenkins' head. But he did not back off. The other two kids stopped bouncing. All three were staring at him.

Chills swept up Jenkins' spine. Suddenly, he wanted to know what had transpired between the occupants of the craft and Dillingham. What had made the man so furious?

"Sadie," he whispered, "what did these kids say to Mr. Dillingham? Why did he get so mad?"

"I can answer that, sir," the dark-haired boy said. "We pinged the people who followed us, and Mr. Dillingham was selected."

"You pinged them?" Jenkins asked.

"Yes."

"Like sonar? Like a submarine pinging other ships?"

"You could say that, sir."

The little girl's voice sounded through the speaker.

"Sir, we threw rocks at the people, and *thunk, thunk, thunk,* they bounced off. But not from him." She pointed at Dillingham, who stood by Montero in front of the crowd. "A rock *pinged* off him." She looked at the brown-haired boy at her side. "That man's Chinese, you know." They collapsed in laughter.

The dark-haired boy kept his serious expression.

"We pinged the crowd, sir, and we selected that man. We communicated with him, only him. I told him he was in a German city, learning how to speak German. In that city, he observed many oil fires in small buckets that firefighters were continually trying to put out. He entered a fast-food restaurant, where he asked, 'Doesn't anyone in this city speak German?' He hadn't heard anyone in that city speak German yet, though, truthfully, he didn't much care. Because of this, he is ours to kill, since we don't have our own yet."

Dillingham burst from the crowd.

"Liar! Liar!"

"He got away from me, Jenks," Montero yelled.

Jenkins faced the onrushing Dillingham.

"That's close enough, sir."

Dillingham tried to force his way around Jenkins, but Jenkins restrained him.

"That motherfucking little—"

"I'll ask you to watch your language," Jenkins said. "These are kids."

"Officer, they're anything but kids. They're the most reprehensible, loathsome, vile—"

With a surge of strength, Dillingham broke free from Jenkins and rushed the saucer. Jenkins seized him from behind and put a choke hold on him.

Dillingham struggled in vain, spraying croaking sounds from his throat, and went limp. Jenkins eased the professor to the sidewalk.

Dillingham, sucking for breath, slowly regained his feet.

"What's this about you being in a German city, learning how to speak German, but nobody there speaks German?" Jenkins asked, eyeing Dillingham, checking for signs of belligerency.

"He was obviously speaking in code, the language of dreams," Dillingham said. "To cut to the chase, Officer, he was telling me I was not taking care of my responsibilities, professionally or personally, that I focused on miniscule things, used others ignobly, and did not exercise self-restraint. In short, I've been grossly irresponsible, and because of this, I am due some calamity that will shake me up and swerve me back to my righteous path in life."

Jenkins nodded toward the dark-haired kid.

"He said they were going to kill you."

"I trust he was exaggerating. They're probably planning some act less despicable than that."

"Ron ..." Sadie Woods walked closer to Dillingham. "Couldn't you at least take some of it to heart?"

"No way, honey."

"Stop calling her honey!" The words shot from the dark-haired kid.

Dillingham lunged at the vehicle, smashed against it, and began screaming.

"Wait'll I get my hands on you, you motherfucking, depraved—"

Jenkins tried to wrestle Dillingham away from the saucer, but it was like wrestling an alligator. Montero rushed up to help.

Dillingham frothed at the mouth, lunged repeatedly for the dark-haired kid, banging against the saucer. Finally, Jenkins and Montero wrestled him to the sidewalk.

Jenkins cuffed Dillingham's hands behind his back, and then he and Montero stood the professor up.

"For your own good, sir," Jenkins said.

"Fuck you, cop!"

Jenkins grabbed Dillingham by the head and slammed him face-first into the saucer.

"Sir," Jenkins said through clenched teeth as he ground the professor's face into the saucer, "I'll pretend I didn't hear that. Now please try to help us. The kid said, 'We don't have our own yet.' What did he mean by that?"

Dillingham struggled to break free, but couldn't, and finally went slack.

Jenkins released him.

Dillingham slid to the sidewalk. Moments later, he regained his feet and wandered around in a daze, blood trickling from a gash on his forehead.

"Yeah, I guess he did say that, Officer. Take these cuffs off and I'll try to explain."

Jenkins removed the cuffs.

Dillingham pulled out a handkerchief, mopped blood off his forehead, and then looked around, pensive.

"Say you've got a hankering to do something, Officer, a real powerful hankering, and your favorite person for doing this thing with—or to—is unavailable. What do you do?"

Jenkins did not respond. He knew the answer, but he wanted to hear it from the professor.

"You find a substitute," Dillingham said. "Apparently, my tormentors are currently without their usual victims and have selected me as the interim honoree. It's no wonder they keep the little felons locked up."

"Professor, you're wrong," Jenkins said. He was amazed at Dillingham's lack of knowledge—for a professor. "Sir, the habitual victim is sought out by the predator. Enraged males have been known to spend years searching for ex-mates who have spurned them. Find a substitute? There is no substitute. No one else will do."

"Wrong?" Dillingham's face flashed anger. He glared at Jenkins with disbelief.

"The predator does not give up the victim easily, sir. Once a relationship with a compliant victim has been established, a pattern is set."

"But they—"

"They?" Jenkins pointed at the children in the saucer. "I'm not talking about them, Professor. I'm talking about predators."

"The kids were just trying to help illuminate your problems, Ron," Sadie Woods said. She took his handkerchief from him and mopped more blood off his forehead.

"Those obstinate, asinine, felons," Dillingham said, pushing Sadie away and grabbing his handkerchief back. "I don't want my problems illuminated by those pint-sized motherfuckers."

"Sir," Jenkins said, "I'll ask you to watch your language."

Dillingham fixed his eyes on Jenkins.

"If you have the temerity to disagree with them, Officer ..."

Dillingham ran to the saucer. Jenkins leaped to block his way but wasn't quick enough. Dillingham put his face squarely to the panel in front of the dark-haired kid. His words came out like venomous snakes striking prey.

"All right, you gutless little felon, give the officer here a run for his money, like you did to me. And after that"—he jerked his head at Sadie Woods—"do the same with her. See how she likes it."

Dillingham spun around, sank into a crouch, and looked about, his eyes registering fear, and then cunning. He rested his knuckles on the sidewalk, and then on all fours ran into the street. A car nearly clipped him. He disappeared into the darkness on the far side.

"Wait!" Sadie ran after him, but stopped. She wandered back. "Did you see him run?" she said to Jenkins. "Like an ape?"

"Yes, Ms. Woods. Mighty peculiar."

Jenkins returned his attention to the saucer. He'd lied to Ms. Woods. Dillingham's running like an ape was not peculiar. This was California. The state was saturated with high-tech slackers who could make your brain stand on end if they wanted it to.

Wasn't the brain like a set of Chinese boxes? Wasn't there a reptile's brain in there somewhere? And then the brain of an ape, layered over the reptile's brain? And wasn't the big outer shell of brain—the thing that made humans human—just a covering for those inner, more primitive brains?

Somehow, the stops had been pulled from Dillingham's brain, placing him face to face with millions of years of evolution. He *had* to get down on all fours and escape into the night. The professor would probably spend the night in a tree.

Jenkins stared into the dark-haired kid's eyes. He looked at the other two. The little monkeys were horsing around. Kids, always horsing around. The brown-haired boy, all twelve inches of him, was wrestling with the girl. She was maybe ten inches. Her long hair, the color of honey in a glass jar, flew about.

Jenkins looked back into the serious eyes of the dark-haired boy.

"My name is Noel Jenkins. What's your name, kid?"

The two little monkeys stopped horsing around and snapped to, their eyes on Jenkins.

"Tell him!" the little girl cried.

The dark-haired boy glanced at her.

"My name is Zelda," the little girl said, smiling sweetly. She sat and bounced on a cushion, and then stood and did a little dance. Finally, she sat and peered at Jenkins. "Zelda. Got that, Noel Jenkins?"

"Got that, Zelda."

"My name is Wilton," the brown-haired boy said.

"Wilton." Jenkins nodded at him.

"I'm Sam," the dark-haired boy said.

"Sam." Jenkins collected his thoughts.

"Where do we go from here, Sam?" he asked.

No response.

"Where'd you guys come from, Sam? Don't you want to go back?"

"Of course we want to go back," Zelda said. "That's what we're doing, Noel Jenkins. We're going back." She looked at Wilton. "Aren't we?" She attacked him and they wrestled on the cushions.

"Noel Jenkins," Sam said, "you are going into a building with two other men."

"I am?"

"Yes, you are, Noel Jenkins. One of the other men is bigger than you. The other man is invisible to you. Once inside the building, the bigger man removes his scalp, his chest, his shoulders, and his feet. Now he has lots of pieces missing. The other man remains invisible."

The image of a man stripped of much of his flesh popped into Jenkins' mind. The man's skull was red and raw with blood, his body a patchwork of exposed skeleton and dripping gossamer tissue.

"Is this a dream, Sam?"

Sam stared at him with his serious, dark eyes. Jenkins wished Dillingham were here to interpret the dream for him. Where was that ape when you needed him?

"Noel?"

Jenkins nearly jumped out of his skin. He turned and saw Sadie standing next to him.

"Sorry, Noel. I didn't mean to startle you."

"It's okay, Ms. Woods. I like being skinned alive. What can I do for you?"

"Call me Sadie. Noel, I couldn't help but overhear. The building is you, you are you, and each of the other two men is you. Understand?"

"No."

"The invisible man is probably closest to the real you."

"This is California, Sadie. It's saturated with high-tech slackers who can make your brain stand on end if they want it to. Don't fall for their psychobabble. Who is this guy who removes his scalp and—"

"He's making himself smaller, Noel. And by doing so, he becomes weaker. Like when you take a condescending attitude toward me and these kids."

"Thank you, Professor Sadie."

Jenkins glanced at his watch. They'd been here long enough. They needed to resolve this.

"Monty?"

Montero walked over.

"What do you think?" Jenkins asked.

"The kids tell you anything?"

"Nothing useful."

"They have to stay inside that thing, Jenks. I've got a bad feeling about this."

"We'll have it towed in and quarantined. Meanwhile, report the vehicle as found. Someone is bound to have reported it missing."

"Will do." Montero ran to his cruiser.

If you have the temerity to disagree ...

Dillingham's words ran through Jenkins' mind. He peered at Sam. The tiny kid stared at him with vigilant eyes. Okay, I'll give it a shot, Professor. Disagree with the dream.

"Sam, sorry to disappoint you, kid, but I believe the dream you cited for me has nothing to do with my life. Maybe it's intended for someone else."

Zelda and Wilton exploded to attention on the cushions. They stared at Jenkins. Zelda's mouth opened in a big *O*. She looked at Sam.

"Bring the woman here, Jenks," Sam said. "I want to grab her ass."

"Sam ..." Jenkins looked at Sadie. She was standing over his shoulder.

"I'm going to grab her ass, Jenks. Bring her here."

"Sam, let's be sensible about this." He put his finger to his lips. *Shhh ... Shut the fuck up, you little bastard.*

"You've got her address and phone number, Jenks. Hand them over. I'm going to call her and put the squeeze on her."

"No, Sam, I would never have done that."

"She'll go out with me if she thinks it's official."

"Not Sadie. She's an intellectual, Sam. She'd never fall for that."

"Women with aristocratic faces have a sense of civic duty—they must cooperate with the law."

It was true—within Jenkins' experience anyway. Women with aristocratic faces like Sadie's were inclined to cooperate with the law. How the heck did the little fuck face know that?

"I'm going to fuck her, Jenks. Bring the woman to me."

"Now you shut the fuck up, you little creep!" Jenkins yelled.

"I'll ask you to watch your language, Jenks. Bring the woman here."

"Her name is Sadie."

"Bring Sadie here."

"Her name is Ms. Woods."

"Bring Ms. Woods here, Jenks. I'm going to fuck her brains out."

Jenkins slammed into the saucer, rocked it back and forth.

"I'll get you, you little motherfucking predator!"

Montero pulled Jenkins away from the saucer.

"Cool it, Jenks."

"Did you hear what that little bastard was saying?"

"Yeah. So did everyone else."

Jenkins spun around and faced the crowd.

"What are you people doing here?" he yelled. He ran at them, pulled out his pistol. "Go home. Get the fuck out of here." He fired a shot into the air. The crowd fell back and then regrouped, their eyes on Jenkins' pistol. He lowered it at them, took careful aim ...

He saw the hard eyes of Mr. Business Suit.

The crowd bolted. Bodies ran helter-skelter, smashing into one another. Several of them crashed to the sidewalk.

Jenkins took careful aim at the prostrate bodies, one by one, looking into their eyes.

They skittered away. The sidewalk was empty. Even Mr. Business Suit had fled.

"We'll have to report a shooting, Jenks," Montero said.

"I know." Jenkins holstered his pistol. "Some asshole in the crowd drew on me, Monty."

"Keep your ass covered, Jenks," Sam said. "Now bring the blonde here, so I can stick my hand up her skirt and feel her ass."

Jenkins slammed into the saucer, screaming at Sam. Montero put a fearsome headlock on Jenkins and pulled him back.

"Jenks," Montero said, still holding him in the headlock, "this is getting bizarre. I don't pretend to know what's going on here, but if you don't control yourself, I think in another minute or two you'll end up doing what that guy Dillingham did. You're going to get down like some gorilla or baboon and run off. An armed cop in that condition ... Jenks, we'd have to track you down. We'd have to tranquilize you. Or maybe kill you."

Jenkins let his rage sink away.

"It's okay, Monty. Let me go."

Montero released Jenkins.

"Jenks, take a breather."

"It's okay, Monty."

Jenkins wandered down the sidewalk a ways. The crowd was gathering again, tentatively coming back. Jenkins saw Mr. Business Suit slinking in from the shadows.

"It's okay, people, come on back. Everything's happy here."

"Bring the broad to me, Jenks," Sam said. "I want to remove her panties and feel her ass."

Jenkins turned toward Sam.

"It's okay, Sam. It's cool. Fine with me." He began walking toward Sadie.

"Sadie ..." he said.

"Officer Jenkins, if you lay a hand on me ..." Sadie stepped behind Montero.

Jenkins stopped.

"It's okay, Ms. Woods. I won't lay a hand on you." He looked at Sam. "You'll have to get her yourself, pal. Sorry."

"Officer Jenkins?"

It was a young voice, soft and feminine. Jenkins turned toward it and looked into the saucer. Zelda was holding up a tiny white kitten. She hugged it and brushed her cheek against its fur. Jenkins crept toward her. The little kitten's eyes stared at him. Two liquid sapphires. Zelda held the kitten out to him, and he planted his face against the saucer's panel.

"Do you want to pet my pussy, Officer Jenkins?"

"Oh, sure, Sadie—I mean Zelda." He petted the panel as Zelda pressed the kitten against it.

Zelda tossed the kitten to Wilton. He caught it, and then Zelda and Wilton collapsed in laughter.

Jenkins looked at Sam. Sam's dark eyes stared back.

"Nice trick, Sam. So, you knew I'd have pulled out all the stops getting to Sadie. Yeah, I'd have put the squeeze on her. I'm a man, Sam. I'm staring at millions of years of biological evolution. It's tough for me, Sam, to be anything but a man. But a gentleman, Sam. That's what I try to be. And I fail at that quite often, I know. I believe that dream was meant for me after all."

Jenkins looked over his shoulder at Sadie, and then at Montero.

"These kids are all right, Monty. Let's give them a break and let them go."

"Jenks, we can't."

"Yes, we can. Sadie, how do you vote?"

She looked at Montero. He shook his head.

"My dream first, Noel." She stepped to the saucer and put her face close to Sam's. "Do you have a dream for me, Sam?"

"You're in bed," Sam said.

Zelda laughed, bounced on the cushions.

"Isn't she always?" Zelda said.

Sam's dark eyes silenced Zelda.

"Ms. Woods, you're in bed," Sam said. "You're dreaming, and you're aware that it's a dream."

"A lucid dream?" Sadie said.

"Yes. You hear an authoritative voice, your own voice, Ms. Woods. You recognize it as such. It says, 'Enemies, I don't need them.' Then you hear another voice, an even more authoritative voice. It says, 'Yes, you do, Sadie. They're important. If it weren't for them, you wouldn't be.'"

"Oh?" Sadie looked at Montero, at Jenkins, and then back at Sam.

Jenkins stepped forward. He wanted to take a crack at interpreting Sadie's dream.

"Sadie, if you have no enemies, you aren't living with any guts. When you have enemies, your life has greater distinction. You stand out better, like the rippling muscles of a prehistoric beast. When you have no enemies, you're as flat and monotonous as a slug on a rock."

Do you have the temerity to disagree, Ms. Woods?

Jenkins wished Sadie would disagree with Sam. He wanted to hear the little monster reveal her innermost secrets.

"I'll buy the dream, Sam," Sadie said. She looked at Jenkins. "Thanks, Noel." Sadie turned back to Sam. "Thank you, Sam. You're free to go now."

Zelda jumped on the cushions and yelled at Sadie.

"Thank you, teacher! School's out! School's out!"

The saucer's panels turned opaque. The whip retracted. A motor hummed to life. The vehicle retracted its wheels and rose slowly into the air.

"Hey!" Montero yelled.

Jenkins and Sadie jumped back.

The saucer hovered about a hundred feet up, as if getting its bearings, and then tore away and disappeared into the night sky.

A strange feeling came over Jenkins. He sensed someone was watching him. He looked around and saw three figures standing in shadow across the street. The kids? How did they get out of the saucer? They looked bigger now.

Jenkins watched for traffic, and then ran across the street.

The three figures retreated as he approached, running deeper into shadow.

"No, wait!" Jenkins shouted.

Three cat-quick shadows disappeared into the darkness. Jenkins wondered who, or what, they were.

Then he remembered Sam's words.

He is ours to kill ...

Dillingham was out there.

They were hunters.

Witherpools

In Lawrence, Kansas, a man stood in the nighttime jungle of shadows that surrounded his house. His powerful body, clad in running shoes, running shorts, and a T-shirt, felt the warm caress of the air. He looked around at the murky landscape and listened to the wind rustle through the trees. The .44 Magnum semiautomatic handgun felt welded to his body. It was in a custom-built holster on his left side, ready for a fast right-handed draw. He gazed at the stars and saw a twinkling orb in the multitude blink out and then relight itself a hairsbreadth away.

Walt Gill shuddered. Odin's signature was in the air. And with Odin came a hellish warp zone. At least Mindy, Walt's wife, would be safe. Walt had woken and dressed without a sound, not disturbing her sleep. He had to draw Odin away from Mindy.

Years ago, Walt had named his enemy Odin. He had wanted to call it something, give it some identity. Odin, the craggy-headed Norse god, came to mind. It put a face on an otherwise faceless enemy.

Odin, stalker of Walt.

Walt ran through his backyard and then through a network of alleys. Block after block he ran. A dog exploded into a frenzy of barking as Walt raced past its yard. Other dogs at scattered outposts joined in, entering into madness.

Walt left the alleys and slowed his pace, running along the sidewalks like any normal citizen. Odin, that most unfathomable of enemies, was thrown off by a good run. Walt discovered this by accident several years ago.

Odin had come on a midsummer's night, sending his musk through the air, and Walt, relaxing at home with Mindy, became enraged. No more locking the windows and doors, he decided. No more huddling with Mindy in the basement like frightened kittens as Odin terrorized the house. He donned army fatigues and stuck a loaded .38 into a holster that rode above his right ankle.

Walt ran through the streets of Omaha, his home at the time, silently imploring the son of a bitch to show himself. Odin's musk ebbed and flowed and eventually fell away. His warp zone lingered, however, producing bizarre effects throughout the city. Walt's lungs and legs screamed. Omaha screamed. Walt went home, vowing to get in shape. The next day, finding out what had befallen the city the night before, he also vowed to find a new home. He didn't want Omaha, or any other decent place, ruined. In a fervent desire to shake Odin off his trail, he moved to Lawrence, Kansas. But Walt found there was no hiding from Odin.

Running along the sidewalks in Lawrence, Kansas, Walt checked the magazines he had secured to his belt, ready for fast removal and insertion. Not that bullets would do any good against Odin, but Odin's warp always drew a diabolical human crew.

Two blocks ahead, a car turned onto the street and drove toward Walt, slowing as it approached. Walt thought of ducking into the yard beside him, but that would only arouse suspicion from the car's occupants, if they were Witherpools. He continued jogging down the sidewalk, giving the car scant attention as any normal jogger would.

They passed one another under the glare of a streetlight.

Walt saw two of them in the front seat. Their faces were grotesque stitcheries. Flesh hung from gaping wounds. Blood oozed from open fissures like slithering maggots.

As the car receded, Walt saw two more in the backseat, pressed against the rear window, staring at him.

Four Witherpools were in the car. *Witherpool,* like *Odin,* a name to give them an identity.

Walt faced forward, felt their eyes bore into the back of his head. Was Odin in there with them? He didn't think so. Odin gave off a peculiar scent. Odin made Walt's blood run cold. Witherpools made Walt homicidal.

He heard the car speed up, turn a corner.

Walt darted through an opening in a hedge, buried himself in the shadows of a front lawn, froze. He was blind. He tried to tune into the night, to get a sense of where Odin was.

Nothing.

The Witherpools?

They were circling. Walt felt their movement like a hang noose tightening around his neck.

To Walt's knowledge, over the years Witherpools had never succeeded in identifying him, and could not track him except by following Odin's musk. But there had been plenty of close calls. Maybe by now Witherpools had him on their radar.

Walt saw Witherpools every day. Witherpools were the curse of humanity. They preyed insidiously on humans, watching for vulnerability, hoping for catastrophe, arranging those catastrophes whenever they could.

And getting off.

Witherpools got off on the suffering of innocent people.

Walt knew that most people did not see Witherpools the way he did. To the average person, a Witherpool looked like anyone else. But to Walt, they were a mass of dripping, uncared-for wounds. The wounds weren't real, not in the physical sense. If Walt were to touch the flesh of a Witherpool, his hand would not come away covered with gore. A Witherpool's flesh would, to the touch, seem like any other flesh. But to the discerning eye of Walt Gill, a Witherpool was a butchered being.

It all started six years ago, the night of Walt's accident. Before Mindy.

Before fortune struck him.

It had been a rainy, gusty night near Council Bluffs, Iowa, a black glove of a night that slapped you in the face and did not want to let go. Walt had been driving home from another thankless round of sales calls, dreading his morning meeting with the sales manager of the bathroom-fixtures firm he worked for.

Afterward, the Iowa State Patrol pieced it together. Rain had slickened the twisting two-lane highway. A car came up fast behind Walt and passed him on a curve going uphill. Ahead, a truck came around a bend. To avoid a head-on collision, the truck swerved into Walt's lane. To avoid the truck, Walt swerved his car into the guardrail. The truck clipped him, and Walt's car flipped over the guardrail and tumbled into a ravine.

Then something happened that the Iowa State Patrol did not piece together. Walt Gill left his body and floated above the ravine. He saw the truck fishtailing it down the highway, its driver fighting for control. The truck stopped and its driver came running back up the highway.

Walt looked the other way and saw the errant car make a return trip. It stopped on the shoulder across from the guardrail. The driver peered out and a flash of lightning lit up his face.

Red, raw, dripping wounds streaked the man's face. Walt, out of body, instinctively knew the wounds were not physical. They were a mark, unseen by most.

Walt stared into the man's eyes. Focused on the damaged guardrail, they threw off rock-hard glints. Walt probed deeper and encountered mind-numbing madness. The man was filled with uncontrollable lust, like that of a child molester who'd finally gotten his hands on his prey.

And Walt knew he had been the prey.

The truck driver ran up. He did not recognize the car or driver, having seen only a pair of blazing headlights. They conferred. The man with the mark upon him pretended to have been coming from the other direction. He spoke glibly to the truck driver, expressing a concern that was absent from his true passions. He wanted to see a dead or mangled body. He was hoping for multiple deaths or injuries. He was engorged with lust.

Walt felt violated. But then a gust or something blew him higher above the ravine, and his earthly concerns melted away. He wondered why he wasn't going anywhere; surely there must be another world for him to go to. But soon even that became a matter of no concern. He was happy to be where he was—in total release from the cares of the world.

Several highway patrol cars arrived. Then an ambulance. The truck driver had called from his cab. They flooded the ravine with lights, then a crew with a stretcher went down. The man with the uncared-for wounds leaned over the guardrail.

Walt saw them remove his body from its resting place in his crumpled car. It appeared to be lifeless. They strapped it to the stretcher and covered it, but did not cover the face.

Well, maybe they forgot, Walt thought as the stretcher bearers brought his body up. Suddenly, with horror, he remembered he had been wearing his seatbelt. Misery swept through him. He stared at his body on the stretcher. *No! Please be dead!*

Then Walt caught another glimpse of the man with the uncared-for wounds. His eyes had grown hollow; his mouth was set in a frown. At the prompting of a highway patrol officer, the man stood back from the guardrail as the ambulance crew hauled Walt's body over the top.

A powerful suction pulled Walt back into his body.

Walt's eyes popped open.

From the agonizing stricture of his body, Walt saw the man with the uncared-for wounds, but saw him now as a normal human, a human with unmarked flesh. The man leaned over Walt.

Walt shot from his body and hovered over the ravine. He stared at the man and saw the raw, dripping wounds. The man was disappointed. He knew Walt was not critically injured. He had suffered bruises and lacerations, but that was all.

Walt battled the pull that sought to bring him back into his body. He had felt helpless lying on the stretcher, strapped in, the recipient of the focused hatred in those eyes. The man wanted Walt—or someone—dead or disabled, and was angry that there was no one in the vehicle down in the ravine that would fill this order. He wanted to reach out and crush Walt's face.

Walt was sucked back into his body.

He closed his eyes and screamed silently. *No!*

He flew into the air, looked down, and saw a form separate itself from his body. It slid off the stretcher and staggered away, a man-shadow stumbling into the night. I am dead, Walt thought.

Now he would go to another world.

He was sucked back into his body and received the shock of his life. With his physical eyes, he now saw the uncared-for wounds of the man. Walt's mind frantically sought an explanation. The shadowy form that escaped him must have served as a filter, blocking this hideous, anomalous view of the world.

The man saw something in Walt's eyes and recoiled.

I know you, Walt thought, staring at the man's torn and twisted face as the stretcher passed him. *I know you.*

Months later, recovered from his injuries, Walt located the man who had tried to kill him. By then, Walt had seen hundreds of Witherpools, Odin had come streaming out of the night dozens of times hunting Walt, and Walt, quite unlike his former self, had become a determined, focused man.

He grappled with the Witherpool in his Minnetonka, Minnesota, home and strangled him to death. He watched as the hard glints went white with death. He was careful to leave no clues.

Walt went home to Omaha. Since the shadow had slunk from his body, his life had become one risky enterprise after another.

Walt became good at killing Witherpools.

After the accident, the owner and the sales manager of the company Walt worked for paid him a visit in the hospital. Walt, fearing the worst, thought he'd be fired. But when they walked into his room, despite his pain, Walt began laughing. He laughed so hard he split open a wound in his neck. A nurse had to summon a doctor to re-suture it. When Walt regained control of himself, he looked at the sales manager.

Red, raw, dripping wounds streaked the man's face. It looked like a pig's head that had been used to mop the floor of a slaughterhouse. *I know you,* Walt thought.

Something shifted in the man's eyes. He looked like a trapped animal searching for a way out.

"Out!" Walt shouted.

The sales manager ran from the room.

To know you is to command you, Walt thought.

The sales manager had always been on Walt's case. Now Walt knew why. He had a need to wound Walt, a craving to inflict damage to Walt's psyche, a lust for Walt's continued discomfort and failure as a seller of bathroom fixtures.

I know you, Walt thought, reveling in his new-found power.

He turned to the shocked owner, asked the nurse to prop him higher, and then asked the nurse to leave.

"He isn't training the sales force properly," Walt said to the owner. "He has a vested interest in planting seeds of failure throughout the company."

Walt gave details, explaining how his training had been sabotaged. In the past, Walt would have shouldered the blame entirely. Now he saw the pattern; he'd been the sales manager's victim. He explained the sales meetings, how the sales manager would rake people over the coals, how the guy had been covering up his own incompetence.

Ideas flowed freely in Walt's mind, ideas for improving sales, for improving morale, for improving products. He talked forcefully for more than an hour. The owner gave him his undivided attention.

"You're the man for the job," the owner said.

Three weeks later, Walt stepped into the sales manager's job. During his first sales meeting, he escorted a middle-aged woman and a man in his mid-twenties out of the conference room and told them they were fired. Both had red, raw, dripping uncared-for wounds all over their flesh. He reentered the conference room and noticed an immediate improvement in the atmosphere. When he told the others what he had done, they thanked him profusely.

A few days later, Walt killed his first Witherpool.

He was watching the local news on television, marveling at the red, raw, dripping facial wounds of both the male and female news anchors, when a story of a rape suspect was aired.

The suspect, in police custody, claimed he was innocent. The story switched to the victim, the man's daughter, a woman in her early twenties. She claimed years of sexual abuse and rape, and said she was coming forward to encourage other women to reveal what their fathers had done to them. If convicted, the father would likely spend the rest of his life in prison.

The father's face was clean.

The daughter's face swam in a sea of bloody, putrid flesh.

The next day, Walt learned where she lived and paid her a visit. It was a big house in an exclusive residential neighborhood. When she answered the door, he said he was a cop. She let him in. Two minutes later, she was dead.

Walt had been careful on his way in, but on his way out, he ran into a laundry deliveryman. He stared at the guy. His face was clean. *What do I do? Kill him?* Walt said excuse me and walked off the steps. He heard the doorbell chime behind him.

The next day, news of the woman's murder was splashed all over the media. The deliveryman was the focus of interviews. He told police and reporters he saw no one in the area. No one at all.

Walt breathed a sigh of relief, but was puzzled. The deliveryman had seen him. Why had he lied? The answer would remain hidden from Walt for a long time.

Walt, blind in the yard, felt the car's return. It cruised down the street, four Witherpools in it, as dangerous as any pack of killers in the world. He wondered if Odin was serving as their outrider.

Walt tuned to the air, searching for Odin's musk.

It wasn't there.

He stood, the .44 in hand.

He peered through the hedge and saw the car. He walked from the yard and ran down the sidewalk. The car made a U-turn and followed him. Walt did not glance back. He ran through shadow and streetlight glare, keeping his body between the .44 and the car.

Deep shadow swept over him. The .44 was hot in his hand. He heard the car's whisper behind him.

He stopped, turned, and raised the .44 in one easy motion. His pulse raced, but his aim was steady, and he squeezed the trigger.

Walt shot the driver in the face.

Tongues of flame shot from the car, an explosion of firearms. The Witherpools were shooting at Walt. The car lurched forward.

Walt emptied a magazine at them and loaded another.

Wild shots zinged from the Witherpools. The car slammed into a lamppost and came to a shattering stop.

Walt emptied a second magazine at them, spacing his rounds, taking careful aim.

The Witherpools' weapons fell silent.

The air around Walt seemed to collapse in one fatal spasm.

He loaded another magazine, walked around the crumpled metal, and saw the car's occupants slumped in pools of blood. He finished them off with a headshot each.

Walt shoved the .44 back into its holster and resumed running through the streets of Lawrence. He thought of Mindy, safe at home in her bed—safe because he'd lured these motherfuckers away from her, confronting them in the night.

Once Odin was after you, once you saw the Witherpools,

you knew you would never be the same. You knew what had to be done.

The sky over Utah churned like a sea of roiling lions. The mountains and flats reflected a brutal dynamic—a thing unseen, but sensed.

Walt felt the power of the Infiniti, glanced at his hands on the steering wheel, shifted his gaze to the racing high-way. The highway was a black oath screaming at him.

He picked out the white flicker of his prey.

Walt was going to kill another one of them.

This one was a woman. No, not a woman. They weren't human. They were something else.

He glanced at the speedometer, edged the needle higher. He looked ahead and caught the white flicker again.

She knew he was coming. She couldn't outrun him.

He had met her in Vail, Colorado, a few hours ago. She said she was a massage therapist from Kansas City, just passing through, on her way to ...

But she had clammed up, excusing herself, leaving the café quickly. Walt had seen the gray ugliness inside her. Funny. Witherpools normally didn't run from him. They normally found him quite charming, in fact.

But, Lord above, things were changing.

Lately, Witherpools had been able to discern him. He sensed their uneasiness in his presence. Their uneasiness sometimes became volcanic fear. Not that Walt killed every Witherpool he came across. That would be impos-sible—there were too many of them.

He'd caught up with the woman outside the café. Something told him to go on the stalk. He poured on the charm.

"Let's have an understanding," he said. "We disagree, but I respect your views." That had done the trick. She softened.

She said her name was Angie Law. Angie Law, hearing Walt's spiel, had smiled the smile of a Witherpool. A smile that drew its power from the pool of human suffering. A warped smile. An ecstatic smile. A smile of the damned.

Walt had watched that smile. Angie Law was beautiful. Raven hair, dark-brown eyes, a creamy complexion, a knockout figure in spandex blue jeans and a blue halter top. The demon that resided inside her—visible to Walt's eyes—was a shrunken, gnarled obscenity.

He looked into her eyes and almost flinched. Her eyes were dead. No one would invite Angie Law's stare.

He couldn't give her time to think. They hadn't gotten around to disagreeing on anything during their short conversation inside the café.

Walt led her to his room at a nearby motel, and gave her a nude massage on the bed, gently running his hands up and down her body.

"Where are you headed?" he asked.

"San Quentin, California. The prison."

"Oh?"

Silence from Angie Law. She quivered under Walt's hands.

He tried to make the massage artful, sensual. He turned his fingers into feathers and played with her body. A treasure hunt. Teasing those areas that liked to be teased. He spanked her ass occasionally, leaving stings to drift in a sea of feathers.

"San Quentin. Wasn't there something in the news ...?"

Angie Law said yes. It was all over the news. Jake Cunningham was going to be released from death row. He'd be a free man in a few days.

"Isn't it controversial?" Walt asked.

"Yes, very. But the law is the law." Angie Law laughed at this. Walt laughed, and spanked her ass hard, walloped it good. She moaned.

"Turn over please," he said.

She turned over and fixed him with her eyes, and then relaxed under the hypnosis of his hands.

"Uh, why are they releasing him?"

Silence from Angie Law.

Walt tickled her pubic hair every few passes, keeping her guessing. "Why are you going to San Quentin, Angie?"

"I'm a member of an anti–death penalty group, Walt. We're going to cheer Jake Cunningham's return to freedom."

There it was. Their point of disagreement.

"I support the death penalty for Cunningham," Walt said. "He murdered at least five people. That's what they nailed him for. But, likely, he killed dozens more. I'd like to see the bastard fry."

"They use lethal injection in California, Walt. Before lethal injection, they used the gas chamber." Her eyes were on him. Cold. Officious. Dead.

"I know, Angie. I live in Northern California, in the Bay Area. I moved there from Lawrence, Kansas, a year ago. You think Cunningham's innocent? That's not what we think there."

"That's not the point, Walt. The point is, the

prosecution fabricated evidence, and someone else has confessed to his crimes." She relaxed, closed her eyes.

Walt had followed the news of Cunningham's impending release. No one seemed to know the facts. Not the press. Not the authorities. Cunningham's DNA was on each of the five victims—it could not have been there innocently. The defense claimed it was all planted. It was outrageous. It stank of Witherpool involvement.

Oh, Lord, things were changing.

Angie's demon woke and rose to the surface. Walt removed his hands from her.

To most people, Witherpools look perfectly human. But to Walt ...

He saw the thing inside them that mirrored—in shriveled, maimed fashion—the dark soul beneath. Sometimes it was barely perceptible, a sleeping ethereal figure. Sometimes it was a hulking, animated presence, jerking its head around, staring with steely eyes, a swirling entity inside its host. *A demon.*

Angie's demon fixed Walt with a look of unbridled hatred, while Angie's physical eyes remained closed.

He picked up her legs and raised them so her ankles were near her ears. Her demon sank back, fell into repose, and she opened her eyes.

"What are you doing?"

"Angie ..." Walt told her she wasn't human, told her he would have to kill her.

"No!" She leaped out of his grasp, leaped from the bed.

"Not here, Angie. I'll follow you."

She raced around the room, gathering her clothes.

"Ugh, I should have known. A death-penalty Nazi. A law-and-order psycho. I'm going to call the police."

But Walt knew she wouldn't call the police, any more than an antelope on the Serengeti would call the police as a lion stalked it. This was too primal. It was too close to nature. Witherpools were Walt's natural prey. They never called the police when he stalked them.

But he had to be careful. There must be no witnesses or things could become sticky. And not in this motel room. Pools, when licking their fear, always ran. All he had to do was follow her and wait for an opportunity.

He grabbed her as she was pulling up her jeans and laid her over his lap. He pulled down her jeans and panties and whacked her on the ass for several minutes, leaving his hand sore and her ass red. Angie Law was crying. He thought she'd had an orgasm in there somewhere so he didn't feel sorry for her.

"Why'd you do that?" she croaked as he released her.

He didn't tell her. It set up a ringing vibration, something he could sense, follow. There was no way for her to hide now. He could have done it another way. He could have beaten the fuck out of her, let her terror become a beacon that way. With male Witherpools, that was Walt's method. With females, especially curvaceous ones like Angie Law, he walloped their bare asses.

He watched Angie Law huddle in a corner across the room, pulling up her panties and jeans. A pitiful figure. She mustered her anger and spat at him. An empty spat. She stomped out of the motel room and jumped into her car.

Walt got into his car, tuned in to Angie Law, and trailed her.

They were close to Nevada now, Angie Law driving a white Honda Accord, Walt in his Infiniti.

Let's finish this, Walt thought. He was getting restless. It shouldn't have taken this long.

He saw the Accord ahead. She was pulling to the shoulder of the interstate. Out of gas. He saw a door pop open, a figure leap out. The figure vanished into the wasteland.

A minute later, Walt cruised to a stop behind the Accord. He got out and locked his car. Angie Law's fear was a tangible presence in the air. He began running after her.

He dashed through arroyos, scrambled over steep banks, following her footprints, sensing her fear. He saw her about forty yards ahead, sliding into another arroyo. His bloodlust rose.

He couldn't do this alone. He had to call on a higher power. Killing was not something that Walt Gill relished— it was his duty. When he had shirked his duty in the past, his life had always taken a nosedive: ill health, financial misfortune, relationships in ruins. But when he had followed his path—pursuing and killing Witherpools—life had flooded Walt with abundance.

He scrambled into the arroyo, saw her tracks, sensed her fear. He followed the trail around a series of bends.

Oh, Lord, things were changing.

A thin stalk of demon stood before him. Behind it, Angie Law lay at the side of the arroyo, gasping for breath. Her eyes were the uncomprehending eyes of an animal that had just given birth.

Angie's demon advanced on Walt, taking mincing steps.

Walt tried to fight the demon, but found it too insubstantial to grapple with. It was like fighting air.

He sidestepped the demon and ran to Angie Law.

The demon grabbed him, feebly tried to strangle him, but Walt disentangled himself from it.

He grabbed Angie Law, yanked her to her feet, broke her neck, and threw her down.

He saw the flimsy demon wander away.

He couldn't kill it—it was too insubstantial. But he knew it would get stronger, knew it would enter the earth dimension fully someday. Then it would stalk Walt.

He checked Angie Law's pulse. She was dead.

He ran back to his Infiniti. In the car, he drank from a water bottle. It was almost like a purification rite.

Witherpools were changing. They were learning how to project their power. In Angie's case, her demon had come out. Collectively, they were able to secure the release of a notorious serial killer.

They were becoming a formidable enemy.

Walt knew he would have to continually hone his instincts to survive. There were plenty of Pools in creation, sucking pleasure from the pool of human suffering.

Walt drove home to his wife, Mindy, the world a little better, another Witherpool consigned to Hell.

He was awake, lying in bed in a guest room, thinking he should never have told Jennifer about his mother. Next, she'd be asking him if his mother was still alive, and why didn't he go visit her? He hadn't seen his mother in twenty years. He didn't know if she was still alive. His early memories were taken up by the naked, drugged, and drunken prostitute that had been his mother. Running through strange homes without a stitch on, she would often steal little things—giving herself a gift, is what she called it—and get herself beaten up by the irate customer who, she always explained to her little boy, Wolf, was his new daddy. Wolf's real father was more than likely unknown to his mother. She was a hippie prostitute, a pothead. She thought nothing of taking her little boy to work with her. She always seemed to be bleeding and bruised about the face. Wolf did not want to see her again. He thought he would still be able to see her wounds.

Wolf got out of bed, did some exercises on the floor, and then dressed in blue jeans, a blue shirt, and white running shoes.

He entered Jennifer's bedroom, stood by her bed, and listened to her breathing—she wanted him to do this every morning, to see if she was still alive.

Sunlight spilled in through the curtained windows, made hazy progress through the room, struck Jen's face and hair with the aplomb of an accomplished lover.

She twitched and curled under the covers. Wolf was like a statue.

No, he shouldn't have told her about his mother.

She opened her eyes, looked at Wolf, a smile on her lips. She rolled onto her back, yawned, stretched her arms overhead, and folded back into sleep.

Wolf left the room and closed the door.

"You're weird, Wolf."

Standing in the hall, he heard her voice. It was not a sleepy voice; it rang.

"Real weird. Did anyone ever tell you that?"

He swung the door open. Yesterday, she'd been gentle, a lamb. Each day she was something different. It had been disconcerting to Wolf at first, but now he saw it as a challenge: he would have to learn to exist peacefully with an expansive, shifting soul.

Jennifer was easing herself out of bed, luxuriating in a circusful of stretches and yawns. She wore mahogany boxer-style pajamas with a button top. The top and bottom were saturated with artful drawings of boxers—the dog, not the pugilist—in various poses.

She ran to the bathroom that adjoined her bedroom. "Back in a minute."

Wolf walked to a window, pulled the gossamer curtain aside, and looked out. The sky was a collection of pale shades, like a nest of robin's eggs. A few houses lay scattered in the distance. No people were up and about, not within his sight. The toilet flushed. The sink ran. Jen rushed back into the room.

"Real weird, Wolf." She danced to her closet, slid the door open, made a dance partner of the sliding door, and then danced into the closet, which was an entire room in itself.

"Jennifer ..."

He fell silent and watched her. Jen spun around in the oak-paneled closet, shedding her pajamas. Her top flew one way, her bottom another, sailing over the hardwood floor with the snap and siren of wings.

"I'm going out for a run, Wolf."

"No."

"Yes."

Echoes of his mother.

She plucked a blue thong panty from a shelf.

"Why do you think I'm weird, Jennifer?" Not that Wolf cared, but talking shifted attention off her state of undress.

"Because of the way you look at people."

A bouquet of Jen's favorite perfume spread through the room. Its elusive scent toyed with Wolf's nostrils. He walked to a window, opened it, took a breath of fresh air. The perfume was on her, on her clothes. Wolf liked the scent, but he liked the outdoors even better.

Wolf watched her slip into the thong. She'd been undressing in front of him since the beginning. At first, he had tried to look away, for the sake of professionalism and modesty, but she had bounced right back into his face every time. He wasn't going to fight it anymore.

"I'm your bodyguard, Jennifer. I have to look at people suspiciously."

She mussed her hair and gave him her practiced dumb-blonde look. Her breasts seemed to magically float toward him.

She pulled on blue jogging shorts, and then cavorted in front of a full-length mirror, admiring her creamy tanned legs and her apple-round hips and behind.

She leaped around the closet, rummaging through shelves and drawers, considering and rejecting several sport bras, and then finally donning one that complemented the blue jogging shorts.

She stood in front of Wolf and twirled around, tapping a lively rhythm on the floor with her bare feet. She stopped and thrust her taut abdomen at him.

"I don't mean when you look suspiciously at people, Wolf."

She sat on a chair and slipped on white socks and white running shoes. She grabbed a white headband from a hanger, smoothed her blond hair back, and slid it on.

She snatched a sport watch from a shelf, strapped it to her wrist, and pushed a tiny button, bringing up the stopwatch function with one silky beep.

"I mean when you look at certain people the way you

do, Wolf." She looked into his eyes. Her blues held his like magnets. "Like they scare you to death."

Wolf followed Jennifer downstairs into the foyer.

She did a series of stretching exercises on the ornate Persian rug that lay in the center of the chamber.

Wolf watched her. She was part tigress, part fallen eagle, nesting and tending to herself in the otherworldly impertinence of the surroundings.

She sprang to her feet. "Let's go."

"Jennifer, please reconsider."

"You always sense danger, Wolf."

They left the house. How could he tell her? This morning he sensed danger not for her, but for himself.

Wolf backed his car, a white Infiniti, out of one of the garage bays. Jennifer ran down the street, heading for the wilder sections of Slingshot Canyon.

Wolf chased her.

She looked back at him every minute or so, her face expressionless. She forgot to drink water, he thought. It was part of her routine before a run to tank up on water. And Wolf forgot to eat breakfast. Jennifer often joked that she had to feed him before taking him outside or the neighborhood pets and children would disappear.

Sunshine ate up the day. A blue sombrero of sky circled. Dun- and ginger-colored brush grew auralike from the undulating land.

Wolf, driving with his window down, kept the Infiniti fifty feet behind her, his foot resting on the accelerator. The car cruised like a big jungle cat, smooth, quiet, flexing its muscles.

She ran with a smooth, rhythmic motion, kept glancing back, making sure he was on her tail.

He saw one. A man. He stood near the front door of a house on the left side of the street, watching Jennifer. The houses in Slingshot Canyon, though opulent, were not enclosed estates. Their yards were open—open to marauding animals, open to passing humans. Wolf saw him clearly. He was a hard case. Wounds lay deep and festering in his face. The blotches and stain of terror peered at Jennifer as she ran by.

Wolf's mind burned. As many times as he had seen Witherpools, it always ignited a rage deep inside him, a rage that Jennifer, oddly, interpreted as fear. An emanation flew from Witherpools. They were connected by web. Each was a jot on the web, a sinking whirlpool of malevolence.

Witherpool. Even the name felt evil. Wolf saw them as butchered beings. Their faces were networks of ugly, uncared-for wounds.

He was seeing more of them lately. They were pooling nearby. Their presence meant death, dismemberment, or ruin for someone. Witherpools wanted ringside seats to the carnage.

He knew he would stand a better chance of protecting Jennifer if she were aware of their presence and the threat they posed. He decided that when they got back to the house, he would enlighten her about Witherpools.

Wolf remembered his first encounter with a Witherpool, at age ten. A car swerved and hit him as he rode his bicycle. The driver stopped to peer at Wolf's lifeless body, lying on the side of the road.

But Wolf wasn't lifeless. His consciousness hovered overhead, watching the grinning face of evil as it peered at his body. He saw the blotches and stain of terror, the lust.

Thinking he had killed Wolf, the man got out of his car and leaned against it, aquiver with passions beyond Wolf's ability to understand at the time.

The man was soon disappointed. Wolf returned to his body. Paramedics revived him and rushed him to a hospital, where surgeons saved his life.

Wolf began to see Witherpools routinely after the accident, though he didn't know they were called Witherpools until much later.

He lived in fear much of the time, until he grew to physical maturity and developed the gumption and skills to deal with them.

Wolf watched Jennifer from his Infiniti. He scanned the neighborhood, his pulse jumping every time a person came into view, until he saw a clean face.

A half hour later they returned to the house. Jen went inside and Wolf drove the Infiniti into the garage.

After her shower, they met for breakfast on the back patio.

"Jennifer ..."

"What?"

"I have something to tell you."

"What?"

"During your run, there was a man watching you."

Wolf told her about the hideous, butchered face that had watched her during her run. He related his experiences with Witherpools, describing the menace they posed to the human race. He told her about the Witherpool watching him die when he was ten, about the Witherpool's disappointment when he revived. He told her about Witherpools pooling in the area, the likelihood of imminent danger.

When he was done, she sank back in her chair and stared at the distant hillsides for a long time. Then she looked at him.

"Wolf, let's eat our grapefruit and cereal. Then go inside."

They ate their grapefruit and cereal, went inside, and sat in the living room.

"Wolf, my mother told me she saw her brother Frank the night he died. She was twenty-two at the time, not yet married. This was before I was born. Frank was a few years older than my mother.

"She said she saw him standing in her living room, staring at her. It wasn't actually Frank, but his spirit, or something. It was a clear image; she knew it was Frank. Within moments, he was gone.

"At the exact same time, unknown to my mother, Frank died in an auto accident in Oregon, hundreds of miles away. She wasn't informed of his death until the next day. Then she made the connection—seeing him at the time he died.

"Wolf, I believed what my mother told me about seeing Frank the night he died. I believe what you're telling me now about Witherpools. Though I don't understand any of it."

Wolf relaxed. The battle was half won. Jennifer was a believer, though she wouldn't be able to discern Witherpools herself.

He got out a legal pad and drew a rough map of the neighborhood.

"Here's where the guy was." He pointed out the house where he'd seen the man who'd been watching Jennifer. "A Witherpool either lives here or was stationed here." He marked it with a red *W*.

"Over the next few days," he said, "we're going to mark the locations of as many of them as we can."

"What then, Wolf? What do we do then?"

He had to be careful. They had to remain within the law. Jennifer was a highly visible celebrity. Wolf was well known as her bodyguard.

"I know a man who deals with them, Jennifer. He's good. I'll get ahold of him."

"Okay, Wolf. Just don't get too involved."

"I won't."

Wolf first encountered the man years ago when he worked as a laundry deliveryman in Omaha, Nebraska. The man had been walking out of a house where Wolf was about to make a delivery.

Wolf always dreaded that house. The woman who lived there had the most hideous face he had ever seen. It was a butcher's shop from Hell—laced with open wounds, split as if by a meat cleaver, a swamp of blood oozing out, maggots crawling in and out of her flesh.

After seeing the man leave the house, Wolf rang the doorbell. Anticipating seeing the woman, he shuddered. No one answered. The next day Wolf learned the woman had been murdered inside the house.

For a while, Wolf had been the focal point of the police investigation. He claimed he had seen no one in the area. Secretly, he planned to track down the man he saw leaving the house. He believed the man also saw these hideous things, and wanted to form an alliance with him.

"Don't worry, Jennifer. We'll handle it discreetly."

Wolf would call Walt Gill. Walt lived in the Bay Area now. Walt would come down to Los Angeles and search out the Witherpools who were pooling in Slingshot Canyon. Walt would know how to deal with a Witherpool infestation.

Street Theater

Late on an August afternoon, with the sun showing no mercy in the sky, Ben Odom stepped from Hun's Restaurant in Santa Monica, California, and shaded his eyes with hands that shook with violent energy. An old lady passing by on the sidewalk gave him a queer look, and he spat at her. She flinched but kept on staring. He took a menacing step toward her, and she bolted. He watched the old scum scurry away and then tossed her from his mind. He drew in a deep breath, and this helped him focus on his problem. A short while ago, a man inside Hun's had called Ben by a new name, *Horse*. Ben spoke briefly with the man, and then left him alone with his girl, Misty Gleeson, and headed outside for a breath of fresh air. That had been a mistake.

Ben yanked the door of Hun's open and yelled inside for the manager, Bob Fat. When Fat came to the door, Ben pulled him onto the sidewalk and described the man who had stolen his girl.

"Throw him out."

121

"My pleasure," Fat said. "I'll break his balls." He went back inside while Ben waited on the sidewalk, reviewing what had happened.

"Horse!" The voice had shot across the dining room with an explosive bang, causing diners to jump in their seats. It reached Ben's table with such force it caused Misty—who'd just raised her schooner to her lips—to slosh some of her ale onto her blouse. She turned an odd color, something like diamonds in bad light. The voice seemed to have jolted her somewhere near her soul. Her eyes told Ben she needed an explanation fast, but that maybe no explanation would do.

"Horse, getting enough oats to eat? Enough water to drink?" The voice was like the crack of a whip. It carried heavy authority.

"Yes," Ben had said. Who was this guy that was talking to him? "I'm getting enough oats to eat, enough water to drink."

He stood and looked at the source of the voice and saw a man on the other side of the dining room wave to him. The man was on the small side, a dapper man, a sharp dresser, as bright and cheery as a pineapple.

The man bounded to Ben's table.

"You didn't pull up lame, did you?" the man asked. "Were you ridden too hard?"

Ben did not answer. He did not know how to answer. More than anything, he wanted this conversation to end. He mumbled a few meaningless syllables, hoping this would satisfy the man's curiosity. Then he tossed his head and scented the wind.

The man laughed, and then began a series of energetic motions that no one in Hun's was likely to understand, except Ben.

Ben felt a vague sense of being lassoed. Then he felt a tug and was pulled away from his table. He whinnied and headed outside.

He left the restaurant, his mind sunk in the blinding grit of the moment, knowing the man had somehow taken control of him and stolen Misty.

Outside the restaurant, Ben jumped aside as the door swung open with tornadic force and Hun's manager, a tough old son of Chinese immigrants, threw the man out. The man went sprawling on the sidewalk, looking rather scruffy all of a sudden.

He got up slowly—too slowly, in fact—which gave Fat just the opportunity he was looking for. Fat rushed him and kicked him in the ass hard enough to raise him off the sidewalk a good ten inches and propel him into the gutter. For a moment, the man lay as if dead, and then oozed to his feet, voicing a succession of high-pitched yelps. He stood in a cloud of hot, steaming anger, glaring at Fat, and then made a move as if to counterattack.

Ben stepped in front of Fat, and the man's face collapsed in indecision. A moment later, he looked determined only to escape, and he began running down the sidewalk at high speed.

Ben gave chase but lost him in a maze of back alleys. After several minutes of fruitless searching, Ben popped out of an alley and gained sight of the man again. He stole close enough to see the remnants of Fat's shoeprint on the back of his trousers.

The man was now walking along in a casual manner,

oblivious to the prospect of danger. He appeared good na-
tured and refined, not the type of scum that would steal
your girl right out from under you. Behind the façade, he
was likely sizing up potential victims.

Ben hit him at high speed from behind and slammed
him face-first onto the sidewalk. He dragged him into a
side street and threw him down a stairwell. He ran down
the stairs and stomped on him for what seemed like an
eternity.

He felt the man's carotid pulse. Nothing.

Ben backed up the stairs, the dead man in his sight.

At the top of the stairwell, he glanced around and saw
Rick Carlisle walking toward him, a cigar clenched between his teeth. Rick was a police detective. Ben shrank
back. He didn't think Rick had seen him.

Ben snuck to the next stairwell and ducked into it. He
poked his head out and saw Rick looking around curiously, and then saw him look down into the other
stairwell, where the body lay.

Ben knew he was sunk if Rick were to look into the
stairwell he was hiding in. Luck was on his side, though.
The stairwells on this block opened onto apartments that
had exits elsewhere, avenues of escape.

He crept to the bottom of the stairwell and tried the
door. It was locked. He jimmied the lock and slipped into
a darkened apartment. He found himself in a playroom,
where a small child was sitting on a couch watching television.

Ben crept from the playroom, his footsteps muffled by
the sound of the television, and entered a shadowy corridor.

He heard a sound behind him and spun around. The
child was following him down the corridor, a little girl.

He had to get out of here fast. If an adult showed up, he'd have to pull his badge and lie his way out of it, one door down from where a dead man lay in a stairwell.

"Krissy?"

The voice froze him. He saw a shape loom behind the child: an older girl, maybe seventeen. She saw Ben and froze.

Ben put a finger to his lips, pulled his badge, and whispered, "I'm tracking a man. I think he entered your apartment."

The girl shuddered, seized the child, and held her close.

Ben whispered, "The front door, where is it?"

She pointed behind her.

Holding his badge so they couldn't see it, he maneuvered around them, slipped down the corridor, and found the front door.

Once outside, Ben breathed easier, but did not relax too much. He knew he had a big task ahead of him. He had to go see Rick.

He walked around the block, the sun pulling his face into a grimace, and saw Rick standing by the stairwell.

He walked up to his partner, intent on saying as little as possible. Rick was writing in his notebook.

"Ben, there was a time when every pen I tried to use didn't work. Each was dry, even new ones. I couldn't find anything that would write. The universe was trying to tell me something. It was testing my resolve. Eventually, I found pens with ink that flowed. I was humbled but not bowed." He nodded toward the stairwell. "What did this guy have happen to him? What was the universe trying to tell him? Take a look."

Ben walked to the stairwell and looked down at the dead man. The man's head was bent grotesquely backward, his arms and legs splayed at unnatural angles.

Ben backed away from the stairwell, avoiding his partner, who now loomed close.

"What happened to this guy, Ben? Did you see it? You were in the area. At least the guy got a good impression of the shoe that stomped on him."

"No, I saw nothing."

Something was waking in Ben's mind. I'm not this guy's partner. I'm not a cop. I'm an actor. What is this? What's going on? That quote is from a movie I made. *At least the guy got a good impression of the shoe that stomped on him.* What did I hold up to that girl? I don't have a badge. He pulled out his wallet, flipped it open. He likely held up his California driver's license.

"We'll have to canvass the neighborhood," Carlisle said, "to see if anyone saw anything."

"This isn't your town, Rick." Ben could talk like a cop. He'd played plenty of cop roles. "Santa Monica isn't your town."

"I know it's not my town. I was speaking broadly. *Someone* will have to canvass the neighborhood." Carlisle shook his pen violently. "Why'd this guy die, Ben?"

That was another movie quote. *Why'd this guy die?* Another one Ben was famous for. Ben looked at Rick. "Isn't that pen of yours working?"

"Nah. It quit. Fuck it. Where's the crowd? Why isn't a crowd forming? A guy is dead."

"They can't see him, Rick. You want me to haul him up for you, throw him into the street? If they're looking our way right now, all they're seeing is two guys with their thumbs up their butts, one with a pen that won't write, that's all. If they knew there was a body in the stairwell, they'd come running."

"You're right." Carlisle twirled his cigar between his teeth. "Does this alter our plans, Ben? Is this guy's death going to snag us?"

That was another famous movie quote that people spun out upon meeting Ben.

Ben looked toward the stairwell, the tight, concise canyon between sidewalk and brick building. "It snags us, Rick."

"Why'd this guy die?" Rick asked again, poking his head into the stairwell.

"I don't know."

"Maybe he took a hit of acid," Rick said. "Maybe he took a flying leap. But I don't think so. There are shoe prints all over down there. Someone stomped on this guy. The prints will show up even better under ultraviolet. With any luck, we'll find the scumbag that did it. Say, where's that girl of yours?"

Though his world was fragmenting into odd little pieces, Ben forced a smile. Rick's line was another movie quote.

"I left her back at the restaurant."

"Better go get her."

"Good idea."

It looked like movie art was playing out on the street. Rick Carlisle was a cop role Ben had created for another actor.

Rick Carlisle's taste in food was meat and potatoes. He had a substantial girth and wore suits circa 1920s Chicago. Carlisle's suit coats fit him snug in the shoulders, maybe too snug. Maybe he'd have to have his tailor let them out some or he'd be bursting them at the seams. His shirts were cream colored, with faint vertical stripes that changed the cream to pink in bright sunlight. The work some people put into their wardrobes.

Rick Carlisle was known for his fondness for all things Chicago, but no one knew why, and Carlisle had never said why. But Chicago was his kind of town. He smoked a cigar that was never lit. No one had ever asked him about that, either. Questions weren't kosher around Carlisle. There was this atmosphere about him of don't ask. You just accepted him for what he was. The Chicago suits, the unlit cigar, the heavy body, the knowing eyes, the smell of cheap cologne and explosive farts—that was Rick Carlisle.

The man beside him was not Rick Carlisle, but a guy who had been passing by on the street.

It was control at a subtle level: street theater.

Ben ducked away. He could do no more; this scene was over. He ran toward Hun's Restaurant, hoping Misty Gleeson would still be there.

Fine Gold

An emergency session of the Sap Watch Committee of the U.S. Supreme Court and various media organizations is in session. On the agenda: the recent Supreme Court decision legalizing medical prostitution. It seems some of the saps didn't fall for it and are in a rebellious mood.

"Highness, we have a petitioner, Fine Gold, who wonders if in light of the recent Supreme Court decision he can now get his chronic pain condition addressed by medical professionals. He says in the past this was well-nigh impossible."

"Show him into chambers."

"Yes, Highness."

Out in the hallway, the orderly says to petitioner Fine Gold, "This way, sir. Highness will speak with you in chambers."

Fine Gold is shown into chambers, where he sits on a large cushioned chair opposite Highness, who sits on a similar chair.

"Good day, Fine Gold," Highness says as the orderly leaves the room, closing the door behind him.

"Good day, sir."

"Please, dispense with formalities. Just call me Highness."

"Okay."

"I am told you have a chronic pain condition."

"Yes. The details take but a minute. Do you want to hear?"

"Yes, if you please."

"Years ago, an avulsion fracture of my right ischial tuberosity occurred—a sliver of bone broke loose, pulled by hamstring muscles. It remains inside me and has ossified: grown large. It is a big detached bone, and it presses on the sciatic nerve, which comes from the spine and branches into both legs. The sciatic nerve enables sensation and strength in the legs. Orthopedic surgeons tell me they can operate, but might accidently cut the sciatic nerve, leaving me with little or no feeling and strength in that leg. In the event of successful surgery, bone might regrow in the same area and renew its assault on the sciatic nerve. Risks of surgery outweigh benefits, leaving no medical solution except pain management, and that is the problem. Massage therapists cannot massage in that area. Licensing restrictions forbid it. It is akin to prostitution. Need I go into further detail about that?"

Highness shrugs, but does not respond otherwise.

Fine Gold looks for reassurance, but finds none. He draws in a deep breath and continues.

"I am suffering so much pain I cannot sleep at night. My leg collapses out from under me. It worsens. I don't want to take medication for my condition—I would become a junkie. Years ago, I got pain relief from my massage therapist because she could massage in that area. But her profession became highly regulated, and ruling powers place so many restrictions. They liken massage in that area to prostitution."

And here, Fine Gold seems to run out of steam.

"What about physical therapists?" Highness asks.

"It's almost the same problem, but slightly different. They are suspicious of anyone requesting treatment in that area for pain relief. They want it by doctor's orders. And then the time spent is negligible, it's excessively costly, and it produces unsatisfactory results. Insurance may or may not cover it. Our society is steeped in prostitution, if you know what I mean, Highness."

Highness nods, and seems to slip into deep contemplation, his eyes drifting far from the events in the room.

Minutes rush by, and Fine Gold raises a hand to get Highness's attention.

Fine Gold speaks, certain he has Highness's attention once again.

"There was a time when my massage therapist could massage in the area of the sciatic nerve for pain relief. They hadn't yet heard it was prostitution. I request that we consider going back to that era, for that is where the solution seems to lie."

Highness stands, gets a book from a shelf, and brings it to Fine Gold.

The light in the room slants differently, and Fine Gold sees a butchered being hand him the book. Highness's face is a hideous mass of raw, dripping, uncared-for wounds.

Fine Gold shudders.

"If you don't like what we in government do," Highness says, "summon the Devil."

The Devil

Jana Woodland stands nude in front of the class, trying to keep her backside to the class as much as possible as she climbs onto the massage table. If it makes it any easier, all the other students are nude, also, and they are all trying to keep their backsides to the class as much as possible as they climb onto their respective massage tables. Jana pulls the sheet over her buttocks and tries to relax. She is doing this as a protest. They are all protesting the wretched massage school they attend.

Actually, only half of the class is nude. The other half is still wearing clothes, preparing to give the massages. They will get their turn, though. Within the hour, they will have to strip down and be nude in front of the class, and they will have to try to keep their backsides to the class as much as possible as they climb onto the massage tables for their massages.

It's a protest. Their massage instructors have outlawed nudity, even of arms and legs. Students are required to drape the client entirely and work through the drape. But they know better—that's not how massage is done in the real world. They are protesting the rules of their wretched massage school. Hence the nudity, except when an instructor is in the room.

Jana's illusions about becoming a massage therapist have been exploded many times by the massage instructors at the Sisters of Bleak Orgasms School of Massage Therapy. Oh, how she wishes she had the Devil to talk to, so she can learn the secrets of real massage. Oh, how she wishes she had the Devil instructing her, instead of the Sisters of Bleak Orgasms.

She would do anything to become a real massage therapist. Anything. Even speak to the Devil.

All of a sudden, Jana hears a whisper in her ear.

"Are you discreet?"

"Hmm ... Yes."

The voice thrills her and terrifies her all at once. Is she about to get her wish? Is this the Devil whispering in her ear?

She doesn't want to look. She thinks it might be Duke Moon, the lone male instructor on staff. Duke is also President and CEO of the Sisters of Bleak Orgasms School of Massage Therapy.

She chances a look. It isn't Duke, whom she suspects of being an enormous hypocrite and womanizer—she's never felt comfortable around him. He's one of those pushing total draping. All massage techniques in the school have to be done through the sheet, no contact with bare skin.

She and the other students know the real world doesn't jibe with that, and that they'll be at a disadvantage with students who went to better massage schools. Hence the nudity in class, whenever the instructors aren't around.

She has to look again, to make sure it isn't Duke. Duke insists on total draping for Bleak students, not just while in massage school, but out in the real world, also. The Sisters and Duke are in the process of taking down names of former students who are suspected of massaging bare skin out in the real world.

It isn't Duke.

"Relax," the man says.

She has to look again, a third time. It looks like the Devil is preparing to massage her. It must be her confused mind, thinking of the Devil, thinking of Duke, who she knows wants to have his hands all over her nude body, but is in denial, and in some kind of dysfunctional territory, forcing, along with the Bleak Sisters, the total ban on skin, the requirement of total draping in the classroom, as well as out there in the real world.

It isn't Duke.

"Relax," he says again.

But she doesn't know if she can relax. The guy has horns. He's burnt a bright red. Smoke issues from his mouth and nostrils. A grin festoons his face.

It must be her imagination.

Jana relaxes, and the Devil uncovers her glutes, her precious butt. Her buttocks are entirely bare to the class— wait, relax, only the Devil can see; the other students are either on the massage tables being massaged, smothered under the drapes, or doing the massages themselves, through the drapes, adhering to the no-skin-on-skin policy of the Bleak Sisters and Duke.

It's the Devil massaging her. *Massaging her bare buttocks! Oh, my God!* Or is it Duke?

She chances another look.

The Devil gently puts his hand on her head and eases it back down, and she rests her face in the face cradle.

"Your name?" she asks, surprising herself, sounding so officious, as if she, Jana Woodland, is going to get the Devil in trouble for massaging her bare butt.

"Henri Gomes," he says.

"Henri, are you the ...?"

"Yes. Don't worry. No one can see me."

"What? No one can see you?"

"No one can see you either, while I'm here."

"Ahhh ..."

Jana rises from the table, exposing her bare breasts to Henri Gomes, and her bare genitals, before she knows what she is doing. With enormous embarrassment, she lies down, hoping Henri didn't see much.

"I saw everything," Henri says.

Jana feels herself turning bright red. She feels that soon she'll be as red as the Devil himself—as red as Henri Gomes.

"Look again," Henri says, "briefly, if it will help you relax."

Jana lifts her head from the face cradle and peers at the man who is massaging her bare buttocks—his hands all over her bare buttocks. *My, God!*

She looks, and Henri Gomes is no longer red, but a mushroom color, as if he had just come in from the outdoors after a healthy run, or a healthy swim, or a healthy bout of chopping down trees or something.

She puts her face back in the face cradle, and she finds herself relaxing, and she feels her own skin change from its bright red of embarrassment to something akin to Henri's hue, something along the lines of a mushroom color, a healthy flesh color.

She hears Henri chuckling, but she senses it's just a chuckle of nothing, as it were. In other words, it doesn't pertain to her. He's just chuckling because it feels like the thing to do, and she shouldn't take it personally.

"I'm just chuckling because it feels like the thing to do," he says. "Don't take it personally."

"Okay. But how can you know my thoughts?"

His hands are working the muscles of her glutes, applying light pressure, and then deeper pressure. *Kneading. Stroking. Kneading. Stroking.* And he's doing it all over, even in the cleft between her glutes, an evil zone the Sisters of Bleak Orgasms and Duke the womanizer had warned the students about—you will be cast into Hell.

But Henri is massaging directly into the cleft between her buttocks, working into the muscles on both sides, doing just exactly what the Bleak Sisters and Duke said not to do, especially not on bare skin.

But Henri is the Devil, and Henri can do whatever he wants, she thinks.

"I can know your thoughts," he says, "because our minds are so alike."

"Oh? So, what are you doing, Henri? I mean, this is school, isn't it? I can ask questions, can't I?"

"Yes, this is school. You can ask questions. I'm doing deep work on your glutes because your glutes are tight. Pain and tension associated with tight glutes is a common problem."

"I know, Henri. Even the Bleak Sisters and Duke mention tension in the glutes, but they warn about addressing any of that tension, lest you be cast into Hell."

Henri chuckles.

His hands are flowing in circular motions on her

glutes, applying deep pressure. Her butt is entirely bare to Henri, the Devil, a man or beast she hardly knows.

"So, what are you doing, Henri? Are you enjoying yourself?"

"Yes, immensely."

"Enjoying the view?"

"Yes, immensely."

"Are you getting turned on, Henri?"

"Well, now that you mention it ..."

"Oh, please spare me, Henri."

"Jana ..."

"You know my name?"

"Yes."

"How?"

"Do you remember Kayla Sawyer?"

"Yes. She graduated from here last year. She's why I'm here."

"She's why I'm here, also," Henri says.

"What?"

She chances another look at Henri. He's burnt bright red again. His horns are back. Smoke issues from his mouth and nostrils.

"Henri, if you're getting turned on ..."

"I am, but more about that later."

He still has his hands all over her bare buttocks, massaging with deep pressure, and it doesn't feel bad at all. In fact, it feels good. She can feel the tension release.

"Okay, Henri, tell me about your experiences with Kayla. Did she turn you on, also?"

Henri chuckles.

This time she catches on that it's a chuckle in response to what she said, rather than it being an all-purpose chuckle.

"Kayla summoned me, Jana, to further her massage career in the real world, and because she felt guilty for leading you on about this god-awful massage school."

"I thought so. I thought Kayla felt guilty about leading me on about this place, the last few times I spoke with her. So, how is Kayla doing, out there in the real world? You know, I can't get into her massage room to observe. What does she do in there? And how did she summon you? I didn't know Kayla had those skills."

"One thing at a time, Jana."

He's massaging her tailbone now.

"Are you sure the others can't see us?"

She pokes her head up and looks around the room. The other students are either lying flat on massage tables or leaning over massage tables, doing the honors, no bare flesh in sight, everyone draped like a corpse on a coroner's table.

"They can't see us for as long as I'm here," he says.

"Oh, please, stay for a long time."

What has she done? She's extended an invitation to the Devil. And now she feels guilty. Guilty over the pleasure she's feeling from the massage.

"You just tightened up, Jana," Henri says. "You went as tight as a spring. Let yourself relax. You will not be cast into Hell. That's someone else's invention, to scare you."

"Okay, I'm relaxing."

She feels herself relax deeply, and at the same time she feels herself getting turned on. She feels her pelvis quiver, and she thinks Henri will notice and say something, but he says nothing.

But this is her school, her training, and she doesn't want to miss out on anything, especially since she has the Devil here to talk to, the Devil who has come to rescue her from the Bleak Sisters and Duke the womanizer. She should ask Henri some questions.

"Henri, I'm getting turned on. Is that a problem?"

"It is if you feel guilty about it."

"Do we need to talk about it?"

"No, we don't."

"What would Kayla say about it? What if it was a female massaging me and I got turned on?"

"You aren't getting turned on because it's me doing the massage. You're getting turned on because it's normal to be turned on during a massage, despite what the Bleak Sisters and Duke would have you believe."

"But, Henri, the Bleak Sisters and Duke actually do say it's normal to be turned on during a massage. They even cite the biology behind it."

"Yes, but they teach it only because they are required to. The Bleak Sisters and Duke stop the massage when they sense a client is getting turned on. I should mention that Duke is heading for trouble with the law."

"What do you mean?"

Suddenly, the veils before Jana's eyes are swept aside, and she sees into a massage room where Duke is massaging a woman lying draped beneath a sheet. She sees Duke slip his hands under the sheet and massage the woman's bare butt, breasts, and genitals.

The scene fast-forwards, and Jana sees Duke's hands all over several female clients, all of them young and sexy, and then she sees Duke in handcuffs, and Duke's massage license cancelled.

"Oh, how horrible for those women," Jana says.

"He was touching them beyond boundaries, and doing it for his own pleasure," Henri says.

"But it's pretty much ..."

"Yes, it's pretty much like what I'm doing to you now, but there is a difference, and the women could tell. He didn't have their permission to touch in those areas. They could tell it was one-sided. There was nothing in it for them. Tell me, Jana, do you feel I'm doing this for you or for me?"

"I feel it's for me. Tell me how Kayla summoned you."

"She went into the forest, drew a pentagram on the ground, and performed a magic ritual. I arrived in a puff of smoke."

"Oh."

She relaxes deeply, and Henri removes the drape completely and sets it aside. And now he's doing long strokes down her back, pausing to rock her body, and then to knead her buttocks again, and to massage her legs, including her inner thighs.

He massages her lower back, extending the strokes onto her glutes, and she shudders under his hands and has an orgasm. She can tell Henri senses this, and that he's doing faster strokes now to prolong her orgasm.

She doesn't think it's wrong. She accepts it as normal. Even the Bleak Sisters and Duke say this can happen spontaneously. But they didn't really mean it. They'd have stopped the massage and called the cops.

Henri asks her to turn over, and she does. She now lies face up, fully nude, and she can feel Henri's eyes on her, on her bare breasts, on her bare genitals. She's grateful no one else can see, but then during a real massage, that is always the case. A real massage is always performed behind a closed door. Only the massage therapist can see.

"Tell me Kayla's experience in the real world," Jana says.

Henri's hands are all over her body, including her breasts, her genitals, and her inner thighs. The Bleak Sisters and Duke the womanizer would have had them both arrested by now.

"She was getting perfectly normal requests," Henri says. "Clients would ask her for nude massage and genital massage, and she was unprepared for this."

"I can understand nude massage," Jana says. "But genital massage is forbidden. Only the Devil can do that."

"If it's done for therapeutic purposes, it's as valid as any other massage treatment," Henri says. "Kayla learned of research being done in this area. She learned the best techniques for rehabilitating this area, and then she went into the forest."

"To summon you?"

"Yes."

Jana feels herself relax deeply under the Devil's touch. His hands are all over her nude body, but she feels safe. She's getting turned on again, but she doesn't feel a need to mention it. She thinks the Devil already knows.

Henri talks about Kayla's experience in the real world.

"Her clients complained that she used too much draping, that she worked through the drape, not on bare skin. They complained that she didn't massage the inner thighs enough, the buttocks enough, or the abdomen at all. They said they couldn't get a real massage from her."

"I see, Henri. Kayla did speak of these things. I'm getting turned on again. Oops, it slipped out."

"Good."

"Are you getting turned on, Henri?"

"It comes and goes."

She feels he's being honest. She doesn't hear much

honesty in the Sisters of Bleak Orgasms School of Massage Therapy. She begins to treasure Henri, the Devil.

"Kayla lost all her clients," Henri says. "Word got around—she was just another loser from this school. Other massage therapists, better ones, snapped up her clients. They were violating all the rules. That's what made them better."

"Oh? What did they do?"

"They massaged the inner thighs deep into the groin. They massaged bare buttocks, including the cleft between the buttocks. They massaged the abdomen. They did nude massage. They did genital massage. Kayla was willing to learn these things, but she was afraid of the police, and of the Devil."

"Afraid of the Devil? But the Devil ..."

"Yes. Kayla wised up and summoned me. I revived her massage career. She's doing fine now, violating all the rules. And now I'm preparing you for the real world, too, Jana."

Jana experiences another orgasm, and she senses Henri is sensing it, and that his hands are helping it out. She quivers for a long time.

Henri is massaging her neck and face now. He's doing a wonderful job. She hopes he won't bother to massage her arms, hands, and feet. There isn't enough time, and she never feels a need for them to be massaged anyway. Maybe that's why the Bleak Sisters and Duke the womanizer focus so much attention on arms, hands, and feet—they don't seem so naughty.

"The most important areas for massage are routinely ignored by the graduates of your school," Henri says, "except for scofflaws like Kayla, and now you, Jana."

She laughs. "Yes, I will be a scofflaw. I will break the law. I will do nude massage. I will do genital massage. I will massage bare buttocks, including the cleft between the buttocks. I will massage the inner thighs deep into the groin. My clients will have orgasms under my hands and I will sense it and help it out."

Ha, ha, ha! She hears her wild, unrestrained laughter, and feels a big grin break out on her face. What a relief it is, she thinks, to finally wake from this nightmare.

She is under the dim illumination of a single light bulb, strapped to a chair, coming to, the truth serum wearing off. Her inquisitionists are circling in the tight, darkened room.

The Bleak Sisters and Duke the womanizer stand before her.

"Renounce the Devil," they say in unison as they throw holy water on her.

"Okay," Jana says, relieved. "I renounce the Devil." Now she won't have to change her massage techniques. She can continue to practice fully draped massages, and touch no skin, and feel nothing.

"Thank you," she says. "Can I go now?"

She watches them look skeptically at one another.

"Can I give you a massage?" Duke asks.

She sees something in his eyes, but quickly dismisses it. She nods.

They release her.

"Renounce the Devil," they say again in unison and toss more holy water on her.

"Okay, I renounce the Devil," she says.

And then the overhead light swings, and the room is cast in new illumination, and she sees them as butchered beings. She sees their raw, dripping, uncared-for wounds. She knows they are Witherpools. She knows they suck pleasure from the pool of human suffering.

Yellowstone

Kristen-Kate McCutchan and Bob Evert jostled for position on the crowded boardwalk that circled Old Faithful Geyser, angling for that once-in-a-lifetime view, or at least the best view they could obtain. They halted in their tracks when the geyser made a succession of hissing sounds, and watched in awe as it blew gigantic jets of boiling-hot water into the sky. Plumes of steam floated through the soft blue atmosphere over Yellowstone, lending a fairy-tale ambience. It was a new experience for both of them. They'd never seen Old Faithful erupt before.

Now they steeled their nerves, for they were about to head into Yellowstone's backcountry. The trail they would take began near Old Faithful Village. Bob thought they'd be too close to civilization for bears or other dangerous wildlife to be a problem, but Kristen-Kate assured him that was not the case. She said there were documented grizzly bear attacks on humans in the vicinity of Old Faithful.

Kristen-Kate was on the mend from a horrendous experience she'd had in Africa. Bob was her psychologist and was trying to get her back to a semblance of normality.

In truth, Bob had no business being here in Yellowstone with Kristen-Kate. He could get in professional trouble if it were found out. Psychological counselors did not go on field trips to Yellowstone with their patients; they did not lead them into danger by hiking into grizzly country. Or did they? Who would ever find out? He tried to tell himself the trip was strictly informal, not a counseling session, and tried to put it out of his mind.

The hell it was. He was going to do his best to help Kristen-Kate heal from her African trauma. He was her counselor, and he was committed to this path.

To all appearances, Kristen-Kate had been on the right path in life, approaching fulfillment of her desires, when disaster struck on her African trip. In Africa, Kristen-Kate chewed on some weird plants and became "possessed," if not outright insane. Since then she's undergone a successful course of medical treatments, yet something still possesses her, a mysterious dimension of fear.

They paused at the trailhead and took stock. It was dark in the forest, shadowy. In Yellowstone, wild animals were a possibility anywhere. Yet people hiked all over the park and slept in tents. So would they before their trip was over.

They set out into the shadowy woods, leaving the bustle of Old Faithful Village behind. Each carried a whistle, which could be used to warn bears of their approach, or to summon help; a knapsack packed with trail food, raingear, and overnight items; and a canteen filled with water.

There wasn't much to worry about, Bob thought. They'd be gone for just a few hours during daylight, but prepared for overnight if necessary, armed with knowledge and a few handy items.

The preparation was Kristen-Kate's doing. She was the daughter of an Army general, and preparation was natural for her. Bob didn't see it as another manifestation of her fear. Only stupid people failed to prepare adequately for danger.

The cloistering effect of the woods served to darken Bob's thoughts. He knew Kristen-Kate's mother had left home when Kristen-Kate was little. It was an undercurrent she would not touch. Her father had told her her mother had to go away. Hearing less and less about her from her father, Kristen-Kate formed a belief: *Profound mental illness. She's not coming back.*

Bob believed confusion and conflict about her mother might be contributing to Kristen-Kate's current crisis. It wasn't just about African plants. No doubt her mother's absence was buried somewhere in her psyche.

Where could he begin? How could he probe without it seeming like probing? He thought he knew a way.

"Kristen-Kate, is your mother still alive?"

"Yes, the last I heard."

"Do you ever plan on seeing her?"

"No, it wouldn't be something I'd look forward to."

"Oh? Why not?"

"She'd be unresponsive. I don't know much about her condition, but I do know she's sick. On rare occasions my father talked about it, but not since I was little. I used to expect her to come back, but eventually realized she wasn't. I began to picture her as dangerous, someone I wouldn't want to see."

"How did your mother's absence affect you?"

"I don't know. My mother was actually absent long before she left us. She was there, but not there. I can't say how it affected me."

"What's your impression of her now?"

"Someone who's hidden away. Someone who's been failed by society. They couldn't help her."

"What is your greatest fear concerning your mother?"

"That she'll come back. That she'll be a danger to herself and to me. That she'll kill me."

They walked in silence for a while.

"Kristen-Kate, what are you most afraid of?"

"I'm afraid of the next major change in my life, whatever that might be. It could be death. It could be disability. It could be anything. It's all so unpredictable."

"Like your mother leaving?"

"Yes."

"What would you most like to do?"

"Manage change somehow, so it's softer around the edges. I can't take extremes anymore. I guess my mother's leaving did affect me. It was extreme. I guess I've been expecting other extremes since then. I guess I've always tried to manage change so none of it is so extreme."

Bob thought he understood her now. Kristen-Kate desires to take that next step, whatever it is. But something holds her back: her need for control, to lessen the impact of change, all this brought about by her mother's leaving all those years ago. She's a young woman at war with herself.

"Sing it, Kristen-Kate."

It was their signal for when they thought a bear might be nearby. Making noise alerted bears of your presence and gave them time to move off, making an attack less likely.

She looked at him.

"I think I heard something," he said.

"I'm not going to sing, Bob. I didn't hear anything."

"Okay. Talk it, then."

"On what?"

"I'll ask questions. Are you making improvements in your life, Kristen-Kate?"

"Yes. I try to make incremental improvements in my life every day. Sometimes something small can mean something powerful."

"You seem, uh, very relaxed, and, uh, very accommodating. There's a bear out there, Kristen-Kate. I can hear it."

"Maybe so, Bob, but I don't think we have to be afraid."

"Oh? Well, you seem very relaxed and very accommodating."

"Yes, I'm usually very relaxed and very accommodating, for myself and others. Relaxation seems to be the key to so much. I can't stand to be around people who are tense. They make me tense. They're broadcasting something that can grab ahold of you and lock you up. It's like being in prison. On the other hand, if someone is a soothing presence, you'll welcome that person more so into your life.

"To me, everyone is an influence, both on the conscious and unconscious levels. Some people imprison me, others free me. I'm very tuned to this. I'm always assessing people as to the influences they exude, both consciously and unconsciously.

"Sometimes I reel from people. Sometimes I shrink from them and go into lockdown. I have these unconscious gestures where I unlock myself, insert a key, turn it, swing the door open, walk out. As I move my hands around, I'm trying to get out of prison, work the mechanism, so to speak."

Bob thought he caught something. Kristen-Kate exhibits two contrasting behaviors. One, the characteristic shuffle and eyes-down movement of a prisoner: isolated, habituated. Two, a sense of fearlessness, as if she were flying.

If she won't sing, we need to keep talking, Bob thought. He can still hear the bear.

"Kristen-Kate, your father is an Army general. How does that affect you?"

"I'm glad for him. I couldn't be prouder. We have a great relationship."

"How do you tell people that your father is an Army general?"

"I don't. I never volunteer that information. If it comes up, though, I'll talk about it."

"Why do you hesitate to mention your father?"

"It's a heavy trip for some people. They don't know what to say. Some people make wiseass remarks. I tell them their prejudice is showing. I've had a few fights. I usually wait until I know someone better, then I talk about my father."

"Would you say you're protective of your father?"

"No. He doesn't need my protection. My father is the acid test. Once I mention him, people show their true colors. Some people are anti-military, some support the military. I prefer the later."

"You must like authority figures."

"Only those who serve us honorably. Some authority figures are worthy of respect, some aren't."

She was silent now.

Bob heard the bear pacing them.

"Kristen-Kate, don't you wish you could sometimes not be your father's daughter and find out what the world has for you?"

"Yes, I do. That's one of my goals, to get out from under his shadow. I know he's pulled a lot of strings for me. But I'd like to see what I can do on my own. I think I'll find out someday. It'll just be me and the world. I'm looking forward to the challenge."

He heard the bear, louder.

They encountered the almost soulful smell of a rotting carcass. It struck Bob full face and stayed with him as he and Kristen-Kate hurried through a dip in the woodland trail. He didn't bother to ask Kristen-Kate if she smelled it. One look told him she did.

The woods became darker.

The sounds of the woods terminated in abrupt silence as they rounded a bend in the trail. They stopped simultaneously, as if they were animals sensing danger.

Bob heard rustling, and edged backward on the trail. He felt Kristen-Kate at his elbow, edging backward, too. Their reactions were animallike, wariness struck to a high pitch.

Bob bent his ears to the woods. No more rustling. The silence was scary. He felt his heart race, like a machine out of control.

And then there was sound again, and it filled the forest. It was the sound of something big moving through the brush toward them.

They ran back along the trail toward Old Faithful Village, which was a good hour away now. Bob knew the danger they were in, and sensed Kristen-Kate knew it, too. No words were spoken.

They burst into a small clearing, went to separate pine trees, and started climbing.

Bob glanced at Kristen-Kate's tree and saw that she was ten feet up, on pace with him. He stopped thirty feet up, looked down, and saw something in the clearing. He could barely see it through the branches.

He made out brown fur, a shoulder hump.

Bob's insides went dry. It was a huge grizzly.

It stood below Kristen-Kate's tree, looking up. Bob scanned her tree and saw her about twenty-five feet up, testing her next handhold and foothold.

She looked down, as if sensing something was down there, and one of her feet slipped off a branch. She caught herself, hung on, and arrested her fall.

She steadied herself and looked down again. The bear stood watch.

Kristen-Kate scanned Bob's tree, found him, and made brief eye contact with him. Then she looked down at the bear again.

One of Bob's feet slipped and rasped the bark. The bear gave a quick huff and bounded to the base of his tree.

Bob held his breath, and peered down through the jungle of pine boughs into the staring eyes of the bear. Its teeth were bared. Its great upturned head was like a lethal weapon.

The bear rose on its hind legs and reached high into the tree. Bob's heart raced at demon speed. He shuddered with fright. For one terrifying instant, he thought it was going to climb up after him. It huffed and puffed and blew out great quantities of air, but did not attempt to climb the tree.

The bear dropped to all fours and lumbered off, disappearing into the bushes.

Bob did not relax; he thought the bear was lying in wait. How could they ever know if it was safe to climb down from the trees?

He tried to catch Kristen-Kate's eye, and saw her on the way down from her tree, hovering dangerously close to the ground.

Bob's heart caught in his throat. The bear was back in the clearing, standing silent, sniffing the breeze. Bob tried to yell, but nothing came out.

He heard a rasp, and without looking knew what had happened.

Kristen-Kate slid down the last few feet and thumped to the ground. The sound immediately drew the bear's attention, and it bounded toward her.

The next few seconds passed with Bob in shock. His blood froze, his body froze, his brain froze. An animal instinct swept his higher centers aside.

Somehow, Kristen-Kate made it back up the tree, unscathed. The bear was at the base of her tree, staring up at her. Bob's heart settled down.

How long would they have to wait? When would the bear go away?

The shadows thickened. The day grew darker by the minute, and Bob had trouble keeping Kristen-Kate in sight. She wavered in and out of view like a storm-tossed ship at sea. She clung to her limb like a sailor to a masthead, showing emotion only in the form of quick, fearful glances at Bob.

The pines began a strange dance, their limbs bouncing up and down in rhythm with the wind as thunderstorms formed over Yellowstone. A lightning display began in earnest, the cloud-darkened sky turning fiery in its dance of electrons.

The bear showed no signs of retreating. But if it did go, would they dare come down from the trees?

The smell on the trail must have been the bear's kill, Bob thought. He and Kristen-Kate had mingled their scent with it. The bear had come after them, protecting its food supply. It was that simple.

He looked down and saw that the bear was gone.

Bob assessed their situation. They were perched in two pine trees, about twenty feet apart. What had possessed them to climb two trees, and not one? The bear knew them both by scent and was probably lying up close by to attack them when they came down.

He figured at some point it would be safe to come down, but when? Danger in the form of the bear was lurking somewhere.

Thick shadows enveloped the ground. He had trouble seeing anything. He had to decide soon: get out of the trees and get back to Old Faithful Village before it got full dark, or spend the night in the trees.

"Kristen-Kate, what do you think? Is it gone?"

"I don't know, Bob." She turned her eyes to the ground and shifted about on her limb, trying to gain sight of the bear.

Bob looked down, willing the bear to walk into view. Not seeing it was maddening.

He decided they would stay in the trees. Each had food and water, and a belt they could use to strap themselves to a branch. If necessary, they could live up here for a couple of days. They could urinate and defecate from their perches. Then what? They had to come down eventually.

No, they couldn't stay in the trees. Bob decided they would have to risk it, or they would be stuck in the trees until one or the other fell out, or until some brave soul passed by on the ground and offered them safe passage. He grew disgusted with himself. They had a duty to warn others.

He climbed down branch by branch, stopping often to look and listen. He saw nothing, heard nothing.

He stood on the forest floor and gazed around.

He walked to Kristen-Kate's tree and watched her climb down, the hair on the back of his neck on end.

She made it down and stood beside him. They looked at each other, and then looked around the clearing.

They walked along the trail that led back to Old Faithful Village, in near darkness now, their flashlights illuminating their path, their skin tingling with the sense of eyes watching.

The next morning ...

Willis Fairchild ambled along the rough wooden walkway that descended the cliff outside the museum at Norris Geyser Basin. Steam rose from the geothermal vents, obscuring the people who ambled past him on their way down into the basin. He wondered who these people were, and what they were like behind the white veils.

He wasn't feeling a thing when his right knee began to act like a misfiring engine popping and sputtering. Then an entire spectrum of pain braced him, and he spied a bench, gingerly walked to it, and plunked himself down.

He attempted to get his mind off the knee, onto other

things. It didn't work. His mind was ever busy plotting for the knee. He'd have to listen to it. *Willis, you left your cane in the car. You'd better go back and get it.*

He was experiencing severe pain and wondered what kind of painkiller to take for it. He'd shucked his knee brace two weeks ago. He'd worn it only during the postop recovery as bones and tissues healed. *After that, all a brace did was build dependency,* his physical therapist had told him.

Willis watched steam rise from thermal vents near and far, watched people amble along the wooden walkway that stretched down into the basin. He would wait a few minutes, and then walk back to his car, pop some painkillers, get his cane, and go down there with them.

Fifteen weeks ago, Willis rode his mountain bike off a cliff in Colorado. He landed on a rock and broke his right knee. His surgeon told him he had a tibial plateau fracture and torn anterior cruciate ligament. Willis knew precisely what that meant and what it would take to recover. He'd known others with the same break and tear. It was a common enough injury.

One week after surgery, Willis began physical therapy to maintain range of motion. He was on crutches and wore a knee brace. Twelve weeks later, he got rid of the crutches and brace and began mild weight-bearing exercises. Now, fifteen weeks after the accident, he used a cane sparingly, determined to get rid of that, too.

But that was not happening. He was disappointed in his progress. His knee was not coming back as fast as he had hoped. He had to be careful; he had to ease it along. Meanwhile, he'd been building his upper body to compensate for the knee.

Willis's upper body was powerful. He spent hours in the gym each week lifting weights and working on his left leg, the good one, careful of the bad one. He was asymmetrical, powerful in upper body, powerful in one leg, not the other.

Willis got up from the bench and began his march back to his car, where he would get three acetaminophen tablets and his cane. After a few steps, his pain exploded and he stopped. It did not ease off. It felt like warring armies in there. He walked some more, and the knee kept exploding.

He considered going back to the bench, but continued to the car, remembering he had a real painkiller in there, something more powerful than acetaminophen. He'd take two of them and drift through the remainder of the day.

At the car, Willis took two prescription painkillers and grabbed his cane. Then he ambled back to the wooden walkway and descended the cliff again.

Norris Geyser Basin looked like a battlefield to him, with steam rising from the geothermal vents, with blood-red taint on the ground, caused by bacteria that lived in the acid pools. The place looked like Hell.

He saw a man with eyes as black as Satan's. He wondered what was wrong with him. Did he have evil in his soul?

It wasn't often you saw evil staring right at you. But it did happen to Willis. He believed he had a special sight for the evil that lurked within people.

Willis knew about evil. Evil killed his wife, Miranda, and his daughter, Juliet. Evil almost killed him, too, riding him off a cliff and demolishing his knee. Willis survived the fall from the cliff two months after his wife and daughter died. Since then, he'd had other brushes with evil. It traveled about. It knew everyone.

He believed evil was heading this way and would soon permeate Yellowstone.

Willis blamed the ugliness, the stupidity, the dishonesty of modern life on the vast middle class. If you were middle class, you had to buy into stupidity to maintain your standing. The middle class was responsible for the evil that was heading this way, the evil that was soon to permeate Yellowstone. Middle-class evil was the religion of life.

The middle class tolerated all that was bad, impeded all that was good in America. Rich and poor needed none of that. Middle-class Americans were responsible for all the wretchedness in society, including the broken-down, busted criminal justice system, the broken-down, busted civil justice system, the laughable institutions of law enforcement, religion, education, and government. Willis knew he was one of them. He was a lowlife, too. But what could he do? He could pretend otherwise. He could pretend to be poor. He could pretend to be rich. Either way he would not have to buy into middle-class stupidity and lies. Rich and poor had no use for middle-class evil, the religion of lowlifes.

Willis despised the middle class: the gutless wonders who stood for everything that was wrong and nothing that was right.

He kept trucking along the wooden walkway that led down into the geyser basin, hoping he would run into someone he knew. That would cushion things. He didn't think he could make it into the geyser basin alone today, even with the cane. It was a long way down there.

Willis almost died in the cliff accident. His injuries were beyond counting; the knee was not the worst. He'd also hit his head. They said he was on the road to recovery. He didn't see Miranda and Juliet anymore.

Anger and resentment hung in his head like clouds from a black cauldron. His wife and daughter had died in an accident. He almost lost a leg in another accident. He was making a comeback. But what was there to come back to?

He'd just visited their graves, laid flowers, before coming to Yellowstone. He didn't believe in God, that was middle-class insanity. He didn't have to believe in God now, because he wasn't middle class anymore. He was something else.

Heading down into the geyser basin, Willis saw stupidity and evil in almost every face he met on the wooden walkway. *Stupidity* and *Evil* might as well have been stamped on every forehead.

Stupidity and evil weren't the only values the middle class cherished. Another cherished value was the lukewarm nature of their lives.

It was axiomatic: the middle class lived lukewarm lives. They couldn't help it; being lukewarm was a middle-class value.

To charge up their pathetic lives, the middle class readily bought into heroes and villains and saviors, while remaining lukewarm within their marginal existences. The mythmakers of the middle class encouraged this sad, pathetic approach to life. Willis was glad he was no longer one of them.

He wouldn't have to buy into any of their half-truths or outright fabrications anymore. He could do things they couldn't do and show them the way. They would soundly condemn him as they adopted his new standards.

The middle class knew nothing except what was given them by those outside their class. Rich and poor showed them the way. Halfwits of the middle class followed along.

Willis hated the middle class, hated his fellow man. His fellow man was responsible for excluding everything virtuous from life. Willis would join the ranks of the rich and poor. If you were rich or poor, you didn't have to observe middle-class protocol. The middle class would recognize you as outside their class and leave you alone.

Being outside their class meant you could show the idiots the way.

The middle class hated freedom, at the same time preaching it. The middle class believed in gods and other absurdities without evidence. Their morality usually rested upon killing mass numbers of people outside their vaporous borders.

But if you were rich or poor ...

Willis walked along the wooden walkway that led down into the geyser basin, something foul in his mind. A black cauldron of hate. He hated the middle-class imbeciles that paraded around him. He hated them with a passion. They clucked like chickens, perpetuating stupidity like it was in their DNA. They were liars, buying into the lies of their imbecilic forefathers. They were the cause of all that was evil and stupid in the world. Without reservation, in mass numbers, they always supported the prevailing stupidity, whether it be mass murder in the name of their Holy Father, or butchery in the name of Stalin, Mao, or Hitler.

They knew nothing except what the rich and poor handed them. The rich and poor led the way. The rich and poor breathed life into the stupid middle class.

He looked into their stupid faces as they passed him by. They were as dumb as cattle. Someday, another Stalin, Mao, or Hitler would come along as their savior, and exterminate them. The middle class would never be the wiser. They would buy into it wholeheartedly.

How could he break from middle-class bondage, being neither rich nor poor? He must pretend he is rich; he must pretend he is poor. That would give him the mental leverage he needed.

Rich or poor, either way he had a chance to change his thinking and leave the idiots behind.

Middle-class thinking did nothing for anyone. The middle class suppressed freedom at every turn. They had contempt for the old ways, too dumb to recognize the traditions that sustained their forefathers. They believed in a Holy Father with no evidence—a Holy Father that slaughtered innocents in biblical proportions. They gave their souls to those who held them in contempt.

Who invented the middle class? Someone must have, for it wasn't normal for humans to be so dumb. The human race would never have evolved if early hunter-gatherers had been middle class. Stupidity would have done them in.

Willis had his work cut out for him. He would find a way to disconnect from the middle class once and for all.

Leaving the middle class behind meant leaving his dead wife and daughter behind. They were gone; it was middle class to hang on to them. Hanging on to them did not honor them. It dragged them down to middle-class ignorance and stupidity.

He could not afford to be middle class anymore. Thinking like a rich man or a poor man would give him opportunities denied by the middle class. Leaving the middle class behind meant he could find a way to rehabilitate himself. The middle class knew nothing of possibilities. They knew only establishment doctrine. They knew only the ways of the slave.

His wife and daughter were dead. He must leave them behind. They weren't going to rise from the dead or return as ghosts. Thinking there was a next life was for middle-class imbeciles. He'd believe it only if there was proof. Middle-class imbeciles didn't need proof.

His knee wasn't dead. That could be rehabilitated. His career as an engineer wasn't dead. That could be resurrected.

He would focus on leaving the middle class behind, and he would focus on rebuilding his knee, and if he found he couldn't rebuild his knee, he would do what he could with the rest of his body. He would build it into something even more powerful than it was now, but he thought he could work on the knee. Breaking out of middle-class stupidity was a trip he did not want to miss.

Today, he would think like a rich man; tomorrow, a poor man. The next day, who knows? Flip a coin. Either way, he was breaking out.

Willis was resting on a bench again, watching the people stream by. He felt heat in his knee. It was time to move on. He gripped his cane with both hands and rose to his feet. He took a step, and then another, and soon he was ambling along the wooden walkway again, wending his way down into the geyser basin, navigating among the hordes of middle-class idiots. He dismissed them by ripping a layer of himself out and tossing it away. Somewhere along the span of history someone had need to invent these people, for there was nothing natural about them.

He reached the bottom of the geyser basin, where the land flattened out and the wooden walkway circled about, more passageway for middle-class morons. Some of them, having reached their destination, stood gawking.

Willis would find his niche outside the middle class, and he would reinvent them in some fashion, and they would willingly go for it, for they could do nothing else. They were an invention, patented a million times, subject to tinkering by those who had insight into the mechanism.

He thought of how middle-class imbeciles dragged everyone down.

If it weren't for middle-class imbeciles, human regeneration would be a reality by now. You could regrow a knee, a limb, or a central nervous system. But the imbeciles wouldn't allow that. Their God would be displeased if human DNA were tinkered with in such a manner. God? Didn't they mean themselves? Yes. The imbeciles always lied.

He would leave his dead wife and daughter behind. He had to. What else? He had to stop visiting their graves. He had to disinter them and cremate them and scatter their ashes. That was the thing to do.

Would he meet up with them in the next world? The next world was a middle-class belief, created for middle-class imbeciles by religious charlatans who routinely conned the middle class into believing just about anything.

There could be a next world. But who could know? The stupid middle class stood in the way of knowledge. If it weren't for the stupid middle class, knowledge of the next world would be revealed by now—by scientific research the middle class forbade.

Willis ambled along the wooden walkway that curved through the geyser basin, past the numbskulls of the middle class, who trooped past him going the other way. Some sped past like demons, in a rush to get back up the cliff. Idiots. Morons. An invented class. Willis would reinvent them. Just give him time.

He would study the curious invention, the middle class, and he would figure his own way of reinventing them, and he would reap a fortune, and then he would go off someplace and work on his knee, and fix it.

He saw evil in their eyes, mixed with stupidity. It was they who killed his wife and daughter, and called it an accident. It was they who ruined everything by grafting their rules upon everything, and calling it morality. *Morality?* A strange word, a made-up word, an invention of the middle class. *Morality?* It was as empty of meaning as their heads were empty of intellect.

The steam drifted across the basin as Willis went farther along the wooden walkway. The blood red of the acid pools reflected the stupid faces around him. It was like trucking through Hell. It truly was Hell—the middle class were here in droves. They believed in Hell. They had to. The ones who invented them insisted upon it. There were others, though, a subset of the middle class, who insisted there was no Hell or Heaven, no God or gods; there were only things you rammed your head into or detected with scientific instruments. They were imbeciles, also. How could they know that's all there was?

Middle-class morons excelled in holding beliefs unsupported by evidence. They had to; they were told to by their inventors, the ones who played upon their deepest fears. Figure out what the imbeciles feared the most and you could reinvent them, reap a fortune, and truck off elsewhere and take care of a broken knee.

The steam was obscuring everything, and Willis had to be careful where he stepped, or he might step on a middle-class moron. The people around him had to be careful where they stepped, or they might step on Willis. Be careful, middle-class morons, he thought as they sped by.

Middle-class morons were easy to fool. All manner of con artists knew how to do it. Con artists fooled middle-class morons all the time, and ripped them off.

Willis hated the middle class, but he knew they needed help. He would reinvent them and help them avoid getting ripped off.

For a typical middle-class idiot, daily life was a rip-off. They were too dumb to know it. They were conditioned to accept it.

The steam obscured almost everything now. Could Willis see anything down here? Careful. People died when they stepped off the boards. The water was hot. The crust was unstable. Animals went in there and died. People went in there and died. Stay on the boards.

Something must have happened to the atmosphere over Norris Geyser Basin, or to the water system in the rocks that fed the geysers. Land and air seemed in chaos now.

The idiots were unseen as they walked by, though Willis could hear them just fine. They were talking their fool heads off, like they usually do, like Willis used to do, like his wife and daughter did, until they died. If only he could have rescued Miranda and Juliet from the middle class.

Then when they died, they would have gone away free, not slaves, not someone's invention that keeps getting reinvented.

What a waste. He'd give anything to bring them back and give them one minute of freedom, so they could think rather than be part of a mindless mechanism.

All Willis could hope for was to salvage his sanity and dignity. He would dig up his wife and daughter, cremate them, and scatter their ashes. No more visiting their graves. He would have memory. That was all he needed.

He would think of a way to reinvent the middle class. He would reap a fortune. He would fade away and savor his insight into these dumb pieces of machinery. He would get his knee fixed.

Willis gripped his cane hard. Some dummies were headed his way. He couldn't see them, but he could hear them. They ought to hear themselves. How stupid they sounded.

They rushed by, and the steam parted enough for Willis to see tattered pieces of middle-class flesh, middle-class clothing, middle-class madness.

These were the idiots who unquestioningly gave their sons and daughters to a parasitic system of education, power, and authority that reduced their minds to dry husks.

More middle-class idiots were passing by, nearly running into Willis. What was wrong with these imbeciles? Did they need road signs?

What could he do for the middle class?

What could he do for these imbeciles?

How could he reinvent them without them being the wiser?

How could he make his fortune doing so?

He would save a life, that's what he would do.

He would save some worthless middle-class imbecile's life.

He would be a hero then.

A man with a cane who saved a worthless imbecile's life.

Of course the media wouldn't term the middle-class person an imbecile. The media would never be that honest. The media themselves were middle-class imbeciles. They were part of the mechanism.

Willis would save some worthless middle-class imbecile's life in Yellowstone.

He would be a hero.

But what if no middle-class imbecile's life was threatened?

Don't even think it.

It would happen.

While here in Yellowstone, Willis would be on the prowl.

Willis stared into the acid pools. Bacteria lived in there. That's what gave the basin its color. Norris Geyser Basin was one of the harshest environments on earth, yet microorganisms flourished. And all around him were plants and birds and animals. The middle class were also all around. But they were a category hard to fit into any ecological niche. Where could you fit imbeciles? They didn't exist naturally. They were a created species. There was no natural niche for dumb bastards. There was no place to put them.

They were like alien visitors to planet earth.

Willis had been one of them once. It was hard to believe that now. But he was no longer stuck within their firmament. He was going to break free.

He would do it, and rescue his precious wife and daughter from the ground, and give them their freedom. No more dance of death for him. Now there would only be life, such as it was.

He would save some idiot's life in Yellowstone and make a fortune. Even if he made nothing, it would be impetus for the next step in his evolution.

Willis kept trucking along the wooden walkway, through the obscuring steam.

Kristen-Kate McCutchan and Bob Evert stood on the wooden platform that hooked around the prominence of Old Faithful Geyser, hoping Lady Luck would be on their side today. They had a good view, but crowds were still pouring in, jostling for position. When the geyser hissed mightily and blew a gigantic jet of boiling-hot water into the sky, their view was unimpeded, their luck never better. Plumes of steam held brief life in the soft blue atmosphere over Yellowstone before dispersing. It was almost magical. They both agreed it was worth seeing again.

Now they would hike into backcountry, on the same trail they had taken yesterday, where they had encountered the grizzly bear. Somehow, today, the bear seemed less scary.

Last night, upon their return to Old Faithful Village, they had informed park rangers of the bear. They said it kept them treed for several hours. Park rangers said they would post warning signs along the trail and at the trailhead.

Word that a grizzly bear had treed two hikers not far

from Old Faithful Village had spread rapidly throughout the park. People everywhere were talking about it.

"Frightened?" Bob asked.

"No," Kristen-Kate said.

Wonderful, Bob thought. A grizzly bear was just the catalyst they needed. What better way to conquer fear? Grizzlies were a wild sort of magic.

They stepped off the viewing platform and hiked to the edge of the woods. Each was armed with a can of bear spray, which they didn't have yesterday. This extra precaution was Kristen-Kate's doing.

Bob didn't see the bear spray as another manifestation of her fear. It was only prudent. When in bear country, pack bear spray.

They paused at the trailhead and took stock. The sign warning of a grizzly bear grew large in their eyes. Slightly apprehensive, they began walking.

After a while, the forest became dark, shadowy, and Bob's nerves were on edge. He thought he heard rustling.

"Sing it, Kristen-Kate."

"I'm not going to sing, Bob. I didn't hear anything."

"I did. Really. Talk it, then."

"Okay. On what?"

"I'll ask questions. Are you usually so relaxed?"

"We've already been through that."

"Okay, but there's a bear out there."

"We have pepper spray."

They walked in silence, each holding their can of bear spray at the ready.

Before long, Bob heard rustling through the woods again, pacing them. He could tell Kristen-Kate heard it, too.

The rustling stopped, and eerie silence struck the woods. They walked another half hour, and holstered their pepper spray. Then they encountered the almost soulful smell of a rotting carcass—just like yesterday.

They rounded a curve ...

Bob heard a sound, and edged backward on the trail, his heart skipping a beat. He felt Kristen-Kate at his elbow, edging backward, too.

They continued to back up. The trail narrowed, squeezed by thickets. They heard rustling nearby, and then huffing.

Terrified, they froze.

A huge grizzly bear exploded from a thicket, and with a deafening roar charged Bob and slammed him to the ground. It bit him repeatedly on the haunches, rolled him face up, and tried to sink its teeth into his throat.

Bob screamed. He punched the bear, rolled face down, and curled up. The bear sank its teeth into his knapsack.

"Kristen-Kate," he yelled, "use your bear spray!"

Frantically trying to keep his knapsack between him and the bear, Bob tried to draw his own can of bear spray.

The bear bit and clawed him, and tore into his knapsack.

Bob had his can of bear spray in his hands, fumbled it, lost it. He flailed his hands on the ground, searching for it.

The bear shook him and dragged him. Bob felt a slippery mess beneath him—his blood.

He heard Kristen-Kate shout at the bear, and caught glimpses of her running beside him as the bear dragged him.

Hope glimmered. She was using her pepper spray.

Down in Norris Geyser Basin, a man with eyes as black as Satan's passed Willis, and paused to speak.

"Say, did you hear the news? A grizzly bear treed two hikers near Old Faithful Village yesterday."

Willis pulled up, thinking he saw steam hiss from the man's orifices.

"The bear kept them up two separate trees for several hours," the man with eyes as black as Satan's said. "Then it went away, and they climbed down and made it back to Old Faithful Village safely."

Willis danced a jig on the wooden platform.

"Park rangers posted signs at the trailhead warning of the bear," the man with eyes as black as Satan's said.

Willis danced a jig, bad knee and all, his cane pounding on the wooden walkway, keeping rhythm.

He watched the man with eyes as black as Satan's wander away, to join the other imbeciles of his tribe.

It wasn't often you had an opportunity like this, Willis thought. A moron passing word of a grizzly bear posing danger.

It was fortuitous. It was part of the evil lurking here in the park.

Willis trucked back to his car and put his knee brace on, just in case. Then he plunked into the driver's seat and jauntily began his drive to Old Faithful Village.

He'd been planning to go there anyway before his trip to Yellowstone was over.

Would middle-class imbeciles venture into danger despite warning signs?

They would. It was one of the certainties in life. It

might as well be branded on their fool foreheads: *Middle-class imbeciles will venture into danger despite warning signs.*

He knew there was going to be some moron in danger because of the rogue grizzly. He was sure of it. And he was going to rescue that moron, and make a name for himself.

He parked his car at Old Faithful Village, and with legs suddenly agile, a knee with new purpose, he tore about, asking about a trailhead that had a sign warning about a grizzly bear.

People told him where the trailhead was.

He found it, saw the sign warning of the grizzly, and began trucking into the shadowy woods.

The trail dipped and rose, and then leveled out.

Something foul hung in the air.

The foul smell lingered for a while, and then dissipated.

He saw no one. The forest became silent. Fear became his companion, and walked with him, brushing him with cool ghostly touches.

He eased ahead, aware that he had slowed his pace almost to a crawl.

Out here, death was a shadow that danced around you. You had to pay attention to it. You couldn't let anyone obfuscate the facts. You couldn't be middle class. You couldn't be an idiot.

Willis hated the middle class, but knew they needed help. He would reinvent them, and help them.

He heard sounds ahead, someone walking. He gripped his cane hard, and relit a thought: *A man with a cane saves a worthless imbecile's life.*

Now he heard two of them walking, heading his way.

Willis came to a halt, his instincts telling him he must go no farther. He must wait right here. With nervous energy, he ground the tip of his cane into Mother Earth.

Like an alien visitor to planet earth, something waited in the sky overhead. Way, way up.

It waited until a grizzly bear exploded onto the trail ahead.

It was a strange oration, spoken by something unseen. The unseen speaker hovered in the air above the trail, mingling with the forest canopy, its voice mechanical, deep and cavernous, as if it came from the bottom of a thousand-gallon rain barrel:

"The damn fools were seen heading out on the same trail this morning, despite the warnings! The same two who'd been treed yesterday! Fools! Middle-class imbeciles!"

The voice sounded angry. It was a searching voice. It found what it was searching for and went into attack mode.

Kristen-Kate was trying to get her canister of bear spray to work. She wished she had read the instructions beforehand, maybe even practiced a squirt or two.

Damn it! Now was not the time to read the instructions!

And yet she had to. The bear was dragging Bob. Bob's life was pouring out of him. An amazing amount of blood lay on the trail.

She read the instructions as she ran alongside the bear.

She thought she knew what to do. She held the canister at the ready and thumbed the safety clip back.

She aimed the nozzle at the bear's face and depressed the trigger, spraying a two-second burst.

An orange mist enveloped the bear's face.

The bear dropped Bob and ran a few yards away.

Kristen-Kate stood between the bear and Bob, holding the canister at the ready.

The bear huffed, and charged Kristen-Kate, but it was a slow, hesitant charge.

She sprayed it in the face again, and the bear turned aside and ran away.

It stopped several yards away and spun to look at her. It pranced about, as if indecisive.

As she watched the bear, Kristen-Kate heard a strange, mechanical-sounding voice in the air above her.

"The damn fools were seen heading out on the same trail this morning, despite the warnings! The same two who'd been treed yesterday! Fools! Middle-class imbeciles!"

At some level, Kristen-Kate knew the strange voice was talking about her and Bob. But she had no time to digest it. She had to focus on the bear, for it seemed to be gathering its nerve again, and was creeping her way.

She backed up, holding the canister of bear spray at the ready.

"Nice bear," she said in a calm voice, willing it to go away.

It charged her.

She depressed the trigger, but saw only a faint mist of orange come out.

The bear leaped at her through the faint mist of orange and knocked her down.

The bear left her alone, and ran off to peer at her from a distance.

She scrambled to her feet.

She was bruised and in pain. She knew the bear could have killed her if it wanted to. Maybe it was just a bluff charge.

She held the canister at the ready, pointed at the bear.

"Bob, can you get your spray out? I think my can is just about empty."

She heard no response from Bob, saw no movement from him. She thought he might be dead.

The mechanical voice sounded again, like a steel drum reverberating in the rain:

"Lie down, middle-class imbecile! Lie down and play dead! The bear sees you as a threat! It mauled that idiot because he struggled! Do not struggle! Do not run! Lie down, play dead! The bear will think the threat has been neutralized!"

Kristen-Kate lay down and played dead.

She thought Bob was either playing dead, or was dead.

The bear kept watch from a distance.

A while later, it wandered off.

Kristen-Kate stood and went to Bob.

She saw that he had massive wounds on his scalp, buttocks, and legs. His knapsack was torn to shreds.

She heard someone on the trail and turned to look.

It was the bear, creeping back.

It charged her full throttle, but in mid-charge, collapsed, as if shot dead.

The mechanical voice sounded again:

"I took the bear out! It isn't dead! Get away!"

"I can't move Bob by myself," Kristen-Kate said, looking around. She saw no one.

"Middle-class imbeciles, get the hell out of the area!"

Kristen-Kate heard a sound and spun around.

She saw a man walking along the trail, approaching her. He had a cane and walked with a limp.

"Help me with him," she said.

Together, they got Bob to his feet, and began the journey back to Old Faithful Village.

One month later, a news story:

Sources say the Pentagon is still trying to figure out how Willis Fairchild was able to commandeer a secret American space weapon and use it to incapacitate a grizzly bear in Yellowstone National Park last month.

Sources say the government will not prosecute Fairchild, as this would make the secret weapon system subject to the kind of scrutiny they want to avoid.

Dexter Sandy, a mechanical engineer and president of the Denver firm Fairchild used to work for, believes Fairchild might have secretly inserted his own computer code into the satellite-based system.

"He might have activated his own code by sending a signal to the satellite," Sandy said. "Our firm was a major subcontractor. Fairchild did a lot of work on the system."

Everyone is wondering how the weapon system knew what to do in the face of a grizzly bear attack. But no one is talking.

"The weapon system is truly remarkable," Sandy said. "Each of us got just a piece of it to work on. Very few people know its full capability. The public has been told its purpose is to help downed pilots escape from enemy territory. But who knows its real mission? It's a well-kept secret."

Why did Fairchild leave the company?

"No one knows why he left," Sandy said. "He was our top engineer. His wife and daughter died in a car accident several months before he left. Fairchild was never the same after that. Then he had his own accident. He rode his mountain bike off a cliff and broke his knee. That might have had something to do with him leaving. We still pay his health insurance. It's our way of reaching out to him. We want him back. People do come back from knee injuries. They do it all the time. Maybe saving the couple in Yellowstone was Willis's way of coming back."

Jack is Badder than Bob

I had seen the little olive-skinned man in the sports center's weight room on several occasions. He was a tough little man and I was looking for an associate, so I kept him in mind. He approached me once while I was on a weight machine. *Can I jump in?* he asked, meaning could he work in with me on the machine, since I was doing multiple sets. Sure, I said. I am much bigger and lift heavier weights, but he was impressive for his size. He was like an eel, long and slippery. When he walked, it was like John Wayne a foot shorter.

Jack is badder than Bob. I'm Bob. I do things for rich people. Jack you haven't met yet. You'll meet Jack later. But for now, you'll meet me. There's this little olive-skinned man at the sports center, a tough little man from the Middle East named Gordy Hussein. He's from an olive country. He is eel slippery. He's Americanized, hence the name Gordy. He came to us from Iraq, along with his wife and son. His son is ten months old. Gordy is twenty-four.

Gordy speaks in a mellow, whispery voice. He'll walk up to you at the sports center and ask, "Can I jump in?" He means can he work in with you on a weight machine. The first time he asked me this, I knew he was Americanized.

"Sure," I said. "Jump in."

I watched as he adjusted the machine and did his set. He is much smaller than me, but tough. He did his utmost, and he used proper technique, which showed he'd been trained and that he cared about results. He walked off without thanking me when he was done: a natural in an age when you expect this. I was impressed. I'd seen him before at the sports center. I'd heard him talking Arabic to other Arab Americans, but until then I hadn't realized he was so Americanized. I like to give opportunities to those who appreciate them. I needed an associate. After getting to know Gordy, I asked him if he could use some extra income. He said yes. He didn't even ask what I did. I told him how much it paid. It would come from my client, a personal check. He looked happy like a dog about to be fed. I guess he and his wife were barely scraping by.

He is olive skinned and has a slender body like an eel, but with sinuous muscles that look impressive, a hard man, a tough man, and yet a little man, from Iraq, here with his wife and tiny son. I saw him with his son in the locker room occasionally. Rules here permit small children of the same sex to enter the adult locker room under supervision of the parent. There is also a family locker room that can be used by parents with small children. Gordy preferred to take his son into the adult locker room, I guess. I don't know why.

He is soft spoken while speaking American. While speaking Arabic, he spits it out like a cobra with bad breath. I sometimes see Gordy congregating with other Arabs at the sports center. But he also hangs out with guys like me: weight lifters. I also teach martial arts. I wanted Gordy in my martial arts class. I talked him into signing up. He worked at it and became good.

He is a sight for a pair of American eyes. Imagine any Western you've ever seen, the good guy walking into a saloon, lanky, eel-like, a tough narrow face, though you know he's a good guy: his features say so. It must be in the eyes. The villain's eyes will be registering something else—something a little villainous. Gordy is a small, tough Iraqi who's become Americanized, lifts weights, goes to school, gets married, has a baby boy, takes his baby boy into the adult locker room at the sports center on occasion.

I wish I had told Gordy not to do that. Not to take his baby son into an unsecured, unprotected environment in America, such as a locker room—unless it's a family locker room, where, in theory, slimeballs can't tread.

I work for a rich man who wants to teach his daughter a lesson. She hangs out with lowlifes who take drugs and play loud music. Sometimes they get busted for it. It's usually the loud music that draws citizens' ire and cops' attention. The cops spy the drugs as they investigate why someone is playing music that can be heard several blocks away.

There are antidrug laws here, and noise ordinances, just like everywhere else. I'm not concerned with drugs. Go ahead, kill yourself with drugs if you want to, good job. Your death is silent. No one hears it blocks away.

I hate your loud music. So does everyone else. So I run this business.

I discreetly advertise my services to wealthy people with teenagers, promising to deliver instructive life lessons. I have another associate, Jack. But Jack isn't here now.

Gordy Hussein and I were on the job. The teenage daughter of this rich client was coolly aloof, pretending we weren't within her awareness. We rented a place out in the country where we could do our work without distractions. We bolted a chair to the floor of the main room and tied a guy, whom we'll call our subject, to it. Then we wired up huge amplifiers and speakers and shoved them right next to our subject's skull.

We stood outside the soundproof room we created around our subject, set music playing, and cranked up the volume. It was morbid. The sound blew out his eardrums and created tiny stress fractures in his facial bones. Blood trickled from his ears and nose like postage due from a bad dream.

The rich man's daughter and her friends were in attendance, watching through a one-way mirror. Our subject writhed like a reptile having seizures and screamed until his voice gave out. We told the daughter our subject had sustained irreparable damage to his central nervous system. One of her girlfriends broke down and cried.

For a while, the daughter's reaction was subdued, unknown. Then she suggested that she and a boyfriend of hers get into torture, also, thinking it's cool. Her father had lectured her on how things were done in America, how there was a shadow government that did whatever it wanted, and that she would have to follow certain rules if she didn't want to get in big trouble and get tortured by this shadow government.

After our demonstration, she conceived of doing torture, not being a recipient. This did not serve as a lesson for her.

Our subject was an actor we'd hired months earlier and told to become friends with the daughter. He did. Becoming friends with her was supposed to pry open feelings like sympathy and empathy, but it never did. She was as cold as a North Atlantic cod during the demonstration.

The torture was a sham. The music wasn't on.

After our make-believe session of torture was over, we dragged our subject from the makeshift soundproof room and dumped him in the trunk of a car, making like we were going to drive away and dump the body someplace. The daughter's old man paid us well. It was a rented Cadillac we dumped the body into. The daughter believed it was real but did not reform. She missed completely what was in store for her: she was next for this torture. She chose instead to cast her lot with guys like Gordy and me, and began talking about torturing people to punish them for not obeying society's rules. I guess in a way she did reform, but not to our liking.

I forgot to mention: Norman Coffey was seeing Gordy's son regularly in the sports center's locker room. Coffey was making arrangements to find a lookalike. He was pulling in favors, arranging things so he could insinuate himself into the life of Gordy's son, Adnan Johnny Hussein. Little A.J. was ten months old. A tiny olive-skinned kid still in diapers.

⌐⌐

Jack is badder than Bob. You've met Bob. I'm Jack. I was studying Jennifer Bancroft through the one-way mirror her father, Vance, had installed in the wall between his study and the observation room. She was sitting on one of the high-back leather chairs he has in there, not paying too much attention to Vance as he lectured her on the proper way for young ladies to behave in our society. He talked about the social order and so on, and honestly, he wasn't doing too bad a job. Her eyes drifted around the room, not looking at anything, just enduring, as usual. Her face was a beautiful kind of putty, shifting, lively with something, but not with what her father was saying, until ...

Vance had prepared me for this. He'd come up with something new to throw at her. *A shadow government.*

"We do whatever we want, Jennifer," he said. "You don't want to run afoul of our rules." Vance told me he'd consulted with psychologists on this. He said young people were impressed with the idea that there was a shadow government that did whatever it wanted.

Jennifer's face changed immediately as the words tripped off her father's tongue, the beautiful putty forming up into a portrait worthy of Rembrandt, her rapt attention on her father as he paced back and forth.

"You've been busted several times for noise-ordinance violations, Jennifer. Don't think we're naïve. We know the deeper secret. When you were little, you acquired a reputation for inflicting pain and emotional distress on your playmates. Over the years you learned to submerge this tendency to avoid punishment. Now you've ventured forth into a new line of work: subjecting people to loud music. Let's not confuse it: loud music is abuse. You're a sadist. I'd hate to cross your path, Jennifer. Are you listening?"

Her face had retreated into indifference. She didn't care. She maintained a high grade point average in high school. She was destined for Stanford, probably. Her father could get her in anywhere. Why should she care?

"Let me explain the facts of life to you, Jennifer."

"Please do." She sat up straighter, her eyes on her father.

"People have to obey rules, or ..."

"Or what?"

"That's what you're going to find out, young lady." He handed her a piece of paper, legal document sized.

I watched as she read it, her eyes growing bigger, but not registering too much. Her lips parted slightly. Her breathing quickened.

After she was through reading it, her shoulders slumped. Still, she did not register fear.

Her father took the paper from her.

"You will be here at seven tonight. *Sharp!* Understand?"

She nodded. I'd never seen Jennifer subdued, and she wasn't subdued now. But she came close.

I'm Bob, Jack's associate. I'm on the job. Before the festivities with Jennifer had a chance to get under way that evening, someone found ten-month-old Adnan Johnny Hussein's body alongside a road out in the country. He'd been abducted, raped, and murdered, his little body discarded like so much refuse.

Norman Coffey was the immediate suspect. He'd been seen lurking around little A.J. in the sports center's locker room and elsewhere. But Coffey had an alibi. He was in a café on the other side of town during all this. Lots of people saw him there. He couldn't have done it.

My associate, Gordy Hussein, was beside himself with grief at the death of his son. He and his wife were in seclusion. I left them alone.

My job doesn't involve Norman Coffey, nor does it involve the murder that Coffey undoubtedly committed, alibi or not. Need I remind you: Coffey was looking for a lookalike. His lookalike sat in that café on the other side of town as the real Norman Coffey took little Adnan Johnny Hussein in hand, raped him, and snuffed him out.

My job is with Vance's daughter, Jennifer, a child whose crime is somewhat softer than murder. Jennifer derives pleasure from playing loud music and destroying the peace of others. Her pleasure derives not from the loud music itself but from how much havoc it wreaks in the lives of her victims. Vance and I can only go so far with Jennifer. Vance's pact with her called for torture, the same as we did to our subject, yet Jennifer knows it will not be torture—it will be a sham; the music will not be on. She knows she won't be harmed. I know this. Her old man knows this. Why bother? you ask. I ask you: Why do you bother with all the weak, irrelevant things you do? Maybe just once you spin the wheel and something comes out right? Is that why?

In any case, Jennifer will not be harmed, at least not by me. But experience tells me she will be harmed by someone else.

It turns out I was right.

Jack is badder than Bob. I'm Jack. I'm on the job now. My associate, Gordy Hussein, heard rumors that Norman Coffey had a lookalike sitting in that café across town.

Gordy shoved down his grief long enough to come and see me, asking where he could find Coffey. He had a gun on him.

"Wait, Gordy. Let's talk about this." I put an armlock on him and disarmed him, or he'd have gone off and killed Coffey for sure. Gordy sat inconsolable, broken-hearted, devastated in his grief as I laid out a plan.

"Gordy, we're going to put Jennifer Bancroft in the torture chamber and ramp up the voltage. We're going to blow her eardrums out and shatter her facial bones. Then we're going to dump her body alongside a road."

Gordy knew it would be a sham, per my agreement with Vance. I told him we'd be doing something extra, though, and it would involve Coffey.

We nabbed Coffey, put him in our torture chamber, and set the speakers close to his skull. But before blasting him into a morbid medical condition, we did something extra. The extra thing had been intended for Jennifer, but with a few modifications, I set it up for Coffey. I did the voices myself. In addition, I flashed pictures of a young woman in a string bikini too fast for the eye to follow on the wall in front of Coffey.

I also flashed pictures of something else, which I won't mention, faster than the eye can follow, juxtaposing them with the images of the young woman in the bikini. You can take a guess at what the other pictures were, but you'd probably be wrong.

I was laying something deep.

Subliminal messages are below conscious threshold and can be aural or visual. If you take total control of the subject, immerse him in a new world you create for him, and give him just one option for escape ...

It's like putting a man in a box and giving him only one direction to run. Even if it's downward into a dark and toxic environment, he will run. He *must* run if you've set the stage properly.

We were banking on Coffey going into a dark, revolting place, but with the promise of eventual deliverance from captivity.

Coffey never heard the subliminal voices—they were below conscious threshold. Instead, he heard the gentle sounds of a burbling brook, which is supposed to put a person in a relaxed state. I also injected him with a drug to calm his nerves, as his nerves were seriously agitated during the early stages of this procedure.

Soon, Coffey was in a deep state of relaxation, the sedative and the burbling brook performing their magic. Then Coffey was bombarded with subliminal messages, aural and visual, which performed their magic, also.

After about an hour of this, we blasted Coffey with the loudest music the system could put out. Coffey strained at his binds like a man being put to death in the electric chair. We did not see charred flesh, but we did see blood seeping from his ears, nose, and mouth. We also caught a whiff of something that must have arrived in Coffey's undershorts in a black heap.

Ha, ha, ha.

We had a good time watching the spectacle, and then we went out and got Jennifer. For the time being, we kept Coffey in the chamber, strapped to the chair.

It was Jennifer's turn. She accepted her fate with aplomb, and went to her doom in a stately manner, regarding the torture chamber as if it were the holiest of holies. She knew it was a sham and was merely playing along, knowing it was what her father wanted. By then we had removed Coffey from the chamber and had scrubbed the place down, removing all vestiges of his blood and fecal matter.

We strapped Jennifer to the chair and set the speakers close to her skull. Then we left her alone and went into the observation room to watch through the one-way mirror.

We fed the sounds of a burbling brook into the chamber, to get Jennifer into a relaxed state, and then we played the subliminal messages I had recorded for her. I also flashed some images on the wall. She was being hit mysteriously, but had no idea.

After an hour of this, we released Norman Coffey into the chamber. These two live in two different worlds and don't know each other from Adam.

The subliminal messages directed at Coffey made him believe Jennifer had tortured him with the loud music, and that she had danced naked in front of him, taunting him.

The subliminal messages directed at Jennifer set up a resonance between Coffey and her father, making Coffey out to be something of a father figure to her. She was always deferential to her father, and had always acted vulnerable in front of him. That's what saved her from the worst that Vance could do.

Norman Coffey has his own reaction to deferential treatment and vulnerability. He sees a little child. Need I say more?

Jennifer, strapped to the chair, didn't stand a chance.

Coffey had his way with her again and again, before Gordy and I intervened.

Jennifer needed counseling for her traumatic ordeal. She recovered and no longer plays loud music, disturbing the peace of others. She has a new focus in life, vastly more mature. I don't know what it is, though. Coffey was charged with A.J.'s murder.

Jack is badder than Bob. I'm Bob. You'll meet Jack later.

That's how I greet all my new clients now. It sets a tone for the relationship. It gives them confidence that the job will get done.

A Funeral for Cymbal

We are not on friendly terms with Cymbal's people now, not after what happened. A team of earth scientists—most of them social scientists—is trying to figure out how to smooth things over, but it won't be easy. Cymbal's people monitor earth constantly, and the hottest jokes circulating inside the Beltway right now have to do with dead aliens.

I knew something like this would happen sooner or later. Earth diplomacy is not a holistic thing. It is a pointed, political, calculated thing—in short, a bunch of lies that do not necessarily reflect the will or mood of the people.

Excuse me if it sounds like I'm proselytizing, but *I am* the President of the United States, and *I am* responsible for the safety of our nation, and by extension, the safety of the entire planet, since we are the only super power.

Please knock off the dead-alien jokes.

How would you like it if, on an alien world, they were knocking them dead with dead-human jokes? Would you feel comfortable with that type of crowd? Realize how difficult it is for me, your leader, when Cymbal's people step in for a conference. I am no different to them than the goons out there who keel over when they hear the latest stupid joke about Cymbal—God rest his soul.

I hope I have won some converts, but in any case, I will bear no further witness to these matters. Instead, I will move quickly into the matter of Cymbal and his funeral. And, for the sake of history, I will give my perspective on the affair.

Cymbal, as most of you knew, was a tireless worker. He did all he could to help bring our vastly different worlds, and our vastly different peoples, together. He was the first alien to become fluent in more than one earth language, becoming widely read in both English and French. He toured the planet, meeting with heads of state, and with the citizenry—the just plain folks of the world.

I guess none of us really got to know Cymbal all that well as a biological specimen. If we had, maybe this tragedy could have been averted. Maybe our focus was too much on the "people" aspect of Cymbal. After all, we were so happy to finally have an egalitarian alien in our midst, especially one as influential as Cymbal. Most other aliens, as you know, tend to look down their noses at earthlings. But not Cymbal, and not Cymbal's people. They seem to be just plain folks, like all of us. And never mind the superficial differences: gray skin, bulbous heads, and ... Well, you know the rest.

As it turns out, deep down, the differences were not so superficial after all. Let us all try to learn from this tragedy. Let us all try to be bio-aware in the future.

Cymbal, as I've said, was a tireless worker, and he kept a whole slew of earthlings—diplomats, aides, bureaucrats, and sometimes yours truly—busy as beavers around the clock as he made his appointed rounds. In fact, he drove us all into the ground, if the truth be known. He was indefatigable.

Cymbal ate. He breathed air. He drank water. He slept occasionally, we know. He eliminated waste—he admitted to this. Aside from this, though, we were ignorant of Cymbal as a bio-being. Like I've said, we were focused on the "just-plain-folks" aspect of Cymbal.

On the fated day, Cymbal came running to a respected aide appointed him by our government. This aide, Donald Triste, received certain hasty instructions from Cymbal. Later, Mr. Triste, under oath, swore that Cymbal told him he was about to die and that a funeral would have to be arranged for him immediately.

Mr. Triste, in consultation with the proper chain of command, went ahead and arranged the funeral for Cymbal, following Cymbal's instructions. This was done prior to Cymbal's apparent death. All was kept in readiness, all was waiting. And then Cymbal, to all intents and purposes, died. He was found lying on the floor in his office, not two hours after his very hasty conference with Donald Triste, and his vital signs were flat.

There was no time to waste. Cymbal was dropped into the barrel of brine and pickled. That was his word, Cymbal's word, *pickled,* mind you. He *was* fluent in English, not to mention French. Cymbal was a very erudite alien.

How were we to know?

Cymbal, as per his instructions, was sealed tightly in the pickle barrel and left alone overnight. The next morning, the lid was to be removed. There were no instructions beyond that.

Imagine what it was like for us, those who sit at the head of government, during these hours. Cymbal was dead. He was undergoing his world's purification rites—funeral rites we took that to be—and in the morning we were to take the lid off the barrel. And then what?

Well, we found out.

We were in contact with Cymbal's people before dawn, trying to explain the situation. They didn't seem to understand. We assumed Cymbal's religion was esoteric or cultish on his world, and not one of the "just-plain-folks" varieties.

At dawn, we popped the lid on the barrel and up bobbed the foulest mass.

It was Cymbal, a zombie we thought, hauling himself out of the barrel, a decayed stalker, brown and green now, not the usual alien gray.

We ran, and Cymbal staggered after us. The Secret Service agents pulled Uzis, but held their fire. Cymbal collapsed on his way down the hallway, falling to pieces. The smell was unbelievably foul.

A commotion broke out in the room that held the pickle barrel. The agents rushed in and discovered that another Cymbal was trying to crawl out of the barrel. They had a solution quickly in hand: they simply lowered the heavy lid on this second Cymbal zombie and sealed him in.

How were we to know that Cymbal was merely having a bowel movement?

Why didn't he use proper technical terms?

Why this impromptu slang for normal bodily functions?

I'm about to die.

I need a pickle barrel to float in.
It will be my funeral, my purification.

When Cymbal's people signaled back with their inter-pretation of our message, we rushed into the room and popped the lid again.

Too late.

Cymbal had drowned.

Apparently, he needed no air during a bowel move-ment.

Apparently, we popped the lid too soon, allowing his bowel-movement product—his bowel-movement twin, if you will—to escape before Cymbal came to and throttled it.

Why the esoteric language, Cymbal, if you're listen-ing? While on earth, why not use earthy language?

Maybe Cymbal had become too acclimated to earth and to the ways of earthlings. Maybe he wanted to "word over" this biological function, this *normal* biological func-tion. Maybe Cymbal wanted to appear more human ... more pointed ... more political ... more calculating ... less holistic ...

There is a lesson in this for us all. Honesty and holistic growth—never be ashamed of either. It might save your life someday.

A Head on the Road

The earth opened beneath Roy Boltjack like a new canyon splitting apart, growing and growing and then collapsing around him like the frantic claws of a thrashing monster. He was packed in tight, a shroud of earth around him, the bright blue sky wiped out by the blazing sun that shined into his eyes. He was on a road, buried up to his neck—a head on the road. A stallion stood over him, and suddenly Boltjack's face was battered by a forceful stream of urine.

"Help! Help!" he shouted. "That horse is pissing on me!"

He gulped for air, and then clamped his mouth shut and waved his head back and forth, futilely trying to duck the stream of urine that shot from the powerful horse.

Finally, after nearly drowning Roy, the horse was through—for now. It withdrew to fill up again at a water trough behind the barn.

Roy sputtered and tried to dry off, but how could he? He was just a head on the road.

The wordy man stood nearby and said, "Roy, that's not very creative. I know little children who are more creative than that. What more can you say?"

Earlier that day, Roy had been in his office, miserable, reading a matchbook-cover advertisement for a creative-writing course that promised instant, fabulous results with no effort on the part of the student. It was tough writing newspaper columns day after day—the same old bullshit. Roy's hand darted toward the phone, but he pulled it back, as if touched by a flame from an invisible fire. He hesitated, read the ad again, looked at the number. It's too good to be true, he thought. He leaped for the phone and soon had the wordy man on the line.

Yes, yes. No, no. Okay. A deal was struck. Roy left for home early. When he got there, the wordy man was waiting. Roy let him in.

A minute later, Roy was cursing himself. Tied and gagged in his living room, he knew he'd been had. He muttered to himself in quiet rage.

Then, a quick trip to the country in the stranger's car—in the trunk—and Roy was plugged into the ground in the middle of a road, staring at the downward-sliding sun.

The horse piss was barely dry from his face when he saw the stallion make his second appearance, rounding the corner of the barn, looking like a professional athlete ready to play. Roy pleaded and screamed. "Help! Help! Get me out of here!"

The wordy man said, "Roy, you can't go back on your word. We have a deal. Don't you want to learn how to boost your creativity?"

The horse approached Roy and stood over him. The wordy man kept up his sideline chatter. "Roy! Roy! Atta boy! Hey! Hey! What do you say?" The urine flew.

Roy clamped his mouth shut, closed his eyes, and whipped his head back and forth, trying to get some air seeping into his nostrils.

It seemed to take forever. His head was being bashed and battered, and he was feeling the effects of several concussions. Nearly suffocating, Roy almost opened his mouth to gulp for air.

Finally, the horse was through. It walked away and went behind the barn.

Roy opened his eyes, shuddered, and gulped for air, hearing the distant sounds of the horse drinking.

"Come on, Roy!" the wordy man said. "What do you say? This is a great way to bring out that inner spark of creativity. Hey! Hey! What do you say?"

"Help! Help! Get me out of here!"

The horse came again and again. Roy sputtered and nearly drowned again and again. The sun sank lower. The wordy man kept up his sideline chatter. "Roy! Roy! Atta boy! Hey! Hey! What do you say?"

The afternoon wore on and Roy became accustomed to his new circumstances. He began to look upon it as a challenge. What else could he do? He was just a head on the road. He noticed that the horse's aim was not entirely perfect, and that the horse often sputtered the urine out in choppy bursts and trickles, especially toward the end of each performance. Roy began to take advantage of these opportunities, feeling smug, turning his head this way or that at the right moment and gulping a huge quantity of air, enough to keep him going until the horse faltered again.

Ha! Ha! Roy thought. *I'm picking up on his rhythms. I'm spoiling his fun.*

The horse walked away after the tenth or eleventh session, seemingly displeased at his performance. Roy waited, pleased with himself. Lately, he'd been breathing in so much air between gushes that it was hardly an ordeal anymore.

The horse approached, weariness etched on his face. The wordy man kept up his sideline chatter. "Roy! Roy! Atta boy! Hey! Hey! What do you say?" The horse took up his position and began to piss. Roy clamped his mouth shut and closed his eyes tight, waving his head back and forth, feeling the strong stream of urine smash into his face, waiting for his chance to take a breath. At last, the horse faltered and sputtered and his aim was off. Roy gleefully opened his mouth.

The eye of the horse, never having left the face of Roy Boltjack during all of the dozen or so pissing cycles, saw Roy open his mouth. The stallion was a Zen master, having trained in the ancient meditative arts for many years. The wordy man and his wife, the wordy woman, indulged him in his fancy, taking him on the road to secluded corners of the land, allowing him to practice his art upon his sworn enemies—which included the idiot before him.

The horse had not even approached his skills today. He had held back, sputtering, faltering, missing—for heaven's sake. Roy's mouth was open. The horse, merging consciousness with action, shot gallons of urine straight into Boltjack's gaping mouth, nearly boring a hole through the back of his head. The force of the urine was so strong that Boltjack's mouth was held open by the stream.

Finally, the horse wandered away with the wordy man, and Roy Boltjack died, having choked to death on his own vomit, which was composed primarily of horse piss.

His ghost shot into the air, and Roy heard the wordy man shout, "Roy! Roy! Atta boy! Hey! Hey! What do you say?"

The Head

Several rock climbers were at a towering cliff beside a broad river, pounding in pitons, climbing upward. One of them, an unskilled beginner, accidently got his rope tangled around his neck. While trying to disentangle it, he accidently undid his harness. As he fell, the rope went taut and snapped his head off.

None of the other climbers saw it—they were all preoccupied.

His head flew out over the river and landed on a passing yacht, right on a table being set for dinner, displacing a salad in a large bowl.

A butler came by, saw the salad on the deck, and cleaned it up.

The diners filled their plates at the caterer's table, and then sat at various dining tables, each of which had its own large salad bowl.

One of the diners saw the head in the salad bowl and pointed it out to the others seated at the table. They'd all had pre-dinner cocktails and were a little tipsy. After some thoughtful consideration, they decided it was a ham made up to look like a head.

They tried to carve it, thinking the servants forgot. They didn't do too well. They sliced off the ears, nose, and lips, put the pieces on a plate, and walked around with it to help out the servers.

The pieces went quickly. People ate them up.

A woman shrieked and fell over. Several people rushed to her aid. She had seen the mutilated head on the table, but none of the people checking her noticed it.

A large man had just filled his plate at the caterer's table when he saw the head. He called the cook, the ship's captain, and a photographer over and pointed out the object to them.

The photographer, not knowing it was a head, steadied his camera and snapped a picture. He keeled over in shock when he realized it was a head and fell into the river.

Everyone ran to the rails. The ship circled and crewmen prepared a life ring and a rubber raft.

The large man stood by the rail, keeping the head in sight. A crow landed on the head and pecked at it voraciously, plucking out both eyes before the large man could chase it away.

As they hauled the photographer out of the river, the large man quickly searched the ship for the body the head belonged to. No luck.

Meanwhile, a hungry diner greedily put the head on his plate, eyeing the others at the rails. He sat and tried to eat it, but found it too tough. Too much bone. He poured lots of sauce on it, gnawed on it, and then flung it overboard in disgust.

The yacht, turning and losing headway, had drifted close to shore. As the head sailed out over the river, an old lady standing on a narrow sandy beach at the base of the cliff saw it and waded in to retrieve it.

The head, washed clean of sauce and trimmings, with its ears, nose, and lips off, and its eyes missing, was hauled out of the water by the old lady.

She knew immediately what it was, having been a school teacher for forty years. It was a large hairy clam they couldn't pry open on the rich people's boat. The leisure class was too lacking in industry to break it open. No wonder the world was in such a mess.

She drove home with it in a plastic bag.

In her dead husband's workshop, she went to work on it, banging, chipping, drilling, throwing it against the concrete floor and brick walls.

She got it open and scooped out the interior.

She ate some and froze the rest.

She put the remainder of the large hairy clam back in its plastic bag and dumped it into a garbage can at the back of her lot. She hoped old Rufus wouldn't come by and mangle her garbage.

But Rufus was watching, salivating. Rufus was a St. Bernard from up the street who frequently broke his chain and ran loose. He waited for the old lady to go, and then snuck up to the garbage can, pawed the lid up, and deftly took the head out. He worked it out of the plastic bag and began to gnaw on it.

Tiring of this, he scooped off the skin and remaining hair and spit it out. Holding the head in his jaws, he carried it home and left it in his backyard.

Back on the yacht, discovering that the head was gone,

the large man requested that they put ashore. He was a police detective hired to act as security. Thinking a murder had been committed aboard the yacht, he ordered everyone to stay put, but they all scattered as soon as the yacht landed, fearful of a scandal.

The detective went downtown and filed a report. While there, he learned that the headless body of a rock climber had been found floating in the river.

The detective questioned other rock climbers who'd been at the cliff and realized what must have happened. He closed the murder investigation, believing the death to be an accident.

But they still had to locate the head. Through careful legwork, the detective tracked down several people who had been at the recreation area at the base of the cliff and got a line on an old lady. The police department offered a reward for the return of the missing head.

The old teacher heard of this quest on the radio, and then saw it on TV. It dawned on her and she keeled over dead.

The owner of Rufus, alerted to the head, saw it in his backyard. He took the head to the police station and claimed he found it in the alley behind the old teacher's house.

The police went to her house and found her dead. Her stomach's contents were checked during the autopsy. Human brain was found. Frozen human brain was found in her freezer.

The old teacher's nickname was Cannibal. Stories of her sucking students' brains out through holes in their skulls were rampant during her teaching days. The detective recalled that he had been in her class. She taught English.

The detective reopened the murder investigation and interrogated the corpse. Cannibal remained rather stiff and formal.

Lulu's Magic Book

Lulu reads a newspaper story her father has pointed out to her. It's about millions of frogs across the face of the planet being born with weird deformities such as missing, extra, or shriveled limbs, missing or shrunken eyes, and smaller sex organs. And the mysterious disappearance of whole frog populations from certain areas. All in the last few years.

What does this bode for humans? scientists in the article are quoted as saying. Changes in frog DNA may be precursors to changes in human DNA. Frogs have been on earth forever.

Lulu shudders. Someone is tampering with frogs' DNA. And now the experiments have shifted to humans.

She thinks the scientists are noticing only the botched cases. Somewhere in the wilderness, Olympian frogs are hopping.

Creature comforts surround Lulu. She is in a bright summer outfit. Mentally, she is in the realm of parables and symbols.

She attempts to reason it out. Anything disharmonious means trouble. Modern culture is disharmonious.

She thinks of men and women in a wild state. She sees them as wolflike, though retaining a basic human configuration. In this state, they are infinitely more interesting and complex, but also more dangerous.

Culture turns us into ciphers, she thinks. We should know no culture except the pack. We should live in the wild. We should chase down prey. We should kill with tooth and claw.

We will be wolves. The pack will rule.

It will keep us eternally energized and complex. We will no longer be ciphers.

We will be magnificent creatures.

There, it is done.

"Seeking balance, seeking balance," she intones as she leaves the bedroom and enters the suite's dining room.

A table is piled high with delights. Lulu watches in delight as the humans descend upon the food. She imagines lots of snarling and snapping. But in fact, there is none. In human society, the fangs are invisible and sunk in secret ways.

She sits by her father.

Detectives Crosby, Kohl, and Meeker of the Los Angeles Police Department are hunting in a pack this evening, as has become their custom. They are in a wilderness area of Los Angeles where wild animals roam the hills and canyons. Large creatures have drawn their attention. The cops are lost in the hypnosis of the hunt, fascinated by the beasts that eerily manage to stay just out of reach.

Crosby received a phone call from a young girl a few days ago, which set off their investigation of the creatures. But the investigation never got off the ground. From the beginning, it was cursed.

Derelict in their duties, each detective expects disciplinary action from the department soon.

None of them cares. Hunting has become their joy.

At a deep level of mind, beneath layers of obscuring clouds, they know someone has been directing them on their present path, as if by magic. They retain this knowledge as a squirrel might retain a seed in its mouth for later consumption.

As pack hunters, they are so tuned to one another they sometimes think they can hear the others' thoughts.

Then that seed of knowledge gets in the way, and for the briefest of moments each becomes a detective again.

But the hypnosis of the hunt calls, and the focus returns to the creatures. If only they could get one within their grasp.

Lulu's father, Vince, rides a bicycle along a dark highway that leads away from the lodge. He wants to see the upper-atmospheric lights, free from interfering glows.

A pickup drives up behind him, bathing him in its headlights.

"Shut those lights off!" Vince yells, stopping his bike.

The pickup stops and douses its lights. Brian and Mike jump from the pickup and join Vince.

They gaze at the sky and see glittering curtains of light flitting about the heavens. The ionic display metamorphoses into brilliant geometrical bursts directly overhead, and they are held in thrall.

The lights are caused by solar radiation hitting earth's magnetic field. All gods need their omens, Vince thinks.

The show continues, but they can't watch it any longer.

Vince puts the bicycle in the bed of the pickup, and they drive back to the lodge.

At the lodge, a strange dance is taking place, a dance of survival, driven by scientific discovery.

They walk to the second floor.

Fearlessly, women and girls are jumping from balconies to the ground below. They do it over and over, landing and running back into the lodge and up the stairs. The women seem to be leading their daughters, as if setting an example.

Vince wonders why they aren't getting hurt. Is this a symbolic way of jumpstarting genes? To scare genes out of hiding? Are quick-mending genes waking up and coming to their aid?

Vince, Brian, and Mike walk through the corridors on the second floor, where they see crazed men, women, and children biting their fingers off. They hear cries and sobs behind closed doors. They also hear cries of ecstasy.

They go back to the ground floor and enter the FBI suite. Vince gets Lulu's magic book. He knew she had it with her. He studies the rituals and tries to deactivate them.

He discovers he can't do this. It scares him. He's always been able to do it before. What has Lulu been doing differently? He runs to her bedroom. She's gone.

"We've got to find Lulu," he tells Brian and Mike. "I want to caution her about the proper use of magic."

He also wants to hear her ideas on what is taking place at the lodge. Lulu has remarkable intuitive powers. She'll know something.

"Women seem to be more into it than men," he tells the two FBI agents as they walk out the door and into the night. "Watch your heads."

They hear two near-simultaneous thumps as two girls land nearby on the sidewalk, close to a woman who is an older version of them. Probably their mother. The three skip away.

"Yeah," Brian says. "Though some of those dudes upstairs biting their fingers off weren't exactly women. They were rich white guys. Rich white guys and women can be the ones to suffer now."

"Sounds like you're taking a perverse pleasure in this, Brian," Vince says. "What happened to that stiff professional exterior of yours?"

Brian slips like a ghost into Vince's path and stares him in the eye.

"My pa had both legs blown off in Nam, Vince," Brian says. "And his country didn't do one damn thing for him or any of the others. Everybody's been pussyfooting around this DNA stuff for years—now tonight we'll have some answers."

"Of course," Vince says. "That's the plan. We'll build our DNA portraits from samples taken from individuals who exhibit spontaneous healing. Once we find out what their DNA is doing, we'll develop the appropriate gene therapies."

Brian continues his speech, his eyes wild hallucinations.

"You're looking for Lulu, Vince, so she can explain this magic to you. Allow me to explain it: there is no explanation.

It's like a dream; it goes chaotically from one thing to another. If you want to see Lulu, go to the Scrumptious Candy Store. That's where all the magic is."

They walk to the Scrumptious Candy Store and travel through the aisles, looking at the wares. They see fascinating potions and spells. It's a mockup, preparing for the new growth industry.

But it's not entirely a mockup.

They stop at the counter in back.

"Has an eleven-year-old girl named Lulu been in here?" Vince asks.

"Yes," the pharmacist says, a young black man with a trim moustache. "She needed something for her nose. Fixed her right up. She said she liked the store so much she plans to come back with all her friends someday."

"Sounds like Lulu," Vince says.

He and the two FBI agents walk to the front of the store.

On the way, Mike picks up a cockroach and lets it crawl around on the palms of his cupped hands. He shows it to Vince and Brian. They marvel at the insect's resilience, its strength, its survivability.

"They've been around forever," Vince says, smiling. "Powerful DNA."

Mike smiles also as he puts the cockroach back on the floor and squashes it underfoot. "I don't want Lulu to get the willies when she comes back," he says.

They leave the store.

When they are gone, the cockroach rises to its feet and calmly walks down the aisle.

Secret Lovers' Tryst

John Plum was an evil man, as evil as they come, and when the bosses wanted the worst jobs done, in the worst possible ways, they called John. There was nothing he wouldn't do for a price.

But even John, as his intimate friends knew, had a soft spot.

He got the call and spent the first night in the emergency-room waiting room. On his return the second night, they sent him upstairs to the intensive-care-unit waiting room, and the vigil began.

She was in critical condition, comatose, not much hope. John was ushered in three times. She looked so small, engulfed in stark-white linens, tubes, and wires. She could have been mistaken for a little child, even though she was twenty-three.

John, periodically, got some sleep in the waiting room, though not much. When he left the hospital for his day job, fatigue dogged him like a sleepwalking gremlin. He fought it off, catching a few winks here and there on the job.

"Stay with her, John," urged his employer, and he was obliged to return to the hospital, grieving, each night.

On the fourth night, he took her out.

The headlines screamed the news the next day.

COMATOSE ACCIDENT VICTIM
MISSING FROM HOSPITAL

John called his employer. "We've got to meet." John set the time, location, and conditions. His employer balked. "She goes back to the hospital, Jayhill, unless you do as I say."

Jayhill relented.

It was in the woods, a mile from the nearest road. Jayhill followed a hacked-out trail: a notched tree here, a broken branch there, mounds of earth, several sharp sticks stuck in the crooks of trees spaced along the way.

John, from concealment, watched Jayhill's progress, tailing him. Finally, Jayhill entered a small clearing. He was sucking his thumb. He'd cut it on one of the sharp sticks.

John crouched in nearby brush.

"Stop right there, Mr. Jayhill."

Jayhill spun around, jumping at the voice. Fear leaped into his face. Then a quick anger took over. He searched, jerking his head around.

"Where are you, John?"

"You don't need to see me."

"Loyalty, John. Remember who pays you unfailingly."

"Shut up, Jayhill."

Jayhill shrugged, his demeanor changing. The expression on his face was like that of a minister in unsettled contemplation, staring at the faithful, yet uncertain of his own faith.

"You did the worst possible thing, John."

"I know."

"The cops have been around." Jayhill continued to suck his thumb.

"I knew they would be."

"Why, John?"

John was supposed to hang around the hospital, playing as if he were Mary Ann's boyfriend, gleaning information from doctors, nurses, and relatives, and being on the alert for any police involvement. He was Jayhill's early warning system, and if necessary, the damage-control specialist. Mary Ann was supposed to have died in an accident. But it had been botched.

"She was your secretary, Jayhill. And your mistress."

"Wrong, John. My secretary, yes. Mistress, no."

"She was finding out too much."

"Wrong, John. My, uh, other business activities are kept strictly separate from my, uh, legitimate business concerns. Mary Ann was just a very efficient, very competent secretary. We're going to miss her."

"Jayhill, she couldn't type without bruising her fingernails. She had the body of an exotic dancer."

"Okay, John," Jayhill said irritably. "Let's not quibble over trifles."

"I have you in a precarious position, Jayhill."

Jayhill's face went blank, as if all thoughts had been sucked from his brain.

"If I bring Mary Ann back to the hospital—and by the way, no one saw me steal her out; it's amazing what an orderly with a pushcart can do, once he learns the routine—they can perform an autopsy when she dies, and the evidence will ultimately lead to you. The electric chair, Jayhill? Or do you prefer lethal injection? The state gives you a choice."

Jayhill's face went around some mysterious bend, into an ultra expressionless state. One could easily have mistaken him for a living corpse.

"Or, if I just dump her someplace, and they never find her, the cops' questions will sooner or later arrive at other chains of evidence, maybe enough to nail you for other capital offenses, Mr. Jayhill."

John paused. Hearing no response, he said, "How do you want your eggs fried, Mr. Jayhill? Over easy or sunny side up? Which will it be? Electric juice or drugs?"

Jayhill's face began to expand and contract, as if he were already feeling the effects of something lethal coursing through his veins.

"Yes, I know," John went on. "Why couldn't I have left well enough alone? Just leave her there. She was comatose. Damn near brain dead. Yes, she'd have been out of the picture, most likely. If she died and the pathologist was unsuspecting, it's likely no evidence of murder would have been discovered. And if she had lingered? Well, who knows? But I jumped the stakes way up by taking her out. Now everyone is curious. They're heating up for major detective work, Mr. Jayhill. I think your goose is cooked."

John fell silent. Moments passed, and then Jayhill, who was now wobbly on his feet and mumbling incoherently, gave a start, as if coming to.

"Hey, Jayhill," John called, "haven't you been listening?"

"Uh ..." Jayhill crumpled to the ground. His body rolled once, and then became a shivering mass, a strange gel-like pool of motion.

John Plum stepped into the clearing.

Feel the sharp sticks, Jayhill, to make sure they're man-made sharp, and fresh, not an accident of nature. I don't want you taking a wrong turn out there and getting lost.

The instructions proved fatal for Jayhill.

While keeping vigil over Mary Ann, John had considered using the rare South American poison on her, silencing her forever, just in case. Unlike curare, this poison shocked the nervous system into uncontrollable activity, rather than shutting it down, before its lethal effects set in, and it was virtually undetectable. An investigation into Jayhill could have implicated John as much as anyone. And with Jayhill now wanting to eliminate potential witnesses against him, John figured it was time for him to part company with his employer. It could be me next, he had thought, mulling things over in the hospital. An accident could be out there right now, just waiting for him to walk by.

John dug it deep.

He got Jayhill's body, and found that it was still quivering. He stripped Jayhill naked and threw him into the grave.

He pulled Mary Ann from the brush. Mary Ann was still quivering, also, the South American poison in her.

She'd been so lively in his hands in the hospital as he secreted her diminutive form on the cart that lustful thoughts had seized him.

But duty called.

Now here in the clearing, John fell upon Mary Ann and knew her carnally. Finished, he threw her into the grave naked on top of Jayhill.

Before beginning the shovel work that would cover them up forever, he stood over them, looking down.

It was John's soft spot. He had always been touched by secret lovers' trysts. The mystery, the danger. The two quivering bodies in the grave seemed inexhaustible in their desire for each other.

With them still quivering, he threw in the first spadeful of rich black earth.

Later, he hid their clothes in the bushes.

Johnny Apple

He had been planning the murders for more than a year, crisscrossing the Sonoran Desert in his car, conducting trial runs. Now it was for real. Johnny Apple was going to gun down four people, two in Phoenix, two in San Diego. A married couple in each place. The wives were sisters. With these four deaths, Johnny was going to send a message to a man. The man's life had intersected with Johnny's a while back, leaving Johnny in desperate straits. In the back of the man's mind there were likely dry and sketchy remembrances of Johnny—things that crawled, things that scuttled. But after Phoenix, and after San Diego, there would be new remembrances. That's all that counted.

The enormity of it hit Johnny on a lonely desert highway. That's when a California Highway Patrol officer pulled him over.

The cop's khaki uniform shimmered in the blazing sunlight as he walked up behind Johnny's Toyota.

"Good morning, sir," the cop said. "I'd like to see your driver's license and vehicle registration."

Johnny's nerves were like frazzled electrical cords as he handed his license and registration to the cop.

The cop took them and walked back to his cruiser.

It seemed to take an eternity.

The cop came back to Johnny's window, leaned in, and handed him his license and registration.

"I saw you weaving."

Johnny nodded. "I had things on my mind, Officer."

"Pay attention to your driving."

"I will, Officer."

The cop stood back from Johnny's window and waved him on, and then walked back to his cruiser.

Johnny drove along the shoulder of the road for a while to pick up speed, and then pulled back onto the highway. The cop stayed behind him for several miles and then faded.

Johnny tried to breathe a sigh of relief but could not. His mouth was dry, his throat was tight, his chest was squeezed. His breaths came in stutters. He couldn't go through with it. He would trip himself up.

His decision made, he breathed a huge sigh of relief and collapsed against the steering wheel. Before long, he saw red and blue flashing lights behind him.

The cop pulled him over a second time. He approached on foot, a perplexed look on his face.

"I think I'm having a medical problem, Officer. Can you help me?"

"Yes."

The cop put Johnny in the backseat of his cruiser, got in front, and pulled onto the highway. "Motorist needs medical assistance," he said into his car's radio mic.

The cop made eye contact with Johnny in the rearview mirror.

"Someone will come out here and get your car. You'll get it back when you're released to drive."

"Thank you."

"They're alerting the hospital of our arrival time. They would like some information. Are you under the influence of alcohol or recreational drugs?"

"No."

"Have you taken any prescription medicine within the last forty-eight hours?"

"No."

"Do you have a chronic condition, such as diabetes?"

"No."

"Are you currently under a doctor's care?"

Johnny found he could not respond like he'd like to, in the honest way. Words spun through his mind.

"No ..."

The cop relayed the information to the dispatcher. A half hour later they pulled into the California desert town of Malta and parked near the hospital's emergency entrance.

A nurse was waiting for them at the registration desk. "Yes?"

"He's suffering from a medical problem," the cop said.

"What's the nature of the problem?"

"I'm not sure."

"Does he know?"

"It's doubtful. He exhibits confusion and goes catatonic at times."

The nurse took Johnny into an examination room and took his blood pressure and medical history.

"A doctor will be in to see you shortly," she said, and got up to leave. She paused in the doorway. "Were you on your way to Phoenix, Johnny?"

Should he tell her? He wasn't going to go through with it, so there shouldn't be any harm. "Yes."

"We've seen you here before, Johnny. Don't you remember?"

He stared at her in stunned silence.

"Remember, Johnny? You keep hitting a barrier here."

She smiled and left.

"Wait!" He ran to the door and looked into the hallway, but she was gone.

A connection to something was lost.

He stepped back into the examination room—the hallway felt dangerous. The nurse was out there somewhere, and she had recognized him. She knew about Phoenix.

Will the doctor recognize him, also? Will he know about Phoenix?

A cold shiver swept his flesh.

The whole thing was crumbling down around him.

He'd have to block everyone from further knowledge. He'd start denying everything. Or better yet, keep mum.

Johnny sat in the examination room in quiet contemplation. He had revived his plan. He would go through with it.

After he saw the doctor he would go see the cop and get his car back. There was no incriminating evidence in the car. No maps, no addresses, no names. The guns were secreted near the victims in both Phoenix and San Diego.

Johnny would send a message to the man.

The doctor walked in. "Sorry it took so long."

"That's okay. I don't have much wrong with me."

"I'm glad to hear that."

The doctor listened to Johnny's heart with a stethoscope, checked his reflexes, checked his scalp for any obvious trauma.

"Any injuries, Johnny?"

"No."

"Drugs?"

"No."

"The cop said he pulled you over for weaving and found you confused and catatonic."

"Yes."

"We've seen you here before."

Johnny kept mum.

"You encounter a barrier on your way to Phoenix, Johnny. We catch you here."

The doctor jotted something down and then looked at Johnny.

"What makes you get confused and catatonic when you hit our little corner of the world, Johnny?"

"I don't know."

"We've eliminated hypertension, hypoglycemic attack, traumatic brain injury."

The doctor paused, his expression grim.

"We have not eliminated schizophrenia or dissociative disorders."

"Is that your area, Doctor?"

"No. I'm going to refer you to a psychiatrist."

Johnny and the cop walked down the hospital corridor.

"I don't want to see a psychiatrist," Johnny said.

"Why? Are you afraid?"

"Yes, I'm afraid."

"Can you make it to Phoenix without a psychiatrist's help, Johnny?"

Johnny wasn't sure. Maybe he should see a psychiatrist.

"Take me to my car. I'll drive myself to the psychiatrist."

The cop took Johnny to his car.

Johnny got in and drove off.

He liked the feel of his Toyota. He did not like the feel of Malta. The place was moribund. He wondered why it had such a remarkable medical facility.

It took him just one minute to drive to the psychiatrist's office. It was around the block.

He sat on a couch across from the man.

"You have an unusual name," the psychiatrist said.

"Yes."

"Johnny Apple. Is it your given name?"

"It is."

"Where do you live, Johnny?"

"San Bernardino, California."

"What do you do there?"

"I'm a cardiovascular surgeon."

"Do you like your job?"

"Yes, though it can be stressful."

"What would you rather be doing?"

"I'd rather be doing what you're doing."

"You'd like to be a psychiatrist?"

"Yes."

"What if a police officer asked you the same question? What would you say then?"

"I'd say I'd like to be a police officer."

"A butcher?"

"I'd tell the butcher I'd like to be a butcher."

"You never get past Malta, Johnny. You never reach your destination, Phoenix. How come?"

"I don't know. Maybe Phoenix is just a blur on my

horizon. Maybe Malta is where I truly belong."

"Go to Phoenix, Johnny. When you get back, tell me what you discovered about yourself."

Johnny left the psychiatrist's office—and saw the nurse waiting for him by his car. She wasn't dressed as a nurse anymore. She wore a schoolgirl skirt, schoolgirl socks, and schoolgirl shoes. Her hair was in pigtails.

Johnny was going to send a message to the man. Did he need this nurse with him? Would she get in the way? He would see.

"Are you supposed to come with me?" he asked.

"Yes."

"Get in the car if you must."

She got in front beside him.

The cop zoomed up in his cruiser.

"I'll escort you to the highway," he said and drove away.

Johnny followed him.

At the highway, the cop pulled over and Johnny sped past.

"I'm your little girl," the nurse said, bouncing in her seat.

"Knock off the act," Johnny said.

"Okay." The nurse slipped out of her schoolgirl clothes.

"Is that better?" She was nude.

"You have to wear something."

"Like what?"

Johnny gazed at the desert rock and sand and saw heat mirages in the distance. "Wear something hot."

"Oh, I get it." The nurse slipped into a red dress a shade darker than the desert. It had a distinctive Spanish flavor.

"How's that?"

"It's okay."

"What are you going to do in Phoenix, Johnny?"

Johnny kept mum.

"If I'm going to be involved, I have a right to know."

"You won't be involved."

"I'm already involved."

Johnny looked her over. He knew she wasn't real. She was a symptom of the disorder he was suffering from.

"Tell me, Johnny!" She bounced in her seat.

"Okay, cool it."

"Tell me!"

"I'm going to kill two people. A married couple."

He saw her sneak a cell phone out of her purse, conceal it in her hand, and start to place a call.

He grabbed her wrist and exerted crushing force. She shrieked, struggled furiously, and tried to twist away from him, but couldn't. His grip was too powerful.

With a desperate cry, she drew her legs up and kicked him in the face. Stunned, Johnny released her wrist and she resumed dialing.

Johnny slammed on the brakes, swerved the car onto the shoulder of the road, and brought the vehicle to a halt. He shoved her out of the passenger door and tumbled out after her. The phone went flying.

Their momentum carried them down into the ditch, where they rolled around in hot, chafing sand, searching for the phone.

She saw it first, grabbed it, and got up to run. He caught

her and smashed her to the ground with a punch to the face. She lost her grip on the phone and it went flying.

He scrambled after it. She flew at him and clawed his face like a frenzied bird with sharp talons.

Enraged, he seized her and body-slammed her to the ground. He jumped on her and they grappled. He broke both of her wrists, snapping them with crushing force. She screamed and scrambled away.

He grabbed the phone, smashed it against a rock, and threw it away. He caught a glimpse of her scrambling into an arroyo, out of sight.

He ran to where he'd seen her enter the arroyo, slipped into it, and searched. She was nowhere in sight.

He climbed out of the arroyo and scanned the terrain, looking for the color of her dress, a shade darker than the desert. He did not see it.

There were lots of arroyos here. She could work her way through an intricate maze. If no one came by, she would die out here. The desert sucked out life fast.

He had to get to Phoenix. He raced back to his car, jumped in, and took off down the highway.

As Johnny crossed into Arizona, he mentally thanked the nurse. She had put her hand on his pulse and had found him wanting. She had prepared him for Phoenix.

He pondered the Malta, California, barrier. What a tough place that had been. He had to conjure up a lot of people back there to shore him up.

He hoped he wouldn't run into any more barriers. Conjuring people wasn't healthy. It interfered with life in a fundamental way. If you couldn't trust your own perceptions, what could you trust?

"Actually, Johnny, we tend to trust our own perceptions too much. Quite often we are wrong and we don't know it."

A big scare blew into Johnny's mind. His veins ran cold. There was a man sitting beside him in the car. The psychiatrist.

"How did you get into a moving vehicle?" Johnny asked.

"You conjured me."

"You can't know that I conjure people."

"Yes, I can, Johnny. I'm a psychiatrist. I have insight into these things."

"You're invading my innermost thoughts."

"I am."

"I'm going to let you out. I'll pull over—"

"Think, Johnny. You need me to see you through this."

"How do you figure that?"

"The girl, Johnny. You didn't conjure her. She's real. She's going to testify against you."

"She's going to die out there."

"She's less than seventy yards from the highway. Once she thinks she's safe, she'll emerge and hitch a ride. It's a busy highway. She'll get picked up."

In his mind, Johnny saw her crawling from an arroyo, her dress torn, flapping in the desert wind.

"She has two broken wrists, Johnny. She's going to talk to the police. She's going to get you locked up."

Johnny felt a sinking sensation. A quiver shook him.

"You need a story, Johnny. It was a lovers' spat. She wanted out of the car. You pulled over and she jumped out while the car was still moving."

"Yeah, okay. I'll tell the police."

"You will tell the police nothing. You will keep the story in mind but say nothing."

"Say nothing?"

"Say nothing. The police will have no choice but to let you go."

"I could ditch the car."

"If you do, it's a sign of your guilt. The police will be onto you. Say nothing. Do not ditch the car. Keep your story in mind. It will play well with your emotions. The police will see it on your face. At subliminal levels, they will get the message: she jumped out."

As he drove through the desert, Johnny was devastated. He'd had a spat with his girl and she'd jumped out of the car while it was still moving. She went down hard and ran off. He thought she was safe, being so near a busy highway. Surely someone would stop and give her a ride.

As he neared Phoenix, he saw a police car trailing him. It kept well back, tucked within the shimmering heat mirages of the desert. When he hit Phoenix, it pulled up close behind him and pulled him over.

"Step out of the car."

Johnny stepped out of the car.

The cop frisked him, handcuffed him, and brought him to a police station, where a detective took possession of his watch, wallet, and keys, uncuffed him, and put him in an interrogation room alone.

Johnny stood on a blue carpet, surrounded by white walls, a mirror on one of the walls. Three institutional-green chairs and a matching rectangular table occupied much of the space. He sat on one of the chairs and waited. He nodded off and woke with a start, feeling a ghostly shiver.

A man in a dark-blue business suit entered the room carrying two bottles of Coke. He had a striking resemblance to Santa Claus, but without the beard. His eyes twinkled merrily and his belly shook like a bowl full of jelly.

"I'm Detective Kennedy," he said with a hearty grin, offering one of the Cokes to Johnny.

Johnny ignored it and stared straight ahead.

Kennedy shrugged and set the Cokes on the table. He pulled up a chair, sat down, and took a long, leisurely drink from one of the Cokes.

"How about some iced tea, Johnny?"

Johnny said nothing.

"Coffee?"

Johnny stared straight ahead, not acknowledging Kennedy in any way.

"Are you sure you don't want anything to drink?"

Johnny said nothing.

Kennedy pulled a pack of cigarettes from his shirt pocket and offered one to Johnny. "How about a cigarette?"

Johnny ignored it.

Kennedy eased back in his chair, the pack of cigarettes disappearing back into his shirt pocket. "I don't smoke myself, Johnny. Bad habit."

Kennedy gazed around the room and then looked back at Johnny.

"You drive a nice car, Johnny. I like those Toyotas. How long have you had it?"

Johnny said nothing.

"Have you ever had any trouble with it? I've never heard of anyone having any trouble with one of those things. Japanese cars are amazing, aren't they, Johnny?"

Johnny said nothing.

"I see you're from California, Johnny. Whereabouts? I've got some relatives in Sacramento. Have you ever been up that way?"

Johnny did not bite.

"Where're you headed, Johnny?" Kennedy perched on the edge of his seat. "We can get you out of here in no time if we get a little information from you."

Johnny said nothing.

Kennedy left the room and returned later.

"What do you want for dinner, Johnny? Hamburgers and French fries? Pizza? We can order you just about anything. Do you want that Coke now? Some other kind of soft drink? Tea? Coffee? Lemonade? A cigarette? That's right. You don't smoke. I don't blame you. One of the other detectives is trying to quit. He's driving everyone bonkers."

Johnny said nothing.

Kennedy left the room and came back later.

"Do you want a trip to the bathroom, Johnny? Soon you'll be pissing out of your eyeballs."

Johnny stared straight ahead.

Kennedy left the room and returned later with a man whose expression chilled the air. They sat at the table. The man studied Johnny.

"Johnny, I'm Detective Marley. I'm going to read you your Miranda Rights." Marley did so, and silence ensued.

"Johnny," Kennedy said, "did you hear the one about the Baptist minister, the rabbi, the nun, and the donkey?"

Johnny said nothing.

"A tired donkey sat down right in the middle of a heated debate between a Baptist minister, a rabbi, and a nun. The Baptist minister commended the donkey for his hard work, and then exclaimed that the donkey would make it into Heaven before either the rabbi or the nun. The rabbi said phooey. He said the donkey would make it into Heaven before either the Baptist minister or the nun. The nun said bull. She said the donkey would make it into Heaven before either the rabbi or the Baptist minister. Then the donkey spoke. Do you know what the donkey said, Johnny?"

Johnny did not respond.

"The donkey said, 'If you admit asses into Heaven without reservation, how can you exclude each other?'"

Kennedy laughed hysterically, Marley cracked a grin, but Johnny did not so much as breathe.

A moment later, Marley loomed over Johnny.

"Johnny, we know what you did. The victim's injuries will require surgery. She's given us a statement from her hospital bed. You're going to go to prison for a long time."

Marley left the room.

Kennedy made a face.

"Johnny, I'm sure you didn't mean to cause any harm. I'm sure you didn't do anything intentionally. Her injuries aren't as bad as Marley made out. It's possible you didn't do anything wrong at all."

Johnny Apple, isolating himself within a cocoon of silence, distancing himself from the events in the interrogation room, thought only of how his girl had wanted out of the car, how she had thrown the door open before he could bring the car to a halt, how she had jumped out, landed hard on the rocks and sand, and got up and ran. He fervently hoped she was okay.

"Johnny," Kennedy said, "I think there's more to it than what Marley implied. Maybe she brought it on herself. Did she have it coming, Johnny? I think I can understand what you went through. It wouldn't be the first time a dame needed a little talking to. I think we can excuse you if it got a little out of hand."

Johnny said nothing.

"I think I know how it went, Johnny. We see it all the time. You two had a lovers' quarrel. She started hitting you, like a dame will do sometimes. You didn't hit her back, though. You took the abuse. Finally, you had enough and you exploded. Is that how it went, Johnny?"

Johnny said nothing.

"No? Okay. I can think of only one other explanation. It's kind of kinky, but it buys your freedom. You're both into rough play. If so, that's mutual consent, not our concern. You're free and clear then, Johnny. All we would need is a little statement from you. Then we let you go."

Johnny said nothing.

Marley came back into the room. "Johnny, I just spoke with the prosecutor. He said if you confess, he won't prefer charges. You'll walk out of here today. If you don't confess, though, he's going to file an attempted murder charge against you. You'll spend the next twenty years in prison. It's an easy choice to make. Confess. It's good for the soul and it keeps you out of prison. You'll be released within the hour."

Johnny remained silent.

Marley left the room.

Johnny was alone with Kennedy.

"You want out of here, Johnny? Was it kinky? Was it mutual consent? If it was, you walk."

Johnny remained silent.

"Are you pissing out of your eyeballs yet, Johnny?"

Detective Kennedy gave Johnny his watch, wallet, and keys, and then told him where he could go to reclaim his car. After Johnny got his car, he drove straight to his victims' house.

Johnny had been in the house twice before, visiting the man and woman he would kill. On the first visit, he had secreted a gun in a bedroom closet. On the second visit, he had checked the closet to make sure the gun was still there. It was.

Johnny knocked on the door. In moments, it opened.

"Johnny," the man said. "It's great to see you again. How have you been?"

"I don't know how I've been," Johnny said. "Maybe that's why I came back so soon."

"Come in, Johnny," the woman said softly, peering at him from behind her husband.

The man opened the screen door, gave Johnny's arm a friendly squeeze, and pulled him inside. "Will you be staying the night?" he asked.

"I, uh ..."

"Your things are still in the bedroom."

"Yes, I think I will stay the night."

"You must be famished, Johnny," the woman said. "I

bet you drove all the way without stopping to eat, just like last time."

"Yes, I believe I did."

They went into the kitchen, and the woman fixed Johnny a sandwich.

Johnny's wife and daughter had been killed by the woman's father, Brock Henry, in a motor-vehicle accident a little more than a year ago. Johnny had told these people—and Brock's other daughter and son-in-law in San Diego—that an attorney would sue Brock and win millions of dollars from an insurance company, the money to be shared equally among them, if they could obtain incriminating evidence against Brock. The daughters and sons-in-law had cozied up to the idea—and to Johnny—instantly.

In truth, it was only a ploy Johnny was using to insinuate himself into their lives.

Tonight and tomorrow night, Johnny would drink deeply of the cup of vengeance. He would taste its bittersweet wine and deliver a message to the man who had killed his wife and daughter.

During one of his court appearances, the killer had given Johnny a look of hatred so intense his eyes had seemed capable of burning holes right through him.

The killer held Johnny's wife responsible for the accident, and portrayed himself as blameless. The California Highway Patrol said Brock Henry was at fault—he had crossed the centerline and was speeding. But Brock had survived to tell his story, and Johnny's wife and daughter had not. Brock blamed it all on the other driver, on Johnny's wife. He said she had drifted into his lane, and he had to maneuver to escape her.

The judge bought Brock's story and dismissed the criminal charges. Johnny's civil suit was pending, but it seemed like a dim hope.

The legal system counted on citizens' preserving their souls and staying off a path of vengeance, but Johnny knew the legal system itself had no soul.

Johnny had cast his soul aside, and was determined that after tonight and tomorrow night, the killer would find solace in nothing.

On sun-drenched streets, Johnny often saw his wife and daughter weaving through the crowds. But it was imagination. They were dead. Even so, he fancied that they knew what was going on, that they recognized how evil sometimes excites the flesh, and that Brock Henry had received a sort of pleasure in killing them.

His wife's life had been cut short. His daughter would never reach adulthood. The killer had preserved her innocence and robbed her of everything else.

But on sun-drenched streets or sometimes in darkest night ...

They sat at the kitchen table as Johnny ate his sandwich.

"We saw my father last weekend," the woman said. "He's busy with a project at Lake Tahoe."

Her father was a civil engineer and owned a construction company. She'd been trying to get him to speak about the accident. She secretly recorded their conversations in case he should reveal anything incriminating.

She looked apologetic. "I haven't gotten him down that road yet, Johnny. But give me time and I will."

"I got him drinking, Johnny," the husband said. "I got

him telling war stories. But he hasn't told the one that counts."

He also secretly recorded his conversations with his father-in-law, to catch whatever might slip.

"There's no doubt he's responsible for the accident," the woman said. "Since he was driving one of the firm's vehicles, there's a great deal of money at stake. Naturally, his attorneys have told him to keep quiet about it."

Johnny nodded. The killer had great incentive to keep quiet.

"There's no doubt he's responsible," the husband said. "His driving speaks for itself. If he's behind the wheel, I refuse to get into the vehicle with him."

"Keep trying," Johnny said. "Sooner or later he's bound to let the cat out of the bag."

They nodded.

Johnny retired to the guest bedroom. He took off his shoes, turned off the light, and lay on the bed with his clothes on. He would kill the Phoenix couple tonight, and then head for San Diego and kill the other daughter and son-in-law tomorrow night. The killings would send a message to the man.

He lay awake for about an hour, and then got up, turned on the light, and checked the closet to make sure the gun was still there. It was.

He slipped on surgical gloves, gathered all his belongings—including the gun—into a satchel, and wiped all the surfaces he had touched to remove his fingerprints. He would keep the gloves on until his night's work was done and he was safely away.

He turned off the light and lay on the bed again. He would wait until the daughter and son-in-law had gone to bed.

Sometime later, he heard bedsprings sigh in another part of the house. He would give them time to drift off to sleep, and then he would go and kill them.

Suddenly, the face of Detective Kennedy was in the darkened bedroom, bathed in soft, glowing light. A primordial chill shook Johnny.

"You're using faulty reasoning, Johnny."

Kennedy's face loomed closer, and Johnny drew back in horror.

"If you kill the daughters, the man will experience a sense of loss, but he'll get over it quickly. He won't suffer like you envision. If you kill the sons-in-law, he won't suffer at all."

"How can you be sure?"

"He's a sociopath. Sociopaths don't suffer unless it's their own ass in a sling."

"How can I make him suffer?"

"Torture him, Johnny. Castrate him. Leave him maimed and absent his manhood. Use his daughters to set him up. If you deprive him of his manhood and destroy his sense of family all at once, he will suffer, but only because it's his own ass in a sling. It's the only way to do it."

Detective Kennedy's face vanished.

Johnny's mind spun in an ever-tightening circle. Kennedy had conned him on every point during the interrogation. Why listen to him now? It did make a certain kind of sense, though. The man was not likely to suffer like Johnny had upon losing his wife and daughter. Maimed, absent his manhood, and with the knowledge that his daughters had set him up, he might suffer.

There was a huge flaw in Kennedy's logic, though. A man in such desperate straits would likely commit suicide. That would put an end to his suffering.

In any case, Johnny's plan had to unfold soon. Strange people floated in and out of his existence. His life wobbled about. The more he delayed, the more likely it was that someone else would show up and wrest control from him. Acting soon would keep his world alive with his own intentions.

He got out of bed, flicked on a penlight, and crept to his satchel.

He pulled out his gun and released the magazine. It made a small mechanical sound coming out. He froze, listened. Nothing stirred in the house.

By the heft, he knew the magazine was full.

He aimed the penlight at it and saw the top two coppery rounds.

He slipped the magazine back into the gun, worked the slide to chamber a round, and thumbed the safety off.

All the while, he listened for anything stirring in response to these small, oiled sounds.

He planned to fire at close range into each victim's head, muffling the gunshots with a pillow.

He put on his shoes, took a pillow off the bed, and opened the door.

His daughter stood in the corridor, bathed in shimmering blue light.

"Abby?"

She beckoned to him and walked away.

Johnny stood still.

The victims' bedroom was the other way.

"Abby, please."

She turned and faced him. Their eyes met.

"Dad, please don't."

"Please understand, Abby."

"Mom and I forgive you."

"Abby!"

She was gone.

Johnny shook with bewilderment and shock. He tried to subdue the emotions that welled in him but could not. They rose like flood waters threatening to engulf him.

The tricks they played on you. They gave you little Abby. Then they took little Abby away from you.

The tricks never ended. They gave little Abby back to you, briefly, and then took her away again, leaving you with nothing except little pieces of her within a heart that was not good for anything anymore.

Johnny reasoned life could not be based on little pieces of Abby coming and going.

Dad, please don't.

What next, Abby? Will you tell me not to burn the toast?

Little Abigail, what would you have told Churchill? What would you have told Lincoln? Jefferson? Washington? Each in their darkest hour, what would you have said to them? You are too young to provide me with what I need at the moment. Why did you come to me?

He steadied himself, gripped the gun harder, and walked down the corridor toward the victims' bedroom.

Abby, you don't know what I am going through. You don't know what I have to do. You are too young to know these things. Come back to me when the time is right. But for now, let me be.

He stopped at the victims' bedroom door and listened. He heard nothing.

He gripped the doorknob and turned it. It clicked as the catch pulled in, and he held his breath.

He eased the door open. It squealed like an alley cat. He heard movement on the bed and knew his carefully laid plan had gone up in smoke.

He cast the pillow aside and burst into the bedroom, just as a small bedside lamp turned on.

He went into a crouch and aimed the gun at the daughter—she was closer. The daughter and son-in-law both shrank back on the bed, eyes wide in terror. He shot the daughter first and then shot her husband.

He continued to fire, body shots into each, and then walked closer, leaned in, and delivered a headshot to each.

He continued to fire into their heads until he heard a click on an empty chamber.

His heart revved like an out-of-control engine, pumping something scary into his veins. The gunshots were sure to draw the attention of neighbors. He figured he had less than thirty seconds to make an unseen getaway.

He dropped the gun on the bed and raced out of the house, closing the door behind him. He had taken precautions over the last few months. Nothing was traceable to him, not the gun, not the ammunition, not the satchel or its contents.

He got into his car, started the engine, and backed out of the driveway, conscious of a light going on in a neighbor's house. He did not look that way.

Once in the street, he gunned it, but caught himself and slowed. Speeding would draw the wrong kind of attention.

He rehearsed what to do if pulled over, but realized his emotional state would give him away. His heart was racing like a runaway locomotive.

He breathed deeply to meet his body's increased demand for oxygen. His chest heaved with the effort.

It was no use—he could not slow his speeding heart.

He fought off panic as he drove, his lungs heaving, his mind filled with horrific images of gunfire and bodies.

Block after block, he encountered empty streets and peaceful neighborhoods. Gradually, his heart slowed, his terror diminished.

The murder site was several miles behind him now.

He had encountered little traffic, heard no sirens.

Johnny Apple was on Interstate 8 a few miles outside of Gila Bend, Arizona, when he sensed that someone was in the passenger seat beside him.

He looked and saw the psychiatrist staring out the windshield at the racing highway, illuminated in the glow of the headlights.

The psychiatrist looked at Johnny.

"What have you done, Johnny?"

Johnny swallowed hard. "I-I ..."

"You killed two people, didn't you, Johnny?"

"Yes."

"What comes next, Johnny?"

Johnny almost choked on his words. "San Diego comes next."

"What have you learned about yourself, Johnny?"

"I-I'm not sure. Did you know I saw my daughter?"

"No, I did not. What was she like?"

"She was like an angel."

In San Diego, Carrie Eagleton, home from work early, took out her cell phone and called her sister in Phoenix.

She got voicemail again, and Penny's greeting. *"Hi, you've reached the Penny and Daniel Smith residence. Please leave a message after the tone, and we'll return your call as soon as possible."*

"Penny, this is Carrie. Sam and I have been calling you and Daniel all day. We've left a ton of messages. You've got us worried. We want to find out how it went with you and Johnny. Please give us a call as soon as you can."

Reluctantly, she terminated the call. It was a connection, however tenuous, with her sister. In recent months they had never been closer.

She felt a sharp barb in her heart, thinking of her. Something had gone wrong—she was sure of it. She was already suffering terrible fear and guilt. This would only make it worse.

She sat at the kitchen table going out of her mind, until Sam arrived home forty-five minutes later with their dinner. The aroma of fried chicken filled the air.

"Sam, I called Penny again. There was no answer. Something's happened. I just know it. What are we going to do?"

"Have you tried calling Johnny's cell phone?"

"No, I didn't think of that."

Flushed with new energy, she dialed Johnny's number. She listened to it ring, a cloud of nervous anticipation building inside her. She got voicemail.

"Johnny, this is Carrie. We haven't been able to get ahold of Penny and Daniel. Are they with you? Please call me as soon as you can."

She terminated the call and sat down with Sam. They ate fried chicken and French fries, devouring it hungrily. They hadn't eaten all day.

As she ate, Carrie felt her stress sink away. She thought for sure Penny and Daniel would be with Johnny.

After eating, they cleaned up, and then sat at the kitchen table.

Carrie set her cell phone in front of her. Before long, her calm mood deserted her, and she became knotted with worry.

Her phone rang. She pounced on it.

"Hello."

"Carrie?" It was Johnny's voice.

"Johnny, are Penny and Daniel with you?"

"No, they are not."

The news chilled her. For a moment, she could not think. Then she heard a new voice on the line.

"Carrie?"

"Who is this?"

"This is Johnny's psychiatrist. I think you better call the Phoenix police."

"What?" Her fear exploded. She sprang up from the table, Sam with her. "Why do you want me to call the Phoenix police?"

"I'm afraid Johnny has done something terrible to Penny and Daniel."

"Done what?"

"He's killed them."

"What?"

"He's killed them."

"I don't believe you. Why would Johnny do that?"

"It requires a rather lengthy explanation. Hopefully, it can wait until we arrive at your house."

"You're coming here?"

"Yes."

Johnny came back on the line, his voice cold and threatening.

"Carrie, what did he say?"

"He-he ..." Fear squeezed off her response.

Johnny's voice became even more threatening.

"Carrie, what did he say?"

She trembled. Her voice quivered.

"He said you killed Penny and Daniel."

She heard a sharp intake of breath, and then a wail that rose like the howl of a wolf.

In panic, she terminated the call.

She reached for Sam, clung to him.

"Sam, Johnny's psychiatrist wants us to call the Phoenix police. He said Johnny killed Penny and Daniel."

Fear rose in Sam's face.

"Sam, what are we going to do? Johnny and his psychiatrist are coming here."

Sam took her by the arm, and they walked into the living room and sat on a sofa.

"Carrie, I'm going to call the Phoenix police. I'll ask them to check on Penny and Daniel's welfare."

"Okay, but don't tell them Johnny killed them."

"I won't." Sam took out his cell phone.

A Phoenix police car pulled up to the curb in front of the Penny and Daniel Smith residence. Officers Griffin and Martinez got out and walked to the door.

Griffin knocked—three loud raps.

He listened and heard nothing.

They were here to check on the welfare of Penny and Daniel Smith. Relatives in San Diego said they'd been trying to contact them by phone all day without success. Neither had shown up for work today, neither had scheduled the day off, neither was known for missing work without calling in. There'd been a report of possible gunshots in the area last night, and that had made the check imperative.

Griffin knocked again—three loud raps.

He listened and heard nothing. He tried the door. It was locked. He stepped back from the door and looked at the windows.

"Walk around the house," he said to Martinez. "Look in the windows, see what you can see. I'll keep knocking."

Griffin stepped to the door again and knocked—three loud raps. He heard nothing.

Martinez walked around the house and saw shades drawn at all the windows except in back where a picture window stood bare.

He peered through the picture window and saw into a living room, where a bureau, two sofas, two easy chairs, and a large-screen television set were in view. He looked for signs of a struggle, or for anything out of the ordinary, but there was nothing obvious.

On the bureau, he saw a laptop carrying case, a purse, and a tote bag—the things a woman might grab just before leaving for work.

He walked to the attached garage. The double doors in front had been shut. There was a walk-in door in back. He tried the door. It was locked.

A narrow translucent window was set in the door, allowing diffused sunlight into the garage. Martinez looked through the window and saw the fuzzy outlines of two cars.

He walked out front and told Griffin what he had seen.

Griffin called it in.

A sergeant told Griffin to wait for backup and then break in.

Two more squad cars pulled up.

Griffin approached the front door of the house, shouting.

"Police! Coming in!"

Griffin swung a sledge hammer at the lock.

Two swings and it broke.

Griffin and three other officers entered the house with guns drawn. They discovered a man and a woman in a bedroom, dead of gunshot wounds.

Detective Wilhelm of the Phoenix Police Department called the residence of Carrie and Sam Eagleton in San Diego.

He listened to it ring, and then heard a woman answer.

"Hello."

"Is this Carrie Eagleton?"

"Yes."

"This is Detective Wilhelm of the Phoenix Police Department. Are you the sister of Penny Smith of Phoenix?"

"Yes."

"Ms. Eagleton, when was the last time you spoke with your sister?"

"Last evening, about nine p.m."

"Did you speak with her by phone?"

"Yes."

"Did she seem upset or give any indication that she or her husband might be in danger?"

"No."

"Was she at her residence when you spoke with her?"

"Yes."

"Was her husband with her?"

"Yes."

"Was anyone else present?"

"Not to my knowledge."

Wilhelm thanked her, hung up, and then called the county medical examiner's office to see if they had identified the two bodies discovered in the Penny and Daniel Smith residence.

Officer Cecil Hayworth of the San Diego Police Department knocked on the door of the Carrie and Sam Eagleton residence.

As he waited, his eyes were drawn to a statue of a bear beside the door. The bear's solemn gaze chilled him.

A man opened the door.

"Yes?"

"I'm Officer Hayworth of the San Diego Police Department. I'm here to check on the welfare of Carrie Eagleton. May I come in and speak with her?"

"Yes, you may, Officer."

The man stepped back, and Cecil entered the house. The man showed him into the living room, where Cecil saw a man and a woman sitting side by side on a couch.

Cecil approached the woman.

"Are you Carrie Eagleton?" he asked.

"Yes."

"Ms. Eagleton, I'm Officer Hayworth of the San Diego Police Department. I was told to check on your welfare. Are you okay?"

"I'm okay."

"Do you want someone to come and see you? We can send over a police chaplain. We can summon your minister."

"I don't have a minister, but thanks. I'm okay."

Cecil looked around and sighed.

"Okay, Ms. Eagleton. If you are okay, I will be leaving."

The man who let him in accompanied him to the door. They stood in the entry.

"It was nice of you to stop by," the man said.

"It's part of our job," Cecil said. "It's terrible what happened."

"Oh? What happened?"

Cecil lowered his voice.

"Ms. Eagleton's sister and brother-in-law were murdered last night in Phoenix."

The man's jaw dropped. His eyes shot wide.

"She didn't inform you?" Cecil asked.

"No. Neither of them did. Not Carrie, not Sam."

Cecil shrugged and walked out the door. What more could he do?

Walking toward his squad car, he watched the bear. Its eyes tracked him across the lawn, made him quicken his step.

Uneasy, he got into his squad car. He caught a vibe in there. Something was not right. People reacted differently to news of sudden death. Some people broke down and cried. Others became numb. Carrie Eagleton had the look of someone girding herself for war.

He looked at the bear one more time before driving away.

Its eyes chilled him.

He drove away and felt a shiver.

Carrie stared at the man who sat across from her. His eyes were like the eyes of a vigilant dog. His face was lean, a fit face, a face she thought of as striking. His nose was straight and narrow. His chin was cleft, but only so. His ears were small and stuck out slightly. His lips were thin. His hair was neatly trimmed. The man looked surprisingly normal. You couldn't get worked up over him too much, unless you knew he posed a threat to you. Carrie reminded herself she must not show fear, or let on that he was dangerous to her, for that would trigger Johnny, a homicidal maniac, one of the man's multiple personalities.

His eyes were gazing with that doglike vigilance, but she was not too worried about this personality. She could always tell when a shift had happened by looking at the eyes. There were other signs, also, including changes in posture, facial expression, and voice. Changes in physique, height, shape of head, face, nose, mouth, and ears also seemed to occur to reflect the new personality. How did the body alter itself? That was a mystery. Or did such transformations actually take place? Was it only perception? She thought not. She was aware of cases of multiple personality where blood sugar changed—a person had diabetes in one personality and was free from it in another. She knew of cases where one personality needed corrective lenses, another did not. The examples were endless.

Multiple personality disorder, now called dissociative identity disorder, seemed to have roots deep within the mind-
body. Some claimed the condition did not exist at all, that it
was triggered by psychotherapists in search of it, others
were ardent believers. In any case, she and Sam had Johnny
to contend with. Fortunately, Johnny was not present at the
moment. She could tell. It was someone else. She wondered
who. She did not recall seeing this one before.

The man lazed on the couch, relaxed yet watchful, as
if home from a hard day's work. He wore khaki slacks and
a blue shirt. Who was he?

Carrie diverted her eyes. It was not wise to look too
much. Looking too much could trigger the protective
personality. That personality was strong out of all propor-
tion to body size, and ferocious as any wild predator. It
scared you and stopped you from doing what you were
doing.

The protective personality could have easily killed the
cop who'd shown up earlier, before Carrie could have
passed a warning, before the cop could have drawn his
weapon.

One of the personalities revealed exceptional insight—
the psychiatrist. If they could get him to come out more
often, he might provide clues on how to stop Johnny.

The protective personality was likely Johnny. If not
Johnny, there was someone even more dangerous than
Johnny lurking in there.

Carrie knew that she and Sam would stand a better
chance of surviving if they were able to draw forth the
personality that knew of the others.

There was a way to do this, but it was risky. You had to
encourage a parade of personalities to come forth, each

taking the stage for a while, revealing its nature and purpose, and then leaving a marker, a way to call it back.

But what if Johnny should appear during this parade and sense he was in danger? What if someone more dangerous than Johnny should appear? It could rush them and kill them instantly.

The man across from her seemed content to remain slumped on the couch. He hadn't moved in quite a while. What personality was he? He seemed harmless enough. She and Sam had to get started on drawing them out. Someone had to start asking questions. She glanced at Sam.

The man sat upright, tension in his muscles. Glancing at Sam had triggered extra vigilance. That was all it took to put them on a spiral to Hell.

Carrie leaned against Sam, as if to rest, let herself sink into him and the sofa. The man on the couch relaxed and resumed his prior position.

Carrie felt safe for the moment. She would avoid looking at Sam. It triggered a protective instinct. Looking at Sam implied she might soon be speaking to him and plotting against the man on the couch.

"What's your name?" she asked the man on the couch.

"Brett Crawford."

"How old are you, Brett?"

"Twenty-five."

"Do you have any brothers or sisters?"

"I have a younger brother."

"How old is he?"

"Twelve."

"What's his name?"

"Jimmy."

Carrie sat up straighter. She wanted to get Jimmy on stage and see what she could learn. How could she pry Jimmy out?

Sam came to her rescue.

"Does Jimmy like to play baseball?" Sam asked.

"No," Brett said. "He hates baseball."

"Does he play any sports?"

"He plays soccer."

"Is he a good student?"

"He's an excellent student."

"Does he have any homework tonight?"

Brett sat upright. "Why do you ask?" There was anger in his voice.

Jimmy is off limits, Carrie thought. Maybe Jimmy would pop up on his own later, maybe not.

The afternoon shadows lengthened. Sunlight arrowed in through gaps in the curtains. For Carrie Eagleton, the world seemed to arrive in thinly sliced pieces. Struggles raged in the man's face, hinting at personalities that seemed all too willing to take over. The man resisted with visible effort and held them off. Then someone new wrested control.

Who was he? Carrie hadn't seen him before. It was almost as if he had stepped in from another world. He exuded power and presence like none of the others, and was also a shocking sight: massive jaws and a powerful battle-hardened physique.

The new personality gazed about the room with a regal air, and then spied Carrie and Sam.

"Well, well, what have we here?" he said in a deep, mellifluous voice.

"Who are you?" Carrie asked.

"Beowulf."

Charming, she thought, the first one with a sense of humor. A strategy occurred to her: get this engaging personality outside, barricade the door, and call the cops.

"Beowulf, you look too energetic to just sit there. Why don't we go outside and play badminton, or go for a walk?"

Beowulf's face changed, becoming wolflike. He slinked off the couch, bounded to Carrie on all fours, and bit her on the right calf.

Carrie screamed.

Beowulf released her calf and sprang back to the couch.

Tears streamed down Carrie's face. She examined her calf, saw puncture marks, felt deep, burning pain. A shiver crossed her flesh. He's with us, she thought, the one that protects all the others.

"Could we have Jimmy?" she asked in a trembling voice.

Beowulf roared with laughter. It shook the house.

Johnny emerged, displacing Beowulf. He looked about, and then settled his eyes on Carrie and Sam. Minutes went by in silence, Johnny eyeing them coldly.

"What are we waiting for?" Sam asked.

Carrie held her breath—it was a direct challenge to the personality. Johnny was fragmented. He did not always know what he waited for. She braced for the return of Beowulf.

The psychiatrist appeared, his expression serene. He sat relaxed, a twinkle in his eye.

"We are waiting for everyone to head off to bed," he said. "When Johnny thinks you are fast asleep, he will creep into your bedroom with a handgun and shoot both of you to death."

Carrie felt a cold wind buffeting her soul. In her numbing fear, she forced herself to watch the psychiatrist for signs of a personality shift. That was the key, she thought, to staying alive.

"Where does he keep the gun?" Sam asked.

"In the bedroom you reserve for him. He secreted it there the first time he visited."

"Is there anything you can do to stop him?" Sam asked.

"I'm afraid not. Johnny is set on killing you both. He feels it's the only way to send a message to the man who killed his wife and daughter."

Carrie knew they had to act soon, before fear paralyzed them, or before Johnny became violently mistrustful of them and their options became nonexistent.

They had to consider a preemptive strike. They could kill the psychiatrist, thereby killing Johnny and everyone else who lurked in there. The psychiatrist seemed easiest. When he was present, they could rush him and ...

But how fast would he change? And who would he change to?

If the psychiatrist did not immediately give way to Johnny, or to Beowulf, they might have a chance to kill him.

She wanted to get a knife into Sam's hands, to make it more certain. She looked at Sam, heard movement on the couch across from her, and looked back at the psychiatrist.

It wasn't the psychiatrist anymore. It was Johnny.

She froze, her eyes focused on the wall beside Johnny's head. She had to get Sam a knife.

"Johnny," she said, "I bet you're famished. Let's go into the kitchen. I'll fix you a sandwich."

The house was taking on a different atmosphere as they sat at the kitchen table. It seemed like a cozier house now. It seemed like the house Carrie's mother had kept when Carrie was a child. That house had been immaculate, a house of home-cooked meals and enchanting smells, not just of food but of soap and bubble baths and other good things. A wonderful house.

Carrie knew she had to think of pleasant things. It would show on her face. It would keep Johnny pacified. The psychiatrist would be curious at some point and make his appearance. He would ask her about the pleasant look on her face. She would then see about Sam doing him in fast and furious. While thinking of Sam doing him in, she would mask it with more pleasant thoughts: the smell of home-cooked meals, of bubble baths, of other good things.

She filled her mind with pleasant memories of bubble baths, of dishes piping hot from the oven, of chocolate chip cookies and apple pie and ice cream, as she slipped a carving knife into Sam's hands under the table. She thought of home-made vegetable soup, home-made beef stew, pot roast, Swiss steak, hot rolls, baked potatoes smothered with butter, mashed potatoes smothered with gravy, asparagus. She thought of peas and corn and carrots and squash—food from the gardens of her youth. Her adulthood could not compare. Where had they gone wrong?

She saw the psychiatrist looking at her. Yes, ask me questions, she thought.

She heard a growl, and her heart jumped.

It wasn't the psychiatrist anymore.

It was Johnny.

Johnny was on his feet, staring at her.

"Where's the knife?" Johnny asked.

"Sam, can you do something now? Can you take him down?"

Sam lunged at Johnny with the knife.

Johnny tried to grapple with Sam, but Sam slashed him furiously, inflicting deep cuts to Johnny's hands and arms.

Johnny spun away and raced for the living room, but Sam tackled him and took him to the floor.

Sam pounded Johnny with his fists until Johnny went limp.

Sam got a rope from the garage and hogtied Johnny.

Johnny came around, gasping for breath, eyes dark with fear. He struggled to rise, but collapsed.

"Why didn't you kill him, Sam?"

"It wasn't necessary."

Carrie looked at Johnny, but it wasn't Johnny anymore. It was the psychiatrist. His voice was calm and soothing.

"Carrie, everyone has a dark dungeon filled with dark secrets. You must enter your dark dungeon and shine a light on your dark secrets. When you do that, you will know that your battle is not with me but with the darkness inside you."

Carrie looked at Sam and saw that Sam was thoughtful now, as if considering everything in a new light.

"Carrie, I think you must do this," Sam said. "You know we've talked about ..."

Yes, we've talked about that, Sam.

"Help me, Sam!"

Secret parts of Carrie were hidden away. Secret parts of Carrie were planning to come out someday.

She knew that she was fragmented, also. She also lay in pieces. It was how she had such insight into Johnny.

And now a more courageous part of Carrie came out and entered her dark dungeon and shined a light on her dark secrets.

She saw Sam in there, of course. She knew Sam would be in her dark dungeon. He was her protector. There was nothing Sam wouldn't do for her.

Carrie walked through her dark dungeon, shining a light on her dark secrets, trying to see what was there.

She saw her father and her mother. She saw her father kill her mother.

No, that can't be. Her father had never killed her mother. Nothing like that had ever happened.

She saw herself and Penny when they were little, in a bubble bath, their father scrubbing them. *But she saw it differently now. Their father was not scrubbing them. He was ...*

She had to get out of here. These things were too dark. Why had she stumbled into this place?

She saw Sam. Sam took her by the hand and led her out of her dark dungeon and into the living room.

Johnny was there, broken free of his bonds. He lunged at Sam with the knife and sliced off a piece of Sam's face. Sam roared, spraying blood, and grappled with Johnny for the knife.

Carrie screamed a nightmarish scream, screamed and screamed and screamed.

Officer Cecil Hayworth drove slowly past the Carrie and Sam Eagleton residence. He took in everything, his cop's instincts buzzing. Then he focused on the statue of the bear that stood beside the front door.

The bear's eyes tracked him, giving Cecil a chill. On impulse, he pulled to the curb and stopped.

Damn you, bear. Because of you, I'm getting ideas. Hear me out, bear. I think the Phoenix killer met me at the door. His display of shock was not an act, but genuine, which means there are at least two people inside him: the killer and another. Don't laugh, bear. I've seen it before.

If the guy killed the sister and brother-in-law in Phoenix, he might kill these two, also. Unless they're in it together.

I dare you to refute this one fact, bear: Carrie Eagleton was awfully cold in regards to her sister's death.

Now, you silly bear, I have to think of a good reason to knock on the Eagletons' door again. We must follow rules here, unlike you in the forest.

Cecil racked his brain, trying to think of a reason to knock on the Eagletons' door again, but came up with nothing, so he drove away and pulled into a Mexican diner for lunch.

He stepped from his police car and shielded his eyes. The sunlight was so bright it looked like a Martian invasion. The brutal rays seemed to tear through everything. The sun is a rascal today, he thought.

He saw through the inferno, and saw his cop friend Dan Kirchhoff arrive in a cloud of dust.

He and Dan went inside the diner and sat at the far end of the counter—their usual place.

Cecil envied Dan Kirchhoff's flair, his savoir-faire, his wicked nature. Dan served as the police department's in-house devil, and was Cecil's mentor.

A waitress in a black dress came by and took their orders: steak fajitas for both of them.

After she left, Cecil described the situation inside the Carrie and Sam Eagleton residence, and his suspicions.

"I don't have a real good reason for knocking on their door again, Dan. Can you think of one?"

"Cecil, have you forgotten your training?"

"I did not. They hammered it into my brain. They swung a big mallet. It's still there."

"Cecil, don't you recall? When we want to enter a place and don't have a good reason for doing so, we become discs of light and go there anyway and hover about."

"You're joshing me, Dan."

"Right, I'm joshing you. We'll barge in, use truncheons, and get the truth out of them."

"Dan, I need a legitimate reason for going back there and knocking on the door again."

Dan took a deep breath. "Okay. Tell me, Cecil, did you see any religious icons in the house?"

Cecil thought a moment. "No, I don't believe so."

"Did you see any artwork? Any paintings? Sculpture?"

"There was a bear."

"A bear?"

"A statue of a bear right outside the house beside the front door."

"Tell me about the bear, Cecil."

"It had scary eyes that followed you."

"It was a trickster."

"A trickster?"

"Yes. You saw what the trickster wanted you to see. Bear means danger."

Cecil and Dan swiveled on their stools, faced the windows, saw their own grim reflections in the glass.

The air snapped with their passage as they raced out of the diner, their fajitas still on the grill.

Cecil cursed the police department all the way to the Eagletons' residence. Why didn't they provide him with training on tricksters and the warnings they conveyed? Why did Dan know, but not him?

They pulled up in front of the Carrie and Sam Eagleton residence and jumped out, guns drawn.

They did a quick search of the perimeter and then looked in the windows. They saw nothing that might give a hint to what was going on inside.

Cecil knocked on the door—three loud raps. No response.

He knocked again—three loud raps.

"Police! Open up!" Cecil shouted.

He heard nothing from inside and was about to force his way in when a flash of light filled the air around him.

Frightened and confused, he looked around and saw several large cars pull to the curb and several large men and women emerge—all with massive heads and jaws, all wearing dark cloaks.

He saw a monstrous limousine arrive and a huge man

in a crimson cloak emerge. He was more massive than the others, his jaws twice as big. He walked toward the house and the others followed him.

Cecil stood on the porch, in their way, fierce eyes boring into him. He leaped off the porch and dashed across the lawn, fear crashing through his mind.

Dan grabbed him and shook him. "Cecil, what are you seeing?"

"Dan, I'm seeing ..."

But Cecil could not explain what he was seeing. He tore away from Dan, slunk around the yard, and kept his eyes on the procession.

Cecil holstered his gun and followed the fearsome entities into the house. They poured into the living room, where a theater-in-the-round stood—a stage in the center, a huge throne upon it, and terraced seating all around.

The man in the crimson cloak walked onto the stage and sat upon the throne, his massive shoulders hunched, his head thrust forward. He beckoned the others to gather around him.

Cecil, still shaken, stepped toward the outer fringes of the crowd, his eyes roving.

A roughhewn altar stood against a wall, dim scrolls of parchment on it. A table was bedecked with meat, bread, fruit, and nuts. A human infant lay on the table, its tiny feet kicking toward the sky.

Little lambs stood afar, grazing on tufts of green grass, and bleating. A creature that was half-man and half-wolf stood by the lambs and seemed to watch over them.

Another creature, half-man and half-bear, crept silently into place beside the human infant and stood there as if protecting it.

Cecil saw human shapes, mostly white, pink, and chocolate-colored, in distant mists. They were motionless, some appearing male, some female.

He saw forms the size and shape of wild beasts, mostly yellow, pink, and black, in the distant mists.

He smelled forests and meadows, saw a vast wilderness veiled in mist, heard the sighing wind, the creaking trees, the pelting rain.

He stood there in his fear and spun slowly, and took in everything again, for he thirsted for a second look, and on second viewing it was all there: a gentle moving feast.

Looking at the various tableaus, it was not difficult to figure out the common elements.

In each scene, there was something attractive that drew the eye. In each scene, there was implied danger. In each scene, there was a beast.

In each scene, there was a sense of life held in precarious balance—would the beast attack or protect?

In each scene, there was a sense of something held in check, a not-quite-ready feeling.

The man in the crimson cloak began to hold forth, and the crowd gathered around to listen, and Cecil once again moved toward the outer fringes, a chill in his bones.

He watched as clouds obscured the man's face and made him seem far away, as if he were on a mountaintop.

The man spoke of the need to protect, of the need to make the beasts protectors. With a few words, he consecrated the beasts as man's protectors.

And then he told the story of the man who had entered

this house posing danger.

Cecil sat on a couch and listened, feeling the heightened pulse of drama.

"There had been a car accident," the man said. "A man's wife and daughter had been killed. Dr. Jonathan Apple came upon the accident and at first did not realize that it was his wife and daughter in the car. He learned the truth and fell into darkness and fell into illness and had to undergo therapy.

"His therapist induced multiple personalities to emerge in him, with the idea that each personality would take on some of the burden of coping with the traumatic events, and that the various personalities would eventually be fused into an integrated, healed whole.

"It did not happen that way.

"The patient, known as Johnny Apple, began unconsciously drawing upon his therapist's techniques and began inducing his own multiple personalities to emerge. He—and they—went about seeking revenge for the deaths of his wife and daughter.

"Johnny Apple was not to be denied: he killed two people in Phoenix and was prepared to kill two more in San Diego when Officer Cecil Hayworth arrived."

Cecil shuddered, hearing the man talk about him. He listened as the man pointed out key opportunities where a god could have intervened but did not because no god was evolved enough.

"A god could have intervened before the accident and saved the lives of Johnny's wife and daughter.

"A god could have intervened during therapy sessions and induced better results for Johnny.

"A god could have intervened before Johnny's murder spree got under way and saved many lives.

"A god, in fact, did intervene, appearing as his daughter, Abby, in the hallway in the house in Phoenix, but it was not well received by Johnny.

"Various other gods did appear, attempting to influence things one way or another, but with limited success.

"Incredibly, some of the gods seemed to take a perverse turn, and seemed to be encouraging Johnny's darker nature.

"What kind of god could have saved Johnny?" the man asked. "It appears such a god was trying to emerge. As matters darkened, a beast in the form of a bear appeared at the front door. But Officer Hayworth failed to interpret the signs soon enough."

The entities left, taking the clouds and the bizarre, impossible scenes with them.

Cecil stood from the couch and saw a tapestry of blood on the living-room carpet.

Three bodies lay on the carpet, a knife protruding from the throat of one of them.

Cecil checked each body for a pulse. Carrie and Sam Eagleton were dead. The man who had met him at the door was dead. It had been a fight to the death, which no one had won.

Cecil looked for Dan Kirchhoff, but knew he had no more existence than the others who had populated the room and had held forth about gods and beasts.

He went outside to his police car and called it in.

"One-eighty-seven," he told the dispatcher, and gave the address.

Dead Colt

Junelle Jamison sits at attention in the front passenger seat of the Ford Bronco, keeps her eyes focused out the windshield, thinks her mother, who is driving the vehicle, has no stomach for this.

"Mom, who is the enemy?"

"I don't know, Junelle. You've asked me a dozen times already. Won't you let up?"

"I want to know who the enemy is. Tell me, Robin."

"I've told you before, sweetie, don't call me Robin. I'm your mom, so call me Mom."

"I know, but I want to know who the enemy is, so I'm prepared. Does Cedric know? I mean Dad?"

Robin laughs. "Have you been talking to your father about this?"

"Yes, I have, about a hundred times. Cedric says he doesn't know who the enemy is, but I can't always trust him to be honest."

"Neither can I."

"He might know."

"Not your father."

"But aren't men good at fighting wars?"

"Honey, not your father. He'd chicken out at the first sign of danger."

"I think he's brave. He hunts big game."

"That doesn't require the kind of courage you need in war. Animals don't shoot back."

"But aren't some men good at fighting wars?"

"I suppose some men are, but not your father."

"Mom, stop dragging Cedric down."

Robin smiles at her daughter, and then puts her eyes back on the road.

"Aren't some women good at fighting wars, too?"

"Junelle, you're only eleven. Don't be thinking of that."

"But what if I'm called to action? They say aliens are invading."

"They won't call you to action. They just want us all to be vigilant."

"But aren't some women good at fighting wars?"

"I suppose some are."

Junelle hears a sigh in her mother's voice and decides to drop the subject. She sees their boxlike home ahead. It's identical to all the other boxlike homes in the Dead Colt trailer court. She hears the old Ford Bronco wheeze, senses her mother stiffen at the wheel. That's all they need, the Bronco going out again. The trailer court is loaded with other Bronco-looking vehicles, many of which do not run half the time.

As they pull into the trailer court, she sees that two police cars have converged on the Yardley residence. This doesn't surprise Junelle—Stan Yardley is a member of a gang called the Blue Dragoons. The Blue Dragoons have a makeshift prison out of town, where they interrogate, torture, and execute their prisoners. But when the authorities investigate, nothing ever sticks.

The Blue Dragoons are easy to identify. They wear army fatigues and have razor-stubble haircuts. Stan is regarded as the most dangerous member of the Blue Dragoons, but he's not the boss of the Blue Dragoons. Everyone knows Stan isn't smart enough to be the boss. The Blue Dragoons have a boss whose name is kept secret. They say he's smart. They say he's the only one who can control Stan. Even the Blue Dragoons need someone smart to be the boss.

Junelle's big ambition is to be a boss someday. She feels her parents screwed up when they didn't try to become bosses. Being a boss makes life so much easier. She wants to be a good and honorable boss.

"Mom, how does Stan Yardley manage to stay out of prison? He killed his parents."

"He's only fifteen, Junelle. And no one knows for sure if he did it."

"Mom, this is Texas. They can hang you at fifteen."

"No, they can't, Junelle. That's too young. They'd use lethal injection, anyway, if they could. I guess they didn't have enough evidence."

"His parents were knifed to death. Stan carries a knife."

"Lots of people carry knives."

"He didn't attend their funeral."

"Neither did you. Neither did I."

"They say he enters the cemetery at night and dances on their graves."

"Maybe he does, Junelle, but that's not evidence he killed them."

"You don't seem to care, Mom."

"I don't have the power to influence things, baby."

"You have the power to influence me."

Robin looks at her daughter. "Do I?"

"Yes, you do."

Robin eases the Bronco around the two Dead Colt squad cars that are parked near the Yardley residence, drives down a gravel lane, and parks beside their trailer.

Junelle helps her mother carry in the groceries. The supermarket was swamped with shoppers again today, piling cart upon cart with whatever they could sweep off the shelves. Junelle and her mother stuck to their list and bought only what they needed. Robin was somewhat flexible, though. As Junelle browsed with wistful eyes, she had said, "Junelle, you can pick out something you like, for you and your father."

Junelle picked out a large pepperoni pizza. She and her father like pepperoni pizzas. But her mother told her to put it back. "Pizzas are swimming in fat," she said. "Pick out something healthier." So Junelle got two frozen dinners instead, with chicken, mashed potatoes, and broccoli in them. Robin hates to cook. Frozen dinners are the specialty in their boxlike home.

Junelle pulls a bag of groceries from the backseat, carries it into the trailer, and sets it on the table. It's stifling hot in the trailer. She hopes her mother will switch on the air conditioner. Air conditioners are essential, but it costs something to run them. Their power bill zooms during the hottest months.

She goes outside and sees Stan Yardley standing in his yard. His skull is shadowy with razor stubble. He's wearing army fatigues. His hands are cuffed behind his back and two cops are standing beside him. A crowd is gathering, drawing forth from the other boxlike homes. Everyone has seen this before. Stan is big. He is all sinew and muscle and has eyes like a panther's. The cops are afraid of him, so they handcuff him. There's been a crime committed somewhere, and they have to roust Stan.

She knows what's going to happen next. One of the cops digs out his handcuff key, steps behind Stan, and unlocks the cuffs. They're letting him go, like they always do. The crowd begins to disperse, and the cops get into their squad cars and drive away.

Junelle feels her mother brush past her. "Come on, honey, these things are going to melt."

She and her mother grab the remaining bags of groceries from the backseat. Her mother slams the Bronco's door and heads for the trailer. Junelle pauses and watches Stan.

She's heard that Stan has started believing in strange things—like aliens invading earth—and that he has to see doctors who question his sanity.

Junelle thinks that's strange. The U.S. government says aliens *are* invading earth. Why would anyone consider Stan insane for holding such a belief?

Stan's eyes meet hers. He's watching me again, she thinks, and she rushes inside.

"Dad, I almost got us a pepperoni pizza today."

"You did?"

"Yes, I did. But Mom made me put it back. She thinks pizzas are unhealthy."

"I've told you before, Junelle. If she thinks you've found one of life's little pleasures, she'll steal it away from you."

Junelle and Cedric are at home; Robin's at work. They've eaten their frozen dinners and are getting ready to watch a Clint Eastwood movie. Junelle pops the DVD into the player and watches the screen light up. Feeling the quiet whoosh of the air conditioner, she grabs the remote and takes a seat beside her father in the darkened trailer.

"Dad, I saw the cops roust Stan Yardley again today. They had him in handcuffs but let him go. What do you make of that?"

"Stan is quite a character."

"Aren't you afraid, living so close to him?"

"No."

"I am."

"Why?"

"He believes in aliens. And he kills people."

"Junelle, most of us believe in aliens these days. It's what our government tells us."

"I know, but ..."

"Do you honestly believe Stan kills people?"

"No, I guess I don't."

"Stan's engaged in a class war. His enemies spread those rumors about him."

"What does that mean, Cedric, a class war?"

"That's a struggle between the upper and lower classes of a society. It happens when people feel oppressed by those in power."

"Do people oppress Stan?"

"Yes."

"People oppress me, too. Can I resent them?"

"Yes."

"Good. I resent Stan. He oppresses me."

"How?"

"He always watches me."

"It could be he likes you, Junelle. You have movie-star looks."

"No, he doesn't like me. He likes to oppress me."

Junelle has the volume off. The Clint Eastwood movie hasn't started yet. Trailers are running.

"Lots of people oppress me, Cedric."

"Like who?"

"Teachers."

"They oppress everyone. It's the system."

"I know, but I'm encountering something extreme. I've been having this dream where an old lady English teacher oppresses me. It makes me so mad I could kill her."

"Who is she?"

"I don't know. I'm older in the dream. I'm in college somewhere far away."

"Is she condescending toward you?"

"It's worse than that, Cedric! She assaults me! She's an evil old bitch!"

"Cool down, angel."

"But I'm having this dream all the time. This old lady hates me. She thinks I'm inferior. She's planning to kill me, Cedric. She's a motherfucker."

He laughs.

"I'm going to kill her, Cedric."

"Junelle, let me introduce you to Stan."

"Aaaa ..."

The movie starts. It's about a serial killer. The Clint Eastwood character has a bad ticker. He gets a heart transplant and is on the killer's trail again, against his surgeon's wishes. His surgeon—a woman whom Junelle finds exceedingly irksome—harps on the danger to his heart if he pursues the case.

When it's over, Junelle says she wants to be a surgeon.

"I thought you wanted to be a boss," her father says.

"I do. A surgeon is a boss. She tells everyone in the operating room what to do. She has to be a good and honorable boss."

"I thought you didn't like the doctor in this movie."

"I didn't. She enraged me. She was always telling Clint Eastwood what he couldn't do. She was a motherfucker, Cedric."

They watch the news, which is loaded with advisories again about an alien invasion of earth. Citizens are told to report wounds that have no apparent genesis, especially wounds that have something growing from them. They are told the wounds are treatable and that the government will pay all medical costs. Citizens are also told to report attacks that seem to happen while in an altered state of consciousness or while asleep.

Junelle goes into her minuscule bedroom and slips into her pajamas. She goes back to the living room, pulls her hair back, and shows her father a big, red welt on the left side of her neck.

"I've had it a few days, Dad. It has no genesis. It's getting worse."

He looks at it closely. "We'll watch it. You should have told us sooner."

"Dad, who is the enemy?"

"I don't know."

"You must know."

"I don't know, Junelle. You've asked me before."

"I thought men were good at fighting wars."

"We are, but this time the enemy is too well hidden."

"The enemy could be anyone, then. Is that what you're saying?"

"That's what the government is saying."

"Do you believe we go on trips?"

"That's what the government is telling us, Junelle. I think it's true."

"The government says they want our trip memories. Do you have any memories of the kind they're looking for, Cedric?"

"I remember episodes in which I've been attacked and had to fight back."

"So do I. Why don't you tell the government?"

"I have. I've called the hotline."

"Do they ever call you in for questioning?"

"No, they just ask me questions over the phone."

"I'm going to tell them about the old lady. She attacks me while I sleep. What do you think they'll do, Dad?"

"They just might call you in for questioning."

"You think so?"

Junelle gets into bed and massages her left heel. She didn't want to tell Cedric about that injury. She thinks she strained it while riding her bike. If so, it has a genesis and the government won't pay. It hurts a lot sometimes and the pain migrates around.

The old lady causes the welt on her neck. She has long, sharp fingers that claw and grip.

Junelle falls asleep.

Junelle wakes, snaps on a light, and reaches for her journal and pen. She sits up on her bed and records the dream she just had.

When I popped out her eyeball, it really sealed her fate.

She wants to do a good job of recording this, for she will show the government her log. Her mind races through the memory of the dream, and her hand flies across the page. She's been recording her dreams about the old lady all along. She figures she had better document everything to make sure the government pays the medical bills.

Finished, she sets her journal and pen aside, snaps off the light, and falls back to sleep.

When Junelle wakes in the morning, the wound on the left side of her neck is bigger and more painful. Cringing, she gently probes it with fingertips. She feels broken skin and wetness. *There's something protruding from the wound.* She pulls her hand away and sees blood.

She gets out of bed, her heart pounding with fright, looks in the mirror, and sees a tiny growth on her neck.

She fights off panic, rushes to the bathroom, and cleans the wound, gently working around the fleshy thing that's flowering from it.

She goes back to her bedroom, slips into white slacks and a green-and-white blouse. She ties her hair back with a green ribbon, keeping the wound exposed, and steps to the mirror again.

She examines the little nub, the little stalk, whatever it is. It's about half an inch long and bends when she touches it.

It hurts a little. It's growing from a puffy slit in the skin. There's something glassy at the end of the stalk. It looks like a little eye, one not yet fully formed.

Junelle closes her eyes and finds that she can see from the little unformed eye, not well, not clearly, but there is vision there, off to the side.

She calms herself. The government did warn of growths. She has to think. Cedric's at his job. Robin's still asleep. Should she wake Robin or just call the hotline?

She steps to the door of her mother's bedroom and knocks.

"Mom?" She slides the door open.

Junelle sits at attention in the front passenger seat of the Bronco, her journal in her hands, her eyes focused out the windshield. She shuts her eyes and sees the translucent sky, the dizzy sunlight, a slash of window, all framed around a pretty mom, Robin, in the driver's seat, all of it slinky and weird, not good vision, but it is vision, and it's getting better. She thinks her brain has to get used to working with the new eye.

Robin has been crying.

Junelle opens her eyes and sees the big, bright world in front of the Bronco. With her eyes open, side vision is nonexistent.

"They might keep me, Mom."

"I know, Junelle." Her mother's voice is swirling in her emotions. "But only for a while. I'll bring your things, baby. I'll buy a little suitcase for you. I'll come and visit you. They won't keep you long."

"Do you think they'll operate right away?"

"I hope so."

"But, Mom, I can see from the eye. They can use this to help blind people. What do you think?"

Robin sniffles, cries for a moment, and then wipes her tears away. "You're right, Junelle."

Junelle closes her eyes and sneaks another peek at her mother. She feels she has an opportunity to help people. She hopes the Army doctors will feel the same way.

She opens her eyes. Within minutes, two police cars intercept them and escort them to the Army base south of Dead Colt.

<center>~~~</center>

"Hello, Junelle. My name is Lisa Stock."

"Hello."

Junelle shakes hands with Lisa Stock and looks around. The room is immaculate. The computer workstation looks exotic and new.

"I'm a psychologist. I'll be asking you a few questions. Is that okay?"

"Yes."

"Please sit down."

Junelle watches her mother depart for the waiting room. Clutching her journal, she sits on a chair near the computer workstation. The white-cloaked psychologist closes the door, takes a seat, and brings up something on her computer screen.

Junelle is dressed in a blue hospital gown and white slippers. She shivers in the cool air. They let her keep the ribbon that's tying her hair back. She's had x-rays and a

CAT scan and has seen a surgeon. The surgeon explained what they would do during the operation. He said she could go home with her mother about two hours after she woke, and that she would have to return in one week for a follow-up exam.

Do you know that I can see from this eye? she had asked him.

Yes, he said, and went on to describe the type of vision she was experiencing from her third eye. Then he left the examination room, and a nurse escorted her to the room where Lisa was waiting.

She studies Lisa. She looks to be about her mother's age. She is slender and has brunette hair and brown eyes, like her mom. Junelle wonders if she can talk to her about helping blind people, but right now Lisa is busy on her computer screen. Finally, she looks at Junelle.

"I saw you limping, Junelle. Did you hurt your foot?"

"Yes."

"Can you describe the injury?"

"I hurt my left heel. I must have done it on my bicycle. Sometimes it hurts a lot. Sometimes it doesn't hurt at all. Sometimes I can't walk on it it's so bad. Sometimes I have to crawl."

She watches Lisa's eyes go wide.

"It's bad, isn't it?"

"Yes."

"What have you been doing for it?"

"Nothing, really, other than to give it rest and to massage it when I go to bed. I try not to let my parents see me limp."

Lisa types something into her computer.

"Do you ..." She smiles at Junelle. "Do you do anything

else for your heel, like do you have conversations with spiritual beings? Do you pray? Do you ask for help?"

"No, I don't. Do you think it might help?"

"I can't make any recommendations."

Junelle steers her eyes toward Lisa's computer. "Do you think you could say my heel has an injury without a genesis so the government will pay for it?"

"I will, Junelle." Lisa enters something into her computer. "The government will cover all costs associated with diagnosing, treating, and rehabilitating your heel injury, but this type of injury is stubborn. Often, there's nothing that can be done, except what you're already doing, rest and massage."

"I'll start talking to spirits, okay?"

"No, don't."

"I will."

"You don't have to."

"I will."

"Junelle, how about this: if a spiritual entity starts talking to you, then talk back to it."

"I will." She shivers.

"Allow it to initiate the contact."

"I will."

"And please let me know if that should happen."

"I will. Did you know that when I close my real eyes I can see from my new eye?"

Junelle closes her eyes, turns sideways, and sees blurry outlines of Lisa and her computer. It grows sharper the longer she looks. She opens her eyes and faces Lisa.

"It's not perfect vision. It's getting better, though. It goes away when I open my real eyes. Do you think if I kept my real eyes shut more often—"

Lisa looks alarmed. "It would develop rapidly, Junelle. Don't do that."

Junelle shivers again.

"Okay, I won't. Do you think if they investigate this, blind people can get their sight back?"

"Junelle, we treat these wounds and the resulting growths as attacks. We document each case during corrective surgery. Growing a new eye and making all the right connections so vision can be restored in vision-impaired people is a possible spinoff. Give us time."

"I will."

"They tell me you're associating your neck wound with an old lady who attacks you in your dreams."

"I am."

"Can you describe these dreams?"

"Okay. At first I couldn't tell what was going on. The dreams were too vague. I was in a classroom somewhere far away, and there were other students there, too, but it was as if the other students were invisible, for the teacher didn't pay any attention to them. She was focused only on me.

"Eventually, things became clearer, and I could see what was going on. I was in an English class at a college far away. I'm older in these dreams, about eighteen. I heard a few groans the first day of class when the old lady walked in, and a few students got up and left. I thought they were leaving because they didn't want an old lady for a teacher, but I was wrong. They left because the old lady is evil."

"How does she conduct the class?"

"We have to write compositions. When I'm through with a composition, the old lady grabs it from me, reads it, and gets mad. Then she writes ugly personal comments about me in the margins of the paper before handing it back."

"What does she teach?"

"She teaches us her political viewpoints."

"Is that it?"

"Yes. She teaches nothing about literature or writing."

"How does she treat the other students?"

"The other students don't really exist for her, except as an audience for my ongoing humiliation. She constantly puts me down in front of them."

Lisa is entering things in her computer. "But it gets worse than that, doesn't it? Do you know her name?"

"Her name is Sienna Spalding. I found that out last night in my dream. It's in my log. I really destroyed her last night."

"What does she look like?"

"She's a small person. Everything about her is small, even her face. She wears drab clothing. She has old-fashioned eyeglasses. She has whitish-gray hair."

"Okay. What else?"

"In class, she baits me in front of the other students. She once asked me: 'Ms. Jamison, can you tell us what the word *acuminate* means as an adjective and a verb?'

"She knew I wouldn't respond. She knew I was a precise person and would prefer to look the word up in a dictionary rather than to rely on faulty memory or guesswork. Not responding made me look dumb to the class. That was the old lady's objective."

"What does she do to your neck?"

"In the dreams, she grips my neck and digs her fingers in as hard as she can. I can never defend myself. It's as if there are rules that forbid me from fighting back. She did it again last night before I had a chance to destroy her."

She hands Lisa her journal, and Lisa pages through it while Junelle continues.

"Last night, the dream moved to Dead Colt. It was a different type of dream. She was a bigger and tougher old lady. She didn't wear eyeglasses. She was keeping me as a pet or plaything. She would keep me nude or seminude most of the time and would put me on a leash and take me out for walks.

"She was planning to kill me last night, but Robin and Cedric helped me out. Robin and Cedric are my parents. Robin cut me lose with a kitchen knife, and Cedric slipped me his utility knife, which I used to finish off the old lady. You'll read about it in there. I also popped out one of her eyeballs. After that, she was in sharp decline. She was really wasted."

Lisa sits up sharply, her eyes riveted on Junelle's journal. "Junelle, I see here that you removed Sienna Spalding's genitals with a sharp cutting instrument."

"Yes, I did. That was toward the end of the dream. I used Cedric's utility knife. She wasn't able to defend herself, with most of her attention on her wounded eye. That's her big weakness—one eye popped out."

"Ah ..." Lisa marks the page in Junelle's journal, closes it, and sets it aside. "This is disturbing." She looks at her computer screen and clicks on something.

"What's disturbing?"

Lisa is typing, preoccupied, and does not answer.

"Junelle, I'll try to analyze your dreams for you."

"Okay."

Lisa stops typing and looks at Junelle. "To simplify, I'm going to refer to the old lady as an antagonist. I'll also call

her an animal. It'll help us both organize our thought processes better. Is that okay?"

Junelle laughs. "Okay."

"Junelle, the antagonist of your dreams resembles an
animal in that her behavior is instinctive. The animal has
done this before, so many times it's like a programmed
instruction. The animal's biochemistry is primed for this
type of behavior. The animal will not permit itself to fail,
for to fail is to die.

"The others in the classroom are forgotten. The focus
of the animal is solely on you. No one else in the classroom exists for her. The animal in charge is satisfied that
no one else present poses a threat to her established authority. She has seen something in you, Junelle, a talent
perhaps, or a characteristic such as honesty, beauty, or
charm that she doesn't possess and therefore resents.

"So, Junelle is the focus of an animal that is expert at
handing out justice—her own brand of justice. This will
necessarily involve the systematic humiliation and eventual destruction of Junelle.

"Junelle must be made to look dumb in front of the
class. Junelle must be made to look awkward. Junelle
must have trials that no one else faces, for she has alien-
ated the animal, and the animal is the ruling power in the
classroom.

"Who is important? This is uppermost in the mind of
the animal in charge. Is it she, or is it Junelle? In response
to the threat Junelle poses, the animal in charge places
everyone on notice that someone has run afoul of her
rules and is about to be destroyed.

"The dream shifts from the college classroom to Dead
Colt, and it becomes bigger than the old lady ever bargained

for. Here, Junelle enters combat. Here, Junelle is on a mission.

"We are dealing with darkness now. Something much darker than the old lady attacked you last night, Junelle. It used Sienna Spalding as its instrument. Now that your dream antagonist is dead, I think you will have to encounter that darkness on more direct terms. Do you know what this means?"

"No," Junelle says.

"Let me make it clear for you. I think you will begin to have memories of trips into other realms. We all take such trips, but we seldom remember them."

"Oh." Junelle shivers.

"Did you know this?" Lisa asks.

"Yes. The government has been telling us we take trips."

"Junelle, through analyzing trip memories, we are learning that consciousness is multidimensional. We are learning that we live in many different worlds at the same time, worlds that run parallel to our own. We believe that by giving you an eye—and it's their eye, remember, that you're seeing from—the enemy is trying to draw you into their world, and if they accomplish this, they will enslave you."

"Lisa, who is the enemy?"

"I don't know."

"You must know."

"I don't."

"I thought the government was good at fighting wars."

"We are."

"Then you must know who the enemy is."

"We don't."

"Do you want me to help fight?"

"Yes."

"I want to join the Army."

"I don't think that will be necessary."

"I want to join the Army."

"We want all citizens to be vigilant."

"I want to join the Army."

Lisa smiles, exasperated. "Okay, Junelle, I'll see what I can do."

"Thank you."

Lisa leaves the room.

Junelle leaps to Lisa's computer. Two documents are open. She clicks on one of them and sees U.S. ARMY INVESTIGATION in big bold letters. It contains information about herself and Sienna Spalding. The old lady lives in Chicago and is a college English teacher. Junelle clicks on the other document:

ANALYSIS OF TRIP MEMORY
By Lisa Stock

Sienna Spalding, based on class distinctions and jealousy, will try to harm Junelle's progress in life. Broadly speaking, Junelle is smart and honest; Sienna Spalding is neither.

In the dreams, Sienna Spalding attacks Junelle viciously, relentlessly. Junelle is not permitted to fight back. No laws protect her. If Junelle's third eye is not removed, Sienna Spalding's world is likely to become Junelle's reality.

In her most recent dream, Junelle reports that she used her father's cutting instrument to remove Sienna Spalding's genitals. She also reports she was on a mission to discover the old lady's weakness, which is to have one eye popped out.

Junelle does not yet realize that her most recent dream with Sienna Spalding was not a dream but a trip into a reality veiled from us.

Mutilation of eyes and genitals and a sense of being on a mission are significant foreshadowing events. Look for Junelle to report trip memories of combat or combat training. She may also begin to communicate with a mysterious presence.

Junelle hears someone in the hallway and rushes back to her chair.

Lisa and a man in an army uniform enter the room.

"Junelle, this is Captain Bull Gordon, U.S. Army."

He holds out his hand to Junelle.

She shakes his hand.

"Lisa tells me you want to join the Army."

"Yes, I do. I want to fight the enemy. And I want to be paid."

"I see. Lisa has told me you're going to have surgery today."

"That's right."

"When will you be able to start training?"

"I'll have to ask my doctor."

"Junelle, we start a new basic combat training class in two weeks. Can you be ready by then?"

"I'll be ready."

"All right." He looks at Lisa, winks, and leaves the room.

"Wait!"

He sticks his head back in the room.

"You know, I was just kidding."

"The Army doesn't kid, Junelle."

"I didn't think this would happen."

"It did happen. Two weeks from now, Junelle. Be here."

"Okay."

He leaves.

Lisa sits down at her computer.

"Junelle, after surgery, the eye will be gone, but you will have a phantom eye that looks onto another world slightly different from our own. There, the war is fought on more direct terms. Are you afraid?"

"I don't know. What am I supposed to do?"

"Do what we all must do. Live in a world of suffering and learn to become a soul."

"Lisa, I think I'm scared."

"You don't look scared."

"I am."

"Come on, we have to get you prepared for surgery."

"I want my log back."

"You'll get it back, sweetheart."

"I want to see my mother."

"We'll go see her now."

Labyrinth

Darkness enfolds Junelle, and she is aware of a presence. But there is more than one presence; many are present, but only one entity is significant. In this place, not all souls are equal; one soul blots out all the others. The entity is like an animal, constantly monitoring the environment she must rule.

A powerful perception erupts within Junelle: the entity is deathly afraid someone will discover its weakness. I know it is weak, Junelle thinks, but I must find out how and tell someone. But whom must I tell?

As Junelle snakes her way through the labyrinth of Dead Colt, an alien landscape plays before her eyes. Everything is either a tree or a shrub or a log cabin or a winding road. There is so much cover in the town: blankets of spruce and ferns, ornamental gardens of Eden everywhere.

But not everything lies in darkness in Dead Colt; there are areas of illumination: street corners bathed in the yellow haze of streetlights, yard lights casting purplish glows.

She maneuvers on foot, on hands and knees, on her belly. She snakes through a labyrinth of ferns, peeks out from the shadowy jungle, looks for the evil one.

She spies the old lady.

Sienna Spalding emerges from her log cabin and stands in the last of the long shadows cast by the run-wild evergreens. For several minutes, she sniffs the erratic currents of dusk, allowing the scents to pillow up in her mind. She smells things sweet, things tangy, things dark and dusky, things that hint at wonders, but she does not inwardly whoop for joy, as is her custom during these evening exercises. No, something is overpowering her mind, something even more wonderful than joy. Soon, there will be no shadows, just darkness, and then Sienna Spalding will kill Junelle.

Junelle is Sienna Spalding's brain-damaged apprentice. Technically, Junelle is not brain damaged, but the schoolmarm has always referred to the girl in that way.

And why not? Who in Dead Colt would object to Sienna Spalding claiming Junelle was brain damaged? Dead Colt is a place where you can do just about anything. Killing Junelle tonight will be no problem, but Sienna wants to make it look tidy, nevertheless.

Sienna has a habit of making things look tidy.

She thinks of the command she had just given Junelle, and the fiasco Junelle had made of it. It had driven Sienna from the house.

She stands near the ferns that border her lot and shakes her head with a great sense of despondency. The ferns reach their flamelike fingers for her thighs, and Sienna wishes with all her mind that the ferns would take her and whisk her into that land of ecstasy she has always dreamed of, but has never found. She continues to shake her head. No, it will never happen. Ecstasy such as she imagines is not for mortal woman; it awaits us in the next world, she thinks.

Damn it all to hell.

They had been in the living room, sitting on the sofa in their underwear, watching television. Sienna had said to Junelle, "Take your underwear off. I want to give you a bath."

Junelle had made it up from the sofa okay, and had gotten herself pointed toward the hallway leading to the bathroom okay, but that had been the extent of Junelle's competence.

Over and over, Junelle—the dumb, fucking girl—had bashed herself into the left jamb of the doorway leading into the hall.

Sienna, standing within licking distance of the shadowy ferns at the edge of her lot, can still hear the club-brained idiot bashing away in there.

Jesus Fucking Christ, will it never end?

Well, let's be reasonable about this, Sienna thinks. Junelle is severely brain damaged. What do you expect?

Fuck it.

In the past, she had thought about trading Junelle in for a newer model. But how? And where? She'd gone through so much to get the girl, how's she ...

Let's face it, dumb girls like Junelle are hard to find.

And killing Junelle ... A shudder works its way up her spine. There were rumors about cops you couldn't trust.

No, that can't be true. Not in Dead Colt. You had to have some-thing you could depend on. But, just in case, an idea had been dropping into her mind. Thinking of it now makes her whole body shiver, but not with fear. Sienna has been beaten up in the past, more than once. She'd reported it—had to, she was taken to the hospital.

I'm going to beat Junelle to death, she decides. To be rid of her. And lay it off on an assailant.

She hears an awful racket: Junelle in there, bashing away.

Her mind steps sideways from the commotion. She thinks of getting a new girl, but the little ape Junelle snaps back into her mind. I'll kill Junelle. That's the first step. A thrill sweeps through her, and she looks at the ferns. They are grabbing at her trousers. Then I'll get a new girl. All things to her who believeth.

Damn it! She is getting weary. She just wants to be rid of Junelle, and she wants a new girl. She doesn't care how it happens. She wanders back to her cabin. She sighs. She'll have to lead the dumb fucker into the bathroom for her bath. Afterward, a bowl of ice cream and a martini as reward—Sienna's reward; Junelle will get nothing. Then around midnight it will be time to take the dumb fucker for her evening walk. The idea flies sprightly through Sienna's mind. *Her evening walk.* Now where the fuck is that dumb girl's leash?

Sienna Spalding wonders if Junelle has finally acquired a brain. It's obvious that she knows something is up. Her behavior tonight is far different from previous outings.

The brain-damaged moron will tug on her leash as if trying to break away, and then she will stop and refuse to go any farther, as if she knew something nasty waited ahead.

But Sienna is having none of that. Whenever the fucking idiot tries to break away, or pauses along the footpath, Sienna whips her mercilessly with the razor-sharp tail of the leash.

"Fuck you, Junelle," Sienna hisses while whipping the girl. "Fuck you, Junelle." Sienna is pissed. Why is this fuckhead all of a sudden acquiring the ability to think, or intuit, or whatever the fuck she's doing?

"Yes, Junelle, you foolish girl with a daisy growing out of your brainstem, you know something is up and you're hesitant to walk. You want to run away or you want to collapse, but I won't let you, you simpleton. We have rules, Junelle. And one of the rules is, when I give you an order, *You obey!* If you fail to obey me, *You are dead meat!*"

She ties Junelle to a fence post in a patch of shadow on a deserted street and looks around. She is sure no one can see them. The log cabins on the street are sheltered by the thick foliage of the trees in their front yards. Yard lights are similarly sheltered, giving off their glows as if limp moons swathed in clouds. The streetlights at either end of the block will pose no problem. Their glows illuminate only the tight spheres of their respective intersections.

But even so, Sienna thinks, what would it matter if anyone saw this event? Things happen in Dead Colt. And people button their lips. If the police happened by, they would watch Junelle take her beating, and when it was over, they would masturbate over her corpse. Oh, and no doubt, if one of Dead Colt's female cops were to happen by, she would grind her genitals against the dumb fucker's dead face until she came at least twice. They were all ghouls on the police force. The town matrons would have it no other way.

But still, you hear rumors.

Sienna recalls the times she has been beaten up in Dead Colt. The cops and emergency medical responders had treated the beatings as sadomasochistic events. They had stood by and watched in pleasure as Sienna writhed—on the footpath, on the ambulance gurney, in the emergency room of the hospital. The attending physician had even asked her if she wanted treatment. *Yes, of course, you fucking idiot!* Sienna had screamed in his face. Sienna Spalding had done a dance for them, a dance of agony—and they had sucked pleasure from it.

Well, be that as it may ...

Sienna finally figures out why she hadn't beaten Junelle to death last night or the night before or any number of previous nights. She had lacked the energy. But tonight will be different. She grabs Junelle's leash and gives it a powerful tug to make sure it's securely tied to the fence. It is. Then she looks into the girl's eyes.

She can't really see Junelle's eyes. The little dummy's eyes are hidden in shadow, as is the rest of her face. Well, I already know what the fucking moron looks like, she thinks, so why get all sentimental at this point?

"Fuck you, Junelle," she says as she turns her back on the girl and walks down the footpath. "You've been a big fucking pain in the ass."

Sienna does some deep breathing and some stretching. Then she runs a little ways down the path. Yes, she needs some more energy, then she can beat Junelle to death.

She begins sneaking around, cutting through yards. Weeks ago, she secreted a blunt instrument in some bushes a block away. She'll get it, sneak back to Junelle, beat the dumb fucker to death, and then sneak away and hide the blunt instrument again.

Then she'll walk back and find Junelle dead. She'll say she'd been assaulted, fought off her attacker, gave chase, came back, and ...

Found Junelle dead.

It will be a nice and tidy ending.

With all this in mind, Sienna Spalding skips down the street.

A death of loneliness lies upon Junelle as she stares into the darkness. She tries to untie the leash from the fence post but can't loosen the knot. It's too tight. The old lady will be back soon. She must do something, but what? Her face comes unmasked, becomes a cauldron of burning hate. She shakes her head in fury, and her hair slithers like knives toward her eyes.

"What am I going to do?" she wails.

Junelle looks around and sees that she is on a winding, hilly road that serves several palatial log cabins. Maybe someone from one of the cabins will save her.

She hears a car's engine blow softly to life.

The car moves toward her, speeding up now.

She hears a thud and the screech of brakes. She sees a body roll off the hood of the car, hit the street with a thump, and lie still.

A pedestrian has been hit.

The driver, a woman, leaps from the car and kneels by the body. There isn't much light, but Junelle can see that the victim is a man. Blood sticks to the side of his head like plaster. He begins to writhe and moan.

The woman is stirring a stick into the bloody stuccowork at his temple. Her lips are parted. Her eyes shine with glee. A twist of the stick—and the man writhes faster, moans louder.

Inhuman wails sound through the night, and Junelle knows she is hearing the primordial sounds of Dead Colt.

The woman jumps back into her car and drives closer to Junelle.

Junelle struggles vainly against her leash, and then presses herself into darkness.

The car stops by Junelle and the woman steps out.

"There are powerful people, Junelle," the woman says. "You are on their list. Leave it be. Let nature take its course. There has to be a place like Dead Colt, where they can drink their fill of darkness and pretend they are bathed in light. They toss a garland of garlic around it to keep the vampires at bay."

She steps closer and attempts to allure Junelle with the cool intelligence of her eyes.

"Dead Colt is everywhere, Junelle. We are all a family of darkness."

She is breathing in Junelle's face.

"Become one of us, Junelle."

She takes Junelle by the shoulders, pulls her from the darkness. She cocks her head, listens. Her eyes glare, malice flows, as if she is hearing something in the night, then she looks back at Junelle, and her eyes become functional.

"I will," Junelle says. "I will become one of you." She manages to inject soft pride into her voice.

"It's like stripes on a tiger, spots on a leopard, isn't it, Junelle?"

Junelle smiles. "Yes."

"What can we do for you, Junelle?"

"You can do nothing for me." Junelle will not change her stripes or spots.

"Good." The woman bites Junelle on the neck.

A secret passes between them.

The woman, Owl, takes a knife out, flicks the blade open, and cuts the leash, freeing Junelle. She steps back, closes the knife, and gives it to Junelle.

Owl drives away.

Junelle races through the night, the smell of conifers in her nostrils. She loves it. The dark running. The smell of everything. She is alive, and she is playing a dangerous game.

She grips the knife tightly in her fist.

She is going to fight back tonight. She imagines what the old lady will look like when she is through with her, and what the police will make of it.

Sienna came home a little woozy from an encounter with a glandular giant in one of Dead Colt's night spots, slipped and fell face-first onto a sharp corner in her own home, impaled herself.

The police will love it. They will suck pleasure from it.

Junelle is on her belly, squeezing through ferns.

She pokes her head out. Light from a lamppost has frozen the old lady in its glare. Before destroying her, Junelle wants to learn all she can about her, so she looks deep into the old one's soul.

Sienna Spalding seizes the club in the bushes. With a club in her hand, the universe opens up new paths for her. Things go her way. It leads to ecstatic encounters. It is happening again.

Unexpectedly, Sienna faces a barrage of strange things flying in from the night. The fragmented bits and pieces of her soul are zooming in from somewhere in the universe, and she is laid bare, pierced by the shards of her own strange being. She is staring into the face of her soul.

Her hands are sweating. Her palms feel stained. Her face twitches as if she has lost all control. She feels naked before the onslaught.

She knows her life has been one of total, unremitting fear and loss.

The wretched things that fly through the night point at Sienna and say, "Sienna, you have always been a weakling."

Sienna sighs and says, "Yes, that is true."

She knows that fear has ruled her life. She knows she has constructed an elaborate bulwark against a frightening world.

Sienna counts her excuses—impaired parents, impaired society—but nothing stands up. Weakness is her own.

She commiserates with herself, but the wretched things still fly through the night, and they hit Sienna, and Sienna does not want to do anything to anyone anymore.

She stands in the fierce winds of her soul, and the winds tear at her, and the winds die, and Sienna Spalding loses herself for a few moments longer before she realizes her soul has become quiet.

No, she does not want to do anything to anyone anymore.

She looks for Junelle.

She sees the shadowy form of her brain-damaged apprentice hiding in the ferns and realizes Junelle has been forcing her to take a look at her soul.

Enraged, she renews her vow to kill Junelle.

Sienna hears the sound of her own running feet, dashing after Junelle. She's forgotten the club. *Fuck it!* She forces one of her sweaty, stained hands into the leather tool bag on her belt. The instrument of torture is still there, sheltered within.

In a bedlam of huffing and puffing, Sienna Spalding tears around the corner of a house, searching for Junelle, screaming in rage.

Her cheeks and jowls look like torn bat wings, beating the air in nightmare rhythms. Her eyes look like crazed spiders.

She sees something in the darkness, attacks it, and discovers it's Junelle.

She grips Junelle's neck with sharp fingers and wrenches it.

Junelle tears away from her and runs into the ferns and hides.

Sienna searches the darkness for Junelle.

Someone watching from the shadows measures the distance, reaches a hand out, and strikes a finger into Sienna Spalding's left eye.

The night becomes a sea of blood.

And screaming becomes its sound.

Sienna no longer has an eye in her left eye socket. It is

empty. But it is not empty. It is red and glistening and pooled with blood.

The darkness sizzles with tendrils of silvery light as cabin lights go on. Red seeps from between the old lady's fingers as she tries to stem the flow of blood. She dances around, her screaming a crescendo of terror.

Sienna Spalding's hands thus occupied, her attacker grabs her by her ankles and upends her.

Her attacker methodically removes Sienna's shoes and socks, pulls the razor-sharp cutters from Sienna's tool bag, and snips off two of Sienna's toes—the smallest one on each foot.

"Run, Sienna, run!" her tormenter shouts, and picks the old lady up and shoves her along.

At first, Sienna's feet run like normal. Then they slow and toddle, as if on a bed of red-hot coals.

Her tormenter upends her again.

"My, my, that was mischievous of me, leaving you unkempt like that. Here, let me prune those toes a mite more."

All the while, Sienna's hands stay glued to her eye socket and the mess inside it. All the while, Sienna's vocal cords split the night with one bloodcurdling scream after another.

Snip, snip.

Sienna goes sailing on her feet again, runs into those red-hot coals again, and falls. If she had bothered to look at her feet, she would have seen one, two, three toes on each foot, the other two attenuated to bloody stubs.

But Sienna is too busy making ungodly babbling sounds to take a peek.

Her tormentor grabs Sienna by the feet again. Sienna lashes out with a foot, striking a molesting hand.

Her attacker grabs her by the throat, picks her up, and slams her against the sturdy wooden post that holds the yard light. Her attacker holds Sienna's hands out of the way and goes to work.

"You fucking whore!" Her attacker cuts an inverted V in Sienna's upper lip, just under her nose. "You mother-fucker!"

Her tormentor releases her. Sienna goes staggering, her hands to her upper lip, her screams now thinning into barren wails.

Her tormentor upends Sienna again. *Snip, snip, snip. Snip, snip, snip.*

Her tormentor stands Sienna upright and encourages her to walk. "You can do it, you can do it."

Sienna's vocalizations become ghostlike quacking, like that of a duck with a split bill. She stumbles, she falls. One hand stays on her face, the other searches for her feet.

Her tormentor rips Sienna's pants and underpants off, rips her shirt off.

Sienna lies naked. Her tormentor props her on her hands and knees.

Sienna's hands try to fight off the molesting cutters, and she tries to crawl away—so it takes a while.

When it is done, Sienna's genitals—and several of her fingers—lie in the yard.

Her tormentor dresses Sienna in her undershorts and stands her up. Sienna stands mute, her ragged hands at her sides, her remaining eye spinning away.

A voice carries through the night. A functional voice.

"Die, bitch!"

Sienna wobbles. Her tormentor yanks Sienna's under-shorts down.

Sounds circle in the shadows. Applause.

A voice cries out.

"Unique! Positively unique!"

Sienna is still wobbling, doing something magical it seems to stay on her feet. And then she topples over in the yard.

Junelle is struck as if by lightning from a cold, deep sea. A chilling, alien creepiness sweeps through her, accompanied by jolts of mind-searing weirdness. She had seen it all, and now, amongst the shadowy ferns, she searches the space around her.

It was Cedric, the man the vehicle struck, the man the Owl stirred. Oddly chaotic, oddly heroic, Cedric had done the old lady.

He saved Junelle from the old one. And now Junelle lies wounded in the bushes, having flung herself to safety, her neck a flaming altar—the old bitch had dug her fingers in before Cedric got to her.

She smiles to herself. In all honesty, her pain is not that bad. And the bitch will never fuck with her again.

The Gingerbread Lodge

Wade Vincentio is perched on a flat boulder five meters from the edge of the rocky shelf, not an exceptional drop-off, two back flips for five-year-old Wade before reaching bottom and crushing his skull, if he goes for it. And Wade is nervous. Wade keeping his kid's binoculars pinned to his eyeballs, his body like a drop of dew suspended on a long blade of grass. And grass does frisk around here on the rocky terrain, in debris-laden crevices where tigers might hide. Wade looking like he might want to run, might have to run, his body leaning so.

A scarce moment later, the sun yawns wide and a chill creeps through the air and Wade's father, Ben Vincentio, seeing Wade leaning but standing too far from him to do any immediate good, calls to him.

But as if terrorized by the air that now reels in the sudden bright mist, the cry strangles in Ben's throat.

"What's that strange sound you made, Daddy?" Wendy Vincentio asks. Wendy is eleven. She's a budding rock climber, restricted to bouldering, a mild form of the sport. Right now she's climbing a boulder that takes up most of the rocky shelf the Vincentios are camped on. She's a meter or so up and climbing horizontally. Wendy is afraid of very little. Bugs. She hates bugs. Crawling bugs. Flying bugs. They give her the willies.

"Grab him, Marie, if he tries to make a run for ..." For what? Ben thinks, having found his voice but now losing his mind as the sun continues to burst across the rocks, throwing up little yellow devils that lick the air.

Marie, Ben's wife, is sitting beside Wade on the flat rock. Her bare legs and khaki shorts catch his attention. She smiles at Ben, looks at Wade, puts an arm around Wade, and scoots closer to him. Was Wade going to give up the boulder and jettison himself into space? It looked like it, but now Wade looks settled, with his mother, her baseball cap shielding her face, cozying up to him.

So Ben relaxes. He has a cool wife. He gazes at the distant cliffs where Wade has his binoculars trained. They are monsters, hundreds of meters high.

His daughter is cool, too, Ben thinks as he continues to gaze at the distant granite cliffs. In fact, Wendy's nickname is *Cool Chick*. Such notoriety for an eleven-year-old.

Cool she is, that Wendy.

The Vincentios are in the Sierra Nevada Mountains, on vacation, hundreds of miles north of their home in La Jolla, California.

Ben gazes at the face of the sheer rock, and then sweeps his eyes higher and scans the ridge, which is topped with snatches of green jungle. Did Wade catch a glimpse of a mountain lion up there, its tawny body oozing around? It will do no good to ask: Wade is a secretive little boy. Wade and his animals, all secretive. Wade in a previous life was probably a saber-toothed cat.

Big Snow is the name given to the area encompassed by that high ridge. Earlier this morning, the sun rising cool to the touch, the world an arsenal of shadows, a man who calls himself a geek rode in on a huge Honda motorcycle. It was his first time on a motorcycle. It felt like a kitten beneath him.

As the geek hid the Honda in a maze of sagebrush, the sun sent a warming touch, and several hundred meters of sheer rocky wall sprang to life. Birds called and soared against the impassive granite face. The geek's ears, the lone set of human ears on the clifftop, bent to catch the sharp, trilling oaths that capered about. It was the first time the geek had alerted himself to a bird's call, or to any sound of nature.

He watched the sky unfold. Never before had he watched the sky unfold. He saw eruptions of various colors at odd, pulsing altitudes, and deep pools of indigo retreating. It was a strange sky, like a birthday party of pink, white, and blue cupcakes.

He walked about, doing a reconnaissance. Scattered growth lay along the long, twisting ridge. Chalky, rugged country stretched out of sight. Green, tender land lay far below.

As the sky sharpened, words and images flared in his mind, tipped with tiny flames, and in panic he drew his knife. A voice inside his head talked of mechanical failure, of fate.

The space shuttle Challenger had a defective seal at liftoff. It sealed the fate of everyone aboard.

He hid in the sagebrush and heard the flame-tipped words again.

They couldn't set the rocket down. Everyone on board was doomed at the moment the puff of smoke issued from the defective seal.

There was silence for several minutes, and his fear faded. He was safe.

He hated the fire-tinged, cryptic thoughts that came to him. Hated them, feared them. They were alien thoughts.

He remembered seeing replays of Challenger's liftoff on television, the puff of smoke from the defective seal, the stir of memories this brought.

Upon further contemplation, he believed the thoughts were not alien thoughts but his own, that he was being driven insane.

To preserve his sanity, he had to focus on his mission.

A family would be arriving at Big Snow soon.

A man, a woman, a boy, a girl.

The geek was going to cut the man's genitals off. He was going to toss the man, the woman, and the boy over the cliff.

He was going to preserve the girl known as Cool Chick. He was going to keep her alive, carry her off, and play with her at his leisure.

Thoughts of Challenger returned, the inevitability of death, of events foretold.

These thoughts so alien and yet his own. Who was this bearer of thoughts, creeping closer to him, spearing him with flames?

Though fearful, he was amazed at the rush these thoughts

brought him. And he wanted to reach out and touch them.

A negligible chill sneaks through the air, not even enough to raise gooseflesh, but Wendy Vincentio, aka Cool Chick, is a child crazy for the heat of the gods, and she is shivering.

"It is many things, Daddy. The Supreme Being, a world at war, a nuclear holocaust. It's the sole survivor at the center of the solar system."

She is romping with grandiose language.

Ben wanders back to the boulder she clings to.

"It's the sun, Wendy."

"Wait, I'm not done."

"It'll warm up, Wendy. Before long you'll feel like toast."

"From the blazing reaches of space, from the mysterious depths of the universe, what is this thing that shines on the faces of the towering rocks that nature has put all around us?"

"Gee, I don't know, Wendy. What could it be?"

She looks down at him and wrinkles her brow. *Don't be such a wiseass,* she mouths. She gazes about with reverence in her eyes. "Nature has put on such an odd face today. It looks like we are in a strange cathedral, with sunlight falling up from the earth, and shadows descending like ethereal plums from the heavens."

She glances down at her father, her face imbued with youthful vigor and innocence. "Now I'm done, Dad. And you're right, it was the sun. Now this is important. What is the worst type of liar you have ever known?"

One meter off the ground, the sleek, bare-legged form of Wendy Vincentio skitters across the face of the boulder, moving faster than the eye can track.

Too young, too soon, Ben thinks as he walks in the wake of her scurrying shadow. Wendy, his inexplicable daughter, in a mad horizontal assault on the rock.

As if realizing she is going too fast, Wendy stops, shivers, and clings to the boulder like a small child, giving out a witchy sound, a yelp that answers itself on a wild journey through the rocky corridors. In the hollow trough of her call, she begins searching out handholds and footholds like the novice she is.

"Run into dicey terrain, did you?" Ben asks.

"Well, you know, it's a craggy face," she says.

Watching her, Ben feels better. She is still his little baby. Yet how could she have moved so fast?

There was a similar incident at home, precipitating the Vincentio's vacation in the Sierras. Wendy had climbed straight up the side of the house, darted right up like a force of nature, reaching a dangerous height.

Ben's mind is still a thousand miles in the air contemplating it. He and Marie decided they would take Wendy to a place where she could do some safe bouldering.

Ben's cronies often say *he* is a force of nature, something like the wind: strong, prevailing, mythical and mysterious, sometimes not even there.

Not even there. Not officially. Not in the maze of science, academe, government, and industry that he inhabits.

Ben is a bootlegger.

You're a swashbuckler, Daddy, Wendy had told him upon hearing him explain what he did for a living.

Yes, I guess I am, he had thought, seeing himself reflected in the glow of Wendy's incredible brown eyes.

Weeks later, Wendy wrote a theme on Ben's occupation for her English class. She received an *A,* and afterward presented the paper to him at dinner, composed in her immaculate scrawl:

My father is a guiding light for the bootlegger fraternity, those creative souls who, while toiling under sometimes severe, unimaginative corporate management, nevertheless manage to spring astonishing new products and processes upon the world, often swiping company time and resources to bring about these miracles. They are strictly unauthorized, hence the name bootlegger.

"The worst type of liar, Wendy? That's a tough one."

"Think," she says, and angles her face upward, as if contemplating climbing higher.

Ben glances at Marie and Wade. They are still sitting on the flat rock several meters away, Marie's arm still around the little guy. Marie is keeping an eye on Wendy. Wade is still peering through his binoculars, scanning the lush growth in the meadows that lie below, and the immense marbled gray cliffs in the distance. He looks intense, like the skipper of a ship searching for hazards to navigation.

Wade had wanted to search for mountain lions that morning, and Wendy had wanted to go rock climbing. Ben, consulting with Marie and drawing upon the Wisdom of Solomon, had allowed Wendy to prevail: her rock climbing would come first, Wade's lion safari second. Wade had not put up a battle. He was a wise little rascal. He knew Wendy wouldn't stay on a boulder too long and that his search for mountain lions would consume the rest of the day. So he had held his peace. Ben had counted on that, and the little guy hadn't disappointed him.

"Come on, Dad, the worst type of liar, give it a try."

He watches her. She's obeying the rules now, reaching for a new handhold or foothold only if her other three points of contact are secure. She isn't hugging the rock; she's keeping her body slung away from it. She inspects her pathway and takes her time. She's showing her skills.

"The worst type of liar, Wendy? Someone who tells lies that get people killed."

She looks down at him and nods. "Step back, Dad. I'm coming down."

Ben steps away and Wendy eases down from the rock.

The geek still lies in the sagebrush, all two thousand pounds of him, his knife back in its scabbard, his brain, feeling its emptiness, beginning to entertain thoughts. His own thoughts, the bearer of fire now gone from his mind.

Two thousand pounds. He still can't believe it. A year ago in the mailroom of the chemical plant where he works, he locked the doors after hours, stripped naked, and stood on the freight scale.

Two thousand pounds. Jesus Motherfucking Christ. I am a fucking geek.

It was unreal.

Yet, he had thought, *I don't feel heavy.* Well, his gut, maybe. Yeah, he had to admit, his gut was like a whale that had hitched a ride. But it was a solid gut. He couldn't push it in when he tensed his abdominal muscles.

That's because the fat is inside your abdominal wall, smothering your internal organs, you fuckhead. That's what the doctor had told him days later. The doctor hadn't said *fuckhead,* but his tone had implied as much.

The doctor told him to lose weight or die. He recommended a high-protein, low-carbohydrate diet, strength training, and cardio exercise.

Under careful supervision, the geek began following his doctor's advice.

Now, a year later, lolling in the pungent atmosphere of the sagebrush near the canyon rim, he still weighs two thousand pounds, but the whale is noticeably smaller, and he feels light on his feet.

He is a large boy. He figures it will take him ten years of dieting, strength training, and cardio exercise to get down to fifteen hundred pounds or so, and then he'll be trim.

Jesus Motherfucking Christ. I am a fucking geek.

He wants a cigarette, candy, and soda. But he holds his discipline. He brought a cooler. He'll treat himself on the way back to the lodge. No one must know he was here at Big Snow. He can't leave any candy wrappers, soda cans, or cigarette butts lying around. The Honda? He glances toward it but can't see it through the wall of brush. He'll leave it here. He'll have other transportation out of here. The Vincentio's Range Rover.

Yes, he is a large boy, and laughing now at his stupid brain, worried about leaving candy wrappers, soda cans, and cigarette butts at Big Snow, but unconcerned about that fat Honda lying in the brush. Fifty years old this year. Newly married this year. For the third time. His wife and daughter back at the Gingerbread Lodge.

Wife and daughter. He laughs louder. He had coaxed wife number two to come along, and she had brought their daughter, at his insistence. His current wife is back in L.A. She couldn't get away on such short notice. He hates to be alone, even for a few moments. He has to have someone within his grasp at all times, or he feels the pangs of a misery that few people know.

He stares at the land through fissures in the brush. The chalky topography dips out of sight and then rises in the distance like a sea gone huge.

Where the fuck are they? The guy, the wife, the brats? They'll be here, he thinks. They had looked delirious back at the lodge when the old cocksucker had shown them the map of Big Snow and had told them about the mountain lions.

They'll be here.

He sees a dust trail.

He feels a twinge of nervousness. It's that old familiar ghost creeping upon him, anticipating events to come. He has never read a book, not once in his life, not even in school when he was supposed to read books. But he does come across wisdom now and then, and steals it. With that ghost upon him, shivering him, he figures it's time to recite some of that wisdom. He pulls out his wallet, takes a heavily creased piece of paper from it, and reads:

The key to overcoming nervousness is to set in motion something outrageously stupid and dangerous. Sooner or later you'll be overwhelmed by your own stupidity, and you'll be too numb to feel anything.

He reads it twice. It never fails to amuse him. It never fails to calm him.

He puts the paper back in his wallet and peers through the brush. The dust trail winds closer. He hears the rumble of a vehicle.

The ghost squeezes his innards.

And the bearer of thoughts creeps closer, unwinding a tongue of flames that licks the outer reaches of his mind.

Wendy looks toward the distant cliffs, shading her eyes with her hands.

"Wade's been watching something," she says to Ben.

"I know," Ben says. Wade is in sober contemplation, his eyes invisible behind the twin orbs of the binoculars.

"He's been watching that ridge," Wendy says, and points.

Ben follows his daughter's pointing finger to a high rim on the far side of the valley. Verdant growth tops the granite wall in places. A hawk or something, almost invisible in the distance, sails in an updraft against the striations of the rocky face.

The hawk drops, and Ben's stomach drops with it.

"Dad!" Wade cries.

"I'll tell you who the worst liar is," Wendy says, a quiver in her voice. "Remember the old man back at the lodge?"

Ben feels weakness all over. Ice touches his flesh. He thinks of running to Wade and grabbing the binoculars, but the show is happening, and he doesn't want to miss anything, however uncertain his view.

He stares at the cliff, watches the spidery objects fall one by one, vaguely aware of Wendy standing beside him. For one feeble instant, he thinks the massive rock shrine is playing host to skydivers. But their chutes would have to be opening pretty darn fast. And nothing is billowing.

Transitory madness seizes him. He wants to get his hands on whoever is responsible for Wade's suffering. He thinks he's going to have a traumatized son.

No, there must be some other explanation. Wade will be all right.

The cliff across the way is blank now. No more tiny spiders zipping down invisible threads. Ben walks to Wade, his body like a cutlass slicing air.

Wade is still looking through the binoculars. Marie seems oblivious to what has taken place. She is the patient wife, waiting on her brood.

"Can I see them, big guy?" Ben asks his son.

A wee voice comes from Wade, so subdued it's hardly a voice at all. "Uh, okay." He slowly removes the binoculars from his eyes and hands them over.

Reaching for the binoculars, Ben studies Wade's face. A little pale. A little unfocused. Maybe it's the chill in the air. Otherwise, he looks okay.

Ben straightens up.

Wade is not okay. There is no chill in the air. It's a balmy day, the sun a tingle upon the skin. He tousles his son's hair and walks back to Wendy, putting the small binoculars to his eyes.

Ben scans the long face of the rock. No movement on top of the ridge. The foot of the cliff is screened by vegetation. The grooves in the far rock stand out in sharp relief. Whatever happened, Wade got an eyeful.

"What did you see, Wade?" Wendy asks.

There is no response from Wade.

"Dad," Wendy whispers. "The liar back at the lodge ..."

"Yes?"

"I think that was supposed to be us over there."

The boy of ten lies hidden in sagebrush, his mind spinning off into madness. His little brother is gone. His older brother is gone. His sister, just a baby, is gone. His mother, screaming hysterically, trying to save them, is gone. His father, something dawning on his face just before all hell broke loose, is gone.

In that moment, his father had roared a single command: *Run!* And the boy of ten had run, as the giant was cutting his father's genitals off, right in front of everyone. He had run and hid in the sagebrush.

His mother had fought like a tiger, but to no avail. His younger brother, his older brother, his baby sister, his mother—each had been a rodeo event that he had heard from the sagebrush, his face buried in scented leaves. Each had resorted to what dumb animals do in the face of danger. He had counted each capture, each scream trailing off. His mother had been hysterical, screaming all the while, a melody of terror. Each child a quiet symphony, whimpering, and then exploding into wails at the moment they were tossed. His father had been silent throughout, except for that one command: *Run!*

He knows the giant will get him. The giant is rooting around in the sagebrush now, looking for him, calling him a stray.

He wishes he had a rifle. He would shoot the giant in the head, kill him. But he knows that wishing doesn't count anymore. Maybe his father had also known that wishing didn't count anymore.

The giant is coming closer. The boy is paralyzed with fear. The fear on his mother's face, he decides, will be the last thing he thinks of when the giant gets him. That and his father's silence.

Moments later, he feels rough hands grab him and lift him from the sagebrush, and the scented leaves are gone from his face, and he knows the stray has been rounded up.

And when he is tossed off the cliff, he barely feels the wind beneath him, so grateful he is to be finally gone.

Ben continues to scrutinize the granite monolith. The scarred face of the rock is showing itself, nothing more, no movement on top of the ridge, no more bodies being cast into oblivion.

The heat and electricity inside him fuse and become one thought: Wendy is right. It was supposed to be us over there.

He feels a monstrous presence in the world.

He removes the binoculars from his eyes.

"Dad?"

It's Wendy. He turns toward her voice. She's peeking out from behind the giant boulder she had been climbing. Marie and Wade are with her.

Ben rushes to them.

"Dad, I told Mom about the bodies falling from the cliff," Wendy says. "Right now the introductions are being made in Heaven, don't you think? I mean, they couldn't have survived, could they?"

Ben puts a finger to his lips, hushing Wendy. He glances at Wade. He's as white as a ghost.

"Ben ..." Marie puts her arms around Wendy and Wade and looks at him calmly. "Are you sure they're dead? Maybe they were making a movie. Don't you think they might have been making a movie?" Hope flickers in her eyes.

"No, Mom." It's Wade. His voice is flat and absent, hardly a voice at all, pretty much the normal voice of Wade. His head is bent over a map of Big Snow that he pulled from his pocket. "The people were hitting eagles' nests on the way down. They can't do that."

"Eagles' nests?" Wendy says. "Ouch, those sharp ledges must have hurt." She shivers. "Wade is right. Hollywood can't destroy wildlife during the filming of a movie."

"Ben," Marie says, "why are we hiding?"

"Marie, in all likelihood, those people were thrown from the cliff. They didn't fall by accident. They were murdered. If Wendy hadn't done her rock climbing first, we'd have been up there this morning looking for mountain lions. If the ones responsible for this learn of their mistake, we'll be in danger."

"Mom, don't you remember the old man at the lodge?" Wendy says. "He said Big Snow was prime mountain lion habitat. He showed us that map, the one Wade has. And that other family kept moseying up, much to Wade's consternation."

"I remember, Wendy," Marie says.

"The old man was directing his words at us and was flustered that this other family had shown up. He made sure Wade got the map, but that other father swiped it and copied it in the lodge's office. Didn't he, Wade?"

Wade nods, still studying the map.

"I knew the old man was a liar," Wendy says. "I just didn't know what he was lying about."

"Someone drew the map up for us," Ben says. "Someone who knew Wade's affinity for mountain lions. Someone was waiting for us over there."

Ben puts a finger to his lips, hushing everyone. He has to think. But thinking only magnifies his fear. His body begins distilling it, squeezing it out of him until a fine mist beads his skin.

And then a strange sensation envelops him, a new resolve. And he knows what they must do.

The Vincentios stand in silence. Ben holds Wendy close. He doesn't want her wandering.

He glances at Wade. The map has lost its allure for him. He takes it from him, folds it, and puts it in his own pocket.

He sees Marie staring at him, fear seizing her face.

"What are we going to do, Ben?"

"For one thing, we need to stay out of sight. We also need to get counseling for Wade."

They break camp. Ben picks up Wade and they begin the journey to their vehicle, stepping down from the rocky terrace and hiking through a forest of black oak and conifers.

They open the doors of their Range Rover, sit inside, and eat picnic lunches as Ben studies Wade's map of Big Snow, the instrument that was supposed to lead them to their deaths.

He fires up the Range Rover and drives along an old logging road that will take them back to the lodge.

"Dad." A small voice.

Ben stops the Range Rover.

They all look at Wade.

His eyes are unfocused, his face touched by fear. When he speaks, the words barely escape him.

"I saw a giant on top of the cliff. I saw him throw those people off."

Ben parks the Range Rover in a knot of pines and tells his family to stay put as he scouts ahead. Walking through the woods, he comes upon a sight that chills him to his bones. He sees the Gingerbread Lodge, its wooden beams and rough masonry, its walls, roofs, turrets, and gabled windows from a fairy tale, the dark and clinging primeval forest that surrounds it.

He walks onto the veranda and peers through the lodge's front windows. Through open slatted blinds, he sees the vast lobby. People are forming up, apparently waiting for the dining room to open.

He walks inside. The dining room is to the right, cordoned off by velvet ropes. The registration desk is straight ahead. The suites are to the left. Something spicy hangs in the air— the smell of gingerbread cookies fresh from the oven.

He sees Marie. She's wearing white shorts and a blue blouse, not the khaki outfit she wore at the boulders. Her baseball cap is in place, ponytail sticking out. Wendy and Wade are with her. Arm in arm with Marie is a man who looks like Ben Vincentio.

The Range Rover is still camped in a knot of pines.

Wendy exits the vehicle, ducking a frosty-green bough that comes swinging for her head.

"Where are you going, Wendy?" her mother asks.

"Oh, just out. I need a good run."

"Well, be sure to stretch beforehand. You don't want any injuries. And don't go too far."

"Of course, Mother."

Wendy looks around. The pines are nymphs of unbelievable beauty. Their delicate needles are like millions of tiny stairways to Heaven.

She runs into the forest.

The Range Rover is out of sight, lost in its jailhouse covering of pines. Wendy climbs a tree and rests on a high branch.

She sees it—the animal that had been watching them at the boulders. Now it's stalking them in the forest. She tries to quiet her heartbeat as it passes beneath her. Its footsteps are preternaturally quiet, its scent wild and overpowering, its imprint on the air as cold as the Devil's. She'd felt its coolness at the boulders, felt it pacing them through the forest all those long miles.

It's lurking near the thick growth that surrounds the Range Rover. She doesn't think it poses any immediate threat. Its interest in the Vincentios, though, is undeniable.

The animal slips out of sight.

Wendy bounds from the tree and races back to the Range Rover. She slices through the pine boughs, opens her door, and slips inside.

Wade is out of the Range Rover, having gotten permission from his mother to take a pee. He has done so, marking a boundary with his scent. Next, he is drawn by sweet music of the air. Or maybe it's a bunch of untuned harps.

He finds a bird's nest in a tree and plays with the hatchlings, pulling their yawning beaks apart and squeezing the small creatures to death. The harps fall silent one by one. He holds a dead hatchling in his hand, studies the bulbous head and soft, runny body. He raises it to his mouth.

He sets the limp body back in the nest without having taken a bite. He isn't hungry after all, but he'd felt a need, something pulling him at a deep instinctive level.

He slinks down the tree and walks to the Range Rover, embroiled in dark thoughts. Wendy had better not kiss him again. She has done that before and he hates it. Better to die.

Then he wishes he had bit the little bird's head off and kept it in his mouth. And when his warped sister tries to smooch him again, she'll find a bird's head going into her mouth. Then she'll know what it's like for Wade to receive one of her kisses.

Wade, at a deep instinctive level, knows this would effectively end Wendy's kissing career, at least with him. She would tell on him, though, so he does not go back to the dead birds' nest. Wendy is a brat and can do anything.

The Occultist sits alone in the dining room of the Gingerbread Lodge, lamenting the passage of an era.

There was a time when a person was a person, discrete to the core, wrapped in the unyielding framework of a life. A man was a man. He lived and he died. A woman was a woman. She lived and she died. But no longer. Now everything is uncertain. Now an individual is a mystery, a multitude, a blur.

A bowl of purple grapes sits before the Occultist on the white tablecloth. He plucks a solitary grape. He eats the grape gently, softly, and gently, softly thinks about what he is doing—eating the grape. A simple act. Its meaning clear.

He swallows the grape and it continues its journey inside him. The grape is food, but eventually becomes something else, and serves other purposes. But for now it gives the Occultist a bit of taste, a bit of energy.

The Occultist wants death to be death, life to be life, men to be men, women to be women. He wants the world to be the world. A grape to be a grape. But now there is uncertainty.

The Occultist plucks the grape of uncertainty and chews on it.

The gods provide us with a framework, and within this framework you have life, you have death. You have this already-slain dragon, this planet earth, which births you and kills you. In between, you tear round and round, and the gods piss on you. In between, your mind reels, and you beseech the gods, and the gods piss on you again.

The Occultist is aware of giants, of other strange beings, of worlds touching. How and why? That is the question.

The Occultist eats another purple grape.

When contemplating the most glorious color in all creation, the Occultist feels more dead than alive. And dead is good. For when merciful Heaven frees him from this slain dragon that is earth, he flies with the wind and becomes the night sky, the twilight sky, the sky at dusk or dawn, the sky before a storm, when daylight darkens to pitiless gloom. To the Occultist, the sky is the grandest color of all.

Purple is an ancillary color. To the Occultist, purple is a color that looks painted on. When the Occultist sees purple, he sees a wound. He sees a playful God delivering hurt to the world. He sees a worrisome dance of creation and destruction.

He eats another purple grape.

The Occultist gets up and walks around. In the dining room, and throughout the lodge, they are used to him wandering. They think he's important. When he leaves a meal behind, they leave it alone. It'll be waiting for him when he returns, possibly warmed-over by a friendly waitress.

He is not walking because he needs to think and thinks better on his feet. If that were the case, he'd be walking all the time, scaring the daylights out of people. An Occultist on the move is dangerous, a force to be reckoned with, especially a purple Occultist.

Something is happening at the lodge, and the Occultist wants to step into the midst of it.

He walks into the lobby and sees Henry Falcon, a man who calls himself a geek. Henry believes he's a geek because he has passed a certain inconceivable boundary.

Bro, I weigh two thousand pounds, Henry has told the Occultist. Henry calls men *bro.* Not everyone. Just those he considers inferior.

Henry Falcon lives in Los Angeles and works as a manager at a chemical plant. Henry as a kid cut up dolls and put pets in frightening situations, tying them up or throwing them onto the roofs of houses.

The Occultist walks up to Henry, who is standing with his second wife and his daughter by that wife. The daughter is twelve, but looks like a woman. Both women are huge and wear colorful, flowing dresses that look like nomad tents in the Sahara Desert. The mother's name is Diana. The daughter's name is Alice.

"Faint heart never won fair lady," the Occultist says, staring into Henry's big, meaty face. Henry chuckles. Henry likes wisdom. "See those two?" The Occultist points at Diana and Alice. "Skunk heart won them." Henry chuckles even more. "The ton sisters. Bertha and Diesel."

Henry doubles over in hysterics, or tries to. His stomach is huge, and he can't quite do it. But he laughs loudly and shakes like a circus tent in the wind.

The four of them walk toward the dining room.

"Have you been porking little Diesel?" the Occultist asks Henry.

"Bro ..." Henry laughs with a high squeaky sound that carries throughout the lobby, his face crimson with mirth.

The Occultist, walking with Henry's entourage toward the dining room, thinks again of the color purple.

Ben's shock intensifies as he watches the *subs,* a term his numbed mind has conjured. Shades of me, shades of my family, he thinks. The implications strike him like lightning from a cold sea.

A storybook family.

They do not seem to notice him. To them, he is probably just another face in the crowd, not worth paying attention to.

Two fat women walk out of the passageway from the suites, sweep past Ben, and send the air swirling. He holds his breath as their perfume launches an assault.

He lets out his breath and looks around. The Vincentio subs are gathering in the center of the lobby, closing up ranks.

He sees a purple man enter the lobby from the dining room. The purple man is wearing gray slacks, a blue shirt, and black shoes. He is loose-limbed, has a chiseled hawk-like face, black hair, and bluish-gray eyes.

The purple man stops and engages in conversation with a giant who is standing with the two fat women. The giant is truly a giant, about the size of a full-grown Kodiak bear.

The purple man gesticulates as he speaks, pointing to the two fat women, eliciting raucous laughter from the giant.

The purple man, giant, and fat women walk into the dining room, followed by the Vincentio subs.

Ben heads for the door.

He runs through meadows and woods, his heart pounding.

The Range Rover draws into sight, standing within a covering of pines. Marie, Wendy, and Wade are inside.

Ben hops into the driver's seat, breathing heavily. He doesn't know what to tell his family, so he says nothing.

He reaches for the ignition key, fires it up, and drives out of the pines, heading for the highway. Beads of perspiration collect on his brow. He turns on the air conditioner, but it doesn't work. He wipes the sweat off his brow, opens the window, and feels the breeze.

Ben drives the Range Rover onto the highway. Cloud shadows creep over them. He realizes how self-absorbed he's been; he hadn't noticed the change in weather.

He sees armed men and barricades on the road ahead, and slows the Range Rover. He had feared this—they are trapped at the Gingerbread Lodge.

Wendy, silent for so long, cheers.

Ben turns the Range Rover around.

Minutes later, he drives into the Gingerbread Lodge's parking lot and parks near the entrance. With a sense of urgency, he gathers his family and leads them away from the vehicle.

They hide in nearby bushes. Great armadas of clouds, silent and heat-thrashing, float over them. The day becomes a prankster, taunting them with brief sprays of sunshine.

Ben sees the subs emerge from the lodge. "Watch," he says, and hears a collective gasp from his family.

The sub Ben Vincentio and family walk down the path toward the line of parked vehicles, head straight to the Range Rover, and pile inside.

The real Ben and family, watching from the bushes, feel the first trickles of rain as their vehicle drives away. The cordon will be like steel, Ben thinks, but the subs will get through. Elementals are about. Doors between worlds have been flung open.

"What's going on, Ben?" It's a voice Ben has heard before, another time, another place. He sees a man holding up an FBI badge.

The man opens a window and pulls the shades against the storm that rages outside, casting the bedroom into a paroxysm of shadows.

He glances about, as if taking in the gray, shifting shapes that now inhabit the room, and then walks into the adjoining suite, leaving the door cracked open. A slender shaft of pale-yellow light shines through.

"Thank you," Wendy says after he is gone, feeling the cool air wash over her. She had asked the FBI agent if they could have a window open. It was stuffy in the room. She had inquired about air conditioning, but was told they didn't exist in the world of the Gingerbread Lodge. She feels much better now.

She sits on one of two beds. Wade is on the other, taking a nap. She wonders if he will have nightmares about the horrors he witnessed at Big Snow.

She turns on a lamp and reads her book. It's about ghosts, and gives her chills.

A while later, sensing an unnatural silence, she sets her book down, goes to the door, and peeks into the adjoining suite.

Her parents and the FBI agent are huddled in conversation.

"Guns and bullets don't work," the FBI agent says. "We've tried them to no effect."

"What will work?" Ben asks.

"We're not sure. The Occultist told us to invoke a shapeshifter from the infernal regions. He says they're the only ones that can slay the giant."

"How does one invoke a shapeshifter from the infernal regions," Marie asks.

Wendy shudders as the FBI agent tells her.

Henry Falcon leads the Occultist and the ton sisters across the dining room to a nook on the far side, where they sit at a table surrounded by French windows.

The ton sisters sit side by side to his left, the Occultist

directly across from him. The windows are closed, the sheer curtains drawn. Henry sees the faint greenery of a garden patio outside, tossed by the storm.

"You look tired, Henry," the Occultist says.

"Fuck it, Occultist. I am tired. I've been up since dawn."

"Oh? Did the ton sisters keep you awake?"

Henry chuckles and shakes his head. "No, it wasn't the ton sisters."

"What did you do so early, Henry?"

"Tending to business, Occultist. The world never sleeps."

The Occultist is getting on Henry's nerves, and Henry is finding it hard to maintain his cool. He hates the Occultist. The Occultist secretly belittles him. Henry thinks it's time to eviscerate the Occultist.

"Diana and Alice, I want you to go to your room now," Henry says.

Diana and Alice stare at him with fear in their eyes, then get up from the table and hurry away.

Henry watches the rapidly departing ton sisters.

He sees the Occultist eyeing them, too.

Henry's hatred for the Occultist boils over. He knows the Occultist is getting ready to say something witty about the two fat women. The Occultist always says something witty about the two fat women. It's his way of being superior. Henry feels a need to compete with the Occultist, to show him up, so he reaches into his pocket and digs out a piece of paper containing wisdom. He reads from it:

"Bro, but for the grace of God, there go you and I."

He waits for the Occultist to say something witty.

The Occultist glances at the departing ton sisters, gives a sly wink at Henry, and says, "There will be no inquiries after the first and second exploding supernovas."

Henry feels a rage building.

He pulls out his knife, unfolds the blade, and locks it in place. He waves it back and forth, nine inches of gleaming steel. When his eyes draw the Occultist's eyes into focus, the steel becomes a slow-moving blur in front of the purple man's face.

The Occultist freezes and turns extra purple. His eyes become elastic, zooming in and out with a panicky focus.

Wendy sits in the bedroom with Wade. An unnatural cast lies over everything in the room, matching the storm-darkened day outside. Two burning lamps create halos that push against the darkness.

She hears the doorbell ring, runs to the window, and looks outside. Her parents, the FBI agent, and a newcomer stand in a pool of light.

The newcomer is the animal that was trailing them.

They come inside, the animal with them.

Wendy peers into the adjoining suite.

They are engaged in a heated discussion about the giant Wade saw on the cliff at Big Snow. Now Wendy knows why the animal is here, why it was trailing them. It can slay the giant, and was summoned by Wade for that purpose.

The animal is a huge werewolf.

Henry Falcon is gutting the Occultist, pulling out his entrails, when something big crashes through the French windows.

Amidst the shower of glass looms a huge werewolf.

With the slash of a paw, the werewolf rips out Henry's throat. A gush of blood darkens the tablecloth, and Henry's head flops to the floor.

The werewolf picks up the Occultist with one paw, his entrails with the other, and departs through the window.

The werewolf deposits the Occultist in the FBI suite. The humans stare in shock at the purple mess, and then render first aid.

Blind Clyde

A god sits in the sky south of the city, not a puny god but one that is godlike in the extreme, and it heartens the little girl who watches from below. She keeps watching, and he goes into swirling motions, and he billows upward. Then, for an instant, in utter inhuman complexity, he reveals himself as a dark-blue horror racing into the mind of ...

Junelle Jamison, the little girl who watches from below.

She needs something powerful to enter her life right now. Her parents are dead, killed in a mysterious accident two weeks ago. She attended their funeral eight days ago. Three days ago, the aunt who took her in locked her out, and Junelle is too frightened to go back.

For three days and nights, Junelle Jamison, all of eleven years old, and small of stature for an eleven-year-old, has been a street waif. She is sunburned to a bright red on her face and legs. Her only meals have been in supermarkets, eating the free samples stores hand out during promotions.

She is hungry, sunburned, and tired, and right now she needs the god that sits in the sky south of the city.

Feeling ludicrously small, she pushes her bicycle along a sidewalk and stops at an intersection.

As lightning tunnels delicate veins through the darkening clouds, and thunder rumbles through the sky, Junelle races across the street and stops on the other side, drawing in a succession of heavy breaths. *He can be a scary god.* She watches the fiery display, fighting hard to keep her mind from mirroring the tumult in the sky.

She jumps on her bike and pedals down the sidewalk, thinking of the wooded lot at the edge of town that has been her home the last three days and nights. She feels safe there, communing with the hoot owls and tree squirrels. She even built a small lean-to with branches and twigs. But she knows it will be no fun in a flash flood, and no fun when the weather turns cold. She knows she can't live there forever.

She stops at another intersection and waits for traffic. Cars are zinging past. She notices a boy sitting on the grass beside a hedge—an older boy with a gash on his face, like he's been in a fight. He's wearing denim shorts and a cream-colored T-shirt. His hair is frightfully short, just razor stubble. His arms are long and sinewy, his eyes observant like a fox's.

He has eyes for Junelle.

What are you looking at?

She looks down. Her legs are red. And hurt so much, now that she thinks of it. He's studying her intently. She looks both ways, sees an opening in traffic, and tears across the street.

She stops and looks back.

He's getting up, looking around. He's trotting across the street. He is tall and looks much older than she had thought.

She hops on her bike and pedals madly for several blocks, and then stops and looks back.

He's loping along, following her. She watches him, her heart pounding. She's tired and must rest. She'll take off when he gets closer.

A lot of boys have been following her the last few days. They all look like the one who's following her now. They have sinewy muscles and wear cream-colored T-shirts and have razor-stubble hair. There's a club for such boys in Dead Colt. They do things to girls, especially pretty girls, things too horrible to think of. Plainclothes cops shadow these boys. Local media covers them and gives warnings. The school tried to ban them but couldn't. A state law forbids it. Her mother and father had warned her, also.

She bursts into tears. The boy stops. He's watching her. It looks like he might be giving up.

She rides away, tears escaping, her throat dry. She could use a soda. Maybe she'll stop at a supermarket.

But the god in the sky has other ideas.

As the heavens grow ever more threatening, a voice enters Junelle's mind.

Oh, I was quite colorful the second day, looking into the mirror at home, blood at both nostrils, kind of like a vampire. My right cheek was swollen. I had blue speckles under my right eye, like a robin's egg. A bright-red crescent joined the blue speckles the next day, turning my black eye red and blue. My hearing was slightly diminished, also.

The voice makes her shiver. But she wants to hear it again.

I felt my first hunger pangs two days later. And on that same day, I felt cold for the first time since waking up from the operation. Before that, I had felt heat. Two days of heat, then cold sets in, and the outside temperature was over ninety degrees. Something told me I was heading for more trouble.

She stops her bike, looks at the sky, and asks God a question.

"Can I come over, Clyde?"

Why am I calling God Clyde?

She hears the voice again.

During the first few days following surgery, I had great clarity of vision in my dreams. Insight? Expanded awareness? The anesthetic? I was contemplating suicide by the second day. Good thing I didn't own a gun. I was second-guessing my decision to have surgery. My tubes weren't opening up like they said they would.

"Tubes? What do you mean, Clyde? What tubes?"

Oh, excuse me, Junelle. Didn't I tell you? I had sinus surgery. Afterward, the surgeon stitched gauze packs into my nasal cavities to stanch the bleeding. They were pre-shaped units with small breathing tubes in them. The tubes were clogged most of the time. I kept spraying saline solution into them, like I was told, but they never opened up much.

"Can I come over, Clyde?"

Junelle hears the urgency—and the fear—in her voice. She listens carefully as Clyde tells her his address.

She rides her bike there, through the pelting rain. It's a half mile out of town. She follows a highway and crosses a bridge over Dead Colt Creek.

It's a big white house with blue shingles, blue shutters, and an enormous covered porch. It's in a secluded area, and occupies a large lot, as do the other houses on the street. Huge cottonwood trees shelter the neighborhood.

Clyde's personal assistant, Guy Sandalwood, greets her at the door. His voice is deep and silky.

"Hello, Junelle. The storm is about to rage, so you are just in time. Clyde will see you now."

Guy's flaxen hair and blue eyes radiate kindness.

Junelle's hand disappears into his as he ushers her into the foyer.

They walk deeper into the house, across a hardwood floor, and approach a big door. Guy opens the door, and Junelle enters a darkened room. She feels a breath of cool air on the back of her neck as he closes the door behind her.

The room is dark, blessedly dark.

Sunburned, tired, hungry eleven-year-old Junelle Jamison walks into a strip of light, sits on a plush chair, and sinks into the cushions.

Clyde had counseled her the night of her parents' deaths, here in this room. He told her he was a psychologist who studied the ways in which misfortune and evil touched people's lives. He also told her of his sinus surgery, and how a complication had left him blind and paralyzed.

But to Junelle, he had seemed more like a god.

She hears the creak of his wheelchair.

The only light in the room comes from a special ceiling lamp that shines on Junelle's chair. *I'm in the light,* she thinks. The familiar, comfortable strip of light that is always the home of anyone allowed in Clyde's presence.

The creaking stops. Clyde, as always, remains in darkness. He talks in a soothing voice, picking up from where he had left off the night of her parents' deaths.

Tales of his own suffering teach her she is not alone; indeed, she is part of a worldwide web of suffering.

"In the hospital and at home, Junelle, I had feelings of being trapped, of being shattered, left in pieces. I got over it, but for a while I didn't even want to live. These feelings had to become more remote.

"I had startling visions after my surgery, both while awake and asleep, visions of ghostlike beings interacting in our lives. And I experienced enormous fear. We take breathing for granted. So when our breathing is impeded, our imaginations quickly invent the next horrible destination: our breathing passages are lost, we panic, we die.

"I seldom slept the first few days of my recovery. I was up and active until fatigue dropped me, then maybe an hour and a half of sleep, sitting up, keeping those precious air passages open. That's all I could manage.

"I was called up to war, Junelle. I was engaged in around-the-clock preparations for combat. Constant attention to duty. Sleep and other considerations were secondary to maintaining this vigil. I kept my ghostly army beside me, all those entities I'd seen in my visions, the entities that inhabit the shadows, arrange our experiences, usher people into and out of our lives.

"I'm learning to manage this condition well, I thought. I've asked for help. I've gotten help. Thank you. Boy, was I wrong.

"What's it like to teeter on the edge of panic, not being certain of your next breath? Whether it would come or not?

"My bathroom sink was my staging area for assaults on my nostrils. I would spray saline solution into my nasal tubes and watch as blood trickled out. Breathing through my nose was impossible; my tubes were hopelessly clogged. I could only suck in shallow breaths through my mouth. Panic had served to constrict my breathing passages.

"Now do you understand why I felt trapped?

"Someone once said that the best thing to do after surgery is to curl up with a good book. Not my surgery. Curl up with a dead rat is more like it. And then pretend you're a victim of the black plague. I got a whiff of the antibiotic I'd been taking. It must have scraped the back of my tongue the last time I took one, before retiring. I'll be taking it with food from now on—flavorful food—to mask its smell and lingering odor. Its smell brought to mind the plague, with dead, burning bodies. I've never smelled anything so horrible. Part of the joy of discovery.

"Shows you how wrong I can be, Junelle. The smell wasn't the antibiotic; it was me. Several days' worth of blood soaking into the gauze in my nasal passages. Drying, encrusted blood. Me dying. Me decaying. Me smelling like the plague.

"As I went to bed—and this was in the middle of the day—kids were yelling in the neighbor's yard, and I was mad at them. I was associating the vile smell with the worst kid out there. While asleep, my ears began plugging up, and I wished for the yelling kids. Anything was better than being closed off, not being able to hear.

"Junelle, an evil smell had permeated my system. It affected the taste of my food and how everything smelled. It just about floored me.

"The pain in my right cheek became prominent at this time. The surgeon had to drill a hole through my right cheekbone to get at one of my sinuses. He did the other sinuses through a scope that he fed into my nostrils. The surgeon made an incision in my mouth to get at the cheekbone and afterward put sutures there.

"My pain pills were almost gone. I began taking them

at further intervals. I didn't seek help. I guess I wanted to prove how tough I was."

Clyde pauses. When he resumes, he seems to have lapsed completely into the past.

"I hope my body appreciates all that I'm doing for it. I hope my sinuses are healing well. I think they are. Now, only clear fluids trickle from them.

"This whole business, though, is getting old. I'm counting the days, hours, and minutes until it's time to have my sinuses unpacked and the tubes removed.

"Then, on the fourth day, I woke around midnight and didn't know who I was for about twenty minutes. I didn't know my name. I didn't know I was recovering from sinus surgery. I didn't know I was on prescription drugs.

"I got up, washed my face, and unloaded the automatic dishwasher, and all this time I didn't know who I was or anything at all about me. And I had that strong bad odor and taste about me.

"I am too scared to sleep again. I am too scared to take more medicine. I need to have these tubes removed from my air passages and be off these medications.

"Confusion is a possible side effect of the antibiotic. Psychotic reactions are possible side effects of the painkiller. I want to stop taking both drugs. Who do I call?

"I called the clinic. A doctor advised me that he didn't think it was a drug reaction. He thought I wasn't getting enough sleep.

"I'm calmer now. I've begun recording food intake and sleep. Hopefully, this will force me to partake of both, since I haven't been getting much of either since the operation.

"The extreme bad taste remains. My breath smells of it. My food and drink smell of it. I'm sick because of it.

"I vomited at the bathroom sink for several minutes. Clear fluids came from my stomach. Wretched stuff.

"I cleaned my bathroom on the fifth day. While doing so, it dawned on me that I wasn't feeling any symptoms. Just then, they came back. The moment my mind was on them, they were there. When I was focused elsewhere, they were gone.

"I woke from a dream. A man was fired from his job because he couldn't breathe through his nose. I felt sorry for him. In this dream, I was a kid, and I couldn't breathe through my nose, either. I thought that was a major problem around the world, people losing their jobs because they couldn't breathe through their noses.

"Somehow, I survived, and on the eighth day my nasal packs were removed by my surgeon. He snipped off the stitches that held them in place and used pliers to pull them out of my nostrils. I had no idea they were so sizeable, both in length and girth. They were huge bloody things, reminiscent of sun-ripened cadavers.

"He plopped them into a stainless-steel bowl held by his nurse and she took them away for disposal. I could breathe freely now. I was elated. But it didn't last.

"Soon after I got home, my head began hurting. Now and then I got a whiff of that horrible smell. I know now it wasn't medicine—it was inside me, my sinuses. My brain being touched somehow. The bones in the sinuses next to the brain are wafer thin.

"I was back in the hospital before I knew it. There was a guy named Jules in the bed next to mine. With the curtains pulled around our beds, we couldn't see each other until the day I left—though I would return. I peeked in on him, the first time I saw him. He was asleep. Later, calling over, he asked me, 'Who was that in the wheelchair?' I told him it was me."

Clyde falls silent, and Junelle hears the creak of his wheelchair as it retreats.

Toward evening the rain lets up, and Guy and Junelle stand in the open doorway of the garage and debate taking Clyde's Toyota Land Cruiser or his Lexus sedan on a shopping trip. Junelle decides on the Lexus.

When they return—Junelle acquired a whole new wardrobe at Clyde's expense—Guy shows her to her bedroom on the second floor. It stuns her. A beautiful white iron bed stands in the center of the room, complete with headboard, bed stand, and lamp. White pillows, sheets, and a bedspread adorn the bed. A dresser, mirror, and wooden chair are along one wall. Three tall windows face the street. A spray of blue flowers in a white vase stands on a small table beside one of the windows. The walls and ceiling are white, the hardwood floor cinnamon. Guy tells her the room is decorated in Victorian minimalist style, as is the entire house.

He asks her if the bedroom is satisfactory. She nods, her heart squeezed tight, a lump in her throat.

Downstairs, she and Guy sit at a long wooden table and eat a deliciously satisfying meal of beef stew and English muffins. There is milk for Junelle and tea for Guy.

"Does Clyde eat alone?" Junelle asks.

"Yes."

"Does he sit in darkness even when he eats?"

"Yes."

After dark, Junelle remembers her bicycle. It's out on the porch. She and Guy go out and put it in the garage. She sees the boy who followed her earlier that day. He's standing in the shadows at the far end of the driveway.

She walks toward him, and the boy steps closer. Junelle hears Guy walking behind her. *He's wondering what I'm doing,* she thinks.

I don't know what I'm doing. This is probably dangerous.

She stands at the outer edge of the garage light, and the boy stands half in darkness.

"I was worried about you," the boy says.

"I know," Junelle says.

"Can I see you again?" he asks.

"Yes."

"When?"

"Tomorrow."

Junelle and Guy go back inside. She showers, dons her new pajamas, and brushes her teeth. She applies first-aid cream to her sunburn, rubs it in gently. It hurts a lot. She looks in the medicine cabinet and takes two aspirin with water. She doesn't know what else she can do about it. She crawls between the sheets and falls asleep.

She has a dream.

A dream of Junelle.

She sees herself curled up on an old newspaper on the floor at the back of Clyde's kitchen. She is sunburned to a bright red on her face and legs. She sees herself rise on her haunches, hears herself say, *Unless you want to stay like this, keep going.*

I will keep going, the dreaming Junelle says.

The first night at Clyde's house, Junelle has another dream, a dream in which she finds herself in a big land where everything—even the buildings and trees, even the land itself—has died and come back as ghosts. Everything is so milky white, and so milky gray, and so transparent and haunting. She can read the very history of each object. Nothing dark has survived, not even the shadows.

When she wakes, her mind is still laden with the recent past when she lived in a lean-to in a vacant lot, and another recent past when she lived with her parents, Robin and Cedric, in their boxlike trailer home.

She looks around and sees windows several feet out, sunlight pouring in through the sheer curtains. The daylight is milky white. Bed seems a good place to stay for a while.

She remembers sitting in a strip of light, staring into darkness. She remembers Clyde, who sits in darkness. Clyde, who speaks to her about suffering.

She reaches out and touches the whiteness around her. Can she touch a shadow? She tries to. But there are no shadows to touch.

Her sunburn ignites, and her hand flies to her neck. Her fingers dip into skin that has the texture of flames. It scares her, and she leaves it alone.

She is fully awake now, and knows she is in an immaculate Victorian house, done up in minimalist style.

She recalls the boy with the cream-colored T-shirt and the razor-stubble hair. She told him she would see him today. She gets out of bed and walks to a window and peers up and down the street. The boy is nowhere in sight, though it's still early.

She walks to the mirror and winces when she sees herself. She isn't just red—she is ugly. She applies first-aid cream to the worst of it, showing special concern for her face and neck. It looks like someone tortured her there. She puts first-aid cream on her legs, too, but they aren't as nightmarish as her face and neck. Feeling hideous, she walks to the bathroom and takes two aspirin.

She looks through her new clothes. There's a lot. She dons white shorts, a blue blouse, and white running shoes. The blouse has a seafaring look. She puts on a blue baseball cap to shield her face from the sun, though she doesn't plan to be in the sun much until she heals.

She walks downstairs and enters the kitchen, avoiding the dark hallway that Guy said she must never breach. *It's Clyde's province. He alone can access it.*

She hasn't explored the kitchen yet—she and Guy ate in the dining room last night. The kitchen has vintage cupboards dressed in pale gray. A stout wooden table sits in the center of the room. Cookware and utensils hang from a ceiling rack. Modern appliances blend with old-world trappings.

She searches the cupboards and refrigerator for food and finds a great assortment. She pours whole-grain cereal into a bowl and sprinkles it with dates, raisins, and pecans. She pours milk on her cereal, pours a glass of orange juice, and puts fresh strawberries and blueberries onto a plate.

The kitchen is a work area, not an area for eating, so she carries everything to a cozy nook off the kitchen, where a cushioned bench surrounds a wooden table, and where open windows give her a view of the flower gardens in the backyard.

She watches out the windows as she eats, feeling the breeze on her face, seeing little bugs crawling on the screens, trying to get inside, their little feet busy, busy.

She hears noises from somewhere in the house. It's probably Guy, she thinks. She doesn't bother to look. She wouldn't be able to see anything anyway from the nook. She keeps looking out the windows, in a dreamy state.

She hears someone walking toward the kitchen. She doesn't look. It wouldn't do any good. Wait. It's Guy. It must be Guy.

She sees Guy outside in a bed of pink azaleas, pruning shears in hand.

Fear grips her. Her heart races as the footsteps draw closer. A shambling sort of person is walking toward the kitchen.

She peers out from the nook, ready to run.

It's the boy with the cream-colored T-shirt and razor-stubble hair. He sees her and heads for the nook. He's wearing denim shorts again, and he's limping. She sees an ugly gash on his left leg, alongside the knee. The whole area is puffy and bruised. The gash looks like it's been treated and then left to heal in the air. She counts about a dozen stitches.

"How'd you get in here?" she asks, regaining her composure.

He points to Guy outside in the garden. "He let me in. He said you'd be down shortly."

"What happened?" She points to the gash on his leg.

"I don't know exactly. It happened last night when I was waiting for you."

She recalls he stayed in shadow. She couldn't see him too well.

"Why didn't they put a dressing on it? That has to be protected."

"I put a field dressing on it right after it happened. I took the dressing off at home, then cleaned and sutured the wound. I didn't have another dressing. I'm going to pick up more medical supplies today."

"Oh?" She gives him a perplexed look. "You sutured it yourself?"

"Yes. Can I sit down?"

"Yes."

He slides onto the bench opposite her.

"Well, I hope you're on antibiotics and a painkiller." She studies him. His eyes give him away. "You aren't? You're not on any medication?"

"No, ma'am. Don't worry. I'll pick some up later today."

She looks at the gash on his face. It's minor compared to the leg wound.

"Why are you so polite?" she asks.

He stares at her. "What do you mean?"

"I thought you'd be tougher," she says. "Outside you're tougher."

"Yeah, I suppose I am."

"Have you eaten anything today?"

He looks at what she's eating and then peers into the kitchen.

"Go get something to eat," she says.

He gets up and heads for the kitchen.

I'm myself again, she thinks. I'm a little doctor. It's been a while. No wonder, with all that's happened. *But I'm not pretty anymore.*

She wonders what the boy will be like outside, in his environment. She wishes she could speak to Clyde about him.

She hears a distant voice.

"You'll find that he's inclined to steer things."

"Is that you, Clyde?"

"Yes, Junelle. I had an early consultation with your young man."

She hears the creak of his wheelchair as it approaches.

"Where are you?" she asks.

"I'm in perpetual darkness. I traverse it occasionally to visit you."

"Oh, thank you."

She waits for him to get closer.

"Clyde, can we talk?"

"Yes, we can talk."

"I'm going ... outside. Will I be safe?"

"We won't lock you out, if that's what you mean."

"Thank you, Clyde."

The creaking stops. She thinks he's very close.

"Oh, Clyde?"

"Yes, my sugarplum?"

"I'm still mystified about you. I don't mean to sound personal, but I only hear your voice. I never see you. It's so strange. Did you let that boy see you?"

"No one sees me, Junelle. My consultations are private, by the way."

"Oh, sorry. I shouldn't have asked."

"That's okay, sugarplum. Not being seen fits my personality. In my youth, I was invisible; no one saw me then, either. Strange or not, Junelle, when people hear a disembodied voice, they pay attention, and this keeps everyone—disembodied voices included—on their toes. If I ever let anyone down, I would be just another voice competing with the wind, and eventually I would die out completely."

Several long moments go by in which Junelle hears

nothing except the buzzing of a bee at a window screen. A whiff of air catches her on the chin. Somehow, she thinks it was Clyde. He's calling me sugarplum. If he could see me, he would know better than to call me that. I'm ugly now.

"Clyde, I just had a thought. I think rich and glamorous people hear voices all the time that tell them how to be rich and glamorous—so why not me? I just know you're going to make me rich and glamorous someday, aren't you? In any case, I don't think they'll be teaching me those skills in school anytime soon, so please keep me informed, will you?"

"My sugarplum, I will keep you informed."

She hears the creak of his wheelchair as it recedes into the distance.

Junelle feels good, having spoken with Clyde again.

The boy returns with a bowl of cereal, toast, and orange juice. He sits and eats.

Junelle finishes her breakfast.

"I'm heading upstairs," she tells the boy. "Wait for me when you're done, okay?"

"Okay."

She rushes upstairs and brushes her teeth.

Before coming down, she looks into the mirror in her bedroom and carefully applies a powerful sun-blocking agent on all exposed skin. She will try to stay in the shade as much as possible.

Junelle, her baseball cap in place, goes downstairs and gets the boy. They run outside, into the breezy oven of summer. She leads him to the back porch, where they sit on cushioned wicker chairs, out of the sun.

The rich colors of the flower gardens enter Junelle's eyes with fairy-tale precision. The aroma, a heady blend of plant and soil, is overwhelming. She scopes out the towering cottonwoods at the back of the lot, and the woods that flow along the banks of Dead Colt Creek, watching the shadows twitch under the rising sun. She's plotting her moves, if she and the boy should leave the shelter of the porch.

She sees that he is looking at her.

"I'll get right to it, Junelle. I'm here for a purpose."

"I didn't know you knew my name."

"We make it a point to know the names of people who wound us."

She feels uneasy but tries to remain cool. "What's your name?"

"Hank Maddox."

"Did I wound you, Hank?"

"Yes."

"You sound serious."

"I am serious, Junelle. I've been given a mission. There are certain matters before the nation, and I am here to uncover your role in them. If you refuse to cooperate, agents of the United States government will force you to talk."

"Oh?" There's an armada of flowers in the backyard. They keep her eyes occupied and give her time to think. She decides she'll play along. She likes his approach, his melodrama.

"I don't think I'll cooperate, Hank. I don't respond too well to threats."

"Junelle, in your efforts to wound us, are you applying conscious or unconscious will?"

She looks at his leg wound. It makes her wince. She points at it. "That was strictly unintentional. I didn't mean to do it. Your face, though ..." She peers at him and purses her lips.

"Junelle, over the last several days, some trivial wounds started to occur." He points to the gash on his face. "This corresponds with the time you were living on your own in that vacant lot. I think you did it. Others also mention you in connection with minor wounds. I don't think you did the leg wound. If you did the leg wound, I wouldn't be here. I'd be setting up an ambush for you. You'd meet your death."

Junelle lifts a timid finger and points to his face. "I did that?"

"Yes, you did, Junelle. Do you have a nickname or something?"

"Well, actually, no. Don't you like Junelle?"

"Yes, I do. But ..."

He needs a shorter name, she thinks. He's driven by efficiency. "You can call me June. But please call me Junelle sometimes, too."

"Okay. Are you going to cooperate?"

"I will, but first tell me more."

"In addition to the more-serious war wounds that we've been receiving from persons unknown, you have been wounding us. We've been tracking you for several days. Now this is something we're good at, tracking the source and then figuring the motive. In your case, we believe it was unconscious and protective. You were afraid of us, so you lashed out. We have to recruit you, June.

Whether you like it or not, you're one of us. If you join us, we'll be more complete. And you'll receive the protection you need by being in the group."

"Hank, let's go for a walk."

They walk through the woods along Dead Colt Creek, and after a while come upon a small clearing. Deeper woods lie ahead. The sun peers through, and Junelle holds back, standing in shadow.

She sees Hank casting his eyes about, scanning the deeper woods ahead, focusing on one particular area. She gazes where Hank is gazing, and is shaken.

She sees a ghostly creature. It seems part human, part animal, but so delicate and flimsy it's almost unseen. The creature has eyes for Junelle, and comes bounding to her. It claws at her face and throat and then dissolves like a ghost fading out.

She lets out her breath, silent, easy. Coolness sweeps her skin. Something invisible plows across her neck. It digs deep and peppers her wound with the chaff of the woods. She reaches a hand to it, but Hank grips her wrist.

"Leave it alone, June. You'll only make it worse."

He releases her wrist, and she drops her hand to her side.

"What was that, Hank? In the woods?"

"It was nothing, June."

"But, Hank, it was something, and it was scary, and it did something to me. This whole area is scary."

He lowers his voice. "June, it was a violation."

"Oh? What's a violation? Some kind of ghost?"

"We don't know. In any case, it's classified."

He scans the woods. "It's a new way to wound people, June. The government calls it a weapon. We have training sites around Dead Colt where we learn how to track these things back to the source. Some areas support this type of weapon better than others. We could use this place as a training site, since a weapon is already here."

"You have training sites?"

"Yes, and not just around Dead Colt. We train elsewhere in the United States, too."

"Anything overseas?"

"I can't answer that. Okay, I'll say yes. We'll call this site June's Ground."

"Hank, I can't join a group of boys."

"There are girls in the group."

"Girls? You're kidding?"

"There are. There are men, also."

"Adults?"

"Yes."

She has to think. This is unexpected. Could he be lying to her?

"Hank, I'm going to have to think about this."

"Take your time, June."

"Why do you guys wear cream-colored shirts? And why do you shave your heads?"

"Originally, we weren't supposed to be identified as a group, but some of us felt we could draw the enemy out better if we were. It's effective. The government supplies us with shirts. A military barber keeps us shaved."

"But not everyone in your group is identifiable, right?"

"Correct. You're thinking of the adults and the girls. They don't wear the uniform. The adults occupy key positions within the command and support structures. The girls, along with some of the guys, constitute our espionage network. They mingle with the enemy, but the enemy eventually sniffs them out, so they have to be combat ready, also.

"June, you would be part of the espionage network, but since you can wound people, your primary occupation would be as a weapons specialist."

"Why do you do this, Hank?"

"We're on the front lines in this war. There's excitement in that. We live on the edge. The U.S. Army considers us an elite unit."

"How much do you get paid?"

"Twelve hundred bucks a month to start. The pay goes up after basic and advanced training."

"Do you get medical?"

"Yes."

"Do you learn a job skill?"

"Yes. But don't expect it to match up with anything in civilian life. It depends."

"Do you get counseling if you need it?"

"Yes."

"Do you get vacation?"

"Thirty days a year, full pay. You don't always get it at a convenient time, though. You belong to the government."

"Who's the enemy?"

"That's classified. Join us, June."

"Why is it people say you do things to girls, especially pretty girls? I've always been warned about that."

"That's a disinformation campaign to draw the enemy out. The enemy hates anyone who's portrayed as conventionally evil."

"What do your parents think of this?"

"They're intimidated."

"You'll ambush them, right?"

"Government agents talk to the parents. They put a scare into them."

"Is it true that cops shadow you? Or is that more disinformation?"

"There are people who keep track of us but they aren't cops. It's classified, June. Join us. You'll discover things then. You'll be glad."

She starts walking back to Clyde's house. She thinks Hank is spinning a tall one. She plays her card. "Hank, I won't join. I suppose now you'll call the government. Maybe some handcuffs and truncheons will persuade me."

He walks after her. "Name your poison, June."

She calls over her shoulder. "You're supposed to call me Junelle sometimes." And then she starts running for Clyde's house.

Hank runs after her. "Junelle, the wound on your neck is a war wound and it's going to get worse."

Hank pulls a small radio out, unfolds it, and keys the transmitter.

"Are you monitoring my location?"

"Affirmative, Hank."

"We were violated."

"What happened?"

"Junelle was attacked, her neck again."

"Hank, she's heading for trouble with that neck wound."

"I know."

"We'll use it as leverage."

"She's a good kid."

"Just the kind we want, Hank."

"I think she'd feel more comfortable if we had a girl recruit her."

"We've got one standing by."

"Money gets her attention fast."

"Her parents didn't have much. They lived in a trailer home."

"If you recall, mine didn't have much either."

"I remember. We'll get her, Hank."

Junelle runs into the house and finds Guy in the kitchen, cutting up chicken breasts on a cutting board. She shows him her neck.

"Guy, I think I have to go see a doctor right away. I think this is more than a sunburn."

He peers at her neck. "Let me put this chicken away and we'll go into town, Junelle." He slides the chicken into a glass container, puts a lid on it, and puts it into the refrigerator. He scrubs the cutting board with hot, soapy water and sets it aside to dry.

They take the Land Cruiser.

Junelle sits in the front passenger seat, staring out the windshield at the speeding highway. Her neck wound is killing her. She thinks it might be suggestion—Hank is evil if he's making this up. She doesn't think he is, though.

I'm getting uglier all the time, she thinks.

"Guy, can other people make you sick, or give you wounds, or make you ugly, even without touching you?"

"Sometimes they can, Junelle. I think Clyde will talk to you about that."

"Good. I need to see Clyde again. I've got this really important decision to make, and I need some advice. Can you set it up for me, Guy?"

"Certainly, Junelle."

Suddenly, a wild impulse possesses her. "Guy, are you and Clyde going to keep me? Can I stay? Can I stay?"

"Junelle, we have informed the child welfare agencies of your situation, and there have been inquiries after you. Clyde has an attorney looking into your case. Ultimately, a court will decide where you will go."

"But he's got some kind of power, right, Guy? Clyde's got some kind of power. I know he does. He can get things arranged, can't he?"

"That he can, Junelle. You are right about that. But this is a nation of laws. Even Clyde must obey the law. Never fear. If things should not go your way in court, we will still fight on your behalf."

"Don't even say that, Guy. If I have to go away, I'll come back. Tell him, Guy. Tell Clyde I'll keep coming back."

"I think he already knows that."

Junelle rolls her window down, hoping the majestic countryside will carry her despair away, but it's a short hop from Clyde's neighborhood to town, and they are already there.

They pull into the parking lot of a hospital that has a walk-in clinic. Junelle registers at the desk and is shown into an examination room. Guy stays in the waiting room.

To Junelle, the examination room is a hard, clunky place, full of menace. She doesn't know how they can do her any good in a place like this; they can only make her worse. There's a metal desk in one corner, a metal sink in another, an examination table, and three chairs, one for whoever sits at the desk, and two for the patient.

Junelle sits on the chair meant for whoever sits at the desk. She knows she isn't supposed to sit on that one, but she doesn't care. She's ugly now and she'll do whatever she wants.

She breathes in the antiseptic smell. The antiseptic smell is the one thing she does like about this place. It fits her mood perfectly.

Hospitals and clinics are always awash in antiseptic smells. She wishes it were stronger. Maybe if it were stronger it would kill her.

She wonders if anyone has ever died from an antiseptic smell that was too strong. She figures no one knows and no one cares.

She figures if she keeps going to school and studies hard and takes challenging courses maybe she'll figure it out someday. But who would care?

A doctor walks into the room, looks at Junelle's folder, and introduces himself.

"What can I do for you?" he asks.

"Look at this." She spins in her chair, pulls her hair aside, and shows him her neck.

He looks at it. "You have a deep abrasion and bruising. What happened?"

"I got a sunburn."

"I see that, but this is an abrasion. Did someone hit you?"

"No."

At his direction, Junelle sits on the examination table, and he begins to clean the wound with gauze dipped in antiseptic.

"How did this happen?"

"I thought it was the sun."

"Something hit you a glancing blow, or rubbed against you. It's a strange place to have an abrasion. We see it on water skiers when the towrope catches them."

He looks at her face. She still has her baseball cap on.

"Will you remove your cap?"

She takes it off.

He gently lifts her hair and examines the skin all the way around her neck.

"Just in this one place. I'll be right back."

He leaves the room.

A minute later a female nurse enters the room carrying a gown and two paper slippers. "Will you undress, except for your undergarments, and put these on."

The nurse leaves.

Junelle undresses, keeping her underwear on, and slips into the gown and slippers. She sits on the doctor's chair, cold and nervous.

The doctor and nurse enter the room and close the door behind them. The doctor has a camera and sets it on the desk. "Please sit on the table," he says to Junelle.

She sits on the examination table. Undoing her gown, the doctor examines Junelle's arms, shoulders, back, and ribcage.

He has her lie on her back and palpates her abdomen, asking her if she feels any pain. She says no.

He examines her legs, front and back. He asks her if

she feels pain anywhere else. She says no, other than from sunburn.

He helps her sit up, and arranges her gown, exposing her left shoulder and neck. He lifts her hair out of the way and snaps a picture.

He looks at the picture, and then snaps another one.

The doctor sets the camera on the desk and applies cream to Junelle's neck. The cream feels cool, and his gentle hand soothes her.

"I'm going to give you a tube of this cream. Clean the area morning and night and apply the cream. Before you leave, I want you to speak to a counselor. The nurse will take you to her. You don't have to come back to see another doctor unless this doesn't heal. I think it will heal just fine. You can get dressed now."

He and the nurse leave the room with the camera.

Junelle gets dressed and leaves the room.

The nurse is waiting for her in the hallway. She takes Junelle to an office where a large, gray-haired woman sits behind a desk. The nurse says the woman is a counselor.

The nurse leaves.

An open file folder sits before the large, gray-haired woman. She studies it a few moments, and then looks at Junelle, her eyes narrowing.

"Sit down," the woman says.

Junelle wants to leave, but forces herself to stay, and sits on a chair.

"Either someone assaulted you, or you had an accident," the woman says, her tone icy. "Which was it?"

"Neither."

"You are a minor child. You can be removed from your home and placed in a foster home until your parents or guardians are investigated. You can help me solve this right now by telling me if it was an accident or an assault."

"It was neither. My parents are dead. I'm staying with Clyde."

The counselor looks at the file and reads off Clyde's address. "Is this where you're staying?"

"Yes."

"How long have you been staying there?"

"Since yesterday."

"Where were you staying before then?"

"I was living in a vacant lot."

"You slept outside?"

"Yes."

The counselor breathes heavily for a few moments, staring at the file.

"I'm going to turn this over to a social worker. Someone will be visiting you at this address within a week or two to ascertain your safety." She looks at Junelle. "There will be other issues addressed at that time, such as your long-term care." She pauses. "I think that with the recent tragic loss of your parents, you had some misadventure and simply do not remember it. That can happen. You told the doctor you thought it was sunburn. Your mind had to fill in something. Maybe you are curious about it yourself. You can leave now."

Junelle stands.

"Oh, just one more question, if you don't mind. If you saw another girl with this type of injury to her neck, what would you say happened to her?"

"I'd say she was assaulted."

"Thank you."

Junelle leaves the office and goes to the waiting room.

Guy asks her how it went.

"Great."

They leave the hospital and walk to the Land Cruiser.

But in her mind, Junelle is elsewhere. She is running into darkness, immense terror swerving behind her, pursuing her. Many swords back there. Someone is wounding her neck. She is unattractive now. People who don't care about her want to take her away from Clyde. She would die if not for Clyde.

She wants to see Clyde. She wants guidance. She wants to know if she should join Hank's group.

The Land Cruiser cruises through the city of Dead Colt and enters the strip of highway that will carry them home.

"We will be eating precisely at noon," Guy says.

"I don't have a watch," Junelle says. "What if I'm out?"

Guy opens the glove compartment, pulls out a watch, and hands it to her. "I bought you one last night while you were trying on clothes."

Junelle examines the watch. "Thanks, Guy. What's for lunch?"

"Grilled chicken sandwiches, garden salad, strawberries, and whatever you want to drink."

"I had strawberries for breakfast, Guy. Sorry."

"You may have them again for lunch if you wish. At precisely 1:00 p.m., you will see Clyde. This, also, is an appointment, and you must be prompt."

She sets the watch's time, glancing at the vehicle's dash clock, and straps it to her wrist. "Guy, I'm in no mood to eat."

"You must eat anyway. Your stamina and wellbeing depend upon it. And don't you worry, sweetheart. Clyde will help you."

"Guy, I'm not comfortable with *sweetheart.* Can you just call me Junelle?"

"Certainly, Junelle. Accept my apologies."

As the Land Cruiser pulls into Clyde's driveway, something down the street captures Junelle's attention. She sees it for just an instant before the Land Cruiser carries them out of sight. It's a black van, shiny and new looking, like it hadn't been driven before today. Its windows were as black as the night sky. She also saw a girl about her own age pedaling around on a bicycle near the van. She looked very much like Junelle, slender with long brunette hair. She wore shorts and a tank top, and had lots of bare flesh and a peachy tan.

They stop in the garage. Junelle grabs the tube of cream the doctor gave her for her neck and gets out of the Land Cruiser.

"Guy ..." She rushes around the vehicle. "Will you take this in for me?" She shoves the tube into his hands. "That's for my neck. I want to go ride my bike. I'll be back at noon."

She glances at her watch and runs to get her bike.

Wendy Vincentio is sticking close to the van, riding her bike in circles. She is watching down the street for Junelle. She is also watching the deep mirror finish of the van. The reflections are spellbinding. Her father and two Army officers are inside, monitoring the situation.

She likes the looks of this street in Dead Colt. It's tranquil and elegant, like some earlier time.

Her father has revealed some things.

The girl, Junelle Jamison, has somehow acquired a mysterious piece of darkness, along with a man who sits in it. There are other such pieces of darkness, with similar entities, around the land, but Junelle's is the most profound. An entity who sits in darkness can pose as a god, and get away with lots of lying, since people invest virtue in their gods.

Her father has said it's entirely possible that Junelle's mind is driving her darkness and the man who sits in it.

U.S. leaders are frightened, for the darkness that Clyde sits in is impregnable and expanding. They believe it's a poltergeist writ large, and if not stopped will eventually swallow up the entire world. They think the only course of action is to destroy it.

How?

Her father did not answer, but she knew. Young girls suffering emotional stress are often found to be the unwitting agents of poltergeist activity.

They would have to kill Junelle to be certain of stopping it.

Wendy volunteered to befriend Junelle and search out some answers before a final decision is made.

Through all this, Wendy vows to keep a place inside her safe, a place where darkness cannot intrude, a place where she can understand Junelle, and keep her alive even if the world kills her.

A beat like war drums enters Junelle's mind as she rides her bike down Clyde's long driveway. A thud-knocker of a heart pumps something scary into her veins as she rides onto the street and turns toward the black van.

The girl has stopped near the van and is straddling her bike, eyeing Junelle.

Junelle pedals faster and her bike becomes a force.

An unnatural cast lies over everything. It's as if none of this should be happening.

Junelle slows her bike. And her heart slows as well.

She stops by the girl. "I'm going for a bike ride. Do you want to go with?"

"You're Junelle, right?"

"Yes."

"I'm Wendy. Let's skip the bike ride."

"Okay."

"They told me to mention Hank."

"Do you know Hank?"

"No, I don't. Junelle, is there someplace we can go where we can talk?"

Junelle looks at her watch. "Come home with me. You can eat with us."

They are in Junelle's bedroom. Wendy looks over Junelle's new clothes and asks if she can try something on. Junelle says yes. Wendy selects a blue bikini and goes into the bathroom to put it on.

When Wendy returns, she belly-dances around the room. She dances toward the windows, spinning around in dizzying circles, shivering, and radiating eeriness to the room.

Junelle watches in awe.

"Wendy, how can you do such cool things?"

"Training and iron discipline, Junelle."

Wendy slips a bathrobe on over her bikini. "It's time to go down for lunch."

At precisely noon, Junelle and Wendy slide into the nook off the kitchen. Guy serves them hot slices of grilled chicken, and they make their own sandwiches.

It has become a storm-darkened day, and the curtains at the windows are billowing in the wind. Two wall lamps push against the darkness.

Suddenly, Wendy jumps in her seat. "A bee!"

A bee is banging against a window screen, buzzing like a squadron of World War II fighter planes. Wendy's voice pours out on a trilling note. "B-b-beee ..."

She clamps a hand over her mouth, halting her verbal spasms.

"It's outside, Wendy," Junelle says, lifting the curtain to take a look.

Guy returns from the kitchen. "What's the problem?"

Wendy points at the bee. "I'm deathly afraid of bees, Mr. Sandalwood. I know it's absurd, but I'm stuck with it. What can I do?"

Guy sinks into the cushioned bench opposite Wendy and Junelle and digs out a black leather notebook.

"Okay, Wendy," Guy says, "if it'll make you happy, I'll set you up with Clyde."

"Oh, great," Wendy says.

"I didn't know you knew about Clyde," Junelle says.

"My father told me about him," Wendy says.

Wendy stands, throws her bathrobe off, and turns toward Guy. "Mr. Sandalwood's eyes keep wandering my way, sneaking looks. I can't say I blame him. In the barracuda light, he thinks he's seeing blue panties and bra."

Guy is clearly uncomfortable. His eyes dart toward Junelle, toward Wendy. He is full of silent denials, his face and eyes working mysteriously.

Wendy puts her bathrobe back on and takes her seat.

"Wendy, how can you say such cool things?" Junelle asks.

Guy shrugs. "Charming, Wendy. Junelle, whenever you're with Wendy, listen for any blood-curdling screams that might erupt. If you hear any, you'd better run. It's bound to be Wendy's victims plotting revenge."

After lunch, Junelle and Wendy go upstairs, and Wendy changes back into her own clothes.

"Wendy, someday someone's going to kick your butt."

Wendy laughs. "Sorry. I'm bad."

Junelle looks at her watch. "We have to go downstairs, Wendy. It's almost time for my appointment with Clyde."

"I have to see Clyde, too, little one."

"I'm not comfortable with *little one,* Wendy."

Wendy laughs again. "Sorry, Junelle."

As they leave Junelle's bedroom and enter the staircase, Junelle wonders what seditious acts Wendy is planning.

"Wendy, are you going to violate the rules?"

"Who, me?"

"Clyde's hallway is always in darkness. We can't enter it. When Clyde counsels you, you have to sit in the strip of light, and he will sit in darkness. You can't enter his darkness."

"Right."

"Please, Wendy, you're my guest, and I ask you to respect the rules."

"I will, Junelle. What are you going to ask Clyde?"

"I want his take on me joining the Army."

"Cool. He's always in darkness, right?"

"Yes."

"I'm going to ask him how he manages to keep his darkness so impregnable."

"Cool."

Wendy pauses on the stairs. "I'll also ask him if he thinks humans should call upon occult forces to help them during times of extreme danger."

"Cool, Wendy." They resume walking downstairs.

At the bottom of the stairs, they walk across a hardwood floor, passing over two Oriental rugs that look gutted of life, a third that looks like it's already a ghost.

They walk through the dining room, their shadows gliding over the surface of the long wooden table, and enter the vestibule to Clyde's dark hallway. The room in which Clyde receives visitors is nearby, its big door shut.

"We're in the staging area, Wendy."

"Cool."

They approach the entrance to the dark hallway, stop, and peer into the black void.

Junelle feels Wendy tense.

"It's preternatural," Wendy says, her voice sinking to a whisper.

"Cool, Wendy."

Junelle hears footsteps behind them, in the dining room.

She turns and sees the tall form of Guy Sandalwood appear in the doorway. His eyes are on Wendy.

"You are not to attempt entry into Clyde's domain," Guy says. "There is a labyrinth of darkness in this house. Be forewarned, it is Clyde's private passageway. It gives him mobility about the house, and you are not to encroach."

Wendy glances at Guy, then looks back into the dark hallway, and steps closer.

A doorbell rings.

Guy takes two thundering steps into the staging area.

The doorbell rings again.

Guy leaves, heading for the front door.

"I think I'm sunk, Junelle. They're coming to get me."

"Oh, no, Wendy."

"There are dangers here, Junelle. You are brave."

"Oh, but I'm not always brave. I get scared sometimes." She hears footsteps coming from the front of the house.

"I'll have to talk to them," Wendy says.

"Who do you have to talk to?"

"My father will be one of them."

The footsteps are getting closer.

"I'm going to the breakfast nook to wait," Wendy says, and dashes away.

Moments later, Guy enters the room with a man.

The man stares into Clyde's passageway.

Junelle watches him intently, taking in microscopic detail. She sees something of Wendy in him. She sees something frightful in his gaze. She thinks he is suffering under a horrific burden, that life and death matters are never far from his mind. She wonders how Wendy can be so cool with this man as her father.

371

The man looks at Junelle.

"Where is my daughter?"

"She's in the breakfast nook."

He rushes away.

Ben Vincentio sits across from Wendy in the breakfast nook. Two Army officers armed with 9mm pistols stand nearby.

"Dad, Clyde's darkness is truly impregnable. I tried to enter it, but couldn't."

They sit in silence, staring at one another.

"Do you know what comes next, Wendy?"

"Yes."

"Go knock on the door."

Wendy leaves the breakfast nook and races through the house, her mind squeezed with terror.

Junelle sits in the strip of light. Clyde sits in darkness. She hears a knock on the door.

"Excuse me, Sugar Daddy. There's a knock on the door. Can I go answer it?"

"Of course you can, my Little Suckling."

They have come up with pet names for each other. Junelle walks to the door, opens it, and sees Wendy.

"Wendy, how did it go?"

"Great. Say, when you get a chance, ask Clyde about Clyde, will you?"

"Wendy, honestly."

"Ask him, Junelle. It's important."

"Okay, I will. See you, sugarplum."

Wendy laughs, and Junelle closes the door.

Junelle walks back to the chair, sits in the strip of light, and stares into Clyde's darkness.

"Clyde, Wendy asked me to ask you about Clyde. Can you tell me about yourself?"

She hears laughter, but it is nothing derisive. Clyde is always polite to her, so she knows his laughter has to be either jovial or self-deprecating. She thinks she hears a brief bout of crying, and then laughter again, all mixed up in one big ball of emotion, and then the name *Guy Sandalwood,* as if whispered by the wind.

Silence. Junelle knows Guy's name accidentally slipped from Clyde. He hadn't meant for her to hear it.

His silence continues.

"Come on, Sugar Daddy, tell me. Is Guy your shadow? Does he go out and commit crimes for you?"

Clyde emits an emotional sound, but Junelle can't tell what it is. Crying? Laughing? It's a quiet, awful sound, and then it's gone. She hopes he will call her his Little Suckling now. That always makes her feel good, and Clyde always sounds so cool when he says it.

"My Little Suckling."

She squirms in her seat. Clyde can see her there, in the strip of light that falls on her chair. She can't see him. She has never seen him.

"Uh, Sugar Daddy ..."

"Yes?"

She gathers her nerve before continuing.

"I'm trying to make this easy for you, Sugar Daddy." She is. She senses Clyde wants to go off in a direction that will be entirely new for both of them.

"Thank you, Junelle."

"You're welcome, Clyde." She pauses. "Clyde, please tell me about you."

"We have unconscious desires."

"Yes, Sugar Daddy."

"Both good and bad."

"Yes."

"And we are unaware of the vastness of these desires and of their power."

Clyde pauses. Junelle discovers she is on the edge of her seat, hunched over. She imagines she must look like a gargoyle to Clyde, perched as she is.

"Civilized society dissociates us from our base instincts."

Junelle feels a jolt through her body. Clyde can't see. But she has imagined he can, twice now.

"Things happen to us, Junelle, that are beyond our control, due to unconscious factors. We are contented, things are going great, everything is falling nicely into place, and then we subconsciously sabotage ourselves, and soon we are in big trouble. Everything becomes a struggle. We get sick. We have accidents."

Junelle stares into the darkness. Can you see me, Sugar Daddy? The possibility scares her.

"And the moon, like a big cream pie, is thrown in our face, and the universe cries, *'The joke is on you,'* and when we try to figure things out, we look everywhere but the one place where we might find an answer."

"We must look inside us. Right, Clyde?"

"Right, we must look inside us." Clyde pauses. "Junelle, what do you say to the idea that all misfortune is nothing more than the universe arranging events to help us refine and develop our souls?"

"I'd say we get hurt for a purpose, then. Right?"

"Indeed, Junelle, we get hurt for a purpose. But what is the purpose? I believe I have a clue. Following my surgery, I had visions so vivid I could not distinguish them from reality. I believe they were reality, of sorts. I believe I will see again, Junelle, and walk again, on the beaches I trod in my mind."

"Clyde, did your shadow emerge during surgery on your sinuses and ..." She has the words but can't say them. "Tinkered with you, leaving you ..."

"In this chair?" She hears him wheel back and forth, quick whiplike sounds. "Yes, that's what I believe, Junelle."

"What did you see on the beaches, Sugar Daddy?"

"I saw the underworld of my soul, Junelle. Let me explain."

Clyde tells her the story of his soul, which is also the story of Junelle's soul: her life from when she was born, her parents' lives, as well. He tells her she has always been a part of him, and he a part of her. He says both their souls cast long, dark shadows.

"Junelle, we do not respect our souls, or our shadows. They are the deeper layers of us. They shape us. They shape the universe. My shadow reached beneath the world and pulled out my eyes. And as a bonus, it left me without legs. Our souls and shadows are powerful—we are but mere infants. When the powerless trample on the powerful, the flow must even out.

"Junelle, we get hurt so we can become whole. I saw all this in my visions following surgery. I see it today: the ghostlike beings on the edges of the world, the ones who play with our lives. They stand on the beaches with a sick hilarity in their minds, and they feel their power. There, I

375

read what was written in darkness. They got my eyes, Junelle. And my legs. But I see other beings on these beaches, also, and I feel their power, as well. They help us escape the wreckage wrought by the darker souls. Junelle, go to these beaches and bring me that power. Therein lies my wholeness, my Little Suckling."

Clyde's voice drops from the exuberant theater in his mind into the room that is half in darkness, and silence hangs like a teardrop, and Junelle is shaken again, thinking blind Clyde can see her.

Junelle adjusts her baseball cap, takes it off, puts it back on. "Sugar Daddy, you're scaring the bejesus out of me. I think you can see me sometimes. There's something on me. What is it?"

"There's a geek on you, Junelle."

"You're right, there is. I'm ugly now. I want to join the Army. What do you think?"

"My Little Suckling, I must caution you. Do not believe any of the advertising slogans of the military. Do not trust recruiters. If you must join, and many do, you will be giving your mind and body to a civilian authority you cannot evaluate or trust. If you enter combat, your life will be in the hands of the most experienced people around you. You can trust some of them, but not all. You might die, or you might be maimed, or you might have experiences that will haunt you the rest of your life."

"Well, *hmmm*, someone told me I might be good at weapons training. The pay is good, there's a war going on, and there's this geek that's on me. Do you know who this geek is, Clyde?"

"Who do you think it is, Junelle? Is it someone who likes little girls?"

"No. That type of geek wouldn't have made me ugly."

"Very astute. Could it be someone who fears you?"

"Why would anyone fear me, Clyde?"

"My Little Suckling, if you are attractive, you will draw enemies. If you are honest, you will draw enemies. If you are intelligent, you will draw enemies. If you are free, you will draw enemies. If you have wisdom, you will draw enemies. Your geek has probably sought dominion over you in the past; having failed that, your geek now seeks your destruction."

"How will I ever find my geek?"

"Look for places where cowards and hypocrites hide. Your geek will reside therein."

"How will I ever defeat my geek?"

"Your friend dropped a hint."

"Wendy?"

"Yes. She wanted to know if humans should call upon occult forces to help them in times of extreme danger. The answer is yes."

"I thought so, Sugar Daddy. You have ears everywhere."

"Yes, I do, my Little Suckling."

"I'll ask the Army a lot of questions before I join."

"Good."

"I'll get commando training. I'll learn how to track geeks and how to lure them into ambushes. I'll bring you that geek's head, Clyde."

"My Little Suckling, please leave the heads of geeks on the battlefield. We have tried them before, but they don't blend well with Victorian style."

"Okay, I will, Sugar Daddy." Her mind is spinning. "Oh, thank you, Clyde. I'm not tough enough for this. I get nervous."

"You will be fine, my Little Suckling."

"Sugar Daddy, tell me about Clyde again."

"My Little Suckling, this darkness, this Clyde. These are terrible forces. They are being used against you. You must learn to use them against your enemies."

"Clyde, Clyde, how can you say that? Someone is attacking me. See? My neck. *Ow!* They're also making me ugly. This darkness, your darkness, is what saves me!"

"My Little Suckling, this darkness is your shadow."

"Clyde—"

The door bursts open. Two U.S. Army officers rush in and stride to Junelle's chair. Wendy's father appears in the doorway.

"Bring her out," Wendy's father says. "Junelle, you must come out now."

The two Army officers bracket her, as if to prevent her from escaping. Junelle stands and walks with them to the door.

Wendy is peeking out from behind her father.

"That was great, Junelle," Wendy says. "You drew important intelligence from Clyde."

"I resent you people eavesdropping," Junelle says. "Clyde's sessions are private."

Wendy laughs. "Honestly, Junelle, is there anything of Clyde that you consider private anymore, or even human?"

"He's human, Wendy."

"My turn, my Little Suckling." Wendy rushes past Junelle and sits on the chair in the strip of light. "We're going to learn how to hurt people, my Little Suckling."

The door closes and Wendy is alone, sitting on the chair in the strip of light, staring into darkness. She is met with silence.

She waits.

Much later, she hears muffled cries in the darkness, and then silence.

Her father told her to wait Clyde out.

Wendy waits a long time.

She checks her watch and waits some more.

And still there is silence.

Her mind is host to strange ideas, but she casts them away. Her father told her to focus on only one idea.

Wendy drifts off to sleep.

When she wakes, she has to go to the bathroom. She hops off the chair, drops her pants, squats, and urinates in the strip of light.

"Wendy ..."

She hears Clyde's voice. It's squeezed with emotion. She finishes urinating, pulls her pants up, and hops back onto the chair.

"Yes?" Her own voice is choked with emotion, sensing Clyde's emotion.

"Junelle is dead, killed with her parents. I couldn't send her off right away. She needed more of a life. Then she can go."

"Go where?"

Silence.

"We're all dead, aren't we, Clyde?"

"Yes."

"Please explain."

"Earth is a slain dragon, Wendy. It happened some time ago. From space, a direct hit, all life extinguished.

What you see about you are ghosts, and the memory of a planet."

"That explains much."

"It explains much."

"All this for Junelle?"

"All this for Junelle."

"Clyde, how much time do we have left?"

"A few weeks."

"Then?"

"Then the shock wears off."

"The shock?"

"The extinction event was the shock. It sprang consciousness into new, ghostly configurations so dramas could continue to play out. It's temporary. It will end soon."

"Then we die?"

"*We* do not die. The body dies."

"So we're going to keep Junelle's drama going?"

"We're going to keep Junelle's drama going."

"Because she's the best of us?"

"Because she's the best of us."

"My father was right. We're dead."

"Life as we knew it was extinguished, Wendy. We live on as ghosts, with partial memories, until the energy attenuates, then we go into the great unknown."

"Tell me about the great unknown, Clyde."

"At night, look at the stars. They provide a clue."

Clyde talks, and Wendy listens.

An hour later, Wendy tells her father what Clyde told her.

Weeks later, a change is upon the world. Clyde's darkness surrounds the planet, chokes the atmosphere. Wendy decides it's time to tell Junelle.

"Clyde was a god sent to lure us back into our fables, Junelle. So we could depart earth with unforgettable memories."

Junelle accepts it.

They go, slain dragons, into the great unknown.

Green Smoke

A husky coil of green smoke announces a presence in the farmyard. A moment later a body barely seen walks across the yellow grass, its motion wavelike. The thing elicits shouts of horror from observers inside the farmhouse, one of whom is Alexis Smith, an eight-year-old girl who has come under attack by these things before. The presence ignores her and the others in the farmhouse and makes for the three men in the yard.

Ty Burke feels a tug as it enters him. His body has played host to these things before. The attacks continually change. Scientists cry for fresh data hourly. The farm is located in California's Central Valley, prime ground for the invaders. Infestation by one of these things makes the skin crawl and raises body temperature. But this time Burke feels nothing beyond the initial tug. It's a new level of expertise, he thinks. These things are becoming dangerously adept.

The presence vacates Burke's body and whirls away in its cloak of green smoke. Burke watches it enter Swede.

It pirouettes inside Swede, faster, faster, casting light outward in delicate displays up to a thousand meters away, creating creatures that resemble humans, animals, otherworldly beings, and figures of myth and legend, all of them ephemeral, lasting but moments. These are presumed fragments of the host's psyche, launched for unknown reasons.

Swede's fragments waver, and then drift into oblivion, but Swede stands unharmed.

The thing leaves Swede, picks up its mantle of green smoke, and enters Sammy. And right away Sammy's energy becomes dark. Burke gets a bad feeling about this.

Sammy's right leg begins to jitterbug like mad, the rest of him tranquil. He looks like he's trying to cry, but something won't let him. And then everything changes, and Sammy becomes still.

Burke watches Sammy. He's looking dangerous, like the rattlesnake he is. Swede is circling behind him. Burke knows he must keep Sammy occupied as Swede circles.

Burke is still reeling from helping Swede bulldoze Sammy to the ground earlier. Sammy is a Canadian with thick, dark body hair—so much hair they initially mistook him for an animal. Sammy showed up at the farm that morning claiming the property was his. Burke and Swede told him to leave, but Sammy wouldn't go, and took after them with a knife. They took Sammy to the turf and pounded him. Thinking him dead they backed off. That had been a mistake. They should have buried him where he lay.

Burke keeps his eyes on Sammy as Swede eases up behind him. Sammy still looks shaken from their earlier altercation. They knocked him senseless, really. They killed him, or so they thought. Sammy's eyes had rolled back in his head.

"How'd you get here, Sammy?" Burke asks as he begins to circle. "You're a long way from home, Canadian. What do you want?"

"You already know what I want. I'm taking this farm off your hands, you ignorant scum. This chunk of California belongs to me. The adjacent chunks, also."

"These are some pretty big, expensive chunks, Sammy. What are you going to do with them besides sodomize the animals?"

"They don't raise animals on these farms, you ignorant scum. They grow fruit, nuts, and vegetables. It makes them rich."

Sammy pulls a knife and flicks it open. On another level, Burke realizes Sammy is not the true operator. Invaders exert the mysterious control.

Swede attacks Sammy from behind and knocks the knife away. He takes him to the ground, and Burke rushes in and delivers a powerful kick to Sammy's ribs.

Sammy's breath explodes from him. He sucks for air and whimpers. Swede picks up Sammy's knife and closes the blade.

Sammy gets up slowly, holding his ribs, sobbing.

The guy is pathetic, Burke thinks. It was too easy. They'll let Sammy go again.

Burke senses something kept Sammy passive at the right moment. It saved him and Swede. There seems to be a mechanism in humans that the invaders are able to access, a control switch that makes a person either passive or aggressive. No one knows how it works, though some psychologists have come up with a theory.

A person's needs are often complex, often buried, hidden from the conscious mind, but not from the subconscious, which is a bolder, more intense, more dramatic mind. The subconscious deals with dreams, symbols, and dramas—things that come from the deepest places. Peer into the subconscious mind and you might see two doors. Enter one, it's dark, it's scary. Enter the other, it's spooky, but not as dark, and there's a control stick in there. The darker door you back off from. It's dangerous. It's a long downward slide into places you'd rather not go. So you enter where the stick is. It's spooky in there, but it's manageable, and the stick is reassuring. Find the stick and you take control.

The invaders are apparently finding the stick and taking control.

Psychologists believe humans in infested areas are also tapping the shadowy realm of the subconscious.

Burke believes he has experienced journeys into the subconscious, but it's hard to tell. It's dreamlike. He has bizarre memories of invading Sammy.

Darkness pervades the mind as a portion of your awareness maneuvers through this other individual. Soon, you encounter two doors. You avoid the darker of these two doors and enter the other one. Sammy wants guidance. So you give him guidance. You tell him to be still, not resist, as Swede takes him down. It works. You have this new skill now. You need to guard it, keep it secret. You wonder about the door that is even darker than the one you entered. You realize that too much thinking will shove this new skill out of sight. You can't let that happen; you need this skill for a purpose. Someone can enter you, influence you, and subvert you. You sense that Swede has already been trying to do this. Sammy?

You have this new skill now, this new awareness, which you call a tool. This tool knows how to enter others. It knows how to work a stick. With it, you can change destinies. You wonder if everyone has this tool. You think so, but you don't think you'll hear anyone talk about it. Too much attention shoves it out of awareness. You don't always know what the tool is doing, though you sense it's relentlessly maneuvering, entering others, having awareness of intrusions into you.

You know that Swede has this thing, too, but don't know how conscious he is of it. *Halt!* Too much thinking about it isn't good. It goes underground and operates secretly when too much attention is focused on it. When it becomes your object rather than your skill, it drops out of sight.

Burke finds this new awareness invigorating, but also scary. He can enter others with it, going in one of two doors, though he avoids the darker of those doors. It's utterly dark, a step down in human evolution. The other door, he realizes, is a step up, but full of hoaxes, relics, and society's control. It's where the stick is. There's always this decision to make: which door do you enter? He feels there will come a time when he will have to enter the darker door. It may contain an elusive truth.

He feels a profound sense of responsibility concerning this tool of awareness. He can enter others, and they can enter him. He realizes he can't think of it too much, or the tool drops off the mental chart. He feels a kinship now with the rest of humanity, as he senses this new awareness is the condition for all.

Be forewarned. Psychologists say you must never think of your skill. Thinking of it causes you to lose it. Simply perform.

But Burke has a degree in a field that rewards thinking, so he thinks of it.

It's a new cartography of mind, dark and scary, hidden most of the time. What if someone comes looking for him? And enters him? Does he have two doors, also? A dark door and a door even darker? Can he know if someone has been scratching at one of his doors? He senses Swede has. But Swede is his friend. Which door has Swede been trying?

Burke wants to see if he can get Swede to do something. He will start small. *Pick up the hoe. Chop a weed out of the garden.* Swede does this. *Raise your right hand and recite the Pledge of Allegiance.* Swede looks perplexed. This is probably too much, too soon. What else can we get you to do?

Burke halts himself. He realizes these are games allowed the conscious individual as something more insidious takes shape deep within. This is comparable to watching television while deep, bedrock controls are being instituted by minds more agile.

The darker door triggers fear. Does it hide the real workings?

He grapples with the complexities of this new awareness and realizes it's a plaything at this level, and has a tendency to sink out of sight unless used.

Did Sammy use it as he tried to take over the property? Maybe he did. Maybe he had a go at it but screwed it up.

Burke watches Sammy. He's in a field, wandering.

"Let's go get Sammy again," he says to Swede. "We need to figure him out."

There's no argument from Swede. He's game.

They drive to Sammy in Burke's Jeep, dismount, and approach him with caution. Sammy pulls a knife and attacks them.

Swede blocks a knife thrust from Sammy, and then grabs his knife hand and wrenches it, breaking his arm at the elbow with a resounding crack.

Sammy screams, and his knife falls away.

Burke rushes in and decks Sammy with a punch to the jaw.

Did I stop Sammy with an intrusion? Burke wonders. Sammy is flat on his back. He stares up with no excitement.

There's something inside him, Burke thinks, deep down, no apparent surface manifestation of it yet. It's doing something for his pain, sedating him.

"What do you do, Sammy?" Burke asks. "Do you have a job? Why have you wandered so far from Canada?"

"They told us to go back to our birthplace," Sammy says. The words issue from him like poorly lit theology. "I was born in that farmhouse."

"I don't believe you."

"It's true. Lots of people were born in farmhouses back then. It was a rage."

"Who are you? What are you?" Burke desperately wants to know the significance of this hairy man showing up at the farm.

"I'm a chemist from Winnipeg," Sammy says.

"Describe sulfuric acid."

Sammy does.

Burke backs away. He fears whoever is doing this is doing it deep and is diverting them by allowing playthings at the superficial level.

While most humans pursue activities unworthy of much focus, someone is creating bedrock controls. They have to stop it with the playthings. Knocking Sammy flat three times was a plaything.

"Sammy, retain something deeper. Look for something deeper in you."

Swede approaches Burke. "We've got to talk. I've noticed something."

"Sammy!"

Swede puts a hand on Burke's arm and grips it hard. Burke tries to shrug Swede off but it isn't easy.

"Sammy!"

"Let Sammy go!" Swede says. "Let him go!"

Burke lets Sammy go. Somehow, he held Sammy in place.

Sammy gets up and tries to walk, but doesn't get far before collapsing. He has a broken leg.

"We'll get in trouble at some point," Swede says, walking with Burke back to the Jeep. "Most of what we did was illegal. The broken leg—I don't remember doing that. Do you?"

"No, I don't."

"We have to hope Sammy doesn't file a criminal complaint."

"Right," Burke says. A trickle of fear enters him. He's not worried about criminal prosecution, but of something else. He feels something was lost back there with Sammy.

When they get back to the farmhouse, they have difficulty seeing anyone other than eight-year-old Alexis Smith. She alone is clear and discernible. The others seem to be present but are like tendrils of mist.

Burke and Swede huddle in the kitchen with Alexis, tendrils of mist drifting by. Alexis performs a magic ritual, placing a ring of protection around the farm.

"That way we are protected," Alexis says, "just in case an alchemist or sorcerer comes from a foreign land and tries to steal our farm. The scum."

Burke nods. He agrees. Protective rituals are necessary.

"How dreadful," Alexis says. "I'm alone again, helpless, and the invaders cloaked in green smoke are coming."

Burke watches the eight-year-old girl, and backs away.

"I'm taking this farm off your hands, you ignorant scum," she says as she flicks open the blade of her knife.

"Tell me what you'll do," she taunts. "Tell me what you'll do." And she backs Burke away with the knife.

As Burke backs away, he watches Swede drift into oblivion on tendrils of mist.

Burke is losing track of everyone, it seems, and he thinks he knows why. They were not of this world. They were fragments from Burke's rich inner world of the psyche. It was drama. For what purpose, he cannot know.

Now they fade. Now they fade.

He looks closer at Alexis.

Alexis does not waver, does not fragment, does not fade.

It dawns on Burke, the darker door opening. He is a fragment from Alexis' psyche and has life so long as he performs for her and does not think.

"Tell me what you'll do," she taunts. "Tell me what you'll do." And she backs Burke away with the knife.

Light Sticks

On his way to yet another trip to the past, Alan Higgins paused in the deserted corridor. The faint hum of the air conditioner was the only sound. The blue light hit his eyes with dreamlike effect. He was waiting for someone to appear. It had to look like a chance encounter. No one must become suspicious. He resumed walking. Just a few more steps and he would be in the chamber that for many had become a deathtrap.

A door on the left swung open. From it stepped a towering man in military khakis, wearing the insignia of a colonel.

Higgins stopped, unsure. In the late twenty-first century, under the despotic rule of the Historians, it was difficult to tell friend from foe. His confederates had promised to relay the official findings of the latest death—if there was time, and if someone dared to intercept him in the corridor.

"It wasn't suicide," the colonel said, his voice low. "He did something outside the mission. We don't know what."

The colonel paused, studying Higgins' reaction, then said, "The light sticks are not separate from your mind. Use them. Experiment. Escape somehow."

The colonel stepped back into the room.

Higgins' pulse quickened, and he resumed walking down the corridor. He must find a way to escape from being sent back to the past again and again for the same unworthy purposes.

He passed through the security checkpoint and entered the amphitheater, which was dimly lit by thousands of tiny lights embedded in the walls and ceiling, creating the effect of a starry night sky.

Three hundred or so Historians sat in auditorium seats terraced around the "flight deck," a raised platform in the center of the room. The body of the current time traveler sat slumped in a replica of a jet fighter-pilot's seat that was bolted to the center of the platform. The time traveler's consciousness was somewhere in the past, inhabiting a duplicate of his body that was created automatically by the light sticks during transition.

Though the time traveler might spend several hours, days, or weeks in the past, the time that passed here was measured in minutes.

The time-traveler's body stirred; the man woke.

Two Historians walked up the stairs to the flight deck, unbuckled the straps that held the time traveler in the pilot's seat, and helped him out of the cockpit.

They took a leather pouch from him and passed it down to another Historian. It contained the light sticks that had accompanied the man to the past. The light sticks held a record of everything that had taken place during the journey. They would be tagged and reviewed by the Historians.

One of the Historians called Higgins' name. "Mount the flight deck."

Higgins walked up the stairs to the flight deck and sat in the cockpit. One of the Historians handed him a leather pouch containing light sticks and strapped him in.

"You have your instructions," the Historian said. "Pay attention to the return time. The light sticks are monitoring it for you."

Two light sticks the size of locomotives sandwiched the flight deck, one a few feet above Higgins' head, the other just below his feet.

At a nod from one of the Historians, an engineer at a control panel threw a switch.

Light shone from both sticks, bathing Higgins in an amber glow. His body slumped and his consciousness transitioned to the past.

The next thing Higgins knew, he was in a river valley in Colorado in 1895, with his feet planted firmly on the ground.

Higgins stood in a grassy meadow and looked around. The sun was setting. Rugged hills lay on both sides of the wide valley. Trees choked ravines and the banks of the river. A profusion of woodlands, interspersed with verdant meadows, ran through the area.

He slipped into a thicket and pulled a light stick from his pouch. He held it to his eye and it began to function as a telescope, its murky surface clearing to reveal a close-up of a distant ridge. A man would be running over that ridge soon.

As twilight set in, a running figure burst over the ridge, brought close by the scope's magnification. The man, whose left arm hung limp, slowed and staggered down the rugged terrain. Reaching bottom, he wobbled on spent legs across a meadow, heading toward a thick covering of trees that bordered the river.

Higgins slipped from concealment, crept through the high grass of the meadow, and sighted the man with his scope.

Wild-eyed and taking panicky glances over his shoulder, the man surged through the grass, fifty meters from Higgins as measured by the scope. Close to the trees, he pitched forward, stumbled, and fell, then scrambled to his feet and vanished into the gloom.

Higgins shot two marker beams with the scope, hitting a tree trunk with each, invisibly highlighting the man's doorway to the woods.

He turned the scope toward the hills and scanned. Nothing yet. He crawled back to the thicket and sat against the trunk of a tree, keeping his scope trained on the far ridge and listening for hoofbeats.

Before long, a horse rider galloped into view, a dark silhouette against the dusky sky of twilight. Higgins' scope zoomed in, its light-enhancement feature clearly showing the man's broad, chiseled face. The rider, holding the reins in one hand, a carbine in the other, searched the terrain with quick jerks of the head, and descended slowly, avoiding the steepest areas.

Reaching the meadow, the horse galloped toward the trees, slowing to a walk as it drew near.

Higgins was fearful of being mistaken for the running man and getting shot, so he slipped deeper into the woods, and gauged the horse rider's position by the noise of slapping reins, clopping hooves, and snorts.

With the sounds diminishing, he crept back to the edge of the trees and risked a look with his scope. The rider, thirty meters away, looked indecisive. He peered about, and then dismounted and led the horse into the trees, out of Higgins' sight.

Darkness settled into the valley.

Higgins waited, hearing nothing save the clamor of insects and the rustling wings of hunting owls.

The moon rose, dimmed by bands of flowing clouds.

With the meadow lit by the moon, Higgins saw the horse rider move slowly toward the hills. He got up from his frozen position and stretched his limbs, feeling the tingle of flowing blood.

He crept along the edge of the trees to where the running man had entered the woods, spotting the two marked trees with his scope. He selected the scope's search function and held it to his eye.

He saw the ghostly figure of the man stumble, fall, and then scramble to its feet, its left arm a useless appendage, a dark smear streaking its shoulder. He followed the reconstructed image as it fled through the woods.

The apparition led Higgins through thickets and dry washes, over deadfalls and boulders, under gnarled, drooping branches and storm-ravaged tree trunks. It passed over muddy ground by the river, paused to drink, and then veered upslope to find firmer footing.

The apparition led Higgins to the running man's hiding place in a wooded ravine.

Higgins' mission was over, and he returned home.

Alan Higgins spent three grueling weeks in the wilderness, tracking men and ghosts through dark woods and meadows, training for yet another mission to Colorado in 1895.

Then came news of another time traveler's death. All missions were scrubbed. All time travelers were pulled in.

Higgins was in limbo, and the thing he feared the most was about to happen—a fitness review.

His training group was sent back to camp, and Higgins received orders to report to Dr. Frederick Luger, the mission psychiatrist.

During the fitness review, Dr. Luger began to probe into Higgins' secret obsession.

"Alan, let's talk about Lillian Abels."

Luger had adopted a friendly approach during the review, but Higgins knew each word came equipped with a barb. He sensed the fitness review was almost over, so he proceeded with caution. He had no desire to be snagged at this point.

"Okay," Higgins said. "After Lillian's husband murdered her lover, and after her husband was hanged, Lillian spent the rest of her life as a recluse, living under a cloud of scandal."

"And you proposed that she be brought back with you to our time to be spared that wasted life?"

"Yes, if she consented. The Historians had been looking for a test case of that sort, to test the impact of intervention, and she'd had no children and no apparent impact on other lives after the murder. I proposed a rescue based on that theme. I thought it was an ideal test case."

"And it was passed all the way up to Jack Duncan and he rejected it?"

"Yes."

"Did he mention why he rejected it?"

"Yes, he did."

Higgins remembered the words of the Historian King, Jack Duncan, a thoroughly cultured though apelike man. "We are not ready for that type of intervention yet."

Higgins had left the Historian King's office disheartened, fearful that a telling comment would be written in his personnel jacket. He had seen photographs of Lillian Abels, had read her journals, and had been captivated by the ravishing nineteen-year-old from 1895. She had bewitched him, and now his dreams of holding her in his arms had been dashed.

The Historian King had seen through his request, had seen Higgins' real motive, and had decided that the light sticks would not be flung through time as Cupid's arrows.

Higgins' personnel jacket lay open on Dr. Luger's desk. He'd be pulled from the mission if there were indications of emotional involvement with a subject.

"You're aware of why all missions have been scrubbed?" Dr. Luger asked.

"Yes. The latest death."

The psychiatrist shifted his gaze from Higgins and stared into space, his eyes unfocused. "Too many deaths," he said. "Three in the last month. The light sticks show how in each instance, of course, but not why." He fixed his eyes on Higgins and continued. "Only the most reliable and dedicated men and women of our culture are allowed to become time travelers. This technology is still in its infancy. We must proceed with caution. Do you have any questions?"

"No."

To ask about the deaths, the how and why, would invite trouble. Each death spurred new rumors of souls trapped in other dimensions. Time travelers were expected to focus on their missions, not on the possibility of death. But were they really dead? Maybe they had simply escaped.

"What did you have planned for Lillian here in our time?"

"Nothing. She would be free to strive, like the rest of us, free of her own time's narrow-mindedness."

Dr. Luger closed the jacket, rose to shake Higgins' hand, and said, "Good luck in 1895, Alan. The missions are about to resume."

In the amphitheater, a Historian strapped Higgins into the cockpit, an engineer threw a switch, and light from the huge sticks that sandwiched the flight deck shone on Higgins, bathing him in an amber glow. His body slumped and his consciousness transitioned to the past.

Higgins landed in Colorado in 1895, in a river valley during twilight. He pulled a light stick from his pouch and put it to his eye. Acting as a light-enhancing telescope, it brought a far ridge close, adjusting the focus automatically to aid Higgins' eye.

A running man burst over the crest of the ridge. The scope zoomed in on his face. It was a sweat-streaked mask of pain and terror. The man's name was Clark Franklin. His left arm hung limp, the work of a bullet from Manfred Abels' carbine.

Franklin staggered downhill. Upon reaching the meadow, he bolted for the jungle of trees that bordered the river.

Higgins swept the hillside for Abels, who'd be arriving on horseback. He saw nothing yet.

Higgins crawled through the tall grass, stopped, and put his scope on Franklin.

Wild-eyed and taking panicky glances over his shoulder, Franklin surged through the grass, stumbled and fell, then scrambled to his feet and vanished into the woods.

At Higgins' mental command, the scope shot two marker beams, each hitting a tree trunk, invisibly highlighting Franklin's doorway to the woods.

Hearing the sound of approaching hoofbeats, Higgins flattened. After the pounding grew fainter, he let out his breath and risked a look.

Through the scope, he saw the broad, chiseled face of Manfred Abels, aboard a large chestnut horse that was prancing near the trees.

Holding the reins in one hand, a carbine in the other, Abels guided the horse with foot jabs and searched the trees with quick jerks of the head. He dismounted and led the horse into the woods, clutching the carbine.

As darkness settled into the valley, Higgins stayed hidden in the deep grass to wait. He heard nothing save the clamor of insects and the rustling wings of hunting owls.

The moon rose, breaking free from shuttering clouds, and lit the meadow with a soft glow. Higgins saw the silhouette of horse and rider moving toward the hills. Manfred Abels would return at dawn to finish his grisly work.

Higgins crept along the edge of the trees and found the two markers. He told the scope to search and the ghostly image of Clark Franklin appeared in the eyepiece. Franklin stumbled and fell, then scrambled to his feet, his left arm a useless appendage, a dark smear streaking his shoulder. The apparition fled, leading Higgins through tangled woods to the muddy bank of the river, where Franklin paused to drink before veering upslope to find firmer footing.

Higgins followed the ghost of Clark Franklin to the real Franklin, who was hiding in a densely wooded ravine. Then Higgins backed off to wait and think.

Since his last trip to the past, light sticks had taken on a mysterious new role. In Higgins' own century, soldiers and ghosts had played pursuit roles during training, shaping a new light-stick architecture. Tonight, Higgins' light sticks were warm and active. Something was afoot. But what?

According to the Historians, no one could stray from a mission without the light sticks being aware of it. But the Historians often lied. Could they be lying about this, also? Did anyone truly know the light sticks' secrets?

On a whim, Higgins peered through a light stick. Trails popped up. He studied them, mindful that he was outside the strict parameters of the mission.

Scanning the area, he had a sense of foreboding. The tree branches began to look like vipers. He heard footfalls and looked toward the sound, his nerves jumping. What he saw sent a chill through his bones.

Lillian Abels was walking toward him, a large dog at her side. She stopped two meters from Higgins and ruffled the dog's fur.

"His name is Blue," she said, looking at Higgins. Her voice was like a melody.

Higgins took the light stick from his eye, put it back in its pouch, took a deep breath, and calmed himself.

He stepped toward her, mesmerized by her beauty. His words flowed effortlessly.

"A fine name for a dog, Lillian. I'm taking you back with me."

Although Higgins did not have a light stick to his eye, the environment acted as if he did. Lillian and Blue were ghostly images, waxy in the moonlight. The real Lillian and Blue were elsewhere.

"I don't know, Alan," Lillian said. She sounded worried. Her face began to look grainy in the moonlight. "I don't think I can go back with you."

Her ginger hair bounced as she turned her head to the side, showing him a somewhat stern profile. Normally, Lillian was all softness, but now toughness ruled.

She spun away and dashed through the woods. Blue stayed with Higgins.

Higgins and Blue pursued Lillian through the woods for a while, and then stopped.

Lillian appearing to him was not part of the mission, unless the Historians were edging toward an intervention.

He reviewed the mission as he knew it. Lillian's lover, Clark Franklin, was holed up in the woods, feverish from his wound, shivering in the night air, frightened of what lay ahead. History ordained that Lillian's husband, Manfred Abels, would be along at dawn with his tracking dog, Blue, to finish him off.

Higgins was here to observe this cruel piece of history, and to guard against interference from other time travelers, known or unknown, from this or any other world.

Had the Historians made a decision to take on the case as an intervention?

Higgins looked down at Blue. Could he get Blue to lead his master astray in the morning and save Clark? Is that what the light sticks wanted?

He merged his consciousness with the dog's, and found that it was like merging with every dreary color this world had ever known. Its browns and grays and splashes of black were truly depressing.

He walked through the woods, his consciousness a strange brew, the night air a cool mist upon him.

Out of the mist, Lillian walked toward him. His heart leaped.

"Come," she said. "There's a cabin. The owners are away."

Together, they made their way to a rustic cabin in the woods.

Lillian patched Higgins' shoulder as best she could. A shot of whiskey blunted the pain. He said good night to her and went into the guest bedroom and crawled into bed.

The whole cabin, except for the fireplace, went dark. He heard soft scratching at the door. It opened. Blue.

The dog stood in the doorway, silhouetted in the dying embers of the fire.

"What's wrong, Blue?"

Blue just stood there, tension in his body.

Higgins dressed, entered the main room, and opened the cabin's front door. He heard the wind. Blue stood by his side.

Higgins crept around the perimeter of the cabin, Blue a ghost at his side. The moon and the stars shone down.

Manfred Abels wasn't supposed to be close at hand until dawn, but things were getting stirred up.

Blue paused now and then to listen and scent the air, to make course corrections, guiding Higgins. The wind in the trees masked their movement. Blue sank low, urged Higgins to change course, indicating an intruder in a thicket twenty meters from the cabin's front door.

Higgins crept toward the thicket. Blue shadowed him. They were meticulous, flowing along like reptiles. Sensing danger, Higgins stopped and listened, backed away, and began to circle toward the thicket.

A low growl rose from Blue.

Higgins stopped, uncertain.

Blue was a keg of dynamite, barely contained. He was going mad, not knowing what Higgins was up to. Blue wanted to take a more direct route to the prey.

A sound. Movement. A human figure rose in front of Higgins and aimed something at him. Higgins sprang at the figure, disarmed him, and took him down.

The intruder crumpled in Higgins' hands, dead of a broken neck. Silently, Higgins lowered the body to the ground. Blue emitted a few chuffs. Higgins held him, calmed him, and then dragged the body into moonlight.

Higgins knelt and examined the corpse, getting a good look at the face. Unremarkable. The man could have easily gotten lost in a crowd. Then a mark of distinction: chest hair peeking above the top of his shirt. Higgins looked at the arms. The man was as muscular as an ape.

He backed away from the body. There was something about the man lying on the ground that made him uneasy. Feeling a tremor in his step, he approached the body again and took another look at the face.

It was the Historian King, Jack Duncan.

Higgins' mind shot in odd directions. A sickness gripped his throat, stole his breath, ripped out his insides. He flattened on the ground. Was there anyone else out there? Did Jack Duncan have others with him? If so, Higgins could be in the crosshairs of a scope right now.

Minutes passed. Higgins thought he was going to die of the sickness that gripped him. Blue stood over him, not picking up anything in the environment. Eventually, Higgins' throat relaxed, his insides eased. Blue was a good barometer.

He lay there, listening to the wind. Nothing. A long while passed. Still nothing. Blue was a relaxed ghost standing beside him.

Higgins crawled a few meters, stopped, and listened. Nothing. He decided everything would have to wait until daylight. The destruction of evidence, everything. He was now reasonably sure the Historian King had been alone.

A silent, deep laughter welled up inside him as he crawled away. *I killed Jack Duncan.*

He laughed quietly, in spurts and jags. Close to the cabin door, he stood, laughing louder. He heard a sound from inside the cabin. Someone walking. And then silence. Blue nudged him. He mustn't laugh anymore.

He brushed off his clothes, his hands sailing around, his eyes frozen on the door. He had no idea what he would say if Lillian opened it. Blue nudged him again, and an idea came to him.

He looked at the dog, but couldn't really see him in the dark. He talked silently to Blue. We heard a noise out there. We were restless and decided to investigate, a little nighttime adventure, that's all. It turned out to be nothing.

Why had I been laughing? Blue made me, with his

antics. You know how dogs are, always doing incongruous things. Blue did a million incongruous things. I couldn't help but laugh.

Higgins entered the cabin, saw the dying fire, the scant illumination. Blue walked to the fireplace and lay down. Higgins' bedroom door stood open, like he left it. He walked in, undressed, and got into bed.

His shoulder was killing him. A free-floating terror worked a path up his spine, chilling him to his bones.

In the amphitheater, the Historians took Higgins' light sticks from him and sent him to see Dr. Luger, the mission psychiatrist.

Higgins sat across from Luger in his office. Somehow, he knew what they'd find in his light sticks. Lillian.

How could he explain her presence?

Luger's phone rang. He answered it, listened for about a minute, said, "Okay," and hung up.

"What happened in 1895, Alan?"

"Lillian appeared. She had a dog with her. The dog played a significant role in the mission."

"Yes, they told me." Luger stood, walked around to the front of his desk, and perched on it.

"Alan, did you orchestrate the events that took place in 1895? The killing of ...?" He let his voice trail off, kept his eyes on Higgins.

"No. Someone else did."

"Who?"

"I don't know. Didn't the light sticks pick it up?"

"No, they did not. You don't know who?"

"No."

"We're concerned, Alan. We see a pattern."

"Someone's interfering, then."

"Yes. Someone else is doing this work, parallel to us. But it's not true interference. They don't stop us. They seem interested in what we're doing. They seem ..." Luger threw his hands up in frustration.

"Dr. Luger, I think we're going to wake up one day and find that there are no more light sticks."

"What do you mean?"

"Control always shifts to another. I think we're already part of someone else's experiment."

"I see. I think we better relay that insight to the Historians."

"They already know. They took control from another a while back. They know it can happen to them, too."

"You feel there'll come a day when ..."

"We won't even know we had light sticks."

"Do you think they'll kill us?"

"No, they won't kill us. We're useful."

"We had such grand ambitions, Alan. I have a file full of ideas."

"Dr. Luger, can you develop a way to assess if we're being taken over? Who is doing it? A way to test for it?"

"I can try."

"The Historians need to be shaken up. Every day we wake up we might be losing more of ourselves."

"Like the Historians?"

"Like the Historians."

Higgins walked out of Dr. Luger's office.

Lillian was waiting for him in the corridor. He took her by the arm and they walked out of the building.

He did not know if the Historian King had decided to fling Cupid's arrows after all. Maybe Jack Duncan had had a hankering for Lillian. Maybe the man had simply escaped. It was the light sticks' secret.

Dark Running

Sam McEwen's mind darkened as he stood in the doorway of his cabin and stared at the darkening woods. The sun was down, though it was not yet full dark. It was his time, a time when he touched nature in a surreal way. More and more, Sam found life shabby, except in its most surreal manifestations. It was dusk, a time of transition, a time when animals came out to eat, and be eaten.

He drifted with his thoughts for a while, and then heard a sound so powerful it was like being struck in the face with a club. It was the sound of a fresh kill. Something had been brought down. The scream and abrupt silence was unmistakable. A wolf or bear or something was feeding. Dare he go take a look?

Sam was not a hunter, though many times he'd entertained the possibility of taking up the sport. He was a nature enthusiast, but not a freak about it. He respected nature and its animals, and gave each room to carry out its destiny.

He wondered what his own destiny was as he stepped away from the cabin. He was going to take a look. He was going to see what had been brought down, and what was doing the feeding.

Don't, Sam! You mustn't do this, Sam!

He heard voices in his head, a confluence of voices. They sounded like the same voices he'd been hearing his whole life: voices that told him what not to do.

The world was good at that—inserting voices that told you what not to do, and conversely, what you must do.

He knew he shouldn't do this, yet he was captivated by the sound he'd heard, the sound of mortal agony, of death, the sound of an animal losing its battle to survive. Now something else would survive in its place.

Sam retreated into his cabin, got a .45 caliber pistol and a flashlight from the chest of drawers in the main room, and once again stood in the doorway, staring at the woods.

He hesitated.

Was he going to do this or not?

Don't do this, Sam!

Was he going to let that voice interfere?

And just what sort of voice was it? A voice a prudent man would heed? Or a voice that harassed, denied, a voice that decreed narrow borders, set up preposterous rules, unfit for man?

He thought the voice was somewhere in the middle of all that, a voice that was cautious, yet not unreasonable. But the warning set up no serious glitches in his system. His body did not shiver, except for a slight shiver of excitement.

All this took about sixty seconds: Sam at the doorway, his thoughts, his fear; getting his pistol and the flashlight; back at the doorway, and more thoughts, more fear, hearing the terrifying sound again—the animal not yet dead.

He wanted to go.

He stepped out of the cabin and closed the door behind him.

Darkness was closing in fast now; he felt its confinement. He also felt confident—he had a flashlight and a .45 caliber pistol in hand. The pistol could bring down a bear.

Only with a lucky shot, Sam.

He'd take his chances.

He would let dinner wait. A pot of beef stew was simmering on the stove. He smelled it, a whiff on the air.

He walked away from the cabin, careful where he trod. He was used to the area by day, less so by night.

Farther out there was a scent in the air, something indefinable. Wait, he had smelled it before.

What?

He knew: it was the approach of wolves.

They intended to feed on the carcass.

He tramped along in a cloud of nervous energy, swishing through the grass. He knew he was making noise. He knew he was bound to draw attention, the wrong kind of attention.

Creatures of fang and claw would not fail to hear his noisy approach, or to smell him from afar—smell his very intent, the arrogance, the gun in hand.

He thought he was incapable of this. Such a deed was for lesser mortals, the ones he looked down upon with contempt. Only they interfered with animals in the wild. Now he was doing it.

He wished he had a dog at his side. A German Shepherd would be his preference. The dog could take the brunt of an attack, if there was to be an attack. He did not care at all about the dog. At least he was being honest with himself.

Honesty seemed to be a pattern—a dangerous pattern—in his life. He wanted to be honest, but knew honesty would get him in trouble like nothing else. Often, he checked his motives: was he up here in the mountains because he thought he could be honest like nowhere else?

He was honest, as well, about another pattern that plagued him. In darkest night, he found himself on a quest to be a voyeur of a thing being eaten alive by a thing that hunted with fang and claw.

He maneuvered downslope, skirted a towering outcrop, and entered the woods. He squeezed onto a narrow trail and proceeded cautiously. It felt like he was in a tunnel. Shadows swirled around him.

He had his flashlight in hand, but didn't turn it on. He seemed preternaturally tuned to the dark. He heard a dry twig snap, and knew a thing of fang and claw was behind him, tracking him.

He was frightened now like never before, for the thing that hunted with fang and claw was smarter than he was, smarter than Sam, who thought he was so clever, being honest with himself, with a gun in hand, a flashlight in hand, and the arrogance of a big brain, but with not much worldly sense at all.

He should have heeded the voice in his head as he stood at his cabin door.

Don't do this, Sam!

Yet the voice had set up nothing traumatic in his bodily processes; it had sent up no clarion call. It had been merely informational: a message in an ethereal bottle.

Now here he was, on the verge of destruction.

He stopped, raised the gun, turned in a circle, his eyes scanning the brush, his ears tuned to the sounds of the forest.

An eerie silence. And then a sound: a dry snap, hooking his consciousness, a shade to the left. He swung toward it.

He saw brush move, or so he thought.

The darkness was hexed by moonlight, which created an illusion of swirling gray mist, wisps of which looked like ferocious wolves.

What was real? What was illusion?

Now he was uncertain of the whole thing. Had he imagined the wild animal sounds, the screams, the death struggle? How much of it had been wishful thinking, a need to watch a thing die and be eaten? Was it a symphony conducted by his mind: the wild animal in its death throes, in a predator's grip, a crescendo of terror? There had been a certain music to it, he recalled.

But he was in the wilderness, where life-and-death struggles took place all the time. That much was certain.

And then he felt a mist of eyes upon him, and his senses sharpened, and his body chugged medicines of survival. He was certain an animal had snuck in behind him, certain it was just off the trail, certain it watched him with intent to attack. He kept the gun raised, kept his eyes on the brush, tried to make no sound.

He turned around, saw swirling gray mist, heard no sound save his own breathing. He saw it—a long, low shape with ears cocked back and teeth bared in a hideous grin. It crept toward him, crouched low to the ground, ready to spring. Its eyes did not stray from his.

He fired at it three times, his hand jerking at the recoil. The wolf vanished, the brush swallowing it up.

Standing on the trail, Sam wondered if anything around him was real in ordinary terms. He seemed to be immersed in a murky world.

Fear swept him. He knew he had to get back to the cabin. There came a time to retreat. That time was now.

He backed along the trail, thinking of his former home, Chicago.

He had learned a lesson from the foreigners he had run into back in Chicago. Don't appease. The foreigners saw appeasement as weakness and would press the attack.

The foreigners had demonized Sam. They had forced him from hearth and home. They had summoned evil forces in the universe against him. Sam had crossed them—just once, and it was accidental—but that was enough to become their mortal enemy.

He never referred to their specific ethnicity—that didn't matter. They were from a culture where mass murder and ethnic cleansing had been everyday facts of life for millennia. It was done to them. They did it to others. And when they came to the New World, they brought their ways with them. If you crossed them, even in innocence, they would target you as their enemy and would dispose of you like they had disposed of millions of others since time immemorial.

That's why Sam kept a loaded .45 in his cabin and a thousand spare cartridges for it. He wished he'd bought an assault rifle, as well, and a thousand rounds for it. But he was new at the game of war.

He backed along the trail, tuned to the forest, the eerie glow of moonlight his only illumination. He thought of turning on his flashlight but decided not to. He needed to sense the overall environment. He could not risk being narrowly focused. He kept it off, and kept backing up.

Something burst from cover and charged him. He fired once, twice, a third time, and saw it drop. He snapped his flashlight on and illuminated an animal lying on the trail.

He crept to it, fear cinching around him. Seeing the creature in more detail, he drew back in fright.

On the ground was a dead wolf, shrunken to a pile of fur and bones, the thing that gave it shape and force in the world gone. Above it, in a fountain of moonlight, stood a wolf far more powerful, vast, and superior.

Sam was now frightened beyond comprehension. The wolf in moonlight was not an ordinary wolf. Its physical manifestation was an extension of a much deeper, hidden reality.

It seemed an odd time for memories to come, but come they did, from when Sam was back in Chicago, and the foreigners were claiming he was stalking their women. They threatened violence if he didn't stop. Sam told them he wasn't stalking their women. He was innocent, wrongly accused. But it fell on deaf ears. The foreigners saw in Sam demons from the deepest pools of their own culture.

Despite his fear, Sam knew he was in an infinitely richer dimension now, here in the forest, and he wanted more of it.

The wolf that stood ghostly in the moonlight was not a thing of ordinary existence, but something primeval.

The spectral wolf growled deep in its throat.

Sam jumped back, his terror exploding. But he wanted more of this richness, and his fear lessened.

He turned off the flashlight. He could see the wolf clearly without it. He clipped the flashlight to his belt and holstered his gun.

In a mysterious fashion, the wolf began communicating with Sam. That's when Sam's world flew into more pieces. Until this moment, he had not known what he was faced with.

The wolf talked at length, telling Sam the foreigners had gotten law enforcement involved. The foreigners claimed Sam had stalked one of their women and had raped her. They claimed Sam's semen had been found inside her, and Sam figured that was probably true, thanks to a nurse he'd been going to for more than a decade.

The nurse massaged Sam's prostate for health reasons, and always took a semen sample from him. She must have stored the semen, for Sam's was found inside the foreign woman. The foreigners must have gotten to the nurse and threatened her, and she must have given it up. For her trouble, the nurse was found dead in a back alley. The foreigners then proceeded to implicate Sam by planting his semen inside one of their women.

The scam was new to Chicago, and was used to frame innocent men. Sam had not been arrested yet because the Chicago police were suspicious of the whole thing.

The foreigners had tried the trick before, attempting to frame a politically powerful man, and it didn't work. Now the prior scheme was in the minds of the detectives working Sam's case.

The wolf told Sam there was no guarantee he would not be arrested at a later date. It depended on how the investigation proceeded in Chicago.

The wolf stood on its hind legs and walked into the

woods. Sam followed it. They walked through the moonlit forest, dark and silent partners.

Sam did not feel fear, but a deepening sense of fatigue. He had tolerated far too much lately, and now he wanted relief. He sensed the wolf would lead him to a power that would set things right.

He felt a kinship with the wolf that he had not felt with another creature in a long time. He knew he was about to be indoctrinated into the pack. He would become one of them. How was such a transformation to take place? He knew but could not articulate it. It was not within language, but a wisdom held deep within the soul.

They entered a clearing, where a circle of wolves stood on hind legs, facing a blazing fire. They joined the wolves and faced the fire. Sam sensed it was a ritual to help them prepare for the hunt.

He watched the wolves and saw their eyes intent upon the flames. He looked and saw within the flames a sight that made him shiver, for he was seeing the whole world as he once thought he might in an afterlife review. Within it, he saw his own journey, and the journeys of the wolves.

The flames licked the air with the image of a large, powerful wolf, and Sam saw that it was his own reflection—he was a wolf now. The wolves around the fire were his brothers and sisters.

They got down on all fours, Sam with them, and they pranced around the fire. The fire grew larger, and they grew larger, and many more wolves joined them, and a clamor rose.

The fire grew bigger and licked the heavens, and Sam saw that it encompassed the entire universe. The fire revealed the nature of matter and consciousness, and Sam understood how he could become a wolf, and how he could live many lives and perform many roles.

The flames licked higher, and Sam knew there were many universes, many worlds. He would take a portion of this flame back to Chicago with him. It was a flame that leaped into the manifest world. Sam would leap with it and be manifest in human guise. He would join the human masquerade, a wild wolf inside him.

He saw the flames shrink back to the original size of the fire in the clearing, and he knew that a new ritual was about to begin.

"A new life is about to begin, Sam," a wolf said. "Your life."

"You will get down on all fours, and you will stalk the ones from Chicago, and you will kill them and leave them for the animals to eat," another wolf said.

"You will leave the gun in the cabin," another wolf said. "You are a wolf now."

The flames shot higher, and the wolves brought forth a drove of bleating sheep, and they killed them and approached Sam and offered him sheep's blood off their paws, and Sam drank the sheep's blood off the wolves' paws.

Then the wolves tore the sheep to pieces and devoured them. And Sam helped devour them. And the pack formed a circle around the fire and howled at the moon. And Sam heard his own voice erupt in the same wild, haunting howls.

The fire dwindled and the wolves dropped to all fours and slunk away, and Sam was alone in the clearing as the fire went out completely.

His flashlight appeared in his hand, the beam showing an empty clearing. He swept the beam around, and he found the trail and followed it back to the cabin.

He went inside and bolted the door. He put his flashlight and gun back in the chest of drawers in the main room. He ate his dinner of stew. Then he sat on a wooden chair and waited.

He waited and waited and his mind entered a silken tunnel. He slept and he woke with a start. He slept again and when he woke again, he knew the reason why.

An animal or something was outside the cabin. Instantly, he was alert, crouched by a window. He didn't have time to think. A plan was already in mind.

He squeezed through an opening between two rafters and eased to the ground outside the cabin. He crouched on all fours and silently made his way around the perimeter of the cabin, his eyes tuned to the dark.

He seemed to have a preternatural sense of smell. It threw him off until he got accustomed to it. Then he knew his prey, knew it every way.

There were three of them, the universe calling this out with signatures on the air.

He stopped and sank low to the ground, not allowing any part of him to move or to make a sound. Wind favored him; it came off the prey.

In the wind off the prey, there was the unmistakable smell of Chicago, and that was to be expected. He'd had trouble back there. People from Chicago were after him.

Sam felt a surge of energy; he felt his mind fill with a strange enchantment; he felt his body infuse with dark pleasures. He could grasp all three of them, crush them in his grip, and drag them off. They'd be helpless, unable to defend themselves, no different than bleating sheep.

Yes, he could do that.

But should he?

It meant their deaths. Was he prepared for that, to be the keeper of their souls? He would have to keep their souls within his, somehow. It sent a shiver up his spine; it was fear of another sort. Could he do that?

He had to think.

Now another fear struck him.

He was afraid thinking would freeze him, like an animal caught in the glow of a powerful light, an animal not knowing what the sudden illumination meant. It usually meant death in that brightness an instant later.

He would not freeze. He would not think. He would not die like an animal caught in the light. He would act, and act quickly.

He scented the air and caught the three moving his way.

He would rush them, grip them, crush them, keep them alive long enough for interrogations; they would be at the mercy of wild nature—his wild nature. Then he would eat them.

But wouldn't that mean he held their souls in his?

Wasn't that a burden beyond his level?

He thought so, yet his survival depended on resisting this evil force that moved his way from Chicago. It was unmistakably Chicago; no other place could make him rage with such hatred. Now, with a crushing force, he could minister to them in kind.

A power erupted in Sam, and he continued his stealthy journey, a plan unfolding in his mind.

He crept in the light of the full moon, on padded paws, clawed toes, something rising in his blood that spoke of other stalks, millions of them, in all their power and glory, successes and failures.

He crept downhill from his cabin and was soon within sight of his prey: three humps that clung to the hillside, a sharp metallic smell of firearms flowing off them like invisible flames.

He was not concerned with their souls now.

He knew nothing of souls now.

He knew only survival, and he became still.

These thugs from Chicago had been sent to either kill him or take him into custody: his semen had been found in the foreigners' woman's body. He couldn't tell if they were cops or criminals, such was the smell of Chicago.

He saw them more clearly now, as each poked a face up into the moonlight and peered toward the cabin. Sam knew they suspected he was still inside.

He scented the air again; still, he could not decipher the smell: cop or criminal? Maybe it didn't matter. It was a threat, and he knew how to deal with it.

He knew he was doing too much thinking, and that frightened him.

Thinking was man's undoing. It led to trouble.

In Chicago, it led to a phony criminal complaint against him: the foreigners putting his semen into one of their women's bodies.

He got a big whiff of them.

The woman was among them.

The other two were males—foreigners or cops here to get the woman to make a positive identification.

He crept toward them. He would rush them, leave broken bodies, and then drag them off one by one for interrogation.

He saw movement.

His eyes sharpened.

He saw the glint of a gun in the moonlight.

Sam sprang at them, just as a shot rang out, the muzzle flash singeing his fur. He slashed one man across the face with his claws, and then leaped on the other man and slashed him, too, both now with mortal wounds.

He faced the woman, took her in his claws, and bit deep into her shoulder. He shook her in his jaws, and he heard her cries and the cries of the other two, who were rolling on the grass, their hands to their shredded faces.

Sam dropped the woman, leaped on the nearest man, and bit him in the arms and legs, crunching bones with his fangs. He did the same to the other man, and left them both screaming in terror, their arms and legs useless.

They could not grip a gun now and use it against Sam, as if that would do them any good, for Sam knew that somehow he was no longer earthly, no longer mortal, no longer human, at least not at the moment.

He dragged one man off, and then the other, secreting them in the brush, and then went back for the woman.

She was crying hysterically, one hand to her torn shoulder. Sam bit into her in several more places. He did not want her too badly damaged. He would interrogate her first, and then the men, if they were still alive.

He carried her to the cabin, took her in through the front door, and sat her on a chair at the wooden table in the main room.

He sat at the table with her, and felt himself changing, acquiring a more human form, though still something of a wolf.

He saw terror on her face, and he bit her on the hand before settling back in his chair and eyeing her. He attempted to speak but no human sounds came out, just a growl.

Sam waited and eventually tried to speak again. This time something resembling human speech came out.

"Are you the woman who has my semen in her body?"

She screamed and he bit her in the face. It was not much of a bite.

He realized he was less a wolf now, more a man, so he slammed a hand across her face, silencing her. He was disappointed—the blow did not knock her off the chair and propel her across the room. That would have sent a message. He raised his hand again, but drew back.

"Who are you? Do you have my semen in your body?"

He waited, patient now. He knew the woman wasn't going anywhere, neither were the two men hidden in the brush.

"Are you a foreigner?" he asked.

She stopped whimpering, slowly raised her head, and leveled her eyes at him.

He saw astonishment there, but also something hard. Her jaw set, her posture stiffened, and then she looked at him curiously.

"Sam McEwen?" she asked.

Sam felt his mouth curl, his eyes widen, his face shift into astonishment. Her voice was a soft, inquiring voice. He had not expected that.

He knew better than to answer in the affirmative. Chicago gave you no breaks. Whether it was the cops there or the criminals on its shores, Chicago gave you no breaks.

"What if?" he said, and realized it was too much of an answer. So he said, as a gruff retort, "What do you know about Sam?"

She looked down, her brow creased, her eyes seeking refuge.

"I ..." she began, but stopped. Her voice was catching. She heaved a big sigh of emotion, something pouring out of her.

"I was brought here to ..." She stopped again, and her emotions got the best of her. She broke down sobbing. "You killed them." Her breath heaved in and out, and she shook so badly the table shook with her.

"They will live." He tried to keep the lie out of his voice, out of his eyes. The words seemed to soothe her.

She was staring at him, her hands cradling her wounds, and for the first time Sam focused on the blood that covered her. She was bathed in it; her wounds would kill her if not treated, but she was in no immediate danger.

"Do you know Sam McEwen?" he asked.

"I did. You were Billie Sue's patient."

Sam tried to show no reaction. Billie Sue MacDonald was the nurse who had massaged his prostate and took semen samples from him.

"I used to work with Billie Sue," she said.

He saw her in a different light now; he saw her as a petite blonde in the health clinic where Billie Sue had worked. He saw her sitting at a desk in the reception area. She had taken his name down for appointments with Billie Sue.

"I was brought here to identify you, possibly to exonerate you."

"You do not have my semen in your body?"

"No, it's in a police lab."

"Okay, I believe you." He did. This woman was not one of the foreigners who were trying to frame him, nor was she part of corrupt Chicago.

He looked at her wounds and saw vast quantities of blood, and he wondered how he could save her.

He realized the two in the brush would likely die no matter what, and she was a witness to the violence.

He gestured toward where he had tossed them into the brush.

"Who are they?" he asked.

"You looked like a wolf, and now ..."

"Are they Chicago cops?"

She looked disoriented; her head bobbed around for a while before she responded. "They are."

Sam stood and paced the cabin. Could he save all three of them? He thought long and hard. He stopped and looked at her. Her mouth was slack, her eyes hooded; he did not like the looks of it.

He stepped from the cabin, into the night. He dropped to all fours, ran into the woods, and let out a howl. He howled until he saw dark shapes converging on him.

Wolves.

Sam spoke with them.

The wolves dispersed, and in minutes had gathered the two cops and the woman.

And now all of them stood around the blazing fire in the clearing, Sam with them, and a ritual began.

The horrible wounds Sam inflicted on the three from Chicago closed up, and the three transformed into wolves—but not very convincing wolves.

Sam watched in dismay; this could not be happening. He was a powerful wolf, illuminated in the roaring flames, why not the three from Chicago?

"Sam," one of the wolves said, "we can only do so much in your dimension. We can save them, but they'll be with us then, gone from your dimension. In your dimension they are dying. You have to make a decision."

Sam knew what the wolf meant, but did not like it.

"Why can't you save them? You saved me."

"You crossed over," the wolf said. "We saved you by giving you back your life. You were ready. These others are not ready. They have not faced what you have faced. You must give them back their souls."

Sam reluctantly took the three faltering wolves out of the fiery clearing and back to the yard by his cabin, where they were no longer wolves, but humans with horrible wounds.

He killed the two men first, snapping their necks.

He killed the woman next, shutting off her screams, and then snapping her neck.

He dragged the bodies into the brush and left them for the animals to eat. He felt their souls somewhere within his, and felt their souls go away.

He got down on all fours and howled at the moon. And he ran into the forest and returned to the clearing where the other wolves were, and they all stood on powerful hind legs, and they all pranced around the fire, and Sam watched their eyes shine with fiery wisdom.

And the three from Chicago were among them, among the undead.

And now things became a little clearer for Sam.

He knew his own body was out there somewhere—the foreigners had tracked him here to the Wyoming high country, and they had killed him. But a raging part of him lived on, and now he would go back to Chicago and have his revenge.

He realized that all humans went through this. It was a transformation derided by culture, a primordial rite of

428

passage that culture stuffed deep below its windowpane existence.

In Chicago, Sam walked the streets as a powerful wolf on hind legs, and he scented the air, all but invisible to the citizens. They saw him fleetingly, if at all, in the passing panes of glass. He looked pretty much like themselves, but for fur and fangs and claws. And they knew something deadly walked among them.

The Bus

He drove the bus through the bleak streets, picking up the occasional late-night rider huddling in a pool of light. A hard rain fell and tarnished everything. It started and stopped, and then fell with a roar that lasted several minutes, and then stopped again, imparting a shine to everything. The rain, the shine, the pools of light, the riders, all came in spurts and trickles, dry spells and floods.

The driver, a tall, muscular black man, was thinking about one of the riders he had picked up a while back in front of a hospital. He had driven a bus for more than twenty years; never before had he seen anyone like the old black gentleman who sat midway down the aisle. The driver was younger than the gray-tufted one by at least forty years, yet felt a bond with him that was hard to explain. He thought the gray-tufted one might be going home, as one might say, might be dying.

Most of the passengers were black, Hispanic, or Asian; some were white, maybe sixteen, seventeen passengers altogether. A white teenage girl with blond hair and blue eyes and a small boy were up front, close to the driver. He had picked them up at the hospital, also. She's probably his babysitter, the driver thought, by the looks of her, her head buried in a paperback, a lost expression on her not unpleasant face. The kid's look and manner, all sly and outgoing, were different from hers. She was the subdued type. The kid was a rascally sort.

The kid, who was about five years old, kept going back to the gray-tufted one and saying something, pointing, and then running back to sit by the blonde. The kid didn't know any better, to be bothering someone. The driver could have stopped the running back and forth, but that would have stopped the fun. The old gentleman, so frail looking at first, seemed to be rejuvenating, seemed to be having fun. The driver thought he knew when to leave things alone.

He could see it all happen in the big mirror that showed the bus's interior. The driver wished more of the riders were as tickled as he. If so, he felt he could let loose with that big whooping laugh that was long overdue to come out without drawing undue attention to himself. If they were all rolling in the aisles, they wouldn't care if the driver pulled over to have a good whooping laugh with tears streaming down his face, his strong body collapsing in helpless spasms against the steering wheel. Maybe even getting off the bus to pound on its side and wander down the sidewalk until the spell wore off. That was the kind of laugh he kept stifling.

It ain't fair, he thought. My innards are killing me.

Now and then he heard a snicker from way in back, and tried to pinpoint its source, hoping to boost it to a chortle or a guffaw with the sympathetic magic he believed was possible in these situations, where strangers were thrown together, trying to maintain decorum in the face of absurdity, each waiting for the other to break through and spark an uproar. Come on, come on, he willed. With an eye pointed toward the ones who snickered, a knowing grin, and an occasional chortle of his own, he kept trying to lead the way.

The kid kept running up to the gray-tufted one, pointing at him, and saying, "You're dead, man, you're dead." And then the kid would run back and sit on the seat beside the blonde, her head still buried in her book, oblivious to it all.

Before the gray-tufted one started responding with his own antics, the driver felt embarrassed for him. He hoped the kid would just shut up and stay put; maybe the blonde would corral him. But no such luck. The blonde stayed buried in her book.

Eventually, the gray-tufted gentleman began to mirror the boy. "Yo mama cakes," he would say, shooting it at the kid, using his hand as a gun, blasting away. "Yo mama cakes. Yo mama cakes. Yo mama cakes." The old geezer would duck and roll in his seat, bounce around, and come back up firing away. "Yo mama cakes. Yo mama cakes. Yo mama cakes." Finally, he would blow on his finger, as if blowing the smoke away, and then sit as composed as if he were sitting on a pew in church.

The driver watched in the mirror as the boy got up and made his way down the aisle to the gray-tufted one again. He watched as the boy taunted the old one, saying that he was dead, and then as the old one taunted the boy right back with *Yo mama cakes.*

Suddenly, a guffaw sounded from way in back.

Another guffaw, louder, longer.

A chorus of guffaws.

The dam burst.

The driver pulled the bus over and made an unscheduled stop, screeching it against the curb. He was splayed all over the wheel, dying, gripped by monumental seizures of laughter. He parked it, popped open the door, and wobbled outside into the cool night. He wandered around, pounding on the side of the bus, scratching his head against a nearby tree—they were in the suburbs now—stumbling around, losing sight and sound of almost everything.

Breathless minutes passed.

He boarded the bus and sat heavily in the driver's seat. He felt worn out. He ached through his chest and shoulders. His face was a stricture of pain. It had been an agonizing bout of laughter, and he was glad it was over.

He pulled away from the curb.

Suddenly, as if by magic, he felt light, loose, exhilarated. He drew in deep breaths and drove on, block after block. It was a dark street, forbidden yards and sidewalks, houses and foliage in deep shadow.

He was puzzled. He would not have guessed ...

The driver looked in the big mirror, worry crossing his face. The passengers were ciphers, no help. They seemed like fragments, reflections of something.

Don't think it.

In panic, he squealed the bus around a corner. Several blocks and two turns later, he parked at the spot where he had gotten out and had his explosive bout of laughter. The passengers stared at him with evil eyes.

He ignored them and got out of the bus.

Wasn't a day that went by without some murder, a black caught unawares in a white section. He went looking, blending with the shadows.

He heard a squeal of laughter in the darkness, imagined a knife plunging into someone.

He grabbed a man out of the darkness and dragged him back to the bus, his heart killing him with fear.

But, glory be, he had someone in tow, a young black man who was injured and stumbling along. He helped him onto the bus and drove away.

The young black man sat across from the driver, facing him, catching his breath, gulping for air. Blood stained the front of his shirt. His arms and face were gashed, weeping blood. Otherwise he looked tolerable. He had a look of gratitude on his face.

"Glad you helped me out, man," he said, grinning fiercely now, having caught his breath. "I don't know what happened back there. It was so dark."

"You were in a white section," the driver said. "You were caught unawares. That's what happened."

"Oh, come on. That's not what happened." The young black man was still grinning, still showing his appreciation.

"What happened then?" the driver asked. "I thought ..."

"Man, that's not a white section anymore. It's a mixed neighborhood now. You need to learn this town better." He laughed.

"I know this town fine. I've been driving a bus for twenty years, plenty of time to get acquainted with the town."

The driver saw the young man shrug, and then saw him look at the blonde and small boy across the way, and toward the other passengers in back, all the while nodding, as if appraising everyone.

The driver looked in the mirror and saw all eyes intent on the new rider, except the blonde, who was still buried in her book. Even the little boy and the gray-tufted gentleman were watching the new rider.

"Watch the road, man," the young black man with the bloody shirt and weeping gashes said, returning his gaze to the driver.

The driver felt a deep tug of fear, not fear that whispered from the imagination, but fear that took a sane measure of life. It was in the young man's voice, the easy delivery, the implied violence if you crossed him. The young man was used to giving orders. With growing horror, the driver regretted bringing him onto the bus.

The driver kept his eyes on the road, but only after taking another look at the red stain on the young man's shirt. It was spreading slowly, like a river's delta.

"Your eyes wander," the young man said to the driver.

"Uh, yeah," the driver said. "Maybe so."

"Glad you helped me out, man. But keep your eyes on the road. I'll tell you when to stop. Just drive. Say, why'd you stop back there, where I was? And why were you laughing so, like a crazy beast?"

The driver glanced at the young man, saw his grin still in place, still showing his appreciation.

The driver put his eyes back on the road, the path carved by the headlights, and then on the mirror, the path carved by reflections. He looked at the small boy, at the blonde buried in her book, at the old man, at the others. *God, I am so sorry for getting you into this trouble.* That done, a prayer of sorts, he put his eyes back on the road.

How could he explain it? Why was I laughing? He felt he must explain it. It would buy time.

"Something funny happened on the bus," the driver said. Come on, come on, he willed, wanting the others in back to lend support. Come on, come on, tell him why we were laughing.

But no one said anything.

"I saw you laughing back there," the driver said to the riders. "I heard it. I saw it. Come on, come on, tell him. Tell him you were laughing, too. Tell him why. Help me out."

There was dead silence on the bus; no one was willing to help him out. The driver's fear rose. But he would try to explain it. He knew he had to buy time.

"The old man is dying," he said to the young black man. "I picked him up at the hospital. The young lady there and the little boy were at the hospital, too. Something funny happened on the bus. It involved the young boy and the old man. It was funny, but it was also a solemn process. I can't explain it; it's not easy to explain to anyone."

"Forget it," the young man said. "Forget it. I get wild at times, too. We all do."

The young man grinned again. The driver saw it, and then his eyes snapped back to the road.

"You laughed, driver," someone in back said. "No one else did."

The driver looked in the mirror and saw heads nod in back. "What are you saying? Only I laughed? But I heard—I saw—"

"My ass! Here, driver, watch." Some joker in back held up a mirror, but it vanished quickly.

The driver strained to see who was jerking him around back there, but couldn't pick him out. There was dead silence again. The bus was like a morgue.

"I'm Nieko," the young man said, breaking the tension, but adding a subtle undercurrent with the inflection of his voice.

Do not defy Nieko.

"I'm Freddie," the driver said.

"Glad to meet you, Freddie. Stop ahead."

"What happened to the streetlights, the house lights?" Freddie asked. "Did the storm take them out?"

"Never mind. Stop right here."

Freddie saw a figure at the curb and pulled the bus over and opened the door. A pudgy man with a limp boarded the bus and took a seat behind Nieko. The man was Asian and appeared to be in his fifties.

Lightning flashed, and for an instant, Freddie saw the bus silhouetted against a building the Asian man might have emerged from. *House of Liquors,* a sign said. The bus looked crumpled, twisted, and torn in the fleeting image.

"Welcome aboard," Nieko said to the Asian man.

The Asian man nodded, and looked around the bus. He seemed somewhat bewildered.

"Proceed, Freddie," Nieko said.

Freddie closed the door and pulled the bus into the driving lane, glancing in the mirror at the Asian man.

The top of the Asian man's skull was blown off. Several fingers on his left hand were attenuated to jagged stumps. A bloody hole decorated his shirt, right over his heart.

Freddie blinked, looked again, and the Asian man looked normal. No blood. No wounds. Got to get a grip, he thought. I'm losing my mind.

Lightning flashed again, and Freddie saw the bus silhouetted again, this time against a traffic accident, where two cars had collided head-on. The bus's silhouette, for a brief moment, was as crumpled as the two cars. It was a bus with bent metal, a twisted frame, and shattered windows. It didn't look much like a bus anymore. It made Freddie shudder.

He stopped and let a woman on the bus. She was carrying her own head, and took a seat midway down the aisle, across from the gray-tufted gentleman, who was rocking back and forth in his seat staring at her.

Freddie blinked and looked again, and the woman looked normal. I'm losing my mind, he thought.

The gray-tufted gentleman held up a mirror, and Freddie disobeyed Nieko's rule to keep his eyes on the road. He stared at the mirror and saw a reflection of the woman. Her head was in her lap. Her shoulders shared space with a bloody neck stump.

Freddie felt his body shake, his mind freeze.

He put his eyes back on the road and drove on.

We've fallen into an abyss, he thought. Blackest night spun all around them. He saw furious energy ahead. Red and blue lights spun through the darkness, drenched the darkness with an unspeakable urgency. He knew there had been an accident ahead. He felt a chill and braced himself.

He slowed the bus, but sensed it was already slowing of its own accord. He thought the bus had behaved as such throughout the night, slowing and so forth as situations developed. Freddie had been just another rider. Illusion after illusion had tricked him.

The real driver was something unseen.

As the bus continued to slow, the surrounding environment acquired more color, more movement, more excitement. The long, languid movements of the bus no longer dominated the senses.

Everyone was staring out the windows. After a lengthy silence, someone in back said, "Look, there are seams out there. Divisions between worlds, this world and the next."

Freddie looked around and saw colors almost magical, blue and yellow tints to almost everything. And there truly did seem to be seams out there, divisions between worlds, this world and the next.

He slowed the bus, his hands, feet, and eyes acquiring a feel for the vehicle again.

He heard Nieko shout, jump, shout again, to express his displeasure at this latest transgression of Freddie's.

I'm doing something wrong, ha-ha, thought Freddie.

The bus eased to the curb, just as traffic came to a halt, likely because of the accident up ahead. The street possessed an aura all its own, hard to say what. It was choked with trendy restaurants. Crowds milled on the sidewalk.

Freddie popped the door open. And right away a man came up and peeked inside. Freddie saw the man's face blanch. And then he heard a squeal, something mechanical arising from the man. It wasn't just noise but something of a complaint. Suddenly, there were odd patterns of color in the man's face: blues and yellows, purples and pinks, reds and browns.

The man stumbled away, and Freddie wondered what he had seen inside the bus that had altered his color, and maybe changed his life forever.

Freddie gripped the wheel hard, bracing for the monstrosity that he was sure would board the bus. His eyes shrank to the dash, to the steering wheel, to his hands gripping the wheel.

He heard the sound of feet on the steps.

Someone entered the bus. Freddie looked up into the eyes of a tall Spanish-looking man—a young man dressed in an elegant manner, wearing a dinner jacket, unbuttoned, loose on his rangy frame. He was clean shaven and had a splash of cologne on him. His eyes were the darkest brown Freddie had ever seen. His features were lean and open, almost like an innocent child's. He looked a bit hungry, as if he'd been expecting dinner about this time.

To Freddie's enormous surprise, on the heels of this man came a young lady in an evening gown of clinging green satin. It fit her figure in the most tantalizing fashion. Freddie could not take his eyes off her. Seconds later, he realized he had stopped breathing. And he gulped for air.

The man who had just stepped on the bus gave Freddie his name.

"Jackson Ybarra," he said. He looked toward the back of the bus, seemingly a bit confused, and nodded toward the other passengers. He walked down the aisle a ways, making room for the young woman behind him.

The young woman, looking worried, stepped up to Freddie.

"Brigida Ramos," she said. She looked around, and then walked down the aisle to join Mr. Ybarra.

Freddie looked around, too, another rule violation, and saw that Jackson Ybarra was making Nieko nervous.

Jackson Ybarra stood about six feet four and had rangy muscles. He looked strong. Currently, he was looking out of the bus's windows, scanning all around.

Brigida Ramos joined him, and they sat down together. They seemed to be a pair.

They died in the accident up ahead, Freddie thought, and now we're taking them somewhere ... somewhere ...

Moments later, Jackson Ybarra wandered up the aisle and stood near the young blonde, who was still buried in her book. He looked her over, a tinge of horror entering his face.

Freddie had noticed that Brigida wore some makeup, but only a hint, as she was naturally beautiful. Both were beautiful, Freddie thought. Why were they on this bus? Most of the passengers did not attain their status in looks or clothing or the air they possessed.

Weren't there different buses for different kinds of dead people? It made Freddie wonder. Maybe they weren't dead. Maybe they hadn't been involved in the accident, but had beaten a hasty retreat from it, and the bus happened to come by at the right time.

Are they dead or what?

Freddie wished he could shoo them away, tell them to board some other bus. That would be the acid test, like holding a crucifix up to a vampire. You dead, or what? Of course there weren't many other buses out there this time of night. He was making his last run, to an unknown destination, and Nieko was aboard, with his chest wound and maybe a gun on him, and Nieko was looking a bit nervous to see these two beautiful people, so obviously out of place, step onto the bus and take seats, and maybe usurp his authority, or rather, his right to intimidate everyone in his cool way.

Freddie stood up from the driver's seat. He was as tall as Jackson Ybarra, and fifty pound heavier. Fifty solid pounds. But he looked like a servant of Jackson's, not someone who could inform him of ...

Of what?

Jackson was still studying the young blonde, her head still buried in her book.

"Were you in that car accident?" Freddie asked Jackson, his voice harsher than he'd intended.

Jackson looked at him, frowned, and diverted his eyes. A look of anguish came over him. He turned and walked back to sit beside Brigida, and he buried his face in his hands.

Brigida placed her hands on Jackson and collapsed against him. The two huddled, quaking, heaving big sobs of emotion.

Freddie looked at Nieko. Nieko looked back, and Freddie saw a look of absolute horror cross his face. Nieko hadn't known.

Freddie sat down in the driver's seat and closed the door. He pulled the bus out into the driving lane. The way was clear; there was no accident scene ahead, no red and blue flashing lights, just darkness and the headlight beams. He stepped on the accelerator and the bus sped along.

Freddie thought it over. The bus had been picking up the dead. It was a ghost bus, demolished in an accident. It had materialized into ghostly form for one last ride. Bus riders became ghost riders. The driver, who'd been decapitated, and who went looking for his head in a misadventure outside the bus, became a ghost driver.

We saw the accident, we saw ourselves die, we saw ourselves in reflections, in shadowy outlines. It was thrown at us piece by piece, presented in fragments along the way. Now we have all the pieces.

We're dead and yet we're still traveling along. We're picking up more riders. Ghost riders.

The bus travels the streets that lie between this world and the next, picking up the dead who still cling to material earth. It offers rides to those not sure of what happened, to those who need reassurance of their place in the grand scheme of things. The bus is a temporary vehicle for this.

I am one of the dead, Freddie thought. I am driving us to a destination unknown to me. I can't believe any of this is happening, yet here we are. I saw myself in flashes of light with my head off. Another person came aboard with her head off. It happens.

We go around collecting the dead.

Some of the riders had suspicions, I know. I never did, until late. Nieko never did, until late. He was probably the last to know. The blonde with her head in the book knew all along. The little boy and the gray-tufted gentleman probably knew all along. The three of them got on at the hospital. In all likelihood, they died in the hospital, ain't it a shame. They either knew right away or learned quickly. For some of us, it took a while.

Well, I'll be. We've stopped at hospitals, at the morgue, at accident sites, at holdups, at knifings, logical places for dead people.

There were clues all along. We stopped only where the dead were likely to be. We never went on any normal route. Most of the riders seemed unaware of their situation. Of course; they wouldn't be here otherwise.

We saw mirrors in the environment, and we saw shadows. They showed us the lost, scattered fragments of ourselves.

Now and then I thought I saw someone hold up a mirror,

but those were illusions. We don't have to hold up mirrors. We are mirrors. Everyone is something of a mirror for everyone else. And each thing is a thing of the soul.

Freddie swerved the bus into a tunnel and darkness was all around them, and a light was in the distance. They traveled through the tunnel, and the things of the earthly world were left behind. They didn't need them now.

They came out the other end of the tunnel, where points of light awaited them. Souls.

They departed the bus. The bus belonged back in that other place. They traveled individually, each to its soul area, and merged with their souls.